Among

the

Silenced

Sacred

JC Santos

ISBN 978-1-7343622-0-6 (electronic)
ISBN 978-1-7343622-1-3 (print)

KCJ Publishing in Seattle, WA

www.byjcs.com

Copy editing, typesetting and cover design by JC Santos

For Kellen – my professor, my coach,
my motivator, my captain.

Theresa

"Are we doing this, Theresa?"

A woman wearing black pants, a short-sleeve black button down shirt and a white plastic collar probed Theresa's eyes, their redness and wrinkled encasings stung with exhaustion. Then, the woman fixed her eyes on Theresa's mouth. It wasn't the positioning of her lips so much as the rapid drawing and expelling of air. On Theresa's face, she read nothing but apprehension. So, she reached for Theresa's hand. It was cold and wet and quivering like a fish that's been out of the water. The woman, whose name was Lania, weaved her warm fingers with her friend's, gave her a reassuring squeeze, and held on until Theresa regained control.

"Theresa, we don't have to do this," she persisted, searching for agreement. Lania didn't feel too sure about going through with the sacrament either. Her own heart rate quickened as she looked at her watch. She could hear it tick, a maddening sound she tried to tune out.

In the deadness and darkness of their surroundings, the only consolation came from the bond they shared with each other. Theresa, the mother; Abraham, the son; and Lania, the spiritual guide, a priest of the Catholic Church.

Abraham had just passed his seven-month birthday. His black locks, ornaments to his soft brown eyes, curled in clumps and stuck to his scalp like embroidered threads. He had no idea of his mother's and the priest's plans, but could only feel their hearts beating twice as fast whenever they held him close.

Certainty long embedded itself in Theresa's heart. She wanted her only son to be baptized into the Catholic Church, but the American Freedom Laws forbade such an act, from any religion. If they were found out, she would lose Abraham, plain and simple. What would happen to her and Lania, Theresa had heard varying accounts. Labor camps, death on the spot, a perpetual cell at an interrogation center — an information mill, rumor held, where prisoners were doped up on some kind of truth serum that slowly deteriorated the mind. Her own fate meant little to her; only Abraham's future mattered.

Lania let the silence brew until she forgot that she had even questioned Theresa's desire to go through with the baptism. Frozen in time, both women stood beneath the streets of Far City. In the early stages of discernment, the choice was simple. But now, in the penultimate moment, regret hooked and pulled Theresa from crossing the threshold of no return.

"I want this," Theresa said aloud, retaliating against her doubt. "My father. He wanted this."

Lania's face fell with sorrowful acceptance. "He did. He always said how fulfilling it was, that he could pass on something sacred to his daughter, and that one day, he hoped you could do the same."

A tearful laugh and an ill memory flashed in the moment.

"Then let's move on," Theresa said. "We're still too close to the subterranean access point." One cold step after another. A pale yellow bulb, reflecting on the surface of the wet concrete, flickered and buzzed just above Theresa and Lania. Puddles and trickling streams splashed underfoot as they ventured without a clear destination. Somewhere to avoid being noticed — they'd know the place when they found it. The women tried to block out clattering footsteps, skittering scratches that got louder, and the cold whipping tails that lashed their ankles.

"Here, sweetheart, let me take him a moment," Lania offered, noticing the dripping sweat from her counterpart's forehead. Theresa took a break from holding Abraham. He was gaining weight fast, already well over twenty pounds.

The child squirmed in transitioning to Lania's arms, opening his eyes and holding them wide for a moment. Lania's thumping heart didn't escape his notice, and he paused from his own slumber to make sure she was okay. Theresa and Lania were transfixed by his face, which conveyed a powerful tranquility in the weak glow of the service light. Then he smiled, and that was all it took. Theresa's uncertainty drifted away in the current of the sewer. Knowing somehow his work was done, Abraham shut his eyes and returned to his slumber.

Light rain fell above them, then swelled to a roar as the drizzle evolved into something more troublesome. The growing trickle of streams into a rush of storm water filled the absence of sound as Theresa's thoughts continued to fall on her mind like waves on a shore — one crashing, another not too far behind, and an unsteady ocean of worry sprawling beyond fathom. But above that ocean, no longer ripped and tossed by the violent storm that raged inside her mind, was her decision. She had made her choice. Her final one.

Up ahead, a storm drain spilled water into the tunnel.

"There," she pointed. "Let's do it over there, Lania."

Lania nodded and took the lead. The storm drain would provide the water, the priest would provide the sacrament. The open air was necessary for the type of baptism Theresa wanted. For one thing, there were no more active churches in which to perform the sacrament, and the abandoned ones had been overtaken by squatters or gangs. There were also private, in home baptisms — a much safer option. But in the context of their society, it made the ritual trivial, especially since baptisms were often open affairs to the community. There were also those bold enough to carry out baptisms above ground in backyards or pub-lic parks. Such brave souls who protested the AFLs had diminished years ago. Only stories of caution now.

Theresa and Lania settled on the most unorthodox—though not un-heard of—setting, which they agreed was a comfortable compromise of safety and openness. Lania arrived at the storm drain, the water still surging from the downpour above. The noise from the pounding of the raindrops brought comfort to the women, but made Abraham squirm.

"Okay, quickly," Lania said.

"Yes, do it."

Lania spoke the words of ritual.

What name have you given your child?... Abraham.

Is it your will that he be baptized?... Yes.

Do you believe... I do.

Do you believe... I do.

Do you believe... I do.

And then, *Abraham, I baptize you in the name of the Father, and of the Son, and of the Holy Spirit.*

"Amen," they said together.

Lania smiled at the completion of the ceremony.

Theresa had one more request. Staring into the eyes of her infant son, she asked, "Lania, you re-member the Our Father?"

She nodded and smiled. It wasn't just the words Lania recalled. It was the man who first taught it to Theresa. A man she loved. Theresa's father. If he could have made the journey into the sewer, he would have been right beside them, sharing the moment.

"Will you say it over Abraham before we end?"

"Abraham." The priest paused a moment and let the name ring in her throat and sail out of her lips. She and Theresa joined hands. Fondly, the woman in the collar smiled once more at Theresa as if she were her own daughter, and they began.

"Our Father, who art in Heaven, hallowed be your name…"

The water from the storm drain above slowed to a trickle, acknowledging the moment with a reverent silence.

JUSTICE

Midland America University

Sophomore Year

Winter quarter, 2079

"Power."

"Why?" Professor Truth's response floats from his lips and hums in my ear like a mosquito. My head twitches. I hate being questioned, and you'd think I would be used to it by now in Freethought class.

Upon the screen in front of the classroom, the word POWER sits proudly in its blocky black bold-faced font. The other words — freedom, finances, moments and love — hover around the word I chose.

"What makes 'power' stand out to you, Justice?" the professor persists. He says to have a reason — a good reason — behind anything I say. I say that's impossible and inconvenient, that there'd be a lot more silence in the world. He says that wouldn't be such a bad thing.

"Who doesn't want power?" I reply, looking around at the rest of the class. Skeptical faces and faces looking at their desks. Apparently, I am the only one in the room with a thirst for authority.

"A thirst for power can dismantle a person and a society. Just like ideas

6

of freedom and justice. Even truth succumbs to interpretation, and that's when the real danger presents itself.

I flinch as he works our names into his explanation. Truth and Justice. We could be crimefighters if he wasn't such a righteous tightass. He gets his wish. Silence. His challenge knots my stomach. I wish I had said something else or nothing at all.

At the end of class, I peer in his direction, and he gestures at me to stay behind for further discussion. Begrudgingly, I linger near the door where he bids farewell to the other students with a cordial countenance. Then he turns to me and frowns.

He's not old — his clothes look older than him. Holes and frays and stray threads appear in just enough places to make his attire look weathered, but not impoverished. The colors, probably once bold and dark, are now foggy. Both his pants and his shirt hang loosely from his body, lightly fluttering in the path of the central air vent on the wall behind him. He's tall, slender and lithe, and when he speaks, it's with a calm voice and a furrowed brow as if he's trying to figure me out.

"Everyone has power," he begins his lecture. "Some use it. Some waste it. Some manipulate it to benefit themselves. Some use it to improve the world around them. I'm curious, Justice, how do you intend to use your power? You're a person with a certain charisma."

"What's that supposed to mean?" I ask.

"Well, obviously that you're a leader. This is a philosophy class, but I'm a bit of a psychologist myself. I like to know my audience before I teach them. I've read up on you, Justice Flint. Your father is a Commanding Officer for the Intervention Force. And you, I can tell, are a man of ambition."

I scoff, but am a bit flattered, so I smile.

"Don't blush now," he cautions. "I do the same for every student."

7

"A bit creepy, don't you think?" I say.

"Well, it's not like I'm hiring a private investigator. You can learn more about people by Googling them than asking them face to face. And should you venture into education, or business, or politics, or any field dependent on relationship, it's not a bad idea to know a bit about your audience."

He pauses to let my mind absorb his advice. I muster a nod.

"You know, in my ten years of teaching this class, I've always been able to determine which student would pick which value. But for the first time, the very first time, I was wrong. You shocked me, Justice. You shocked me with power. And I want to know why."

"Well, if you had really read up on me, I think my choice would be pretty obvious."

"Would it though? What if I saw something better than power?"

"Like what?"

"The one with four letters."

"Love?" I say as though I just drank spoiled milk.

"It's the best word up there. And if you're going to be happy, it's the one to go for. Yes, Justice. Maybe you don't see it, but somewhere in that dark heart of yours, I got the impression of love for others."

I'm a bit overcome. It sounds too noble a quality for me.

"You don't think you deserve such an attribute?" Truth says, reading my mind a second time. Another awkward moment of silence transpires. "Thank you, Justice. I just wanted you to know that."

"Thanks," I say, still confused.

PRESENT DAY

Power. It's been an ambition of mine since I first learned about God-seekers. And with the exception of one class I took in college, I've never flinched at that goal.

I remember my very first Civics and Freespeak class in the fourth grade. I turned in my first interventionist — an eighth grader. Quiet kid named Max. I caught him with a cross around his neck that escaped the gap between the buttons of his shirt. He tried to claim it was the letter "T" for his last name, Tunay. Well then, it should have been an uppercase T. Who knew good grammar would lead to my first interventionist bust? The name Max also gave him away. It teetered on the edge of illegal, since all traditional names had been outlawed almost a decade before, thanks to the Generic Name Act.

When his parents came to pick him up from school, Intervention Force were already waiting. They took the whole family, including his little brother in the third grade.

And with that, I lived up to my name.

Justice.

I was never crazy about my name, but it sure as hell fits. Doesn't feel like a name. When I was a kid in school, all the historical figures we studied bore interesting names like George and Abraham or Amelia and Simone. The Generic Name Act wiped all those names from existence. It became mandatory to name your kids after stuff, like Mesa or Sky or Rhythm. It was a subtle way of wiping religious names from existence, without being overtly discriminatory. You'd be shocked at how many people I know named Grass or Sunrise. You could round up a group of people, string their names together, and make a lovely poem.

Names are the least of my worries about this country. To think that there are still Godseekers — interventionists, faithies, bapticks — practicing in open society, makes me feel like I'm living in a messy house. Stains and dust bunnies invisible to the public eye rarely escape my attention, and I like to keep my city clean.

That's where my ambition to power landed me. I started out as an Intervention Force officer responding to calls of Godseekers attempting to convene in secret. Then I moved up to an IF Elite officer with higher jurisdiction and security clearance. Now, I'm an IFE field specialist, and I'm moving up the ranks fast, toward real power.

Power. That would have been a good name for me, too.

I've arrested 382 Godseekers in my ten-year anti-intervention career. I'm proud of that accomplishment. No one else in any city across this country can match that number in the same amount of time. Not even close.

My parents groomed me to dream big and go for the best. Someday soon, I'll make Commanding Officer, but that is only a stepping stone to the real end. To be Supreme Commanding Officer, in charge of all domestic security and anti-intervention in the entire country, that's when I could just die and be satisfied. But I'm not looking to go anytime soon. Once I become the SCO, I intend to hold that position for a good long while. It's important to me, to keep the peace, and in order to do so, there can be no trace of organized religion in society.

I couldn't imagine living in the chaos before I was born. Conservatives hating Islam, Liberals hating Christianity — it took a bold leader to put an end to it all. He was one of the first to change his name. President Greatness. First name President, last name Greatness. And you thought I was an arrogant son of a bitch. After isolated anti-Christian, anti-

Muslim and anti-Semitic attacks had appeared all around the country from Far City to the quiet towns in the mountains and plains, President Greatness signed an Executive Order, establishing the American Freedom Laws.

No citizen, inhabitant or traveler within the borders of the Great United States of America may practice in public or private any semblance of an organized religion, by way of ritual, prayer, service, idol, gathering or any action that is connected to a deity of any tradition.

There it is, in plain English.

When the law gets violated, the consequences are brutal. And it starts with me. I don't tolerate people who think they are above the law. So before the interrogations, before the prison cells and labor camps, they meet me. I am their first experience of pain.

Justice.

I suppose my name fits after all.

I sleep with my shades open about a forearm's length from the top sill of my window, allowing morning light flood into my room. My dad called it waking up with the power of a star. I hated it when I was a teenager, but now I get it. I start my day productively. Strategically. With goals I set, and challenges to conquer. Don't laugh. Don't roll your eyes. Out of all the people I know, I'm the one who gets the most work done. So many others hit the snooze button over and over. Not me. As soon as the sun's up — or before — I'm up.

This morning, it's not the red of the sunrise glowing on my wall that wakes me. It's the sound and flash of my phone. My partner, Beamer. What's he doing up?

"Justice, get your ass out of bed!" he says urgently.

"I get up earlier than anyone. What's up?"

"Leonardo's. Fifteen minutes. We have a lead. Major. I'll tell you about it when you get here."

"Got it."

A major lead. Beamer usually doesn't attract inside knowledge, though that's probably why he wants to meet me so early. You know the people who hit the snooze button? Well, he's the worst. The fact that he's calling me three hours before our shift makes me get dressed a little faster than usual.

Under the electric blue glow of Leonardo's neon sign, the large panel windows showcase the patrons nestled inside the booths. Absurd stacks of pancakes occasionally catch the eye of a passerby. Cops, teachers, morning business meetings, reading groups, breakfast dates — all these and more fill the tables at Leonardo's. Everyone loves this place. The food is inexpensive, but hardly cheap. Fluffy pancakes, thick sliced bacon, and their specialty, the shuffle, which is a layer of hash browns, sausage, cheese, veggies, an egg, then repeat. I've only had it once in my life. Doctor doesn't like me eating stuff like that.

The diner has been a fixture in the Northlake neighborhood for almost a century, and is one of the few establishments privileged enough to maintain its original name, despite clearly violating the Generic Name Act. I wonder what kind of person would be attached to such a name as Leonardo. I would think an artist or a scientist or an engineer. Not a hole-in-the-wall diner owner.

A server approaches our table. Beneath the metal wires coiled through her purple brows, her eyes squint at me. Her black lips open wide to yawn as she arrives at our table. Hatching a smile, she greets us cordially. "Beamer beat you this morning," she says. "Something wrong, Justice?"

The smile on her face stretches, and I reciprocate.

"Guess he's finally getting it together," I quip. Beamer smirks and I ask for coffee as server tops off Beamer's mug.

"IF special, as usual?" she says before leaving.

"Yes, Silver, that'll be great," I say, assuming Beamer hadn't yet ordered food.

Beamer rests his hand on the handle of his coffee mug and stares off into the distance. Redness coats his eyes above puffy bags. His black terra suit, wrinkled and oversized, outlines his body, which could be described the same way. The sculpting gel in his hair has dried, mingled with his sweat, then dried again, and tiny white flecks of adhesive make it look like he accidentally brushed his head against a dusty wall. He must not have made it home last night. Pearl shouldn't mind — her husband never works that hard.

"So." I'm just about to snap in front of his face to grab his attention.

He shakes his head, snapping out of his daze. "An RI. Tonight. On public property."

"In public? Who'd have the balls to —" I'm alarmed and also a little furious that I wasn't privy to this information before Beamer. I have several contacts in this city. Not a single leak about a Ritual Initiation. Thought those bapticks would have learned by now. You can't hide a public RI from Intervention Force. This will be easy. But I'm going to have to pay some of these so-called informants a visit. Any kind of initiation into a religion is a Class A violation of the AFLs, and I *know* somebody knew something before Beamer picked up his tip. Two years ago, Central City had a blown RI and they never even found the baby.

13

That CO was terminated and their Intervention Force "reorganized." Know how many times that has happened in Far City? None. Under my watch anyway. The SCO won't stand for negligence or half-assed work. Neither does the future SCO.

"Where did your lead come from?" I ask.

"He's doubling as an old store owner and exchanging information to keep his shop open. He sells historical artifacts to private buyers. Some of his artifacts contain icons just generic enough to pass as legal, and religious enough to appeal to faithies."

Sounds compelling enough, but my past experience isn't reassuring.

"A doubler, huh? And you're sure we can trust him? Where did you meet this guy?"

"Pearl and I were walking through the Hills District—"

"Gross. What were you doing there?"

"A stay-cation, all right? Anyway, we were window shopping when we came upon this place called Etc. attached to an old Chinese restaurant. Some of the stuff looked suspicious, so while Pearl went to get her nails done the other day, I went back. Dude was terrified when I showed him my IF badge, but he tried to play it cool. After a few threats, he offered me information about the baptism."

"RI," I correct.

"Whatever."

"I'm just saying, I've worked with the doublers before and the success rate isn't all that great. Observers and plants are more trustworthy. They don't have any attachment to the Godseekers. Doublers collapse under all that guilt, especially if they're selling out Catholics."

"Come on, Justice. Maybe back in the 1950s. Besides, if this is a busted tip, we bust him and his shop shuts down. It checks out, he'll keep feeding us info. Win win." A short stare at Beamer, then I nod at him.

"Not bad," I say, as he exhales a sigh of relief. "What about specifics?"

Beamer holds out his mobile media device and projects a map of the city on the diner table. He taps on a saved template, and a dozen city blocks become highlighted in yellow with red lines in between, which I recognize as sewer lines.

"This is our target area," Beamer says. "I tried to get more out of him, but he said that was all he knew."

"Well, this is pretty precise — as much as we'll get. It's typical for a public RI. The only ones who have the exact location are the priest and the parents, but that's determined after they meet up a little before. Your doubler probably has no idea where this is going down, beyond what he offered. I'll bet it's underground."

"A Rat?" IF talk for an RI that happens in the sewers.

"Most likely. The sewers are prominent and wide in this part of town. Any information about the exact meeting time?"

"Only that it's happening tonight."

"No. It's not going to happen tonight." Again, Beamer smirks at my confidence. He knows how highly I think of myself. "We'll need some additional Elite agents, but I'm sure some *regulars* will be there too. They need to be quick-moving, and plain-clothed. We can't make it seem like the area is swarming with the law. I'll talk to the IF Commanding Officer this morning and set up the operation."

"You sound like the Commanding Officer already. And you do realize this is my tip, right?"

"Did you want to meet with the CO then?"

Beamer scoffs. "You kidding me? I'm fine with letting you do that, even though it is *my* lead. I know you want to move up in the world. Maybe even rule it."

"You don't?"

"Not really. I'm in it for the adrenaline rush. Not sure why you want to leave it. You're so good at hauling in interventionists. You really want to waste those skills behind a desk?"

"It's not the desk I want. It's the power that comes with it."

"Yeah, you are a power-hungry son of a bitch," he belches. "We all know that!" Power hungry. That's not quite the type of son of a bitch I was going for. Arrogant? Sure. But power hungry? Well, I guess he's got me there too.

"Better watch your mouth, Beamer," I grin. "When I'm SCO, I can keep you on IF Elite or have you laundering uniforms."

"But seriously, Justice, why does that job appeal to you? What good is all that power anyway?"

The server interrupts Beamer's question and carefully sets our breakfast on the table. She can tell we are dancing in a deep conversation, so she just smiles and checks on the next table.

Beamer ignores his plate and pries for an answer. I ignore him and start eating. I don't mind shooting the breeze for a while, but he is digging a little deeper, and I'm not interested. I don't need to answer to him or anyone. We've been partners for just over a year. He doesn't get to ask that question yet.

He begins to move, and I assume it's safe to look up. Exhaustion continues to weigh down Beamer's face, despite the empty coffee mug in front of him.

"I'll be right back," he says. "Gotta wash my hands."

I nod. Good. When he returns, the topic of my ambition is

forgotten. We finish our breakfast talking about his family and how I'm married to my work. We speak about the Intervention Force 5K happening in a couple weeks, a few IF regulars who make good fodder, and the fishing trip he has planned next month. We keep the topics on the surface. I don't mind talking about what I'd do as SCO, but whenever someone asks me why — why I want that kind of power — well, I've produced several answers to that question, and none of them have ever felt genuine. There. There's something about me you can take to the bank. Ever have a goal, but no idea why you're chasing it other than it looks nice and you have the ability? That's my greatest fear. That my strongest ambition is hollow. That I'm a fraud. That I'm striving to be something I'm not. I tell myself every morning, I believe in the AFLs, and dammit, I do. My mom was a prominent politician and a strong proponent of the Freedom Laws. My dad was a commanding officer himself and hated interventionists. Both of them saw when I was a child, an eleven year old boy, how good I could be at busting Godseekers. They were proud that I brought down Max Tunay, and I was pleased to make them feel proud.

Beamer is sitting in front of me. I had no idea he had returned from the bathroom, but already, he's chewing on his last bite of pancake.

"I'm out," Beamer says, collecting his coat. "We don't start for another couple hours and I have to take Sonic and Reflection to school. Get going on that lead though. No initiations in this city."

"All right. I'll see you at headquarters in a bit."

My doubts fade as one dominant thought pervades my mind. No initiations in *my* city.

JUSTICE

Midland America University
Sophomore Year
Fall quarter, 2079

    I find myself staying behind again. Even though I'm only two weeks into Professor Truth's Freethought class, it's my favorite one. Of all time. No exaggeration. I hear he offers the same course at three levels throughout the school year. I'm already looking forward to taking the winter and spring extensions. Rumor has it that ProTruth offers a window into the mind of Godseekers, and his class navigates the ideals of the criminals I'd be after as an Intervention Force officer. Freethought, I guess, encompasses all thoughts. Even illegal ones.

    But beyond my initial motivation, Professor Truth does something else. I'm thinking in ways I've never thought before, and I can tell, because I catch myself, well, thinking thoughts I've never thought before. Like, maybe believing in God isn't such a bad thing. Of course, I catch the insanity of such an idea, but the fact that this teacher is able to bring such a notion into my head impresses me as a student.

"Freespeak and Freespeakers. Defenders of the right to say and do as you please. Except in our own minds." How contradictory! His first words to the class made me wonder — what if he's right? What if his idea of Freethought really means we aren't as free as we believe?

The stuff we discuss in Freethought class simply can't *be legal, but somehow, he gets away with it. We talk about deities, religious practices, history and rituals all from a philosophical perspective. It's not objective at all. And people are actually interested in this stuff. Little do they know, my father could round up the whole class and have them at the Interrogation Center. But I'm not saying a word. I can't have my dad shut down the most thought-provoking class I've ever taken.*

Now, here I stand for the fifth time in six days with yet another post-discussion question. He must think I'm obnoxious. Or dense.

"What is God?" I ask plainly.

"Civics and Freespeak," Professor Truth replies with the programmed response. My question needs a little work, as he would say.

"Okay, well, you've been teaching about Godseekers — errr, Muslims, Jews, Christmen —"

"— Christians —"

"— right — for the last few days. You talk about their rituals, their prayer, their practices, their traditions, their rules. But you don't mention anything about their God. I want to know what the big deal is."

Professor Truth thinks it over for a few moments. Every response from him takes ages. I don't see how he grew up in the Age of Instantaneous Internet. Finally, in classic ProTruth fashion, he responds with a question.

"Why do you ask?" he says.

"I thought you would have an answer."

"I will answer this question, but my price is your motivation."

"I don't know if I'm willing to pay that," I say, overvaluing my reasons.

"Then I trust you know your way out and I shall see you in class next week. Good day, Justice."

He walks to his desk and plops his slender frame into a cracked red leather chair, the upholstery peeling like sun-burned skin, flaking and curling. One of these days, that seat is going to collapse, but I swear he hangs onto it like it's been in his family for generations. His laptop is open and he begins to type, paying me no attention even though I'm still standing right in front of him, watching him ignore me.

I surrender.

"I want to know what you think."

"What I think?"

"Yeah, you. I mean, you teach about it. You must have an opinion about it." My sincere curiosity quickly morphed into an unintentional witch hunt.

"I've no opinion whatsoever." The most disingenuous words I've heard come out of his mouth. He raises his eyebrows. I can tell I won't get a response from him, but in a way, he did respond. That sustained lift of his eyebrows was a footnote. I had only touched the surface, and that gesture cracked the facade of his secret like a pebble pelting thin ice.

"I want to know what you think so that I have a better idea of how to approach it."

"It?"

"God, I suppose."

"God, or your ambition to Intervention Force?"

"I said 'God,' didn't I?"

I mean God, too. I don't blame him stating the obvious. He knows my career path. But more and more, ProTruth's class has been a place where

I can step back, observe and evaluate without having to worry about the appropriateness of my thoughts and words. His class is like a sideline, and he's my coach going over the last play with me.

"I'm sure if you have listened closely, I've taught nothing but facts and logic." I nod; he proceeds. *"Any thought beyond fact comes purely from each student. S'why my class is so dangerous."* He grins deviously. *"I can tell you what I've found out about God, as I've learned from others in my tenure as a professor and in my own life."*

I nod again, accepting his discretion.

"You know, I grew up before the AFLs were passed. So, legally, I believed in God when I was just a bit younger than you."

"You did? Why?" It's no surprise, but I'm still shocked to hear him say those words. *Time and progress paint an ugly portrait of even the best people.*

"Well, back then, believing in God was a lot more common than it is now, of course. My parents also believed God. That's where I got it from."

"What was it like?" My curiosity is getting the best of me, but I've never had access to the mind of a pre-AFL Godseeker before, and I may not have an opportunity like this again.

"It felt pretty normal, until it wasn't. I was a Christian. I believed that there was a man named Jesus who died for me and rose from the dead. I believed in an afterlife, that is, life after death. I believed that if I was good in this life, that I'd have a good afterlife."

"But if you were a Godseeker, didn't you argue with people? Other religions? People who didn't believe in God? Didn't you think that your God would punish them for not following him?"

"Justice, maybe I'm the first one to tell you, but it was nothing like that. Most people believed what they wanted to, and that was that. Most people

let their faith enrich their lives, and the lives of others. You know, freedom of religion was protected under the First Amendment before freedom from religion."

"But freedom of religion was found unconstitutional and even dangerous by the PG Administration. I mean, it wrought so much dissent and conflict."

"President Greatness." His eyes roll up and he makes no further comment.

"Do... do you still believe in God?" I ask, hesitantly. "You don't have to tell me. In fact, that was a stupid —"

"Of course not, Justice. It's against the law."

I breathe a sigh of relief. That's right, professor. It's against the law. Only, I don't know if I'd treat him like I treated Max Tunay in the fourth grade. The way he describes believing in God makes it seem as though it wasn't such a bad thing.

A team of five IF Elites and about a dozen regulars assemble in Monument Park. I wish I could swap those numbers. The best Intervention Force officer would be hard-pressed to make as much impact as an Elite. But at this point, these are all the resources available to me. The city's on a budget, yada yada.

Residential high rises and a slew of strip malls populate southeastern Far City, but at this hour, most of them are empty and dark, save for a few late-night markets. Traffic sparsely sputters by in this older region of town, though earlier in the day, the main arterial buzzes with people trying to make their way in and out of downtown. Just off 24th Street and Garden, our search begins. We're traveling on foot, and I've instructed the team to inspect storm drains without using their flashlights. I'm certain that this will be an underground initiation. It wouldn't be the first one I've come across.

It's true that many ritual initiations happen inside private homes. Those are much more difficult to prevent, and the government lacks the money and time to run residential surveillance for such dangerless crimes. Maybe those resources were available back in the earlier part of the century when terrornoia entranced the public and the intelligence agencies used phone taps and microcameras to keep tabs on known threats. The Freedom Laws struck down that practice as too severe an invasion of privacy. I don't mind. I've been successful enough at my job without needing an eye into someone's home.

Public initiations are my business. A parent and priest will only opt to perform an RI on public land if they are trying to make a statement against our government. Treason — that's their first objective. An expression of hate for our country. They want to sabotage our way of life, and I won't stand for it.

Sewers are the first place to look. They're without cost, concealed, and dark no matter what time of day. Of the eight initiations I've broken up, six were attempted beneath city streets.

Still, I check the windows of businesses, whether they're opened or closed, lights on or lights off. Businesses are the more costly option for these families. Our economy is on the verge of recovering, and any opportunity to make extra money on the side appeals to the desperate business owner. They can charge astronomically high prices for common citizens looking to rent a private space for business of their own. The leasing party signs a waiver that places all legal responsibility upon the shoulders of the renters. This is a loophole the government allows, purely to support the practice of Business Baiters — corporations that will rent their property to wealthy families looking to conduct a religious ritual, and then, after depositing the check, blow the whistle to the IF. The culprits are then found and apprehended, and the families don't get their money back.

To be honest, I always thought Business Baiting was pretty messed up. In more corrupt scenarios, the business would receive an undocumented tax cut for narcing on the faithies. Obviously, I'm a shark for those who break AFLs, but taking their money and providing tax incentives is an abuse of power. Only once did I make a bust from a business tip, and I didn't forward their tax ID to the IRS for doing their duty to their country. Maybe that's why Beamer's getting the tips and not me.

Speaking of Beamer, I catch him from the corner of my eye leading a team of Peace Force through an alley away from 24th Street. They jog through puddles and trash that litter the ground, whisking their heads in every direction and occasionally stopping and crouching to look and listen beneath a dumpster or into a storm drain. They're doing their job thoroughly, and I'm a bit impressed.

I meet Beamer at the end of the block. The guy needs a break. His eyes, flushed red and squinting, struggle to meet mine, and he sways with his feet planted on the ground, still wearing the same clothes.

"Man, I've never seen you work so hard," I say, grinning at my backhanded compliment. "You trying to get some kind of award?"

"What can I say? I'm inspired."

"By yours truly, naturally."

"Naturally," he concedes droopily.

The raillery draws a perfunctory smile from Beamer, which quickly fades in his fatigue. "Your team is doing a good job, Beamer. I'd say we could handle this without you, but you look like it would take a shit storm and the apocalypse to get you to go home right now."

"It's my tip. I'm going to see it through."

"Atta boy. Keep at it."

I might joke about Beamer's work ethic, but in all honesty, he's very good at his job. If I'm the bad cop, he's the good one. Almost pleasant to the Godseekers we haul away. He used to be a regular beat cop who took down violent criminals. The Commanding Officer loves to poach skilled police officers into the IF. Instant Elites, most of them. If there's one comment about Beamer that came up from all his references, it's that he treated all his suspects with a degree of dignity that some cops don't believe criminals deserve. I don't share the same sentiments as my partner, but I respect that about him. He still pursues justice, but in his own way. It's a good thing we got paired together. I sort of balance him out. And I know he respects me. Even looks up to me. I've tried to push his ambition, but he keeps telling me that this is it for him. Intervention Force Field Specialist Elite. If he ever gets another job, he says it'll be something completely different like a chef or a teacher. Whatever floats his interesting little boat.

Beamer and his team turn a corner down L Street, and I start to prowl in the opposite direction.

It's after midnight, and the sidewalks are spread with graveyard shifters heading off to work and buzzing pockets of late night partiers already well into prefunk. A few vagrants wander back and forth searching for a place to sleep, and some have found refuge in the doorways of an old abandoned church.

Its old bricks stack on one another, lit orange by the pale street lights. Cracks in the weathered rectangles fan out like bolts of black lightning, some grooves as thin as a hair, others wide enough to peek through to the inside of the old sanctuary. Not so invulnerable anymore. I'm surprised the building survived the Freespeaker Movement, let alone time. It seems this ruin should be an apartment building or at least a parking lot by now.

Our Lady of Lourdes. That's a town in France. I heard in one of my university English lit classes that the residents of the town believe a mysterious woman cast a spell on a nearby stream, giving the water healing properties so powerful, believers from all around the world would make it a point to visit the remote village just to bring home a vial of the liquid. Our teacher assigned the story during a unit on mythology. The tale fascinated me. How miraculous it would be, to be healed from a disease just by drinking water from an ordinary stream. Even if it were just the common cold. I would probably travel halfway around the world to take a swig of that magic water.

For some reason, in the 1900s, the Far City Council allowed believers to erect this building and dedicate it to Lourdes and name it for their Church's mother. There's a glaring example of intervention — let's just claim an entire city in the name of a religion. Bapticks.

With perfect timing, in the middle of that very thought, I hear a rhythmic splash under the layers of aquatic sounds — the fall of rain, spilling of gutters, draining of stormwater. It comes from beneath the grating I'm standing on, as subtle as mist. I bound off the metal ridges and plant my belly on the concrete, the cold water quickly seeping through the gaps in my coat. Peering between the jagged slats, I search for any sign of human life ambling through the murky pipes. No voices, just a dim, steady light. It's a common feature of the tunnel — nothing to get excited about.

But as I push myself up, I notice a pronounced flicker, then another following closely behind. My eyes widen at first, then squint, and I can feel the edge of my lips curl into a smirk.

Two figures, walking underground. One is short and husky. The other is tall and appears to be wearing extra clothing to cover up her actual body type. She walks aggressively with her back upright as a tree trunk while the shorter woman attempts to keep up. This should be a piece of cake.

I press the mic button on my lapel. "Backup. Just outside the old church."

Theresa

"And lead us not into temptation, but –"

Mother Lania cut off. A jittery yellow circle, patterned in parallel shadows landed on Abraham's face. At once he let out a cry. Panic swelled as Theresa placed her hand over Abraham's mouth.

"I told you we'd find some rats in the sewer," a man grunted, squatting above the storm drain grating. His jaw was a rounded square and his shirt was not made for his neck. He rose to his feet and stood over the trio, taunting them with petulant grinning teeth that roared into a spitting fleer and snort.

"Over here!" he hollered at his team. "Cover the access points at 23rd and Terrace."

Theresa and Lania backed into the shadows while the man's head was turned. Didn't matter. Abraham was still whimpering. They bolted.

"Intervention Force," Lania said, already drawing deeper breaths. "If they were tipped, Elites will be with them."

"We gotta move," Theresa acknowledged. "The closest maintenance holes are just up ahead — a block and a half. They're bound to have those covered. But the ventilation opening over there — the one we

28

looked at last week. It's a tight fit, but there isn't much else."

They plodded through the underground stream, wading through drainage, plastic bottles, and prickly teeth and tails as they entered the narrow shaft. Old bricks suffocated them, while the smell of sour waste made them gag and cough. The encompassing darkness and ominous trickles of water whittled at their spirits.

They crawled through the cold and dank underground, hands and knees scraped and sticky wet. Theresa led the way with Lania close behind, but their getaway made little difference because Abraham started wailing again.

"Theresa—" Lania said calmly. "Let me hold him."

"They're right behind us. We have to move!"

"He's crying. Just 20 seconds."

Twenty seconds for Lania to work her magic. It was all she needed. Theresa rested Abraham in her friend's arms. Lania took a patient moment to settle the boy. Yes, magic it was. Whenever Theresa couldn't pacify her baby, Lania's embrace carried him to instantaneous quiet, punctuated with the child's long and curious stare. Her eyes went off into infinity — vast galaxies that spun love and compassion. And her touch — something about her touch calmed him, even more so than her eyes. Even in the cold of the sewers, she mustered some warmth that comforted Abraham, and his temperament cooled as she slowly drew the cry from him like a demon being exorcised.

She was graceful when she held him. It was always tight enough to make him feel safe. That's how anyone felt with Lania. Safe. Infants, and adults. Even in this moment, Theresa felt safety intertwined with her feeling of dread at their imminent capture. At least I'm with Lania, and Lania always knows what to do. The priest nodded and pushed forward.

Theresa, standing still in admiration, let her companion take the lead.

"Come on," Lania whispered. Theresa followed. "I don't know if we can outrun them, but I have a few tricks up my sleeve."

"What is that supposed to mean?" Theresa shot back to no response.

They approached the end of the ventilation shaft, but before exiting, Lania signaled for Theresa to stop. A light. Two of them ahead. Getting brighter.

Back! Back! Lania mouthed. "Turn off your glow stick," she added in a faint whisper. The water flowing through the sewer shrouded the sounds of their escape. Good thing it was still raining. They didn't get too far before the officers' flashlights made it into the shaft, at which point, the two women promptly froze and prayed that Abraham would not make a sound.

"Are we going to have to go in after you?" a stern female voice called from the end of the tunnel. "Come out now, and we won't be as pissed off when we catch you!"

Still, no sound. Like sculptures, they froze. Lania, in the cover of shadows, dressed in all black, crouched in front Theresa.

"Last chance!" the woman called. Her team came near.

"Find anything, Sky?" a man spoke.

"No, nothing in here."

"Good thing. Smells like cooked shit over there."

The crawlspace had curved just enough to keep them from line of sight, and the officer's bluff didn't carry. They lingered for several moments before deciding to flush themselves out.

"That was close," Theresa said. "Thanks for the heads up."

"Think I'd let anything happen to you? I told you when we started this thing that I'd keep you and Abraham safe." Theresa smiled and hugged her friend.

How long, they wondered. How long before the pursuit in the sewer would end? Before the IF would assume their prey had made it above ground or wandered to an opposite section of the sewers. Outside the ventilation shaft, Theresa and Lania were disoriented, but relieved to be out of the cramped crypt.

Another light, however, made their respite short-lived. The opposite tunnel intersection was too far to make it in time.

"We have to go back again," Theresa whispered curtly. "Maybe they've dispersed in the sewer and cleared the starting point."

"Maybe," Lania reluctantly agreed. "We're not having much luck in this labyrinth."

As they crawled back to where they began, Lania's breath failed to hold up. She pressed on out of love for her friend, but could feel her lungs writhing for lack of fresh air, her head spinning from the methane and absence of oxygen. She worked hard to stay physically fit, but along with her asthma, she suffered other limits to a 63 year-old body.

Theresa could offer her friend little help while trying to soothe Abraham and crawl at the same time. She halted now and then, allowing Lania to catch up.

"It's just up ahead," Theresa reassured.

Back at the entrance, there was only the steady soft yellow glow of the maintenance light. And silence. Theresa put her nose on the vent opening and scanned for law enforcement. At this point, she toyed with the thought of surrender, just to leave the sewer. Must be the fumes. No way in hell she would give up Abraham to alleviate her discomfort.

Not a soul in sight. She opened the gate and gently stepped out, with

Lania right behind. The two breathed in a breath of not-as-foul air. Still a relief.

"The Garden access point, just past Forest Avenue," Lania suggested. "I have a feeling."

Theresa nodded. Now a burst of energy found its way into Lania's step. She galloped forward, sensing that their window of time was closing. Past Terrace, past Village, past Governor avenues. Past Forest, and here they were just off Garden Boulevard in an alley access point.

"Let me go first," Lania said. "Wait down here. I'll let you know if it's safe."

"Well, what if it's not?" Theresa called after Lania who was already moving forward.

"Stay there with Abraham. You have to protect him."

Theresa nodded, Abraham somehow asleep in her arms.

Lania ascended the ladder and pushed up the sewer plate. She pulled herself out to the surface and breathed the clean air. Then she slid the plate back in its place.

Theresa looked upward, alone with her child. The moment confused her. Was she supposed to wait? Was Lania going to signal her? Then the obvious sunk in. Were it safe, she would have signaled. Instead, Lania didn't even look behind her as she sealed the exit. She knew what she was doing — she was giving Theresa a chance. Fret filled the young mother's head, but she wouldn't let it command her good sense. She backed around the nearest corner and sure enough, the lid was removed again. A bright light shone through accompanied by a head swiveling left and right.

"No one," the distant voice called.

No one. Then an argument between Lania and a man.

"Where is she? Which direction?" The man's voice boiled with aggression. A smack and a thud and an elderly woman's heaving gasp. "We don't need you alive, you know that, right?"

His words squeezed Theresa out of the shadows, but Abraham's eyes were open now, and she held back. *He* held her back.

"I won't say a word, unless you give me yours that she will not be harmed," Lania coughed. "She's my daughter. I won't see her killed. You will not take her child from her. And if you —"

"Daughter?" a snide voice remarked. "You don't have any kids. You gotta... for that to happen." A brief pause in the middle of his comment invited laughter of the other Intervention Force officers. Theresa wanted to pummel him for whatever gesture he made.

But Lania began shouting, feigning anger to keep Theresa away from the altercation. In the middle of Lania's tirade, Theresa noticed the wall across from her light up. It was too close to move without being heard. She froze in her place as a loud voice shouted, not twenty feet from the corner behind which she held her breath. Again, the ambient sounds of the sewer allied with her evasion. Steps coming closer. Fifteen, now ten feet away. Just around the corner.

"You find something up there?" the nearby voice called, recognizing the open access point ahead.

"We got the priest!" replied the surface. "Come back up — the baby and mother resurfaced back at Governor."

"You sure?"

"Yeah, the priest coughed it up so long as we stop beating her and don't harm the mother. 'Less you like it down there!"

"Yeah right!" The officer said passing the corridor where Theresa was hiding. If he had merely turned his head to the right, he would have seen her, but luck sided with Theresa. Still holding her breath, she waited until the officer had made it all the way up the ladder and to the surface. With her back to the wall, Theresa dared not move nor make a sound. She could hear the officers above taunting her friend, mixed with blows and Lania hitting the ground.

"Get up!" a man yelled.

Another kick.

"I said get up! We're moving."

"Well she's not."

"You hit her too hard, man."

"Or she hit her head on the ground."

"She's not moving."

"She's done."

"No she's not. She's just out."

"Check her pulse."

"Probably would have died anyway."

"Well, pick her up and —"

The access plate clanked back into place, and she was left with her son, alone. The stream in the middle of the sewer floated gently above the grave silence. Theresa looked left and right and left until she realized she was only shaking her head. Her eyes fell on Abraham, then lifted to the sky. But there was no sky, only the darkness underground. She felt sick. She wanted to vomit, but there was nothing in her stomach. She hadn't eaten all day. Her breath pounded on her lungs like a trampoline and leapt out of her mouth. Then she screamed a soundless scream, only a steady weak flow of miserable air snuck by her vocal chords. Tears streamed from her eyes, landing on Abraham like rain, then joining the drainage below. She collapsed to her knees, holding her newly baptized baby close. Her prize. What she risked everything for. A pyrrhic accomplishment she wished she could return to the universe.

Not an hour ago, she had an unbaptized baby and the woman she considered a mother, alive and well. Now began the agony of living with her decision. Too soon, she thought, too soon. Too much! Not worth it! She clutched Abraham to her chest tightly, as if using him to hold her crumbling heart together.

Lania did it. Made good on her promise. Theresa had always felt safe with Lania. Because a mother would do anything to protect her child.

JUSTICE

Midland America University

Sophomore Year

Spring quarter, 2080

"*Why do you teach about God?" I finally confront ProTruth.*

"*As I recall, you once asked me about God after class, last fall, was it?"*

"*You remember that?"*

"*How could I forget? I almost gave away my secret life as a doubler. Oh — I think I've said too much."*

"*You better watch your mouth around me." I laugh playfully, but the nagging suspicion is always there. I tell it to pipe down. ProTruth is a free thinker, but he's not a law breaker. This is the third straight quarter I've taken his class. I'm a level three now. He pretty much knows my deepest darkest secrets and has pegged me as a power-hungry egomaniac. He's right, of course. But I've got him pegged too. A sentimental old man in a forty year-old's body who just sits around and thinks too much. At least he's got a sense of humor.*

"*So, you were questioning my practices," he says.*

"*Yes, I was. In our modern society, where God is not just an archaic concept, but an illegal one, how can you possibly justify bringing it up in class?"*

"For starters, I haven't broken any laws in speaking about God as the 'concept' existed. Plus, it's my class, and I've been given free rein to teach as I please, as long as I get my students to think for themselves. It is my course title after all — Freethought in the Late 21st Century."

"Fine. But why God? Why not other freedoms, like the right to bear arms or more about Freespeak? I mean, there's so many other ways to look at freedom in our country than some old anachronism."

"Nice word. What's wrong with delving deep into a subject matter of illegal proportions? Do you fear you might turn into a seeker?"

I take offense and stand up.

"Sit down!" he commands. "You sure are sensitive when it comes to this topic."

"Well everyone is! Look around society. No one talks about God. It's against the law. We're breaking the law right now, and you're doing the same in your class. I'm surprised you haven't been locked away already."

He smirks.

"You—"

"Look Justice," he interrupts again before I can ask about his criminal record. "God isn't any less real just because Godtalk is punishable by God knows what. And neither are the people who followed or continue to follow that school of thought. I am not afraid to teach about God because I believe that in order to think freely, especially in this society that is so bent on freedom, you have to understand as much of the truth as you can get your hands on. And the ability to tell truth from perspective has dwindled so much in the past few decades. The news isn't even news anymore. It's entertainment and gossip." He searches my eyes for approval.

"You're getting off topic," I point out, something he's been doing a lot more lately. "Why God? Can't you teach us to think freely without mentioning God?"

"No. Because how can you think freely if you can't think about God?"

His logic punctures my impression of the law, and wouldn't you believe it, he's making me think.

"If it makes you feel better, Justice, I'm not trying to convince you to believe in God, or even of God's existence. I'm only asking you to open your mind. And there's nothing wrong with that, I hope."

The silent body in my back seat tugs at the restraints around her hips, legs and torso. Her cuffed wrists are held in place by a strap and buckle embedded in the cushion. I'm hoping she doesn't regain consciousness before we reach the City Interrogation Center. I don't think she will. We knocked her around pretty good.

Still, the baptized baby. Somewhere in my city. Exactly what I set out to prevent. I need to find it fast. A future SCO doesn't lose initiated children. With over fifteen officers on hand, I'm confounded that we lost them. We had the advantage. I knew the priest was lying, but nobody wanted to spend another minute in that sewer. This one will talk though.

We have Beamer's source, and if nothing else, the Truth Committee will have their way, and we'll know every location she has ever been with the mother. It takes a special kind of person to join the Truth Committee. The interrogations are a mutated form of infinity, and I mean for those who are asking all the questions. Sure the drug they use on prisoners slows time to a geologic pace, but the way the committee members search for answers is like searching for one person in the most crowded city on earth. You've got to be so precise in how you word questions, but I think the first and worst qualification for the job is the ability to sit on your ass for a ridiculous number of hours, asking circular questions and hoping your subject coughs up new information. I'm glad I'm only delivering the package.

I pull up to the City Interrogation Center at about one-thirty in the morning. A wired fence with a razor coil snaking across the top support beam encircles the premises. The four outer walls of the cube-shaped building, painted a sterile white, reflect the glimmer of the surrounding street lamps. Citizens call it The Box and consider it the eyesore of downtown. For the common Far City dweller, this structure is far too ordinary — not enough color, not enough protrusions.

Two windows flank the main entrance, the only two windows installed in the building. It baffles me, why the designers bothered to implant these glass panels, long and narrow like skinny towers. They are tinted, allowing filtered light to project a cheese orange glimmer on the floor inside. But only for about an hour. Afterwards, all natural light is hidden by surrounding skyscrapers, and it's all fluorescent after that.

Get me out of here — the dreaded home of the Truth Committee, where prisoners go to lose their minds and endure the painful side effects of *eternatae*, the recently outlawed mind alteration drug used to draw truth from the lips of AFL prisoners. In the minds of the Truth Committee, the drug is too effective to be illegal. I would bet most Commanding Officers couldn't care less if the drug makes its way into interrogation rooms. Many Intervention Force staff and old school detectives still carry single-use syringes in their belts. I have never had the misfortune of that poison rushing through my system, but on a few occasions, I have employed it on my detainees. Information begets

39

incarceration, and I believe I have a right to do whatever it takes to protect my society, even if my local senators and representatives are a little
soft.

I pull up to the security tower where the guard scans my identification card, then slide my bulky Ford Enforcer into one of the dozen
parking spaces near the entrance. After shutting off the ignition, I look
with dread upon the building before me, and even more so at the blur
on my windshield amassing as the rain raps on the glass. Then I look
back at the woman. Still unconscious. I retract my wish for her uncon-
sciousness and hope she wakes at this moment so she can walk to the
door on her own accord instead of me having to carry her.

She lies still, her head drooping from her neck like an overripe piece
of fruit about to fall from a tree. Her short, curly hair is a tuft of white
and gray. Along her neck, two other colors stand out to me. Navy blue
and goldenrod line the collar of the shirt she wears beneath her priest
garb. I'm familiar with the colors. I wore them proudly as a student of
Midland America University. Something we have in common. Whenever
I'm reminded of my alma mater, a memory wanders into my head. I hate
the memory, but I can't say the same for the person to whom it's attached. It's this old professor. A man who made me think in ways that
would get me fired and probably locked up. A man who thought my
dream to be Supreme Commanding Officer was a bad idea. A man whom
I loved, because I knew he'd do anything to help me live my life to the
fullest. Only his idea of living my life to the fullest came into direct conflict with my own. You know what — enough about that.

Seeing my old school colors around the priest's neck transforms my
apathy toward her. I've arrested hundreds of Godseekers and broken up
initiations so many times that it's merely a series of routines that I

follow. But something about this moment is different. A foreign force has infected my usual attitude. In all my busts, I've never felt a sliver of sympathy for my adversaries or guilt about what I do.

It takes a minute, but I shake my head and shut down that feeling. I've done that numerous times, whenever that old man pops up into my head. I've been coached on how to handle these feelings, neither of which are productive to my purpose. None of which are conducive to landing the job I want.

Who is this woman to me, anyway? Nobody. She's no one. She is a law breaker, and she deserves this. But the colors. Professor T— I won't say his name. Not even in my head. He taught me that freethought in a Freespeak society is essential. And that freethought can only exist if I respect others' beliefs. What a crock. If that were true, then religion wouldn't be outlawed. But it makes so much sense. Why should my view on life be any better than this priest's. It's not as if she's hurting anyone. Only helping herself.

Maybe I can let her go. That's the craziest thought I've ever had. I'm not exaggerating. What would I say? She regained consciousness, somehow beat me in a scuffle or outsmarted me, both of which are impossible for an old God lady? I've done this hundreds of times. She'll be number 383. That's all she is. Just a number.

I close my eyes and draw in a gust of air. Supreme Commanding Officer, Justice. It's my dream. It's my destiny. With that thought, I get out of the car. At least the rain is warm, but it doesn't take long, even in the moment I frantically close the car door and unlock the back, for the shower to form tributaries that roll down my cheeks and fall from my chin. I lean in and begin unraveling her from the restraints, then drag her out by the legs in one sweeping motion. I squat and dig my shoulder into her gut, then lift her body, using one arm to support her and one to shut and lock the door.

Her body is large and unwieldy. I thud through the puddles to the City Interrogation Center entrance, a metal monolith of a gate. I buzz the intercom, and no one answers. I hit the button again, and just as I'm about to leave her body in the rain on their doorstep, a click and buzz release the deadbolts, and the portal is opened. I wait for someone to pull it open, but apparently I have to do that too. At least it's hinged inward so I can kick it open, and standing in the corridor as I enter is a tree of a man who looks strong enough to have assisted me with the body-transporting duties. I shoot him an impatient glance. He sits at a desk behind a window of tempered glass and wears a goofy grin on his face.

"Papers," I say as I let the woman drop on the floor. I hate papers. Handwriting is pretty much extinct, except when you have to file official captive registration forms at the Box. "Get them quickly. The mother and baby are still at large and I need to get back out there."

"Justice! It's been a while. Yeah, let me get those papers going for you."

I've never met — or noticed — this man in my life. I've been in here only a handful of times. How does this guy remember me? He's too friendly for my urgent circumstances and already he irritates me.

"Come on!" I yell, not making an attempt to sugarcoat my urgency.

My elevated voice causes him to fumble around, but soon he regains control of his brain and puts all the paperwork together.

"Do you need anything? Coffee?" he asks.

"Get some guards out here to take this woman to a holding cell. They should have been on hand already. And give me a pen."

My self-doubt back in the car spawns the irritability I'm unleashing on this poor clerk. If I hate having to come here in the middle of the night, imagine having to be here every night. A moment of sympathy for the man comes and goes. I'm sure I won't be met with the same greeting next time I come in here, which I hope is a long time from now, if ever.

In the foyer where I'm standing are a few tables and chairs for field agents to trudge through the least interesting part of our job; anywhere from 30 minutes to three hours of handwriting. The files go to the Truth Committee to prepare their interrogation, and I have to be legible and painstakingly meticulous. Every observation, interaction and interpretation I have need to go on paper — another way her car nap benefits me. Some criminals I apprehend don't understand the importance of the words, *you have the right to remain silent.* If I were on the Supreme Court I'd change the word *right* to *obligation.*

Straining my mind for information, I spill out all I can in under an hour then hand the clipboard back to the man behind the desk who, although we are in the same room, pretends I don't exist. Now that the paperwork is all filled out and I don't have to be in this pit anymore, I try to be courteous. Don't want him to think I'm a complete asshole.

"Hey, thanks a lot, Court," I say, catching his name engraved above his badge. "Sorry to be such a jerk when I got here. I'd love to catch up, but I need to return to the field and have my partner update me."

He nods solemnly and turns to filescan and deliver my report to the Truth Committee. I hardly notice that the priest's body has been moved, but I don't let such details interrupt my stride to the other side of that metal door.

I check my phone to see if Beamer has an update. There's only one message.

Back at headquarters. Combed the entire radius with a four block cushion and with back up. Gonna have to regroup and do some legwork.

Dammit.

Theresa

Dawn hadn't yet broken and already, birds sang a morning hymn. Abraham squiggled and hollered, entertained by a flickering glow flashing outside Theresa's window.

An unholy bonfire — a political statement so common, it was now passé — whipped and snapped across the street in front of the old St. Catherine's church. Boards crossed the frames where stained glass depictions of the church's namesake once filtered eastern sunlight into the building. Nails and needles littered the grounds like boobie traps for any unknowing wanderers.

A statue of Catherine of Siena overlooked dried piles of human feces and stains of urine lining the walls of the walkway between the church and the rectory. Her head was covered in a habit and her eyes aimed downward, not with judgement, but with a munificence that embodied her legacy. While the walkway reeked with human waste, her effigy remained untouched.

The church, preserved out of historical sentiment from residents of the neighborhood, was finally set to be demolished later in the summer. The Far City Council had won that long-fought battle. It was about time, thought Theresa. Nothing historical or holy had happened there in years. The block would soon sprout high-rise micro apartments and street level retail. Many of Theresa's neighbors were hoping for a Healthwide, a popular national grocery store that sold only lab produced foods. Locals had always griped at why it had taken so long to remove the old abandoned eyesore of a church. Even Theresa wanted to put the space out of its misery.

She had walked into St. Catherine's only once, before she became a mother. It wasn't her home parish, and the priest delivering masses was strictly traditional at a time when Catholic Progressivism caught fire. The advancements were all for naught. The state ushered the congregation out by rule of the American Freedom Laws. All metropolitan places of worship and prayer were to be vacated, shut down, and repurposed. Churches would be compensated for their property, but their sacramentals and images of God and religion would need to be immediately demolished. The compensation promised was significant, but met delay after delay, indecision and technicality. That type of money never leaves the pockets of the ones making the promise.

The flashing of the fire died down, and Abraham woke as the sun burst through Theresa's bedroom window. He seemed rather peaceful, in stark contrast to his mother who could muster no dissimulation of her grief in front of her child.

Lania. The thought of her name, its five letters, floated and dispersed in Theresa's mind like a cloud of smoke. Then Lania's mouth. Her eyes, and soon her entire body. Her smile. The clothes she wore the night of the baptism. More and more, Lania's features revealed themselves. They shattered Theresa's heart and made it soar at the same time. Lania's absence filled Theresa with emptiness.

Abraham's peace exited his body as he sensed his mother's sadness. He began crying. Theresa limped out of bed, pulling herself together as best as she could. She approached Abraham's crib and picked up her newly baptized baby, singing him a soft, minor hymn.

The Lord is my shepherd, I shall not want.
In the fields of green, he gives me rest.
In waters still and deep, he is my breath.
My shattered soul, he shall restore.
On paths of life, he walks before.

The Lord is my -

It was a psalm of life after death. Theresa had always found it lovely. Lania had just been ordained a few years before being introduced to Theresa as a young girl who lived with her widowed father. Theresa's mother had died when she was barely five years-old. Cancer. A natural way to go. At least her mother's fate was not engineered by hate and fear. Biologists, philanthropists, even governments spent billions of dollars and countless hours researching a cure for the loathsome illness, until finally they found a way to eliminate it altogether.

Shame, the lonely mother thought, a shame no one had found a cure for the driving force behind Lania's killers, or bothered to make such an effort.

Theresa had a routine whenever she visited her father. The 45 minute trek to Marina Town could be tedious in traffic, but it was Sunday morning, and the gridlock stacked in the opposite direction with people from the suburbs flooding downtown Far City for the annual Freespeak Parade. She wanted no part of that. Along the way up north, she passed a handful of landmarks as she sped by on the interstate, ones she and her father would frequent in her younger days.

Center Bay. A fitting welcome mat for Far City, the skyline of which still looked like a cluster of stalagmites surrounded by forest, mountain and sea, despite rapid development earlier in the century. Theresa and her father rode the ferry together at least once a month when she was younger. The water held some special significance to him, and then to her. Neither of them would entertain living in a place away from a large body of water. How many times they crossed the Sound, Theresa couldn't count. She only knew that it was enough to immortalize the bay as a perpetual reminder to give some part of her busy adult life to her father. She'd catch herself staring out the window of her car as she crossed the Old Seattle Bridge on the way to work. She'd see a ferry sailing slowly across the Sound. Then she'd know it was time for a visit.

Midtown Shopping Center was the next attraction on her drive. She spent most of her time there with friends, but her dad always drove. The weekend before a high school dance or a friend's party, or sometimes just to hang out, she would ask her dad for a run to the mall. He never said no because Theresa always had a grasp on when not to ask. Family gatherings and school work took precedence.

On the left side of the interstate, Heathland Athletic Center housed recreational sports games on evenings and weekends. Theresa played basketball for the Heathland Seagulls rec team from fourth grade through middle school. Her teammates became lifelong friends. Now as adults, she met with them for brunch just about every other month, a practice they continued even now. They were supposed to meet in a couple of weeks, but Theresa doubted she'd make it this time. Wouldn't even give it a foolish hope as a fugitive. The HAC girls, they were called by staff at the center. At nine years old, Theresa didn't want to go out for the basketball team, like many young people fear trying new things, but her father pushed her to try. He had played growing up, and wanted another way to connect with his daughter, especially an activity that got her out of the house and moving around. Once she made the team, he never missed a game, and often played with her outside in their alley or at the school.

The last landmark on the tour up to her father's residence was Our Lady of Lourdes Catholic School, where Theresa went to elementary and junior high. In Theresa's eyes, the greatest gift her dad gave her was his faith. He grew up a PC — Progressive Catholic — a movement that led to many changes in the church, both small and great. His faith taught him to love, to include, to serve, to be compassionate, to uplift, and to pry open the rusty hinges of old Catholics who clung to outdated traditions and beliefs. In a society that put so many disguises on discrimination, Theresa's father had a faith that demanded he accept — truly and unconditionally accept — everyone, no matter their difference. Instilled in Theresa were these same values, and in no other place were they more richly cultivated than at OLL Catholic School. As a teacher at the school for nearly two decades, Theresa's father was a deeply rooted member of the community. Hundreds of students, parents, staff, former priests, and parishioners showed up to the final destination on Theresa's drive from her home in Far City.

The gates of St. Francis of Assisi Cemetery were always open. Even though the American Freedom Laws ended organized religion in the United States, and buildings fell and streets and cities renamed, the one sanctuary still untouched by the government was the religious cemetery. The line had to be drawn somewhere, and it was drawn by the dead.

Theresa never brought flowers or knick knacks to place at her father's grave, only her words. In fact, it took a long while after his burial for Theresa to even visit. She didn't feel like he was there. She wanted to believe she could find him in every sunset, in the old basketball they used the play with, which she kept in her living room. She felt his presence at church, until that was taken from her. Then, she thought he would be in the places where they used to eat and shop. But after a while, she could no longer find him in those places. Only his memory and the ache of missing her father. Now at last, she found him only within the walls of St. Francis Cemetery, the last place she saw him in person. The only place she knew she could be with him like she wanted to. Next to him. Even if it was just sitting on the grass next to last month's rotting flowers, counting the dried petals on the ground, doing her best to feel alive with him.

She missed him still, twelve years later, just as much as she did the day he died. She felt the same grief, cried the same tears, wished the same wish, that he would be back for one more day. The sadness that was a part of her was a painful, yet happy companion. Painful because he was gone, but happy because in those moments of grief, they were together.

It seemed fitting for many reasons that she visit her father the day after Abraham's baptism, and the day after she lost Lania. Without him, the baptism would have never happened. Without him, she would never have met Lania, and definitely would not have been as close to the priest, close enough to call her Mother.

She pulled in along the graveyard, took Abraham in her arms, and walked down three stone steps toward her father's grave. It lay among the blades of grass, flat and humble among the taller tombstones.

Abram Paulo Torres

May 29, 1981 - February 21, 2048

"Love one another, as I have loved you."

"Hey Dad."

"Your grandson — he's baptized."

She clutched Abraham tightly to show him.

"Your dying wish... I did it."

She couldn't hold it together. The words *I did it* encompassed so much, and in her mind *it* began to unravel.

I did it. I took Abraham, your grandson, into the sewers beneath the city, and Lania baptized him. It was as public as it was going to get. But you wanted a public baptism. A middle finger to the AFLs and to the Free-speakers who took your life. Abe's a full fledged Catholic now, in a world that will give him hell for that. No one was there except me and Mama Lania. But that was enough...

I did it. I initiated the first Catholic in Far City in over two years. Abraham is just one child, but maybe we can save our church and other faiths too. Either way, I'm going to teach him how to love others and serve others first. Just like you taught me. Just like Jesus...

I did it. I found my courage and my strength. I stood up to the

Freespeaker Movement. To the Freedom Laws. To the system, to the man, to the government. I did it. Like you always wanted. Because you thought people should be free to practice their faith. I believe in that too. Because of you. So I did it. I didn't care about the cost. I did it. Because I felt like you were with me when I did.

"I did it," she spoke. "I did all of it. But I —"

She tried to console herself by looking at all the positives of baptizing Abraham. But it wasn't enough. She collapsed to her knees with Abraham in her arms. He began weeping too. The birds and the wind joined in. A small moth, fluttering around Abraham's face, landed on his head. Every time she visited her father, a moth would land on her shoulder. It was a small and simple sign, but Abram was never one for the grandiose.

"— I lost my mother. I lost Mama Lania to the Freespeakers."

"First you. Now her."

What will I do if they get Abraham?

Someone had recently cut the grass at St. Francis Cemetery. Even though the state permitted its existence, there was no entity to maintain the landscape. No new burials were allowed. When a loved one died, the hospitals sent the body to the cremation wing, and ashes were distributed to families in vials, if they wished to keep them. Sentiment for the dead was a thing of the past. Most of the society cared little for the elderly, so why care about the dead? Social security was eliminated first, then driving rights, then healthcare — there was little left to revere about being, when someone has been for so long.

Still, many underground religious memorialized their family and friends. Some would sneak into St. Francis, which was tended by volunteers who claimed to maintain it for aesthetic reasons.

Since burying someone's remains or any semblance of a ritual was a grave violation of the American Freedom Laws, many religious, not just Catholics, would bring the remains of their loved ones along with an artifact to mark their place at the cemetery. Lania's ashes would not be possible, so Theresa brought a rosary that Lania had given her when she was confirmed. She took a small hand shovel and began digging a hole next to her father. This too, would make him happy, she thought. In life, and in death, they could be together.

"Here, Lania," Theresa said through subsiding sobs. "I know it's not you, but this rosary is a part of you. Dad would be happy you are by his side."

Theresa

The affluent neighborhood in northeast Far City remained untouched by the neo-architecture of the mid-21st century. A tall brick barrier encircled the blocks that made up Old Lakeview, and residents vehemently upheld the long history of the area.

With all the money — old money — and long standing family presence in the neighborhood, a developer couldn't afford a permit to build a box-shaped house without a prolific bank account or two. Even then, one would need power and community status in order to achieve such a feat in one of Far City's oldest neighborhoods. Homes there, even the most modest, would sell for over five million, but then again, no one in the neighborhood was interested in getting rid of their property.

The parked cars gleamed in the sunlight, lining both sides of the street, making statements about the tastes of their owners. Fast, luxurious, futuristic, cavernous, classic - anything but a practical car that could take you safely from point A to point B at a reasonable speed. When Theresa drove through in her sedan as she had many times before, she felt out of place — an anxiety about brushing up her old Honda against a six-figure hunk of shiny metal.

With Abraham in tow, she arrived at an old Spanish style villa overlooking Lake Mossgrove. She pulled up to the black iron-bar gate and pushed the intercom button.

"Bolden Residence," a cheery voice said.

"Hi Fern, it's Theresa."

"Oh Theresa! Just a moment, dear."

The gate slowly crept open. Theresa coasted along the driveway and approached a roundabout that encircled a fountain covered with blue moon wisteria. Purple flowers draped above the water, some low hanging branches dipping in at the intermittent breeze and breaking up the perfect reflection. Theresa wondered whether the fountain was inspired by some famous painting, or if the fountain had inspired an acrylic she'd seen at an art gallery show a couple years before her first acquaintance with the Bolden estate.

August Bolden was a frugal rich man perpetually house sitting for his parents who seemed to be on perpetual vacation. He always had everything he could ask for and then some, and while Theresa never lived in poverty, she felt out of place whenever she found herself in her former husband's circles. Their conversation bounced from moorage fees to private island vacations, to buying private islands and other topics that made Theresa cringe to think about all that money being talked about in this quiet, gated part of town, when just ten minutes away were homeless shelters and rehab facilities struggling to stay open. It was another world, because in her imagination, had she the same wealth, she would have used the money to build a school for disadvantaged children. And a trip to Tahiti.

Whenever the topic of conversation amongst August's friends

managed to fall upon some tragic story in the news about violence or broken youths, they would engage Theresa for her perspective as a social worker.

Gang violence, a fading nuance of the early 2000s would make headlines to the shock and fear of August's entourage.

"We spend so much money locking up those religious fanatics," Theresa once heard from one of August's associates. "Why not put some of our tax dollars toward locking up these savage youth?" Coming from the lips of a woman whose family business was a privatized juvenile reform center.

The eyes in the circle gradually gravitated to Theresa, and an awkward silence until, "You work with people like that, don't you Theresa? Horrible, I'm sure."

Theresa would shrug, and August would rebuke his friends for being so ignorant. His friends would roll their eyes and change the topic. August didn't have many friends.

Her former husband was different than the circles that appeared in his home like periodic rashes. Somehow, despite his wealth, August managed to stay down to earth. He never flaunted his money, though he wasn't ashamed of it either. He'd waited a good long while before revealing his financial status to Theresa. Sure, he drove a nice car, but just about anyone in the city could be driving a BMW or Tesla. It wasn't until they were officially dating for two months that he said those alarming words to Theresa: "I'm rich."

He'd grown to accept his family's affluence and was quietly generous with his money. Some of his own projects were public art galleries and performance halls, where the contributors were children and amateur painters, poets, dancers and actors. He believed that the more people were in touch with their inner artist, the more successful they would be in life. His tone in conversation angled toward the world and what could be done to make it better, often stemming from his view of the news or the latest book in his hand. Among the many properties his parents owned, a generous wedge in their own budget was dedicated to philanthropy. As for work, he held a degree in the arts and spent much of his days relentlessly painting in his studio at the Bolden Estate.

He did not identify with any religion growing up, so the transition to the era of the American Freedom Laws didn't pose much of an obstacle. Not until he fell in love with Theresa.

He was searching for his own purpose when he found her.

The Downtown Youth Care Center was where their paths first crossed. Theresa was instructing a program for teenage runaways, and August was looking for a place and people with whom to share his artistic talents. Before he even laid eyes on Theresa, he heard her voice, encouraging a young foster child who had run away from home. He fell in love with that voice. It was like a song to him — the tone and tempo, the pitch and melody. He heard it all together, a harmony he couldn't get out of his head. Foremost were the words of encouragement she directed toward the youth, words he knew could never find, even if he tried. When it came to giving of himself for the sake of another person, he admittedly had a lot to learn. And he wanted to learn from her.

After his first day volunteering at the Youth Care Center, August came back on a weekly basis, then twice a week, hoping for a coincidental encounter with this woman he found so fascinating. The very next time he encountered Theresa was nearly a month after he first met her, and he asked her out. She said yes, more and more as she got to know him. Yes to his eagerness to change the world. Yes to his honesty and integrity. Yes to his own love for her. After dating for a year, they were engaged, and Theresa became pregnant with Abraham. There, their paths divided. Theresa was set on baptizing Abraham. August was more than afraid. Not only would his child be put at mortal risk, but Theresa and he himself could face a prison camp or worse.

He couldn't go through with it, and asked politely for a divorce, a practice common in his day and age. The ubiquity mattered little to Theresa. She was heartbroken to find the extent of August's tolerance of her Catholicism. She admitted that she asked for a great deal in having Abraham baptized, but she believed that August's love was enough.

She was wrong. Or he was.

The marble floors and ivory columns of the Bolden Estate resembled the Vatican in grandiosity. Theresa entered with her shoes on, which always felt weird to her. In her house, shoes were not allowed, for cultural and practical purposes. "Don't drag the rest of the city into the house," Theresa's father would say, echoing his mother, who echoed generations before.

The Boldens had staff to take care of the dirt problem. In fact they had a dedicated hospitality worker — Fern — a cleaning crew, a maintenance crew, rotating culinary specialists, and an aesthetic team. Theresa never had any idea of the latter's job description, but she noticed the artwork on the walls of the main hall rotating every two or three months, along with the houseplants and music played over the built in sound system.

Fern wasn't too much older than Theresa, and she had yet to sprout a single white hair. A jovial woman who acknowledged all the niceties of etiquette and social hobnob, Fern managed and maintained the estate while August simply lived there. She greeted Theresa with a smile. The two were on friendly terms, and during August's parties, Theresa would opt for her company over his friends'.

"Theresa, it's been a long while," she said with a Mary Poppins proper accent. She sized up her friend, then frowned. "You look a mess, but Abraham is happy as ever." Theresa laughed and Abraham stared up at Fern's perfect grin then to his mother's sleep-deprived eyes.

"Yeah, a well-deserved mess," Theresa said.

"You did it then?" Fern asked, ignoring Theresa's observation. "You baptized Abraham?"

A nod and a proud smile at the first person who acknowledged her secret op. "I did. Or — *we* did."

"Lania?"

The triumph of Theresa's nod only a moment ago evaporated like a droplet of water on a frying pan. Fern went in for an immediate embrace. She evaluated her friend.

"Good God, I'm so proud of you," Fern said. "I wish I had the same nerve as you and Lania. The same courage."

"You don't know how much that means to me, Fern."

"I think I might. Like I said, you look terrible. I can't imagine what you've been through. I'm not sure I'd like to find out, either." They entered the villa. Under the archway of the front door, the two walked on a painted tile floor.

"Come to the kitchen first," Fern said. "I just baked a peach pie. You are going to have a slice. I'll make you a cup of coffee, and don't say no because I know you need it. Did you have lunch yet?"

"No not yet," Theresa chuckled, overwhelmed by Fern's kindness. "I just came by after visiting my father."

"Then you're going to eat too. There's some chicken en croute in the fridge. I'll put it in the oven."

Theresa felt safe for the moment in the care of a friend, especially after running through the Far City sewers just last night. Fern held Abraham while Theresa ate, then pulled out a bottle of milk from Theresa's cooler bag and fed him while Theresa recounted the baptism. Everything from the stench of the sewer to losing Lania.

"How horrifying," Fern said. "You're on the run then. You need a place to hide out."

"No. I should be fine. I heard them. Lania didn't give me away before —"

Fern nodded. "Are you sure? I mean, are you sure she's not still alive? There's a chance, I mean, maybe they just wanted you to think she was dead."

The thought never occurred to Theresa, and it moved her to silence.

"Don't lose hope, dear," Fern added. "I have a feeling you're going to need it with the life you're choosing to live. Do you want me to let August know you're here? He's upstairs painting in his studio."

"Yes," Theresa answered while shaking her head.

August Bolden combed his cocoa brown hair over to the right, and the top of his head was just about eye level with Theresa. He kept in shape, playing racquetball and running on the lake trail just outside his residence, but mostly with his eccentric style of abstract painting on wall-sized canvases. He would twist, jump, splatter, reach and stretch to get his work of art just right. In the process, he would not be disturbed, except under urgent circumstances. For Fern, who would judge the appropriate level of urgency, Theresa's situation was over the top.

He made his way into the kitchen, his hair out of place from the last few hours of painting, and sat in front of Theresa. Their most recent exchange didn't end well, and he carried a reserve of guilt with him. He had admonished her for wanting to baptize Abraham. Living a private faith life was fine, but taking part in the ritual was too much. His decision to leave her was anything but final, however. Guilt rapidly took residence inside of him and spread like weeds in a garden. Throughout his days, it gnawed at the fibers of his consciousness.

As of late, his paintings had a dark theme to them, with patterns uneasy and disjointed. It resembled the troubled state of his heart, and her, the noble Theresa — he believed her heart to be too pure. She always had the best of intentions and would treat people kindly. Never harmed a soul, nor harbored any bitterness. Mockingbird, he would call her. He wanted her to adopt the name. She told him there wasn't a chance in hell.

"So, this is our newly baptized child?"

"Yes, he's *our* newly baptized child," Theresa glared, the wound of their separation still fresh. August spared any reaction.

"Let me hold him," he said. It felt odd to Theresa, handing over the child that he abandoned. But she needed August to remember what it felt like to be a father. This simple exchange wouldn't suddenly activate his sense of paternal responsibility, but it would be a start.

Abraham took kindly to his father. He offered August a look of wide-eyed excitement and a loose giggle that spurred a swell of pride in the man. August's face lit up with surprise, and he laughed himself. He hadn't held Abraham in two months and was afraid his first born had forgotten him. But no, the connection remained, and August felt an odd juxtaposition of guilt and joy.

"Why did you have to risk it Theresa?" he asked. "Well, it doesn't matter. You didn't get caught. You're here. You still plan on teaching him to be a Catholic?"

"I do." Unexpectedly, the words came out of Theresa's lips like a question.

"This is so dangerous — you know that," August said. "I just heard on the news that the Intervention Force apprehended a priest engaged in a baptism last night and are searching —"

He had made the connection well after Theresa expected.

"You. They're looking for you and Abraham. See. I knew —"

He stopped himself. She'd heard it before. He'd said it before. The results were ugly. No need to repeat.

"What do you need?" he said, breaking the tense silence. "Money? How much? Whatever you need."

It was the guilt. Surely it was the guilt, but it also felt like something else. Love. Yes, he still loved her. Perhaps he had been a fool to leave his family for a fear.

"I don't need money, August."

"Then what do you need? Anything to protect you and our son."

"I need you to do exactly what you're doing. I need you to hold him. I need you to be a father. Take Abraham, just long enough to make the Intervention Force think I've sent him off. I'll need maybe a week. Can you do that?"

August glanced down at Abraham. The confidence to be a father — a good father — had always eluded him. He knew that was the underlying reason he left Theresa and Abraham. Uncertainty seeped into his mind, then troubled and entangled his emotions. The words were out of his mouth before he made his decision.

"Okay. He can stay here." He felt the warmth Abraham generated in his chest, abdomen and arms. This can't be too hard, he thought. "You need to go, Theresa."

"I was never here."

JUSTICE

Midland America University

Sophomore Year

Winter quarter, 2079

"*I know what I'm doing, dad.*"

"*That's fine Justice. Do what you want. Just don't do it with my money.*"

"*It's a Freethought class.*" Maybe I should have taken Advanced Rhetoric. I never thought I'd have to defend my favorite class to my number one financer.

"*I've never heard of Freethought, but I'll tell you what — it sounds like a fluke. What do they teach in a Freethought class anyway?*"

"*How Godseekers think. Why they think they're right and not breaking the law. It's a good class. You still want me to become a Commanding Officer just like you, right? Freethought is the way to go. There's studies that show —*"

"*What studies? How can it help you make Elite if I've never even heard of it? If it should impress anyone, it should impress me.*"

It's hard having a dad who knows it all.

"Look it up," I say, "It's the next thing in the anti-intervention field."

Classic delay tactic. I'd keep arguing, but I don't have time for this, especially when I know I won't win this debate with my father. He's right, mostly. I haven't done any research on Freethought. I just figured it would be interesting, and I was right. From what I know there is little research about Freethought and no correlation to Godseekers, other than my own personal hunch that it will help me track down AFL violators. I still hold to that rationale, but the deeper reason why I'm taking this class is because it's so damn contrary. I like having my mind challenged, and my beliefs, especially to the point where I might be on the verge of changing my mind. And ProTruth's class does that for me. My mind is in the process of changing. Into what, I have no idea.

High-fives snap about headquarters as if we accomplished something significant, but I'm not quite satisfied. My expectations are much higher than breaking up an initiation and apprehending a clergywoman. The mother and the child are still at large. No one seems concerned about that right now. Well, maybe one other person. He walks into my office and shuts the door.

"I know that little celebration outside must be making your head feel like it's about to pop," Beamer says. "I also know you have a plan."

"We've got to talk to your lead. It was a good lead, Beamer, but we need more."

His face lights up at my approval, and he hands me a scrap of paper, pleased at his own preparedness. It's an address in the Hills District. Figures. That neighborhood is known for its religious associations. There is always some rumor of Godseekers floating around there. A prayer group, a private RI, a community club that actually partakes in old rituals. The majority of my busts have come from the Hills zip code, which is why I love paying a visit to that part of town.

It's the closest to a ghost town you can get in Far City. No modern architecture or developments. It's as if the entire neighborhood is stuck in the pre-Millennium era. I'm surprised most of those buildings are still standing.

Beamer and I don't even need to look at each other. We get up at the same time and walk out of my office, heading toward the exit acknowledging no one, not even smiling. Every moment I spend around here repulses me, and I don't really give a damn if they can tell by my cold stares looking down on them. It's intentional.

"Where are you two going? Back to work already?" Rock asks, sitting in his cube with his two buddies who are just as middling as he is. Rock. Dumb as rocks. Ha — never gets old, especially when he lives up to it so often.

"Well, there's a baby out there still," I say in a voice I would use to talk to a puppy. "Someone has to think about its future. Not to mention what happened in Central City a couple years ago. I'm covering our asses too."

I don't wait around for a response, though I can hear Rock still mouthing off. Some conciliatory remark intended to make himself and his friends feel good. Meanwhile, Beamer and I make our way out to the Hills District in search of his doubler. The layout of the neighborhood is pretty simple. It's made up of three hills — surprise surprise.

First Hill contains all the modern homes and apartment buildings that managed to nudge their way into the neighborhood. It's the only decent area, one where you can find healthy restaurants, retail shops, and of course Starbucks.

Once you start descending the hill, however, you see a transition. The houses are these tall and wide structures made of exposed wood and brick. Some blocks hold only five houses and they have these inconsiderately large yards of just grass and flower beds and play areas for young kids. That's what parks are for. It seems pretty selfish to be taking up so much space. Go live out in the country if you want to do that. City living is all about volumes of people who need to be near the buildings where real work actually happens.

Next we head directly to the heart of the district. Beamer's doubler also doubles up on work, and today he's hosting at an old restaurant called the Golden Garden instead of working at his antique shop. We pull up just outside.

"You think he'll run?" I ask.

"Maybe," Beamer replies.

"How fast is he, do you think?"

A slight smirk and side glance populate Beamer's face. "I would guess he's pretty quick, but who's ever outrun you in a chase?"

I nod my head proudly.

"Let's go in together and just tell him we need to talk. It shouldn't be too alarming. He's used to working with me, but your presence might make him nervous."

"Good. He should be nervous. And if he runs, I'll catch him. If he knows what's good for him, he'll sit and talk to you *and* me."

I follow Beamer into the restaurant and he makes his way straight to the host stand. A small collection of patrons wait to be seated, and the dining room buzzes with conversation and laughter. Aromas of garlic and fish fill the air, and the crackling clatter of hot pots echo in the large hall with several round tables, seating large families. The customers are diverse and I can hear four or five different languages being spoken at once. I've always admired how food brings people together, and this restaurant is a prime example. Maybe I'll come back for lunch when I'm not trying to interrogate one of the employees.

Three customers hover over the host stand. Though the restaurant is full, there aren't very many employees working, and the ones who are zip around like flies from table to host stand to kitchen. I can tell which one is the doubler. Longer hair streams from his scalp and it's tied back in a ponytail, streaks of grey cascading down between his shoulders. He wears a serious face and a black and gold name tag with Chinese characters just above his English name. Chameleon. How appropriate. More than his name, his eyes give him away, because I immediately see them flash toward Beamer, then me, then he goes about his business in a more rushed and nervous manner. As we get closer, his eyes scan the area, blipping whenever they cross us.

"Just a moment please, I'll be right with you fellas," he says and briskly walks toward the kitchen.

"He's going to run," I lean over and tell Beamer, who nods his head while watching Chameleon slither into the kitchen. "Is there an alley exit or a way out from back there?"

Beamer nods, and with that I'm out the door. Once I look to my left, I see him book it out of the alley and away from the restaurant. He's fast. And he's running uphill. Expletives ricochet in my brain, but I'm already in pursuit. I never really enjoy the start of a chase, especially one as undesirable as running on an incline through the Hills District. But a few strides into pursuit and I'm sprinting, a predator, stalking its prey. A slight grin forms on my face. I *do* love this. I've never met anyone who's faster than me. I'm already gaining on him. He hears my footsteps, and whips his head back and forth to check my distance. Doesn't matter buddy. I'm gonna get you.

As I'm closing in, he can feel my proximity and pulls out a pretty fancy move by grabbing onto a stair railing and tethering himself to it, swinging his body around and changing direction. I slip as I attempt to stop, but quickly right myself and begin to close in on the small amount of distance he earned from his agile maneuver.

Now, he veers off the sidewalk into live traffic, weaving through cars and at one point flipping over one and somersaulting over another. After landing on his feet, however, a car illegally passing in the shoulder clips him, sending him airborne. In a blink, all traffic comes to a halt. I track him down, pick him up and carry him to safety. The driver of the errant car is decent enough to check on Chameleon, especially since he knows he's screwed with an Intervention Force agent as a witness. I'm less concerned with him, but tell him to remain at his car while I radio the police.

More important to me is my target. We move to the sidewalk where I prop him up on a park bench. It takes a moment to catch my breath. Though I am pissed at him for running, we share a mutual respect, like two athletes battling it out on the track. He kept distance for a while, and I hold him in higher esteem than other criminals I've arrested.

He looks at me, grimacing in pain, but remains coherent with no sign of serious injury. He earned some scrapes and perhaps a couple broken bones. I'll let the paramedic take a look. Meanwhile, I have questions that need answering.

Where is Beamer? This would be much easier with him.

"Chameleon. That's a perfect name, I've got to say."

He doesn't speak.

"There's really only one thing I want to know, and I'm going to get out of you. It's up to you if you'd like to volunteer the information and spare yourself the pain of—"

"Torture? Is that what I can expect from the Intervention Force? Glad my tax dollars have been funding shit like that. You've caught me, and I know exactly what people like you do, you asshole."

He takes a heavy swing at me, but I grasp his wrist. He groans in pain as I twist his arm, and his defiance surrenders.

"Look," I say, releasing my hold. "You seem like a good enough guy. You're already a doubler. Just point me in the direction of the mother and her baby so you can stop being in the center of my attention."

"No. And I'm no doubler. I'm on one side of this game, and you're on the other. So if you're going to try to beat the truth out of me, whatever. I hate you. You hear me? I *hate* you! You goddamn freespee!" He screams expletives and creates a scene.

"This is about more than a mother and a child," he says through clenched teeth. "You IFs, you Freespees — you think you're so righteous fighting for freedom. You *kill* freedom."

The last three words fire from his rage like bullets from a gun, and he speaks them, cold and calculated with a hoarse voice directly into my eyes. He thinks I'm the bad guy. He's really convinced. But it's not his conviction that gets me. It's the look on his face, now — the transformation from livid suspect to prosecutor. His eyes, for only a second, grab me, pin me and force me to pay attention and think. *You. Kill. Freedom.* Those words belie what I've dedicated my life to. How can someone so passionately say this to me? I would take "die shithead" or a good old fashioned "fuck you," but this is more than insulting. What does he mean, *I* kill freedom?

Thankfully, Beamer runs down the sidewalk, and he interrupts my train of thought. The hill left him pretty gassed as he arrives, struggling for air.

"I thought you said this guy is a doubler," I say, ignoring the fact that the man I'm speaking to sounds like he's about to hack up a lung. I give him a few moments to breathe. Seriously Beamer, the treadmill or something.

"He is... Come on Chameleon... Talk... We need to know where we... can find that baby..."

Beamer's breath deepens and slows. His attention sticks to Chameleon who makes a silent gesture with his face.

"I know you can tell us where the mother is hiding out," Beamer says. "Just point us in the right direction, and we'll be on our way."

The game of ping-ponging heads and not-so-subtle expressions continues.

"Enough — I can fix this." I remove a small vial from my belt. "This is going to end right now."

"Hey what is that?" Beamer asks anxiously, pointing at the tube of silver liquid between my index finger and thumb. "That's the E drug — you can't use that, Justice. That's illegal now."

I swing my arm back to jab the needle into Chameleon's leg, but before I can pierce his skin, Beamer's hand clenches my wrist.

"No," he says. "This is against the law, and even more, it's wrong. You know what E does to people, especially the platinum version."

I ease up for a quick moment, but then shove Beamer out of the way and complete the task.

"Even after its outlaw," I reply as the liquid forms a tiny dome on Chameleon's thigh. "We all know the Truth Committee still uses it.

Reforms only happen when we make busts, and for that to happen, we need information. Besides, he won't remember a thing in a few hours. Maybe I'll even let him go."

My prisoner's eyes go glossy and his face droops as if it were melting. He lets out a sigh and couples it with a smile; the sedating effects of the E drug must be absorbing the pain from his injuries. He looks up at Beamer, then swings his head like a wrecking ball toward yours truly. His mouth stretches into a toothy smile at first, then his eyes go back to that cold-blooded look.

"I see how it is." Chameleon speaks with a misplaced tone of victory. The drug works fast. But before he turns into a completely docile creature, he uses his words to pierce me with a needle of his own. "I used to have the right to remain silent. You just took that from me. How does it feel to be a *freedom killer?*"

Theresa

Lania awoke to a throbbing headache and a red flicker through her eyelids. She froze as she felt light breathing, fluttering the hairs on the back of her neck.

"Out cold," shouted a bold voice of a woman. "Whacked her real good. Still alive though."

Am I? Lania wondered, but then quickly accepted her survival, resolving that there was no way she could be dead and in so much pain.

The guard's footsteps faded. A door shut with a sharp clang, startling Lania. Locks clicked, and the room filled with a silent darkness. Her body lay crooked and still on the cool concrete floor. Gradually, her eyes adjusted enough so she could see a weak light coming through a crevice in the ceiling.

She stretched her limbs to a cacophony of cracks from her crinkled joints, crunching and crying out like a sizzling frying pan. Her back was stiff, so she slowly twisted and contorted and pulled until she felt pliant enough to sit up. She inhaled the dry, frigid air.

Water, she thought. *I need water.* She called out, but only stale wind and a soft wheeze emerged from her throat. She wanted to bang on the door, but lacked the strength to stand. Instead, she dragged her body to a wall where she could prop up her back, and continue relaxing herself into stretches. As her forehead landed on her knee, her mind spun back to the moment of her capture.

Abraham. He has to make it. Theresa must have left town by now, but Lania realized that was a point neither of them had discussed - what to do if one or the other gets caught, or if they are split up. All preparation went into studying the routes through the sewers and making sure their timing was just right, but no mention of leaving Far City if the baptism ended with an abduction. It wasn't as if either of them had much or any experience committing a treasonous sacrament. Godseekers rarely took the risk. Their friends considered them brave, but would talk amongst themselves about the foolishness of Theresa and Lania.

Lania knew the risks. She agreed that it was foolish, or dangerous, to be more precise. She envisioned a bright future for Abraham — a future where he could grow up with real freedom. And to achieve that, some foolish risks needed to be spent, otherwise change would never happen.

She thought his baptism would be a foundation for overturning the AFLs. There was no magic behind the sacrament. Or maybe there was. Maybe a power planted itself inside the baby, one greater than himself. One that drew its strength from the boldness of his loved ones to do something sacred in a place where the sacred no longer existed. Someday, Lania believed, this child will save us.

A firm confidence elevated Lania's spirit. Her friends had made it. She found hope in this conviction that her sacrifice was not in vain — that Theresa and Abraham were safe somewhere, far away. That thought gave her strength. But not enough to stand.

"Who is Abraham?" a voice asked.

Unaware that she was uttering his name aloud, Lania responded, "How did you... Who?"

"Relax. Don't force your voice. You're right — you do need water, and really, you won't be able to speak until you get some. Here."

The voice transformed into footsteps, light and swift. Three booms reverberated, then echoed down the hallway outside the metal door.

"Water!" the voice cried out, then floated back to the corner.

Within moments, a series of latches clinked until a sterile light, eclipsed by a human figure, illuminated the cavernous tank. The shadow seemed to hover in Lania's direction until finally she caught sight of the guard's eyes peering down into her own. It was an empty gaze, full of indifference and ever so slightly vexed. Still, an arm extended toward Lania's lips. Water spilled from the container into her mouth, then her tongue, then down her throat and into her stomach. She could feel it as the moisture gave instant rejuvenation to any tissue it touched. Lania reached out to grab the canteen, but it was abruptly jerked away.

"You drink as much as you're given."

The woman's words were daggers, her hefty voice like murder, but Lania wasn't intimidated. It's probably in her job description: *Must be able to sound like murder.* The canteen returned to her lips for a few more swigs until the guard moved back toward the door.

"Get yourself together," said the guard. "You meet with the Truth Committee in half an hour." Then the door slammed and Lania was left alone with the voice once again.

She hadn't fully swallowed her last gulp of water, but instead let it soak in her mouth until her tongue and cheeks were saturated with the fluid. She turned her attention to her counterpart.

"Thank you," she squeaked.

"Thank *you*, actually." This time, Lania paid closer attention to the voice speaking to her, and she clearly heard a young man. A boy even. *Too young to be in this cell*, Lania thought. "I haven't had someone to talk to other than myself and the Truth Committee in — well, I don't know how long I've been here. But I've been hopeful ever since I overheard the guards talking about possibly releasing me."

"Who are you? What's your name? I'm Elania, first off. Don't mean to be rude."

"It's okay," the boy said, hesitating. "Genjin is my name. And keep your voice down. They'll hear you"

Lania nodded. "Genjin? Is that a Buddhist name?"

The boy hesitated. "Yes."

"How did you end up in here?"

"I'm a monk," he said plainly. He wanted Lania to ask a different question, not a follow up. He got neither. Just a sobering dose of silence. She heard the charade loud and clear in the boy's shaky voice. His words landed unsteadily on Lania's ears, and she knew that if she waited, his story would present itself. It wasn't her first time listening to a memory worth hiding.

"I... I'm not a monk," he proceeded with the truth more quickly than she anticipated. "I don't really even consider myself a Buddhist. Or I do consider myself a Buddhist. But I'm also a Christian. I grew up in the Church, while it lasted anyway." He paused a spell, and Lania did nothing to urge him to continue, except for practicing patient quiet.

"I'm also a Muslim, then," he continued. "I'm also a Jew. Also a Hindi. A Taoist. A Sikh. Whatever I want to be. That's supposed to be free speech, right? To choose something I believe in and to be able to believe in it. *Freely*."

76

His voice swelled and Lania grinned. It was dark in the cell.

"Good thing all sanctuaries were outlawed, otherwise you'd have no social life," Lania quipped. "Be in church all the time. Or temple."

That drew a smile from the boy. Something in her voice was reassuring and friendly. His gut told him that she was safe. Lania had a tendency to make people feel that way, and it never took much, and it never took long.

"My real name is Daniel. I had a friend. Well, a teacher, and he was the Buddhist. He was the real Genjin. Haven't seen him in years, though. Intervention Force, you know."

"Oh I know, all right. And I see you know as well. I'm sorry... Daniel is your name?"

"Yes. Though I really like the name Genjin. He told me the meaning of it — to reveal one's true humanity. And he's not dead." Daniel paused a moment, trying to convince himself of his own statement. It didn't work before and wasn't working now. "Elites took him, just like they took my parents. Just like they took me."

The boy choked on a word and Lania was moved to compassion. Forgetting the pain in her joints and muscles, she stood, walked near to him, and sat. She put her hand on his shoulder, then on his chin. He couldn't have been older than fifteen. Lania's eyes widened and though no one could see it in the darkness, it flushed red with outrage.

"I'm 14. I know, right. Pretty messed up."

"Fourteen." Her chest tightened and fists clenched. She'd come to expect anything from anti-interventionists. But a teen? Someone's child. Again, she thought of Abraham and Theresa.

"Fourteen," she said again. "How in God's name did a young man like you ever end up in a place like this?"

Daniel's eyes glimmered in the sliver of light cutting into the cell. The mention of Genjin and his parents worked like an enzyme, stirring up his insides and riling him up. It brought up memories of his loved ones, and they were all gone. Well, almost all of them.

"My parents are Godseekers. They were taken when I was nine."

"Taken how?" Lania asked.

"They would organize mass for Catholics and Episcopalians. Maybe not every week, but at least a couple times a month."

"Really? Who were they?"

Daniel didn't respond.

"I'm sorry," Lania said. "I know many people who've gone in and out of the Interrogation Center. I know some who haven't come out. But for me, it's my first time in here. I understand. You don't have to answer any of my questions."

She smiled warmly, and the boy could see her this time, now that she had moved closer to him.

"It's okay," Daniel spoke. "Anything I'm telling you right now, the Truth Committee already knows. We were members of St. Augustine Parish."

"St. Augustine," Lania said with mild distaste.

"I know what you mean. Like I said, I grew up in that parish. It changed a lot after Father Eric died."

"Eric Lam. He pushed for so much reform within the church, including the Canon Law allowing women to enter the priesthood. He was also a strong advocate for religious tributarianism."

"Tributarianism?" Daniel wondered.

"It's the belief that all religions are separate paths that lead to the same truth."

"The same *God*?"

"Not exactly. Not everyone calls their truth *God*. But for Catholics, that's how we view it. People like Eric believed that we had more in common with other religions than we had differences. He pushed inclusivity and shared traditions."

"It's weird to me," Daniel said, "to hear you call him Eric."

"You know, he was just a normal person like you and me."

"I guess you're right. But Father Perrington would have never allowed that."

"*That's* where my bitter history with St. Augustine begins." Memory pulled Lania back to a sour place. "We butted heads a lot, he and I. He didn't think women should be priests. He wasn't a tributarian — in fact, he was the complete opposite."

"I know," Daniel said, turning his head away. "My parents told me so many parishioners left our church. It was such a shock going from Father Eric's open-mindedness to... well, Father Perrington."

"He set the church back," said Lania. "Our communities needed to broaden themselves by engaging with everyone. He looked down on other religions and nonbelievers. That's when people inside the church decided it was easier — safer — to not believe in anything. Father Perr—" Lania stopped herself and shook her head. Daniel read her frustration.

"My parents were, what do you call them again? The ones who believe in the multiple paths?"

"Tributarians."

"Right. They would come home frustrated at the same things you are mad about. So they continued their ministry underground, without the approval of Perrington."

"I guess that's of no consequence now. That man is out of a job. And so am I. There's no Church left in our country anymore."

"Oh — you're a priest too?"

"I am. I suppose that's not saying much these days."

"No - that's actually impressive. To stay loyal to being a priest? That's why you're in here?"

"Yeah, like being a monk."

Daniel smiled. He felt a connection, one he craved in the cold walls of the interrogation center. Three months, he had spent in the dark cell. Not long, but an forever for a youth. At last, he felt light and warmth.

"After the church shut down, my parents continued their work, and they led the underground efforts to keep the mission of St. Augustine — the old St. Augustine — alive."

Lania's curiosity was amplified, and she very much wanted to know the names of Daniel's parents. She had a hunch.

"I was priest at Our Lady of Lourdes. Our churches are both in Far City, and I knew many people who led rebellious lives and orchestrated faith experiences despite the AFLs. I did it. Hell, it's why I'm in here. People started calling us Martyrs. Then it became sort of a label. I don't much care for being deemed a Martyr while I am still breathing. Makes death feel even closer."

"You were a Martyr?" Daniel asked eagerly. "People said the same about my parents, and I got involved myself. I kinda like the title."

Lania's eyes rolled back, but figured it didn't matter in the dark. "It's a small world, I guess. Well, no wonder you're in here. It doesn't seem like there are too many Martyrs left. Me and some other religious leaders pushed the movement soon after we lost our places of worship. Not just Catholics, you know."

Daniel nodded. He always admired that about the Martyrs. They weren't some exclusive secret order — though they certainly had a secret order name.

"I had just baptized a baby before I landed in here," Lania went on.

"Publicly?!" Daniel exclaimed.

Lania nodded her head. "In a sewer, but yeah, in open air." Her eyes had adjusted to the dark and she could see his features better. Dark, straight hair in a disheveled thatch on top of his head. A skinny face with boney shoulders. Pencil neck. Definitely still a child. Though the boy seemed genuine and safe, she didn't want to reveal her friendship with Theresa and Abraham. In fact, she lamented he already knew Abraham's name from her earlier mutterings. She felt uneasy about sharing any details that the Intervention Force hadn't already known. Nevertheless, Daniel was impressed.

"An open air baptism. You're gonna be in here for a long time!"

His words seemed harsh, but that didn't make them any less true. Everyone knew that getting caught in a sacrament was an automatic life sentence to a labor camp. Her response was another smile.

"Well, for me, I came home from school one day," Daniel recounted. "It was Good Friday — I remember because my parents were in the middle of organizing a marriage to be held in the cellars beneath Brighton Winery. Seems kind of off to do a marriage on Good Friday, I know."

"I'll say. Kind of ominous."

"My parents always wanted me to stay clear of their church business, with the Freespeaker Movement growing and more and more reports of disappearances. But I couldn't. And they couldn't shut me out of their work. Their work was their lives, and I wanted to be involved. Or I wanted them to be involved with me.

81

"Anyway, I got home, and they weren't there. I told myself over and over that they were working late, but I knew what really happened. Just too scared to admit it. The hours drifted into night, and I panicked. I wanted the garage door to open so badly. I wanted them to walk through the door like they did every other day. But they didn't. Instead a knock came on my front door. I was afraid to answer it because I was only nine at the time and I knew my parents were taken by the Intervention Force. My first hunch was that they were coming for me, to take me away. To be with another family. One that would put it in my brain that God does not exist.

"But there was only one man standing outside, and he looked familiar. He was ancient and called my name from behind the door. Said his name was Marcel and that he was a friend of my parents and Genjin. I opened the door, which might not have seemed the smartest idea, but I had seen my parents talking to him on several occasions. He said my parents were captured and that Intervention Force officers were only a few minutes away.

"He took me outside across the street and we watched as Intervention Force showed up at my house, knocking on my door, then breaking into it. As they entered, we left. It was the last day I saw my mom and dad. I had no idea our last moment would be our last moment."

"Daniel, I'm sorry, honey." Lania moved closer, consoling her young cellmate. Then it hit her. "Lisa and Edward."

"You knew them?" Daniel sounded enthralled.

"Only by word of mouth, dear. But I was well aware of the work they did. Catholic circles are very small you know. I'm sorry to hear they were abducted. That was five years ago?"

"Yeah."

He paused from his story. A moment of painstaking silence always accompanied the memory of his parents' capture. It collected from the reservoirs of his strongest emotions — anger, resentment, hostility, sadness, despondence — and surged through his blood. For years, the waves would hit him and unleash an outburst in the boy.

Lania reactivated her patience, but cushioned the conversation with pleasantries.

"I don't think I'll ever adjust to it, but Marcel — that guy who pulled me out of my house just in time — he has been a good guardian in their absence. Been taking care of me ever since. It was through Marcel that I first met Genjin. Marcel enrolled me in the school where Genjin taught sixth-grade social studies and really helped me find little bits of peace after losing my parents. He taught me to meditate, and that's been a huge part of my life. I meditate every day and it helps me stay focused, but it's also why the IF came after Genjin.

"One day, after the last bell went off and I was leaving school, I saw Genjin in the office with the principal and two Intervention Force officers. The principal pulled me into the meeting and the IF questioned me. They asked me up front if Genjin was *intervening* and imposing belief on me. I told them no, and that was the truth. He was teaching me something I wanted to learn. He wasn't intervening and he wasn't imposing. It was true, however, that he let me meditate in school, but I left that detail out. Didn't matter though.

"After I was released from the office, I saw that nothing I said to the IF mattered. One officer pulled Genjin out of his chair and struck him on the back of the head with a baton. He was cuffed and dragged out of the office, and that was the last I saw of him. I feel like I'll be saying that statement a lot more in my lifetime."

"I think that's something we have in common, unfortunately," Lania agreed after listening closely to Daniel's story. She asked, "If you knew that was how life would be, why do you choose to keep living that way? Obviously, you did. You ended up in here."

"It was my parents. It was Genjin. It was Marcel. All the greatest influences in my life were connected to God or spirituality. And each of them fought for the right to practice. Doing what they did after they were taken was the only way I could keep them in my life. I figured if I got caught, I would only end up where they were anyway. And Marcel always supported me. More than I could imagine. Without him, I'd be on my own. Or in the government foster care system."

"There's a new strand of foster care developing — Freespeak Foster Care," Lania said. "I don't know much about it, but it's meant to 'rehabilitate' children of Godseekers. I'm glad Marcel took you in, and your loved ones are proud of you. I know it."

Lania searched the narrow expanse of her mind for some way to heal Daniel. To heal his pain, his guilt, his sense of loss. But, she feared, that type of science would take a generation or more to figure out.

She felt her time with Daniel dwindling, but she had one very important question to ask: What is the Truth Committee and what will they do to me? She hadn't asked the question, opting to listen to Daniel over acquiring the important information. Daniel read her mind for her. He knew what was coming.

"The Truth Committee. You're going to see them. Soon. I'm sorry, Lania. It's not going to be fun."

Voices murmured in the hall and footsteps approached.

"Don't lose your mind," he whispered looking up at the corner of the room at a small glass oculus. "It messes with your sense of reality.

You've got to find a memory. A *real* memory. And hold on to it. Repeat it to yourself. Somehow, you have to find peace in the chaos of it all. I've been drugged several times over the past few months. You can meditate your way out of it. Marcel and Genjin — they both taught me how powerful meditation and the mind can be. But if you give in to the drug, you'll be lost and give away everything you know."

"A real memory? What do you—"

The door opened. Time was up. Three guards entered this time. They grabbed Lania by the arms, pulled her up and herded her toward the door. She didn't look back, and if she had, she would have seen only a shadow of her young friend. They bagged her head and once again, darkness.

Daniel sat back in the corner of the cell, alone again. He had spent the last three months having the truth extracted from his lips, and every meeting with the Truth Committee felt like all the blood was drawn from his body. He would return to the cell and wake up hours later, or perhaps days, weeks even. He did not know.

But Lania's ears were different than the Truth Committee's. She listened with love and empathy, and though he knew she would come back in the same blind daze as he had so many times, he couldn't help but smile because at last God had answered his prayer. He wanted to feel love again, and Lania's listening brought him back to life.

Theresa

Daniel's words lingered. As the firm grasp of the guards dragged her through the long corridor, Lania pondered her task and began searching for a memory potent enough to anchor her to some sense of reality.

Her grandmother's house, an image untouched for years, materialized immediately. The beige brick chimney, the bright red siding, the ever present smell of garlic and onions or a pan of cookies, and the sounds of her cousins running through the hallway — it had felt like ages since Lania recalled her own family when she was just a child.

Images of the Catholic church hung from the walls as paintings and crucifixes, and beyond that, her grandmother radiated an air of things holy, even though her aunts and uncles never really went to church.

But it was those moments when she circled the dining table, dodging her younger cousins and collecting portions of a Thanksgiving dinner, a Christmas crab feed, an Easter brunch, that she recalled a time that made her smile, even under the heat lamps, even with the bracing pull of these strangers, even inside her body, still sore and mending from Abraham's baptism. The warm air of the old house came to her and settled her joints, cushioned her steps, and made her crack an unlikely smile on her way to her fate.

Emotion, she thought. That is the key. What could be more real than our emotions? Raw anger, sadness, elation — at no point is our sense of life more tangible. That is the connection to reality she required. That is what Daniel meant when he said a *real* memory. Any time she blocked access to her own emotions, she felt disconnected to what was real in her life at the time. So Lania stayed at the party. In the old house with the green carpet and the gentle drone of the stove hood vent, with the laughter of herself and her cousins, her raucous aunts talking trash and her own mom finding a spare moment to tell a story about how well Lania was doing in school. A classic family party.

Such were Lania's thoughts as she lay strapped to a cold aluminum table. Her wrists, ankles, below the knees, her thighs, waist, abdomen, biceps, and wrists all pulled flat to the cool metal by leather straps. She wondered if there were bands to tie her fingers down as well.

Around her neck was a collar that afforded little wiggle room, and another band on the table to restrain her head. The cranial restraint did not quite wrap around her scalp, but instead, two metal dimples wedged into her temples. Lania tried not to think about them.

She struggled against the restraints like a beetle on its back. It was of no use, but at least it was something to do. She could open her eyes, but only a two-way mirror and a table in front of her with an arc of chairs revealed themselves. The room was stale, a cavity of nothing — only an old woman and her thoughts. She tried to cry out, but her throat had gone dry. More water, she wished.

Stillness and silence her only company, her thoughts unwound and refused to yield to the frantic voice in her head doing all it could to calm her down. That self talk, that positive self talk, rehearsed in times of safety for other times of unorthodox anguish — it either fails to register or is forgotten altogether.

"Breathe," she said aloud, and the sound of her own voice made her feel less alone. So she spoke more to the empty room. "Relax. Breathe. Breathe. Relax." Had she more energy, she'd have sung to herself, but as it was, she could barely hum a tune. Heavy in, slow and steady out was all she could muster. In between breaths, she grimaced, but not from any pain. All the mental anguish that flourished in anticipation for this "Truth Committee" she tried to expunge with each exhale.

That image. The party. The laughter. Where did it go? She had lost it a moment, then brought it back. Every time it slipped from her fingers, she picked it right up.

She shut her eyes tightly as if sealing the memory in her own head and wondered, would this Truth Committee have access? This thought — could they infiltrate her brain so deeply that they would join her in the dining room, find her hiding in the coat closet, hear the words she remembered from her family members, taste the flavors of her grandma's Thanksgiving turkey?

Enough! She commanded herself. A scream built up in her chest, then, with a shredded and hissing pitch, she howled to the empty space, sound ricocheting off the walls and back into her ears. Shame hovered over her at the thought of giving the pleasure of her grief to whomever watched behind the two-way mirror. Were they laughing? Disinterested?

She breathed heavily. The exhaustion from her mind pushed and pulled on her lungs as though a child were jumping on her stomach.

The party. Stay there. Stay in the red house. Gramma, stay with me.

"You're in the Devil's Hand," interrupted a man over a speaker.

"Make yourself comfortable. You'll be here a while." Then he chuckled, and that made Lania laugh. *How typical*, she thought.

Before her laughter subsided, the metal dimples pressing on her temples began to heat up and her head spiked with a stinging pain, like a strand of rusty wire being pulled through her head from one ear to the other. She cringed and cried but could make no sound.

"Stop! Please," Lania begged in a deathly whisper, regretting her reaction to the man's cartoonish threat. Fifteen seconds was all it lasted, then the voice returned.

"That pain, that physical pain — I promise you, at some point, when we finally interrogate you, you will beg for that, only to feel something, anything, again."

The man's words cut a slow incision into Lania's mind as she wallowed stiffly on the table. Her skin beneath the restraints was now painted crimson, and she could only feel the burning sensations at each part of her body. The wrinkles on her cheeks sagged downward as she gave every ounce of focus to her breathing.

Then, as the pain of the head restraint faded, a new wave of torture settled in.

Time.

How long had she been lying on the cold aluminum? Lania's heart picked up tempo, her hands trembled with a cold sweat. She had thought to sleep, but her mind raced too fast for a respite.

The party, she reminded herself. But the party wasn't sticking. No memory could cohabitate with the prospect of this Truth Committee. No image, no face, no words. All she had left was her faith; she turned to God, praying. The holy rosary would fight this battle for her, she resolved. It was her tool of choice in the face of darkness.

"I believe in God, the Father almighty…" she mumbled to herself.

"Our Father, who art in Heaven, hallowed be thy name…"

"Hail Mary, full of grace, the Lord is with thee…"

Decade after decade. The fourth, the fifth, then a sixth and seventh — a twelfth, a thirteenth, then she lost count, but kept repeating. Repeating. Repeating. And in between decades, she raised up her grandma. Raised up her mother. Raised up the red house. Then, before the start of decade thirty-something, Abraham and Theresa wandered into her prayer, and she started —

"Hail Mary, full of grace…"

And repeated more. She kept going, as long as the image of her friend — the woman who treated Lania as a mother — kept her grounded to the earth, beneath the metal legs of aluminum, beyond the captivity of the leather straps and imposing walls of the chamber, and with love that invaded whatever evil watched her mumble the words of an outlawed meditation.

Find a memory, Daniel had said. *Meditate,* her recent friend had advised. *Find peace in the chaos…*

Her young friend was right. Peace became her. And she kept on with the rosary. The rosary was her anchor. The rosary fought for her. Mary fought for her. God, the Father fought for her.

But then, she fell asleep.

Lania awoke to a haze that filled her head as whispers began skittering in her ears like cockroaches around an abandoned banquet. They babbled a breathy dissonance, but slowly, one voice at a time, she could decipher brief messages — words from her past, words she'd never heard before, words she feared.

We won't kill you…

Until we have the child...

Until you watch Theresa die...

The silence in the room gave the voices all the more time to sing their song of terror.

You sold us out...

They've caught everyone...

We have all become martyrs. It is all your fault.

The voices grew louder and louder, and tears sneaked from her eyes. The sleep had done her a disservice — it separated her from the peace and broke her rosary. Now the onslaught of words was joined by scenes, like clips from a movie. Parishioners — ones she loved, ones who did and didn't love her — all encircled her in accusation and condemnation. Theresa was among them, and in her arms, her child. She extended Abraham toward Lania, and Lania reached to hold him. Then as she took possession of the baby, all the other faces dissolved, and the three of them were back in the sewer beneath Far City.

Lania took Abraham in her arms, but he felt frigid, as though she were holding a block of ice. Terror gripped her as she looked at the child, his face stripped of all color, a pale corpse as silent as stone. She hollered and moaned and looked to find Theresa, who was now being pulled up the ladder through the sewer access point.

"What about the priest?" a voice from above inquired.

"Leave her."

It was Theresa's voice.

"She killed my son. Leave her in the dark. Forever."

Then the metal plate locked into place and all was darkness.

A whirring vent but no draft stimulated Lania's consciousness and she opened her eyes to the white walls and two-way mirror. Back to reality, she guessed. The vent seemed to be pulling air from the room instead of blowing air inside. Her mind was blank, an empty canvas, an open field. No thought, no image, no memory, no meditation presented itself to her. It was as though her memories had been completely erased. Or taken.

The Truth Committee had won.

"She didn't scream the whole time. She's tough," a female voice observed from behind the glass.

"Not so tough," replied a man — the same one who had threatened her before. "Look at her — she's drenched. And the marks on her wrists where her bonds are. Whatever she was thinking, we're going to know it. We're going to find out who she's protecting and more importantly where they might be hiding."

Lania's stirring drew their attention.

"She's waking up," the woman said.

"Another round of *eternatae* gas," ordered the man. "This time use the augmented batch. That last round took almost an hour. We need to speed this up. The Commanding Officer wants an update immediately."

"What's the rush?"

"Didn't you hear what happened in Central City? Two years ago, they blew up the Intervention Force admin staff because they couldn't find a baptized baby. Any officer who was deemed inept was let go. You want a job, don't you? Once the CO gets a hold of the mother, he's going to execute her and this priest at the same time. Wants to do it publicly, but I don't think he'll be able to. Too many softies out there."

"*Execute*? That's…" Her counterpart shot her a side-glance as she hesitated. She quickly hit an orange button and the vent began pumping fumes back into Lania's lungs. "That's exactly what they would deserve," the woman agreed.

Lania opened her eyes. Again darkness, but this time, her limbs were bent at the joints, and she lay curled on the concrete floor. The shard of light passing through the ceiling of the holding cell cast a faint glow on her face.

"You awake?" Daniel's voice.

Lania didn't respond, though she rolled over, trembling, expecting her body to be engulfed in the same hurt as before. Instead, she felt remarkably rested. She sat herself up against the wall with little trouble.

"How long?" she asked the boy.

"Three days," Daniel said. "Just like Jesus."

"I've been gone that long?"

"No — you were gone for about two hours. You've been out for three days."

"Asleep?" Already her mind struggled to make sense of Daniel's words, but asleep for three days? "Are you joking with me?"

"If only," Daniel tittered. "It's the drug. I told you. Messes with your sense of time. I'd never know how long I was out whenever I'd wake up in the same corner you're in. Now I know."

"You're welcome."

He laughed. So did she.

"They are releasing me," he said, a bit unenthused at the sound of freedom. "Later today. Cell's going to be all yours."

"That's good Daniel."

"I'm sorry, Lania."

"For what?"

"Just that you're in here. For what happened to you. That I have to leave."

"Oh — you mean you feel bad for me."

"Yeah, that's right." He understood the correction. "I hate to leave you alone though."

And that was the truth. Daniel didn't know Lania, but he knew she what side she was on. They hadn't spent even an hour together — consciously, anyway — but he'd always remember that hers was the first friendly voice he'd heard in months, and though he should have spent their earlier encounter preparing her for the Truth Committee, he chose to talk about himself. What made the difference to Daniel is that she chose to listen. That's the mark of someone who is truly selfless, Daniel thought.

"I can't remember anything," Lania said.

"You will. You're still out of it. But in a few hours, you'll start to remember. And that's... no fun."

Daniel put his hand at the base of his spine.

"The first thing you remember is the needle," he said. "Your body probably feels great right now, but soon the high will wear off and the first thing you feel is where they injected you with liquid eternatae at the base of your spine. It burns like crazy.

"I'm sorry — I don't want to frighten you, but it's just what happens." He sat next to her, took her wrist, and held it up to the light. The skin at her cuff looked raw and frayed, coated with crusted blood. She pulled her arm back from Daniel, mortified. The pain medicine allowed no indication that her body was so marred, and she raised her other wrist to the light, then her ankles. One by one, she recalled the restraints. Then the thoughts. The awful thoughts. Theresa leaving her for dead. Abraham cold in her arms. The searing metal prods on the sides of her head.

Then the interrogation. Her body went limp.

"I told them everything." She stared at the wall in front of her. "I told them —"

"So did I," Daniel felt her shock. The same shock he felt when he realized the same after his first interrogation. All the information he spilled about his parents, about Genjin, about the Martyrs, and about Marcel.

"I tried — you told me to meditate and I tried," Lania said regretfully.

"It's no guarantee. Eternatae is like an opponent — it can be strong at first, but once you've had it a few times, your game plan changes and gets more effective."

"You're pretty smart, you know."

Daniel's face gleamed at the compliment.

"They're going to find Theresa," Lania said. "They're going to find her and Abraham."

"Maybe," Daniel said. "Did you two have a separation plan? If you did, you already told them. But for the last three days, you were mumbling in your sleep. Over and over you bulleted your interrogation." Daniel wondered if he himself did the same thing after his own pow-wows with the Truth Committee. "Didn't sound like you had a separation plan. Not once did you mention an exact place where Theresa would be."

"There was no separation plan. I never brought it up to Theresa. I figured if one of us got caught, it would be best for neither of us to know where the other would be."

"That's good."

"I hope to God she left town though. I know just about all the places she would go in Far City, and now, so does the Truth Committee."

"And so do I."

They looked at each other, her eyes adjusted to the darkness. He nodded in her direction. She leaned over and hugged him, and as she did, she whispered in his ear.

"Don't go looking for her. You don't belong in a place like this."

He whispered back.

"Sure I do."

JUSTICE

Midland America University
Junior Year
Fall quarter, 2080

"Unfortunately, you'll never know your whole self," ProTruth
instructs.

"Well that sucks," I blurt, my vocabulary reverting to a ten year old's.

"I agree with you Justice," ProTruth responds. "It totally sucks that you
spend your whole life here and you will only know your whole self for a
split second at the end."

I sit in shock and lean in, expecting him to continue.

"You can only know yourself completely once your life is complete. Until then, you know only part of the story. That's the beauty of tomorrow.
You always have a chance to change your story if you don't care for the
day before."

"Doesn't leave a lot of room for happiness if you're always trying to
change until you're dead," I contest.

"Ultimately, it's a matter of being satisfied with who you are in the
moment — flaws and all — and being willing to change at the same time."

"*That sounds contradictory.*" I mean honestly, ProTruth. Even you can't reason your way past this paradox.

"*It isn't contradictory,*" he says. What else should I expect. Of course he's going to defend his own nonsense. "*Satisfaction is always temporary. Would you agree with that?*"

I have to think about it, and before I can produce an answer, he assumes it for me.

"*If satisfaction is temporary, then you're constantly looking for new ways to get what you want out of life.*"

"*I won't be satisfied until I become Supreme Commanding Officer,*" I offer, knowing that will get under his skin.

"*That's a firm ambition. What makes you so sure that being the SCO will make you happy?*"

"*I know it will. It's what I've wanted all my life.*"

"*I'm not so sure about that. Plus you haven't really lived that long yet.*"

My attempt at getting under his skin backfires. Now he's getting on my nerves. How does he know what I want and what I don't want?

"*So you're telling me that my dreams and goals are meaningless?*"

"*Oh quite the contrary. They're very meaningful. But never equate accomplishment with happiness.*"

"*That doesn't make any sense,*" I say more bluntly this time. "*You win something — you're happy. You graduate — you're happy. You get a date — you're happy. Whenever you accomplish something, you're happy. Accomplishment equals happiness. It's practically mathematical.*"

"*I understand that accomplishment is often accompanied by happiness, and failure is accompanied by inadequacy. But don't let these be your default emotions when you accomplish or fail at something.*

"*How many prominent figures in history have accrued great*

accomplishments at the expense of others — often those less fortunate than they? Yet in these accomplishments, they blind themselves to the full reality of their 'success' in order to sustain their happiness. Could you maintain your satisfaction if it cost you someone you love?"

ProTruth always has a way of making me think. Usually after making me angry.

"No," I say, after a moment of hesitation that I hope went unnoticed. "No, I couldn't. My family — they mean everything to me. If I had to sacrifice one of them... I wouldn't do it. Absolutely not."

"So here's a harder question. Take a person you've never met. A person who's been good to their family and to others. A person who's made the same sacrifices your parents have made for you for the ones he or she loves. A person who is someone's mother or father, son or daughter. This person whom you never met before — would you let them pay the cost for your happiness?"

"What do you mean by pay the cost? Like if I am more qualified and they don't get the job?" He knows I know he's not that stupid. He tilts his head down then looks up at me.

"And then there are those who aren't as decent. Ones who are law breakers, who don't fit in with society, ones who may or may not be upstanding citizens. You have to be able to give them... justice."

He pauses before using my name. How dramatic, Prof.

"The costs I'm talking about are the costs of doing what's right, and oftentimes, in positions of great power, those costs are dramatically elevated. Being SCO isn't like being a doctor or a business manager or a waste management specialist. It's one of the most cutthroat, ruthless positions in our country. It's a job that can be done well, if you're radical enough. And by radical, I mean able to listen. You, Justice, are radical."

"How do you know?" I can't tell if he's complimenting me or putting me down. I hate it when he speaks so fast.

"Because you're ignorant, but at least you're willing to listen. And that's a lot more than I can say for many of your peers."

"That's not the nicest thing to say."

"You're right. I'm not nice. You know why?"

"Because you're kind of an ass?" We both laugh. I guess I can get away with that since I'm not his student anymore.

"You think you can get away with that because you're no longer in my class?" He reads my mind.

I'm not really embarrassed, but I can still feel the blood rushing to my ears, which he can undoubtedly observe.

"Once a student of mine, always a student of mine."

"Awww, that's sweet, teach."

"I'm not nice, Justice, because I actually care about you. You could always use more people in your life who are less nice and more loving. I think you'll do great things someday, but how you'll be remembered in history depends on the placement of your heart."

I have no words. For the first time in my life, I start to question why I want to be the Supreme Commanding Officer. I look at this man before me. He's not too old. Not too young either. I have great respect for him.

"What did we just talk about," I ask, confused about how our conversation jumped from finding yourself, to my ambition, to accomplishment, to him being an asshole.

"Life," he replies. I nod.

Beamer looks uneasy. He stares at Chameleon as though he's watching an ugly car accident or a tornado — something enormous and devastating, but something he was powerless to stop. He sits on the park bench fidgeting while screwing his head back and forth nervously, and I'm anticipating the moment when I find out what is making him so damn antsy. The connection between Beamer and Chameleon hovers in the air around us, and the tension makes us all breathe a little faster.

I consider the situation. Chameleon is the doubler. Maybe Beamer was trying to protect his one and only informant. That would be reasonable, but my gut is telling me it's something deeper than that. The look on Beamer's face spells an external concern, not an internal one. I waste no time getting the information I need.

"The mother involved in the ritual initiation — tell me where I can find her, and where I can find her child. Be exact."

"They are... in... Far City... inside their skin... on the floor..."

I wonder if it's the eternatae or if he's just being a smartass. Doesn't matter. I still punch him in the gut. I don't have time. When he regains his stature, I ask my question differently with more volume.

"I need the addresses in Far City where the mother involved in last night's baptism can be found."

The precision of my question and using faithietalk yields two addresses. One is a home address, the other for a child care facility. Both addresses are within city limits. I could apprehend the child myself if I wanted to, but something tells me I won't find the kid or his mother. At least not right now. She'll probably lay low. Unless they've skipped town, however, I'm pretty sure she'll return to one of these places eventually. As long as she doesn't feel like she's being watched. A week. Maybe two.

I'll order the IF to place covert surveillance at these two locations. Soon enough, they'll be spotted, and if they don't return, I know there are other ways I can go about tracking them down. It's not like I haven't tracked fugitives before.

Turning back toward my entranced prisoner, I seek to satisfy another curiosity.

"Who is this man sitting next to you?"

"His name is Beamer Atkins."

"Justice, what are you —" Beamer urgently interrupts.

"Tell me, how do you know him?"

"I provided him with information about the initiation you had just asked about."

"But you knew Beamer before you doubled for him, didn't you?"

"Yes."

I look over at Beamer and his concerned expression is no longer there. It's replaced with an ambiguous blob of anger, fear, resentment and shock. He's flushed, and it's not because of the hill he just ran up. He and Chameleon share common knowledge they wish was buried under a rock. But all I have to do is ask the right question, and that information is mine. I guess I'll have to find a new partner if Beamer gets locked up for whatever he's hiding. Still, it will look good on my resume to catch a two-faced traitor as high up in the rankings as Beamer.

"How did you know Beamer?"

"Beamer is my —"

"Your... your... what?"

I realize that it's not his voice that's fading but my hearing. I put my hand on my thigh where I feel a slight sting. A tranquilizer dart. I have just enough time to glance at Beamer's utility belt to see he's missing one. The last expression I read on his face no longer hides behind ambiguity. It's a plain look of desperation, as well as a look of good-bye.

He had better hide somewhere I never find him, or kill me now. Because when I find him, that's exactly what I'll do to him.

He starts to go blurry, then double, and colors blend together like a splotch painting. My eyelids shut, and the last sense to fail is my hearing which dissolves as the sound of their footsteps grows more and more distant.

I wake up to the glowing night sky of Far City. The warmth of the summer night must have made me real comfortable, because I'm left in the same spot where I lost consciousness. The tranquilizer works for about four hours. What puzzles me is why am I still in this park? No one alerted the police or even called for an ambulance. No one cared enough to even pick me up and put me on the bench. What is the matter with people? I start looking around for apathetic faces to scold.

A white envelope newly tucked in my jacket pocket intrudes upon my intrapersonal tirade. It has my name on it. I sit on the bench, tear through the seal, and unfold the thin, white paper. I immediately look at the bottom to see who sent it to me. No one is claiming to have written this note, and the message is plain and simple:

Dear Justice, I hope you're feeling better. That tranquilizer can certainly leave a drumline going off in your head. Now then, if you wish to know the truth about your partner...

I don't care about the truth so much as I care about finding him and locking him up.

... you should probably know a couple other things. First, even though it seems like he double-crossed you, Beamer is on your side. He thinks and speaks of you in the highest respects...

It doesn't *seem* like he double-crossed me. He did. There's no

103

dancing around it or dolling it up. He stabbed me in the back, or whatever, the leg, and ran off with my prisoner. For that, I will never forgive him.

... Second, you're probably very angry at him. Perhaps you'll be able to deal with this anger back at the restaurant.

There is no signature at the end of the letter, but I start the jog back to the Golden Garden.

JUSTICE

Midland America University
Senior Year
Winter quarter, 2081

"I can't think of anything else right now," I tell Truth. He's always made time for me. When I took his Freethought class two years ago, I would take advantage of his open door policy to discuss all things life related at least once a week. Now it's down to once or twice a month. I have to schedule these little conferences now since so many students want to talk about challenges of growing into adulthood. I imagine they experience the same agitation at his challenging responses that I felt when I was their age, but I always see them walk out with a hopeful look on their face.

"You're taking the Intervention Force Academy Test in a few weeks, I hear."

"I am."

"Nervous?"

"No — not even a little. I'm ready for this. I can't fail."

105

"It's actually not that bad of an option."

"Are you kidding me? It's the worst option! Who wants to fail at any-thing?" He's said some audacious things before, but this is my — well, I guess it wouldn't be the first time he's thrown my ambition into the mud.

"Who hasn't failed at anything?" he asks.

"Me." Now I'm just being defiant for its own sake.

"You've been successful at everything you've ever set out to do in life? Every sport you played, you won? Every test you took? Everyone you ever tried to date? These have all been successes?"

"Well, no, but I don't consider losses failures. An A minus, maybe, but otherwise..." He cracks a small grin. Report cards come out next week. Still, I notice I'm smiling at my own feigned contempt.

"What do you consider your failures, then, as I understand it?" Truth asks.

"Undesired outcomes," I state even though the words leave my lips curled up in a question.

"Semantics," Truth dismisses. *"Failure is just a word, and one that gets a bad rep for what it actually does for humanity."*

"What does failure do? Except prevent us from getting what we want out of life? Or, what we think we want." He gives me a look of pity. A poor-stupid-soul look. I hate when he does that.

"I understand. You grew up in a culture where the phrase, 'Failure is not an option' is broadly emphasized, and not in competition. In upbring-ing. Parents are so afraid to have their kids mess up or lose, that we've numbed ourselves to messing up and losing. But the sting of failure is crit-ical. It's what makes you better. Makes you stronger. 'Failure is not an option' is complete and utter bullshit, my friend, and until you fail and fail hard several times, you haven't lived. It pushes you to go after something

you really want. Or it will tell you to chase another dream."

*"That's what you want, isn't it? What you've always wanted for me —
to change my dream." The words come out of my mouth like knives.*

*"If you truly want to join the Intervention Force and ultimately be-
come SCO, it shouldn't matter what anyone else wants for you Justice. As
long as you pursue the path you choose and are content with that choice."*

"So do you?"

"Do I..."

"Do you want me to be SCO or not?"

"Are you asking for my opinion?"

*"Yes." Not really. I want him to say yes. Yes, Justice, follow your heart's
desire and rule the world.*

"No. No I don't want you to be Supreme Commanding Officer."

"It figures. I didn't even need to ask." I start to get up and walk out.

"Mr. Flint —"

*He calls me that sometimes. It's usually when I'm storming out. Some
sucker I am. I always stop and turn around. This time, I hang for a moment, but I refrain from looking back. It's a long moment, but I realize he's
not thinking of what to say. He's moving. Moves right in front of me. I wonder what my face looks like. He's got to be used to my cherry red cheeks
and offended eyes.*

*"I wish you the best." He doesn't smile when he says it. Instead, he al-
most looks defeated, and not in the kind of way I would gloat over. His look
was lamentable, as if he's losing a student, a friend. And it really hurts him.
He clasps my shoulder, then walks back to his old leather chair.*

After calling headquarters to relay the two addresses I extracted
from Chameleon — even though he and his rat friend have probably

already told the mother and her baby to steer clear — I arrive back at the restaurant, looking for the person who wrote the letter.

It's easy. There's only one person inside. The letter I received had every indication.

"So, you have another lesson you want to teach me?" I say to my old professor with a hint of resentment and guilt. Silence. "You own the place? It looks like it's closed."

He says nothing but stands up and looks gravely into my eyes. His face is long and weathered, and he almost glares at me with a look I can only interpret as contempt. I've never been on the receiving end of such harshness from my old teacher. Only his sadness, once. Today, he hates what I've become. He doesn't need to say a word.

"It's been too long, Justice."

Then he hugs me, and now I'm confused. I slowly lift my arms to reciprocate, but this greeting feels undeserved.

I always had incredible respect for Truth. I loved how he made me think about life during college and into my early adulthood. Never mind all the times he pissed me off. He was the first person to get me to ponder the big questions of life. Before I took his class, my ambition to run the Intervention Force drove every move I made. I didn't have time for much else except for working hard in my political science and sociology classes, and I only took his "Freethought" class as an elective. No universities offer those types of classes anymore. They were phased out with the Moving Forward Education Act a few years ago. But the thoughts and ideals I learned in Truth's class spoke to some of the greatest wonders I had about life. He made me reevaluate my end game, and for a while, all I was interested in was learning more about how our principles made us great or terrible.

Now here he is, right in front of me all these years later. He is exactly the same. That makes one of us.

"That letter made me think of you, but I never thought its author would actually *be* you," I finally reply. As I'm saying this, I realize the man whom I hold in such high esteem is a criminal. I could arrest him right now. But I don't. I want to hear what he has to say. I'm curious about why he left the letter. Maybe he'll lead me to more Freedom Law violators, perhaps even the mother and child and their conspirators. All these thoughts sprout in my mind, but one lonely feeling in my heart is the true reason I don't tranq my old professor right here and now and take him into custody. I care about him, genuinely, after all these years, more than my aspiration. What is he even doing here? He must have no idea how far I've wandered from that idealistic and open-minded college kid. I understand the world much more clearly now.

"You know Beamer and Chameleon," I say.

"The interrogation begins. I thought I was the one who got to ask all the questions."

I crack subtle nostalgic smile. His remark activates a memory of a simpler time. A time before I made such a name for myself. I feel I've come so far — I can't change my path now. Why is that thought even in my head? He's why. The only person who had the balls to disagree with me. The strong will of Justice Flint. Now this old man — probably sixty-something — stands before me, frail and weak. A lamb before a lion.

"No questions this time, ProTruth. Only answers. Especially since you're aiding and abetting two or three or who knows how many fugitives."

A flood of guilt crashes over my accusation. I wish he would say something to wash it away somehow. Instead, Truth's eyes fall from mine to the ground and his lips purse, bracing themselves from the impact of my cold charge. He thought we were friends. I thought we were too. But time and interests created an ever-growing river between us until neither of us could see the shore on the other side.

"I do know Beamer and Chameleon," he admits. "I also know the baptized child, his mother and the one who baptized him."

"What are you doing? This information would get you sent to an interventionist camp — probably to an execution room!"

"You asked, my friend. You asked." He lifts his wrists to me, offering to let me take him as my prisoner. My cuffs remain in my belt.

"Do you know how many violators I've put away for committing crimes far less significant than what you're doing?"

"Well, if you count the priest your team apprehended, I believe that brings your total up to 383," he floats a spear of a remark that cuts deeper than my accusation. I can't believe how he knows this. I thought I was the only one keeping count. "I think in some way, by some connection, I knew just about all 383 of those people. You know, we religious types have to stick together. There aren't too many of us left, thanks to you."

Instantly, I unholster my tranq gun and whip my arm toward Truth. His antagonizing words do it for me. They push me over the edge, or rather back me into a corner, and I'm shaking. *I hate this man.* Everything he's done to me to the core, to make me question myself, to break the iron of my confidence and will. He has no right to speak to me that way — I've earned my position and it comes with well-deserved respect. For a moment, I forget who he is to me. Who he was to me. The jury's still out on that verb.

I aim right at his heart even though I don't need to shoot him there, and I look dead into his eyes that are now void of all fear and sadness, but solid with a calm confidence. The fury I felt at Beamer's betrayal possesses my brain and I feel my jaw clench, my arm tremor. I look at the string of an old man standing in front of me. He's sacrificing himself. He won't let me take his life. He's already given it to me.

But I'm not pulling the trigger. If this were anyone else, *anyone*, that culprit would be on the floor, unconscious. Number 384. But he still holds some power over me. Part of me hates that, while another part feels, for lack of a better word, safe. Safe in someone else's power and control. That's never been like me. Or maybe it has. There is a certain comfort in dependence. And yes, part of me still depends on him. The part of me that could dismantle everything I am — unthread my uniform, rebrand my badge, change my mind.

"Justice," he finally says, padding the intense moment with his gentle voice. "Are you going to put me down?"

His eyebrows tilt like a drawbridge going up over his nose and his lower lip cowers under the clamp of his teeth. He inhales deeply through his nostrils and doesn't break eye contact, though I can see a lacquery coating in his pupils. Not a single tear falls. Instead, the sheet of saltwater acts as a magnifying glass into our history. In his eyes, I see all our past discussions, all my confusion and frustration that he so capably erased just by making me think about my problems in different ways, and even if he was unsuccessful in molding me into the person he saw, he still hasn't given up. This moment is proof of that.

All those years he made me question my goals and motives in life — I loved those years. I loved opening my mind to his ideas of freedom. They tempted me outside everything I had been taught — lured me from the iron bars of the AFLs and made so much more sense than the contorted view of Freespeak. But I got lost in expectation and desire for power. He saw the path I chose before I took a single step and did everything he could to help me escape it.

This moment right now will determine what I do with the rest of my life. I'll either take down an old friend, or figure out why he's really here in front of me. If he gets sent to a camp, with his rap sheet, he's a dead man, and I'll be left with questions, and who am I kidding — regret. That's what I'm really afraid of. But I've come too far. If I let him go, I'll never have what it takes be SCO.

My finger flexes and tightens around the trigger.

Stop it. *Stop!* The thought floods my mind and I can't tell if the command is for him or for me. I spew out the air that had been growing stale in my lungs and lower my tranq gun. Suddenly, I feel sick and fall over on a chair, heaving air in and out of my body, resting my elbows on the table and my head in my hands. He's won. I'm all ears.

"Okay, professor... I'm listening."

For a while, we say nothing. Then Truth turns his back and walks toward the kitchen. He returns with a pot of tea and two cups. He pours and waits for me to drink.

"C'mon," he encourages. "It'll help."

The porcelain warms but doesn't burn my fingers. I dip the tip of my tongue into the liquid and it's barely hot. In a long gulp, I consume the entire cup and the tea radiates heat into my chest. The simple floral scent of jasmine settles my nerves and the warmth of the tea melts the stiffness in my chest. It feels good, just what I needed in that moment. Placing the cup back on the table, I release a deep sigh and return my attention to Truth.

"You have a lot to learn, Justice, and I don't mean that in a condescending way. There is, in fact, much you do not know about, when it comes to myself, Beamer, Chameleon." He pauses, stopping his breath short of his statement's destination.

"You were going to say more. Who else do I need to learn about?"

He initiates a long gaze into my eyes as if he's about to tell me that everyone I've ever known is now dead. "Yourself, Justice. You need to learn about yourself."

"Yeah. You always told me that. I need to find myself. I know you think I've lost who I am, or at least who you want me to be."

"Can't remember a time when you didn't seem lost."

"Is that supposed to be an insult?"

"No. It's just the truth."

And he bears his trademark grin, only I'm too exhausted to share his humor.

"You know, I've been lost too," he shares.

"Yeah? How long have you been lost? Ever since I stopped keeping in touch with you?"

"I'm sure you'd like to think so. But no, I've been lost my entire life."

Here it comes. Another discussion. The hinges of my mind, rusted and stiff, creak as he slowly pries them open with his backwards thinking. Always lost? My wise old professor? I don't buy it.

"Justice, no one can claim to have it all figured out."

"Me most of all. I went from aspiring SCO to conspiring with an interventionist, I think in record time, if anyone else ever did what I'm doing right now."

"Thank you for that, by the way. Hey." He doesn't let my fleeting attention veer off from the sincerity of his gratitude.

"I do not trivialize what you are doing for me right now. I know that decision to lower your tranq was not an easy one. I wasn't sure you'd do it, but I put my faith in you."

"Don't talk like that to me," I snap. "Don't use that word!"

"Faith?"

"Yes. I might have put my gun down, but I'm not one of your... colleagues, I guess."

"What's wrong with the word? Why are you so viscerally opposed to a word as innocent as faith?"

"Innocent? I know what I learned in school. I know that —"

"Faith means," he interrupts, "trusting someone or something. That's all. Faith isn't always about God. Faith is something we place in others as well. Where has yours been all these years?"

I pause and think, but I don't need to. I know exactly where my "faith" has been, only I don't know how many more punches my pride can withstand.

"Myself," I confess.

"There's nothing wrong with having faith in yourself. But if you invest all of your faith in one entity, especially yourself, you can end up lost when your goals change, when your situation changes, but especially when *you* change. I think all of that has just now happened to you."

"Thanks to you," I smirk, but he takes me at my word.

"Don't mention it. You've been treading water long enough. Are you ready to move in a direction?"

"I thought I was moving in a direction."

"You were. You were sinking."

"Are you trying to proselytize me?" I ask flat out.

"You?" he laughs. "Are you kidding? I'm not here to help you find

God. Even I know that would take a miracle. No, Justice, I'm here to help you find yourself. Again."

"You mean you don't do that only once in life?" I remember our talk, years and years ago. He does too. He softly smiles and his eyes go back into his memory.

"I suppose you could. But that doesn't leave much room for growth, don't you think? Especially for you. Hate to break it to you, but life isn't that easy. You've got some searching to do, and what you will find will amaze you. Or break you. I'm not really sure. But wouldn't it be fun to find out?"

The clock reads 10:24. The sidewalk outside the Golden Garden has been vacant for the last fifteen minutes. I haven't eaten since breakfast, but here I sit, entertaining and old teacher over tea. An old friend. A possible enemy.

"No you don't," I say, shaking my head.

"I don't what?" Truth asks.

"You don't hate to break it to me."

Theresa

The silence woke Theresa, the still staleness of the air circulating in her bedroom undisturbed because of the absence of her son crying in the middle of the night. It woke her to a strange peace. One that cloaked her anxiety like a pain killer.

It was nine in the morning, Monday, the second morning she had awoken without Abraham, the third without Lania. She was to arrive at work by noon. She had slept for nearly ten hours.

The warm light of the sun rested on her face like the hand of a parent and nestled itself on her cheek and forehead, her ear and neck. It felt good.

The softness of her sheets glided smoothly along her legs as she kicked into a stretch, an impossible smile plied from her cramped frowning lips. Sleep had been hard to come by, let alone ten hours of it. Having a child, the plans for his baptism, her split with August, and aging into her mid-thirties all robbed her of sleep. But last night, a special kind of exhaustion put her to bed and gave her the best rest since before she could remember.

Abraham, the last baptism in Far City, safely slept in a palace under the capable care of Fern with his father nearby. Before she left Abraham at the Bolden estate, she and Fern created a way of communicating on social media. Fern, a frequent presence online, would post a picture or random status three times a day if all was well. Should she stop posting for a period of six hours, Theresa should check in. Fern hadn't stopped posting and left ambiguous messages over the weekend to reassure Theresa.

A flower in front of last night's sunset with the status, "All is well at the estate," was intended for Theresa. Another status read, "This baby slept well last night," above a picture of her new car. Theresa smiled at that one. Abraham rarely slept through the night. Maybe Fern was embellishing so that Theresa wouldn't feel as though she were inconveniencing her. Nevertheless, the posts kept the anxious mother calm in the absence of her son.

Yesterday marked the first day she had to herself. Sunday. The Lord's day. No way she would meet up with the Martyrs as she had in previous weeks. She barely wanted to pray on her own, but she did in her own mind. Halfway through the prayer, she paused. It was a dark feeling that held her back — an underlying anger that wanted to give God the silent treatment. She stopped the prayer altogether and listened to the thought. She heard nothing back, but only felt reserved betrayal that reduced into a bitter hatred. The feeling was new to Theresa. She had never been angry with God before, but now that her dedication to her faith had cost her another loved one, she rounded up all the suspects. God ended up as an accomplice. Innocent until proven guilty.

She let the thought slip and went about her Sunday with her original plan. Rest and restore. A book. Takeout. A movie. A nap. Leftovers. Chocolate mousse. A glass of wine. Another glass of wine. Another glass of wine. Then out.

Now, on a Monday morning when the sun already simmered the air, Theresa felt refreshed. She stayed in bed for another hour before she put down her book and fanned the blanket off her body. Two more hours. She wondered what to wear to work.

After rest and restore, Theresa's next goal that began with the letter R was routine. So back to work. She dare not miss a day to spark suspicion because without a doubt, many of her co-workers at Far City's Department of Social Wellness practiced anti-intervention and leaked incriminating anomalies to the IF. Nowhere did gossip travel faster than at her workplace.

A few months back, an employee, one whom Theresa avoided because she often saw him at private liturgies, no longer showed up to work. It was around the same time when the liturgies, led by Lania, had to be moved to another location. A member had been exposed. Later Theresa found out from one of the congregation members that IF Elites waited for him to return home from work, and the last anyone saw of him was a neighbor saying he had been escorted into a car by a handful suited men and women. A week later, Theresa overheard some of her work friends talking about the man and how they overheard him whispering what sounded like a prayer to himself while he was in the bathroom. Careless mistake. Foolish. You don't do that. Certainly not at work.

Everyone who met in secret, especially government employees, knew that the workplace is the last place to engage in prayer or anything resembling Godseeking. Normalcy was necessary, and Theresa dressed her troubled heart with a fake smile as she got ready for work.

Theresa obtained her master's degree in social work from Seattle

University — now Far City U. She endured long hours and worked mostly with juvenile criminals as part of Far City's Department of Social Wellness. It was ironic to her, that she could work in a job that intervened in the lives of others and essentially put Jesus' teachings into action, yet any sign that religious teachings had influenced her actions and the ire of Freespeakers would burn in her direction.

Though she loved her job, Theresa's work didn't come without pain. The pain of watching her 'kids,' as she called them, continue to make bad choices. The pain of showing up to their homes while their parents were strung out on drugs. The pain of sitting with them in the city prison. The pain of attending their funerals or their siblings' funerals or their parents' funerals. She hurt with each youth she lost — the type of hurt that changes who you are, that messes with your heart and mind and makes you wonder if you're doing right by the world or if the world will ever do right by the ones who deserve it the most. The pain wore out many of her colleagues, but even though Theresa had her moments, she felt only a stability in her purpose in life. *They're always going to need me, like I'm always going to need them,* she thought.

She would endure the pain of her work, because love is only made stronger through pain.

A young man taught her that lesson. Servando pushed cocaine in Far City's University District and Capitol Hill neighborhoods, two of the most dangerous areas in the city. Theresa met him soon after he was caught and locked in juvenile detention for a second time. His parents were gone — deported when he was only seven years old after their naturalization documents were revoked. But since Servando was born in Far City, he was allowed to stay. Instead of moving back to El Salvador with his family, he remained in the States in hope that one day, he could bring his parents back to their home. He lived with an acquaintance of his parents who ended up using Servando to sell drugs when he was only ten years old. Six years of abuse followed. On the streets, he found refuge in a neighborhood gang, and rarely returned home. To the prison corporations, Servando was an easy target; they tracked him as a potential lifer and hired police to be a little more partial to his location after he was released from juvie the first time.

Theresa came into Servando's life during one of her volunteer prison visits. Servando never had visitors, and when he heard that one had turned up, he hoped so desperately that it would be his mother. At first, upon seeing Theresa's profile, his heart leapt, but all he saw was the deception of similarity. He sank into the chair and cried for the first time since he was separated from his parents.

But as they spoke, and he illuminated small corners of his life to her, he realized more than a physical likeness between Theresa and his mother. Her compassion and gentleness and most of all her genuine concern for *him* awoke some long forgotten memories.

"Are you sure you don't know a Terecita Valenzuela?" he asked her.

"No, I'm sorry honey, I don't," Theresa said, knowing how deeply deflating her honest response was. "She is your mother, though?"

Silence. More tears.

"I'm not your mother, Servando. But I'll tell you what — I'll keep visiting you."

Each week, Theresa came back. He illuminated the dark corners of his life, and she shared with him her story as well, losing her own mother and father. They became close over the grief they shared, and together, the burden was lighter for both. When Servando was released seven months after they'd met, Theresa knew exactly where he could find a safe home. A diminishing church in the Hills District of Far City run by a woman who knew what it meant to take in an orphaned child.

Soon after, Servando located his parents in their native El Salvador. Theresa and Lania raised enough money to reunite the family.

"I was born here," he said to Theresa and Lania as they pulled into the airport. "I've never felt at home since my parents were deported. They wanted me to stay because they thought I'd have more opportunities here, but in the last nine years, I've only felt genuine love once — from you two. I'm alive and I'm free, and it's all because of you."

Theresa wanted Abraham to grow up without the pain she witnessed, or at least not as much of it. She felt the best way to accomplish this was to teach Abraham Gospel values as her own father taught her. Being a light in the darkness. Giving hope to the hopeless. Rest to the weary. Healing to the sick. Visiting the prisoner. All the qualities about Jesus she had romanticized when she was a child. All the dispositions society now embraced as long as they weren't God's virtues.

An hour to go. She started getting dressed. Black blazer, black pants, red blouse. Her power colors. Makeup too. She never wore much, just enough to cover the aging skin around her eyes. She hated makeup and thought for a long while about giving it up. But today was not the day. Today was absolutely a day for *ordinary*. Today, she would return to normal, whatever that was.

She made her breakfast and ate at the counter instead of the table next to Abraham's vacant child's seat. Two fried eggs and more leftover gallo pinto. She tried to stop thinking about Freespeakers and baptisms and priests and Abraham and hate and prison and death — side dishes to her morning's meal. She breathed deep and went to nowhere, a place

121

in her mind where she would minimize her thoughts to going through the motions. A sterile way of living, void of feeling.

She silenced her hatred of Freespeakers and rinsed her plate and fork, leaving them in the sink. She silenced her rebellious thoughts of public baptism and lament for Lania, and she picked up her car keys making her way for the front door. She silenced the sound of Abraham cooing and crying, though the image of his face wasn't going anywhere, then unlocked her car door and climbed into the cabin warm with the morning sun pouring in for the last few hours. She started her engine, leaving at home the thoughts that busied her mind over the weekend and distracted her from all else in existence. As she sped off, she passed an old sedan, a lot like hers. It took her notice, since she had never seen it parked on her block before. Inside was an old Asian man sat in the driver's seat, reading a hard copy of the newspaper.

They still print those? Theresa wondered.

JUSTICE

Midland America University

Senior Year

Spring quarter, 2081

"My pride's hurt more than anything," I confess.

"Well, the bigger the pride, the bigger the hurt."

"Yeah, I know. I just... Well, I just messed up. Big time. And I feel really bad about it. It's something I don't normally do — it's... it's uncharacteristic... it's —"

"It's very characteristic."

"Not of me —"

"Yes of you. Yes of me. Yes of everyone. You remember our talk about failure just a few months ago? You, Justice, are a hard worker. You don't shy away from challenges and that's why you will try new things. You'll get good at them. But they won't always turn out the way you want. Those are the times when you need to pick yourself up and refine your craft. Those are the times when you reinvent yourself."

I find myself agreeing with him, but I'm still lopsided over my ineptitude. I wouldn't have told anyone else but Truth that I failed my entrance test for the Intervention Force. My dad knows. That's more than enough.

"I shouldn't be messing up like this. Not now."

"You're too proud to be imperfect, Justice, and you're only able to change one of those. You'll become spiteful toward yourself if you don't learn to forgive yourself, and that's dangerous. You are allowed to be imperfect. We all are."

"Yes, but I want to be the best that I can be."

"So did you try your best? Did you give it your all in the critical moment, even though you came up short?"

I say with all conviction I have, "Yes, I did."

"Then as much as you're honest, you're free from shouldering the blame. Sure, it could have gone differently, but sometimes our best in one moment is different than our best at other moments, or maybe, believe it or not, our best is just not good enough. You haven't disappointed me. In fact, you've made me proud in this moment. It's nice to see that the Great Justice isn't quite so infallible."

My eyebrows twitch at the Godseeking nature of his last word, but I'm more interested in accepting his compassion and encouragement at the moment — qualities my professor shares abundantly with me.

"You need to come with me," ProTruth says. He isn't making eye contact. Tells me he thinks I won't want to go.

"Where." I say it more so than ask. I'm listening to him. I'm listening to him propose too much, and I don't like it.

"I can't tell you where, but I promise you will have answers there."

"That's not enough. You have to tell me something."

He looks me straight in the eye. "You want to know who you truly are? Then come with me."

"What do you mean who I truly am? You really don't want me to be

SCO, huh. You have to understand, this makes me uncomfortable because you're breaking the law and now you're asking me to break the law."

"I offered myself to you."

"Maybe I made a mistake."

"Well I'd say that's a quick turnaround."

"It's because you're holding back. You say to go somewhere with you and you won't tell me where. Tell the truth. Isn't that what you're supposed to be about? Where do you want me to go? Is it close? Is it far?"

He hesitates, but still maintains his stare into my eyes. "It's far."

"That's it? Why can't you tell me?" I know the answer. He doesn't need to say it. He doesn't trust me. And he shouldn't. We're about as far into our opposite sides of the law as we can be. "Look, I took a risk in letting you have this conversation with me. Why can't you do the same and give me even a small idea of where you're trying to take me?"

"If we're balancing risks, wouldn't you say I took an equally great one in meeting you? Forgive me, Justice. I can't tell you because I can't put that much faith in you. Not yet at least. This conversation is a start."

"Then I guess we're done here. I won't go anywhere unless you tell me where we're going, and you won't even tell me how long I'll be out of commission from work."

I'm getting worked up.

"Justice, please."

He knows he's losing me. But it's not just a logistical issue. I feel if I go with him, I'm finished. No more Intervention Force. Might as well be a fugitive myself. So the only answer I offer is silence.

"You know, I care about all my students. I've helped many of them through life. Not just in my class, but through real issues. Loss of loved ones especially. I help them find hope. Help them find a way to persevere. You've never lost anyone close to you, have you?"

What does that have to do with anything? My parents are both alive. I was an only child. No wife. No kids. Never knew my grandparents or got close to any other relatives. I have friends, but my best friend is my work. That's why I'm so good at it. And he's taking that away from me. He can't. He *can't*. I reach for my tranq. He sees my arm moving, but still doesn't break eye contact.

I do it quickly this time, without a thought.

"Remember when I told you I didn't want you to become SCO?" He doesn't wait for me to respond, but I remember that moment so clearly. It was when I started to drift away from him. "It was selfish. Forgive me. Please. Forgive me…"

The dart does its work quickly.

"I'm sorry, professor," I say to the silent room. "It was too much for me. I tried to listen. But I couldn't quit. *You* taught me that. That if I fail, it's just an opportunity to make myself stronger. I know you won't understand. I don't expect you to. In a way, I saved you, or at least protected some of the people you care about. You were about to show me something, take me to a place where there are people like you. I know it. But I didn't want to go, because once I went, there would be no option left for me but to leave everything I know and love and want out of life. And that's just too much.

"You can't ask that much of me, Truth. I'm sorry."

It looks like he's dead.

Most of the faithies I tranq have a look on their face of peace at minimum, almost happiness. The look on Truth's face, however, is a snapshot of his heart and mind the very moment after he realized what

I was doing. A look of disappointment. A look of failure. I try to believe it's directed at himself.

Honestly, I probably would have listened to him all the way through and used the information to my advantage. I bet, with whatever he was about to divulge, I could have easily shortcutted through the ranks and become SCO next week. Instead, I did him a courtesy — more than that — in the name of our old friendship. He's not a bad guy — at least I don't believe he is. I'll try to make the Intervention Force Commanding Officer see it the same way. Only I won't, I'm sure, when the time comes to make that decision. That will only make me look soft, and that's exactly how people get stuck behind desks or get demoted from Elite status. Not gonna happen.

I squat beside him, and using a few napkins, dry the sleeve of his jacket where his cup of tea spilled as he fell over. Straightening out his glasses, I scoop him off the ground, but before I lift his limp body, I hear the creak of the old wooden floor behind me. I turn around and find my traitor partner and his slippery friend glaring right at me from a distance. I let go of my old teacher and think to reach for my firearm, but their pistols are already drawn before I complete the thought. My hands rise slowly to the ceiling.

I analyze the two of them. Chameleon's face is the tamer of the two. He looks focused, eyes steady and mouth pouting with no lines of strain or sheen of sweat. It's Beamer who gives me greater concern. He has the upper hand for now with a gun in my face, but what really makes me nervous is that he looks pissed. Beyond. The kind of pissed off abandonment that could end my life right here in this restaurant.

"You son of a bitch," he shoots. It's a cold shot of settled anger. "You really don't have a heart. Professor Truth could turn a war criminal into a World Peace Award winner, but he can't turn Justice Flint into a hero, let alone a decent human being. Didn't you learn anything in his class?"

"Don't patronize me. I don't need that from you. *You* are a criminal. And so is he. From the moment he knew I wanted a position of power, he's tried to stop me from achieving my greatest goal. That's exactly what a teacher *isn't* supposed to do. What makes you think I want anyone telling me what to do with my life? Not him, and especially not you. You're nothing Beamer. You have no ambition."

"You have no idea who I am. We've been partners for more than a year and you know nothing about me because your concern is always with yourself and with your obsession you call a dream. What kind of person wants to be SCO anyway? Locking up and torturing people who don't even commit crimes worth the time it takes to catch them."

"So this is the real you? You're going to tell me you're an interventionist too? A Godseeker? A Baptick? I admit, I've always had my suspicions. You've never locked up anyone. I thought you were just spineless. Now it's clear that you're a traitor. If I had my gun —"

"You don't. And I might be a little out of my mind right now, so if I were you I'd shut my mouth and listen."

"What, are you going to kill me? I don't think that's what your *God* would want."

"I don't have to kill you. God might not want me to, but I wonder if he'll have a problem if I put a bullet in your leg. How will you ever be SCO if you're not able to walk anymore?"

"No!" Chameleon's interjection surprises both of us. "Enough of this, brother."

"Wait — you two are brothers?" Beamer lasers a stare at his sibling, but quickly directs his disdain back at me.

"Yes," Beamer admits. "He's the lucky one. He's only had to double for the last few years, but I've been losing my mind ever since I joined the academy. Justice, you think you have everything and everyone figured out. That's a load of bull. And the person you have least figured out is yourself. Bet on that. Professor Truth may be naive to believe he can reach you, but at least he cares. He saw something in the great Justice Flint, something that I've never noticed in the entire time I've spent as your partner."

"Really?" I ask with a noticeable change in my tone of voice. "What's that?"

"He always thought you would change the world, or at least our country, for the better. He said you had the drive, the determination and confidence to make our society a place where all people could live freely in peace. Only, the one part he saw lacking in you, the one part he tried to instill in you was never going to happen."

"And what was that?"

"What do you think, Justice?"

Beamer reads my face and knows I know the answer to my own question. Love. Every time Professor Truth and I would discuss some part of life, he'd remind me to temper it with love. If I have power, wield it with love. If I'm to enforce the law, enforce it with love. If I'm going to achieve great things with my life, make sure I do it with love. I always thought it was some cute little tagline he put at the end of each lesson. Sort of like, 'be nice to everyone,' but now I start wondering what he really meant by 'love.'

"Now get away from him," Beamer orders.

My hands still raised, I step back generously. Beamer collects Truth from the floor. It's the only time during the whole exchange that he breaks eye contact with me. Chameleon's pistol still locks in on my chest, and I swap my attention between him and the scene before me, which I can actually appreciate, strangely enough. Beamer reverently lifts Truth onto his shoulders and begins to walk away.

"Beamer."

He stops, but doesn't turn around.

"He was your teacher too, wasn't he," I ask.

"He was," he replies continuing toward the exit.

"I'll find you. You know I will."

"I know you will. I'll see you then."

With that, I feel a needle jab into my thigh, almost in the same spot I was tranqed just hours ago. I see Chameleon walking backwards, holstering his gun and placing a tranquilizer in his coat pocket. As the room goes dark, I wonder if there are negative side effects from being knocked out twice in one day.

JUSTICE

There's a spider in the upper left corner of my bedroom. I watched it make its web in the twilight not one week ago, the silk secreting from its spinneret, its legs extending and attaching one strand of web to another. It's mystifying. Something to do when all you can think about is work, and work is all you can think about. I left the spider there — didn't kill it like most people would have. In a strange way, it helps me fall asleep, usually an hour or so after I try. I stare at the web, moonlight reflecting off its perfect lines, while occasionally, a passing car's headlights illuminate the entire thing.

It's a shame, really, all the spinning the spider did to create its home. There's no way I would tear it down. But soon, it's going to die. There are no flies in my room. It's a beautiful home, the spider's, symmetrical and functional, but the damned bug built it in the wrong place. So I lie here awake, watching it die in ignorance, until one day I recline to sleep and see an empty, sagging web. Then I'll sweep it off the ceiling. It'll be gone, and I'll have no other distraction from my musings about Truth and his band of Godseekers.

For now, I'm not focused on the fugitives like I should be — it's that spider. I can't stop thinking about the insect, because, well, I identify

131

with it. I relate to the spider. I've built my web in anti-intervention. I've caught many flies. Three hundred eighty three, in case you forgot. But I'm not satisfied - there's still a hunger inside of me and I have no idea how many lock-ups it will take until I'm finally happy. What if happiness is the real fly, and every time I arrest a Godseeker, I am eating a ghost? And like that spider in the corner of the room, I'm starving in a place where I'm never going to find what truly fulfills me. I'm 36 years-old now. I should have this figured out.

I don't usually say this to other people, but I think it. All the time, I think it. And I know exactly who to blame. I hate him and love him at the same time. I know those are strong words. I think the strength of the latter is the only reason why I didn't bring him in. Sometimes, I don't know who I'm more pissed at. Him for being who he is, or me for being who I am.

It's been nine days since I last saw his face. I had the upper hand at the Golden Garden. But he broke me down — again. Deconstructed me. Not with a wrecking ball, but piece by piece. One belief at a time.

It was my experience, though, that validated his arguments. Before Chameleon, I never met a hostile, let alone resistant, Godseeker. All of them, all 383, came quietly once I caught up to them. No fighters, no tongue-lashers to call me a freedom killer. That still stabs at my con-science. A *freedom killer*. I'm a Freespeaker, and I work for and fight for Freespeakers. How could I possibly be killing freedom? Except, when I jabbed him with the eternatate needle, as the serum made a bulge in his thigh, I felt I was what he said I was. I stole his ability to speak freely, and I never felt more contradictory in my life.

There was an old word ProTruth taught us in his course — hypoc-risy. It's when you believe something and say you believe something, but what you do is different. The complete opposite, even. And that's how Chameleon made me feel.

Then, of course Truth had to show up and make me question my ambition all over again. I *hate* how he does that. Not because he disturbs this comfortable path I'm on, but because he challenges the integrity of my decisions. I'm doing something I'm good at. I'm doing something I love. I'm doing something that helps society. Then Truth comes along and makes me ask, *Am I?*

The objective face of the clock somehow manages to mock my anguish. I remember two-twenty-four and one-forty-three and twelve-fifty-eight. The flatly lit aquamarine digits, slim reminders that I'm captive to my own obsessions, now read two fifty-three. The clock counts down to the buzzer that will sound in just over two hours, but a different alarm has been jackhammering in my head all week. *That* alarm had grown into a commonplace ambient sound like a freight train wailing on its horn or an aircraft growling overhead, city noises I've grown so accustomed to, I no longer hear them. But now, *that* alarm blares louder and more distinct than ever. It won't let me sleep until I acknowledge its existence — hear its voice. I've tried to bury it, but the damned thing won't shut up, won't let me sleep.

I tilt my head up and open my eyes. Three oh-five. This last thought has shaved another twelve minutes from the clock. No way I'm falling asleep tonight.

I throw back my sheets and blankets, kicking my legs out of bed. It takes a moment for my head to orient itself, but I emerge from my bedroom, lethargically lumbering toward my short-term solution and knowing full well this is a problem in and of itself. Above my refrigerator in the cabinet, I pinpoint my cure. It's in a tall, green bottle with a crimson cap and a coat of arms on the label. I pour whiskey into a glass meant for a beer, stare at it, and ponder why I didn't just drink from the bottle. I extinguish that thought, and consume the smooth libation in separate gulps, the liquid igniting my throat on the way down. It scorches like a brush fire spreading all throughout my chest and arrives at my belly, sitting there like magma in a lava chamber. Pressure builds. It goes straight to my head and erupts in a dizzying stupor. I haven't eaten since the apple I had for lunch yesterday. Maybe I should have just had a cup of tea.

Then, another strange thought invades and attacks my psyche, but I let it, simply because I've got a good buzz going on, and it's so crazy that in the morning when I wake up - if I ever fall asleep - I will not remember the thought, or if I do, I know that I can blame it on the liquor.

I want to quit.

I stand on top of the words as though they are a mountain I've been climbing for the better half of my life. You would think, after all the hard work it takes to scale that mountain, after all the training, conditioning, the hours and the sacrifices, that once on top of it all, I would see some glimpse of heaven — not the religious one, obviously. The word heaven has come to mean an idea of perfection. An effort like mine deserves — no, *demands* — a profound reward like heaven. But here at the summit, all I see is fog, like I'm in a cloud. For all I know, I'm at the base of another mountain. To me, that would be the worst outcome — that all I've worked for means nothing in the end. Nothing to *me*.

It's late, I'm drunk, and I find myself slipping my bare feet into a pair of sneakers and walking outside my front door in pajamas. A walk.

That'll do me some good. Some fresh air to circulate in my lungs while I take crooked steps along the porous pavement.

The summer night makes the outdoors pleasant in pajama pants and a long t-shirt. It's clear, the stars are out, but the city and the moon are so bright, I can see only a small handful of them. I walk by my neighbors whom I have yet to meet. I've been living here for a year, but have been too busy to do anything neighborly. A cheery couple came by to welcome me when I moved to the neighborhood. They brought freshly baked cookies, and I've wanted to return the favor for eleven months now. Don't think that's going to happen.

Even though I'm rarely home, living in south uptown has its benefits, like a late night pub just around the corner. I look down at my attire, self conscious about my flannel printed drawstring bottoms, but alas, I've come too far. I've decided that alcohol is more important than appearances.

The heavy wooden door of the pub has a Celtic cross engraved on its upper half. The City doesn't make them shave off the carving, they say, because it is historical, iconic, but mostly because they serve good booze to anti-intervention enforcement at a good price. Plus, the owner is an old Irishman who swears he'd shut — or *burn* was his exact word — the place down if he was forced to get rid of his grandfather's original door. No one wants to lose such a fine establishment, especially me at four in the morning.

The bar is not empty. Two other early-morning patrons sit on opposite sides of the counter. One man's thinning curly hair frantically zigzags off his scalp, his back a rounded hill curving down from his neck from which more hair peeks just above his collar. He sports a royal blue long-sleeve business shirt, which would have been a sharp choice except for the dark, damp circles swelling at his armpits. The other man huddles on himself next to the wall. He wears his hood. He burps and stumbles out of his seat before he realizes standing is not such a great idea. Oh, the company I keep.

"Officer Justice Flint," I'm greeted by Sultan, the late night barkeep. "What in the hell are you doing in here? In pajamas? My God. I oughta send you home to your mama, but you look like you're going to spend some money here tonight."

Sultan doesn't bat an eye as he makes a Godspeak infraction, and neither do I. He scans my eye with his retina pay gun, lifts a clean glass from the counter and starts pouring bronze bourbon.

"Double," I say firmly. He obliges and I throw it back like a frat legend.

"Jesus Christ, man!"

"Relax Sultan," I say in a drunk droll. The words come out like my voice is on autotune. "That's two strikes, you know. But don't worry. I won't say nothing. Bigger baddies out there." I pause to laugh. Alliteration tickles me. "Plus you're the boozy man." I twirl my index finger, requesting a refill. He looks at me as if I'm asking for his first born.

"Here — drink this," he offers me a tall glass of water. I squint my eyes in irritation, but I lift it to my lips and down the whole thing. He refills it immediately.

"What is it, Justice? I've never seen you this fucked up."

I shake my head, too inebriated to recall what brought me to the pub in the first place. I shrug, then growl. Whatever brought me to this moment, I remember it being something I don't wish to share.

"I'll let you alone then," he says. "But Justice —"

I lift my eyes and they reach for him like a hand stretching for help.

"I don't know what you're going through, but sooner or later, you have to face the truth."

It's as though he sees the stake over my chest, then slowly steps down on it. And now, I'm dead. He walks off and leaves me that way.

I have all the power in the world and I'm better at what I do than anyone, but here I sit at a bar, four in the morning, and I'm all alone. No time for a woman, no time for friends, no time for family. Only my work and my goals lay claim to my sorry drunk ass.

I tap a monitor on the bar counter and tip Sultan for his services. The room is spinning now, and I have to work in a few hours. As I burst through the door, I hear Sultan call from behind.

"You take care of yourself, chief!"

I laugh at what he calls me. Laugh all the way home.

I awaken on my couch, half my body draping off the cushions and an open bottle of SoberX on the ground. I must have taken a few. It doesn't do much for the memory, but it works wonders on headaches. It's bright in my living room and the sun punches through my window at an angle that causes me to sprout up immediately. It's almost noon.

I find my comm on the kitchen counter, a yellow light flashing on the screen. Messages. Four of them. The IF Commanding Officer.

Surveillance recommends an interception around noon. Come in at 8 for details.

Shit. I dial the CO's direct line and put him on speaker while I throw on my uniform, which I left conveniently on my couch. He picks up just as I walk out the door. Yeah, I'm that fast, and just like that, I leave the previous night's musings, whatever they were, within the walls of my house.

Theresa

Theresa's father wasn't wealthy, but he owned a generational home which she inherited. The rain-pelted white siding needed replacing, and the roof looked as if it were molding, spots of moss forming little tufts on the shingles. A bay window jutted out from the upstairs bedroom, and throughout the entire home, there was no better view of Lake 14, which sprawled out to the east. Theresa had always been a night owl and loved waking up to the persimmon glow of the sun painting the walls of her bedroom.

This house — the walls, the smells, the scratches and stains, the furniture — was Theresa's life. For her, walking through each room was like reading the story of her past, a chapter for each memory and dialogue written by the conversations with her father, aunts, uncles, and family friends.

On the ceiling in the living room, a slight but noticeable puncture remained, an eyesore for Theresa who wanted her father to fix it, or at least patch and paint the imperfection. But Abram, who authored the wound, looked upon it fondly, a memory of when the Seahawks won their second Superbowl on a late game interception. The hole in the ceiling was a scar of celebration, and a scar like that was one hell of a story that Abram loved telling guests. Theresa had thought of finally filling the hole after her father died, but no way would she ever do that. It was now a memory of her father, and every time she looked at it, she'd only see the elation on his face.

In Theresa's childhood bedroom, which she had hoped one day would become Abraham's room, the northern wall opposite the window held a mural of nature — trees and birds, flowers and a lake, sun and clouds and rain, butterflies and spiders. The colors on the wall were bold and bright, not soothing, but lively, vibrant with the bustle of the outdoors. When her birthday would come around, Abram would have her add to the mural, which they started on Theresa's fifth birthday, the same year Abram turned 35. He painted the grass, she the sky. That whole year, whenever she'd stare at the wall, she'd imagine a flurry of purple butterflies coming over the green blades of grass. She asked her father if she could add the image on her sixth birthday. And so she did. When Abram turned 36, he added a bed of lilies — his mother's name — and daisies, for Theresa's mother.

A more common tradition they shared was etched on the kitchen door frame, where Abram had carved grooves in the wood to show how tall his daughter had grown each year. Theresa had seen it in a movie once as a kid, and asked her father why he'd scratch the house in such a way.

"Why not just mark it on a poster or a separate piece of wood?" a young and curious Theresa asked.

"Because this house is part of your life," Abram responded. "It's important. It's where we became a family."

"But I thought material things shouldn't be that important."

"You're right," Abram responded. "They aren't the most important. But years from now, when you look at this kitchen door, you're going to remember something. You're going to remember me measuring you. And if we do it every year, you'll remember not just that I measured you, but the time when you didn't grow at all for a whole year, or when you shot up four inches, or the day you will grow taller than me. It'll make you feel happy, maybe sad, but ultimately, it will be a good feeling. And no, it's not the wood that is important, but it gives our memory something we can see and touch instead of simply imagine. We need stuff like that in life, to remind us that certain parts of our past were once as real as the thing that sparks the memory."

After eating breakfast, Theresa walked by that same kitchen door and as she did every time she passed it, slid her fingers over the tradition she shared with her father. The grooves had grown soft to the touch.

Theresa wouldn't be in Far City for that long. Tomorrow, she would meet Fern at the Bolden Estate and pick up Abraham. Then the two of them would be off to Mile High City, where a temporary safe house and reidentification process would give her and her son a chance at living a life in society without being surrounded by constant suspicion. It was the Martyrs' doing. They took care of their own. They also arranged for a renter to live in the house, someone trusted but not connected to Theresa.

It's just wood and nails, she told herself, but her father's sentiment made it difficult for Theresa to imagine someone else taking residence in her childhood home. Up the stairs she went. They were getting old, boards creaking like a sore spine. Theresa sighed deeply as she entered her bedroom, shut the door, even locked it, and perched herself in the bay window, wrapping her legs in a soft chenille blanket.

She pulled back the shades. The wind-blown trees interrupted her view, but her eyes found the water and fixed themselves on the blinking white crests forming and vanishing throughout the surface of the lake. The waters leapt, unruly and undone. It made her nervous. Whenever the lake appeared disturbed, something bad always seemed to happen.

Only once did Abram recount the day Theresa's mother died in great detail to his daughter. At the top of his story, he would explain the uneasiness of Lake 14, how it twisted and rolled, turbulent under the rumble of thunder and constant prodding of purple lightning bolts. Another instance came when Theresa was in elementary school. A storm had wrinkled the surface of the lake on the day she broke her arm falling off the monkey bars. A few more similar coincidences and Theresa found enmity with the raging waters. The morning of the attack that led to her father's death, however, solidified her hydro-paranoia.

She was visiting Abram as she usually did on a Sunday morning. Another tradition they shared — breakfast and church, or church then breakfast, depending on what time she awoke. The day of the attack, the waters had appeared grey, blue and several shades in between, except a rusty red hue that crept out from the northern shore into the middle of the lake, dispersing itself like a drop of blood in a glass of water. She remembered gawking at the anomaly after eating breakfast that day, not wanting to leave the house because of the portentous moodiness of the lake. Abram reassured her that there was nothing to worry about, so he insisted they go to church that morning as planned.

"I don't care if the waters are yellow with swirly red dots," he said,

141

his dismissive attitude giving Theresa anxiety.

"It looks pretty rough, dad," Theresa sputtered. "You know how I feel about the Lake."

But her father insisted, and to his defense, there had been numerous times when the lake was under duress, but no harm fell upon the family.

The mass was typical, except the music, which was particularly loud and boisterous. Wind slapped the west side of the building and the congregation, during moments of silence, could hear the beams of wood snap and crack against the nails holding them in place. But as the mass continued, another uproar surrounded the building. A large Freespeaker protest gathered just outside the main doors of Our Lady of Lourdes Church.

"One nation without God!" was the chant this time. Ann Waldie, the music director, felt a flare of defiance and cranked up the monitors and amps. She walloped a G Major, starting a song of post communion reflection, then the drummer kicked in the beat, followed by the bass and guitars. "*Your Grace*," the singers belted, and the ensemble, though small, and the congregation, though sparse, shouted the song with more spirit than they ever had any other number. Ann repeated the refrain and Natalie, one of the vocalists, improvised as the cycle rotated back and forth.

Then the song ended. The chants were still echoing outside, but everyone smiled at each other, and Lania, who was presiding, started an applause, thanking Ann and the band for the vivacious number.

A final selection for the recessional, an encore, and then mass was over. Despite the looming opposition outside, everyone wore a smile on their face. Lania didn't want anyone going out alone. She brought the worshipers — about 40 of them — together in the narthex of the church.

"These people are our brothers and sisters," she said. "But don't do anything to provoke them."

The protesters sounded particularly angry that day. The sharp key of their cries, shrill and full, seeped into the cracks of the doors, then the ears of the congregation grew more anxious, as the moments stretched and it became evident that the protest wasn't dying down anytime soon.

The doors opened.

The congregation walked out in solidarity, some with arms linked.

A word to instigate from a protester.

No response.

A word and a push.

No response.

Theresa walked close to her father, who had shifted her from the outside of the migrating flock to the inside.

A man screamed at him.

Yeah you!

You fucking baptick! Fucking wetback! Who's the whore you're protecting? We know your savior fucked around with whores and homeless and...

Abram couldn't resist. He turned his head. He took a step. That was enough. A riot. A baseball bat. More chanting. No more songs.

Police had surrounded the volatile group, but took their time intervening. Took too much time. Abram was on the ground over creeks of blood. Theresa cursed the clouds.

"An ambulance!" she cried. *The lake. The lake, Dad, the lake.* "Get help!" Lania was on the phone and parishioners were pleading with police. *The lake. The goddamned lake.*

As the anxious waters trembled outside, Theresa felt betrayed by the lake. Not because of all the tragedy it foretold, but because of its silence the day she lost Lania. In fact, the water's stillness gave her comfort, as if mother nature herself were validating her decision to baptize Abraham. There was no voice in the waters, she concluded. And even if there was, nothing significant would happen today. It was the day before she would reclaim Abraham from the Bolden estate. Not the day of. The storm was a day early.

Except, her phone rang.

It was Fern. She and Theresa agreed that no contact was to be made unless under dire circumstances. Before reaching for her phone on the side table next to her window seat, she glared at the lake and shook her head. *Don't do this*, she implored.

"Fern? What is it?" Theresa thought nothing of formalities.

"August took Abraham to Anna's," she replied. "I'm sorry Theresa, I had to run a simple errand for Rhody and Curt. August knew he would have Abraham all day. I called to check on him. He just told me."

Theresa's skin felt like the lake now. Restless, cold, chaotic. Her heart began hammering against her chest, and instantly her head began to ache. Her hands were tingling, and she thought a stroke was preparing to take her life. Anna's Ladybug Daycare. How many times had she walked with her son through the glass doors, the multi-colored decals and cloud-shaped letters inviting her in with a feeling of joy and safety? Surely the Intervention Force had staked out the place and informed employees about who they were looking for and why.

"Okay, I'm going," was all Theresa said. In her head raced so many more thoughts, clamoring but not making it through the phone receiver. Many of them unpleasant and directed toward August.

"No Theresa! Someone is bound to be there."

"Then what? What else can I do? I have to go."

"I told August to go. You hang back. You can't be seen with him. They'll take him *and* you. He'll probably be left alive. You won't. Theresa please!"

There was nothing to think about. "I can't stay. I'm going Fern."

"Let *me* go—"

But Theresa had already hung up. She was already running to her car. Already starting her engine. Already topping the speed limit.

She parked two blocks away around the corner from Anna's Lady-bug Daycare, ejected herself out of her car, and bounded down the sidewalk.

That moron. That absolute moron. Fern had to leave for one day, and he couldn't even handle that. That asshole. How dare he? His only son. My only son. What was he thinking? He wasn't thinking. He didn't care. Why did I marry such a careless, selfish man?

Stop it, she told herself and quieted her vindictiveness. Her focus needed to be on pulling Abraham from the daycare.

Her steps quickened. She wasn't running, but she passed a handful of pedestrians, including a jogger.

Please be safe. The waters from the morning flooded her thoughts. *The Lake. He's got to be okay. They don't mean anything. He's there. He's got to be there. Please let him be there, God, please let him be there.*

She approached the corner. Now she was jogging. She had to see. Now. Twenty steps away. Now ten. Now five.

The sight around the corner spurred her into a sprint. Abraham rested in the arms of a uniformed officer who strode toward a large

145

black SUV. She hadn't hit her full speed before a young man crossing the street intercepted her. He stopped right in her path, like stepping in front of a rolling boulder. He looked her right in the eye as he put his arms out in front of him, clasped her arms in his hands and halted her.

"Turn around," he said urgently. "Turn around now."

His eyes looked sad and wide, his face a teenager's. It was Daniel.

Theresa held her ground and gave the young man an aggressive look. She worked free of his grasp and tried to sidestep and go around him. Then he called her by name.

"Theresa, you have to trust me. We have to leave *now*. They're already here."

She felt a shift in her momentum. She knew exactly who 'they' were, but wanted to play dumb. Didn't give a damn at all. Still, her own safety could be her only chance at seeing Abraham again if *they* had already taken him. Like a bowl of water tilting back and forth, her determination to get to Abraham pushed her forward. Back the other way, she was pulled by the exigency in this stranger's voice, this stranger who called her by name, and most of all, by the sincerity and conviction in his eyes. They pushed her back, and she fell back. Into retreat. Her own will gave no such permission and she felt as though a parent was pulling her away from a treasured toy. But something swept her in the opposite direction of her son. Not the boy. Something inside her. A powerful fear. A fear telling her that she had already lost. A fear that any mother would ignore, but Theresa found her body faltering.

"My son," she said with a voice as creaky as the stairway in her house, eyes desperately looking into the boy's. "My son." Her second utterance was much clearer.

"I'm sorry," Daniel said mournfully. Then he pointed at the building across the street from Anna's. Its tall tinted windows at the street level were the mark of architecture of the time. Visual security — no one looking in. In the clean glass, the reflection in the window provided Daniel's retort to Theresa's plea. Three Suburbans with purple lights flashing huddled around the entrance to the daycare center. Intervention Force Elites.

"They took him not five minutes ago. And a man too." *August.*

"We have to go Theresa. They know who you are. They'll recognize you. Lania. Your friend. She told me you might be here. We have to move."

The boy's referral zapped Theresa into motion and the two ran down the block. Theresa's mind remained. She could feel her legs moving, her body pouncing away, away, away. But her mind — it was still in the tinted windows. Still at Anna's Ladybug Daycare. Still in the sewer beneath Far City. Somewhere between St. Francis Cemetery and the Bolden Estate. It was anywhere but in the moment that was carrying her away from Abraham.

Get caught, she thought. *Maybe I'll get to see Abraham one last time.*

She stopped. Daniel reached the end of the block before he noticed that Theresa was not right behind him. He turned around in time to see the desperate mother spin into a one eighty and begin stumbling back toward the corner, back toward the daycare. Toward three men in suits who had just rounded the corner. Daniel was fast. He was already in front of Theresa with his back to the agents. Good thing he was a bit taller than her.

"Elites," he muttered. "No way in hell they let you see Abraham again. We have to find another way."

Theresa caught a glimpse. She remembered the uniform. She'd seen them before two weeks prior scattered in the sewer system. One last look at the ground level tinted windows of the skyscraper across the street. There were only two SUVs now. They had her son, and he was gone.

Theresa

The sun burst through the clouds at the most inopportune moment, casting long afternoon shadows and awakening the air, warming Theresa's skin. The sky's hopeful gesture poked with insulting irony, the sun pressing unpleasantly on Theresa's face. That weary hot, the kind that withers alertness and favors afternoon siestas dragged the sullen mother with it to the asphalt.

And there she wanted to stay, a puddle or smudge on the sidewalk — something on the ground, trampled and defeated. Her feet planted themselves, deep and firm into the asphalt, immobilized. But the boy took hold of her, grabbed her arms and uprooted her like a bulb and ushered her onto the air-conditioned 7-bus where the cold air snapped her back into reality. As they drove off, Theresa caught a glimpse of her car about a half block from the intersection where the boy intercepted her. Three agents surrounded her silver Toyota like flies around abandoned meat. *Take it*, she thought. *Take it, like everything else.* Things no longer meant anything to her. Even her house, a living hall of memories she would likely never see again, was on the selling block. She didn't care what they did to the place when they would undoubtedly ransack and strip every room, from her bedroom with the painted mural she shared with her father to the living room where she produced school projects and term papers, to the kitchen door frame where her father measured her height each year. The IF would learn so much about her, find her concealed contraband of crucifixes and rosaries and journal entries and videos of Lania and her father. She wondered if she could get back to the house before the Intervention Force and set the place on fire. Who else would be at risk with all the evidence stored within the doors of her childhood home. If the walls could talk, they'd be witnesses.

She laughed. At first a giggle stirred in her gut, then erupted in a delirious fit of coughing and snorting. Her head throbbed and she grunted with all the depth of a grave. The bus brakes yawned a high pitch and the driver called over the speaker to see if Theresa needed an aid vehicle.

"She's okay — just exhausted," Daniel hollered back. Hesitating and holding his gaze on the cabin mirror, the driver eased off the brake and the bus hissed, lurching forward.

He put his hands on Theresa's shoulder.

"It sucks. I'm sorry." His whispered words harnessed a genuine yet worn out empathy, one that was void of shock and despair, but somehow still communicated love. He squeezed her shoulder. "Lania. She led me to you. Wanted me to keep you safe, if I could."

In the moment of separation from Abraham, she forgot that he had mentioned Lania's name. The effect it had on her physically. The power so strong that it moved her away from her son. All the air in Theresa's lungs rushed out of her mouth, and tears flooded her eyes. It was too much. She drew the awkward glances of the passengers, and immediately Daniel regretted divulging Lania's name, only he felt Theresa's heartbreak so deeply, he wanted to give her *some* sign of hope. Now the stares from other passengers were accompanied by looks of concern and confusion.

"Theresa, people are looking at us. Come on. Please. I don't want to go back. Not to them. You know what will happen. Please. Hold it together just for a little while."

Those words jolted Theresa. *Not to them...* She knew *them* and hated *them*. This boy seemed to be familiar with *them* and she would walk through the gates of hell before losing another innocent child, even one she had just met, to *them*. All it took was a deep breath, and she willed her tears away.

"I have a lot to explain once we get to where we're going," Daniel said, keeping his hand fastened to Theresa's shoulder. She tightened her clasped hands, which were hot and damp, and toggled images of Abraham, Lania and her father like a slideshow.

The bus ride lasted about half an hour until they reached their stop. Southwest Far City - the Global District, as it was called. The boy led Theresa to the neighborhood junction where a number of businesses — restaurants, dental offices, boutique shops, weed cafes, and coffee shops — lined the sidewalks. They came upon the Voices Mural, a famed wall covered in krylon by local artists, illustrating dozens of people, all from different backgrounds, simply speaking. An icon of freedom, it was, only among the various personages, it contained the likes of women in burkas and hijabs, men in yamakas, monks in robes, and a dark man who held a striking resemblance to images of Jesus - a crown of woven brambles may have given it away. The mural was commissioned by Far City before the AFLs were established, and when presented with the choice of whether or not to remove the religious figures from the wall, the City Council opted to let it remain. It was historic, beautiful, and residents of the city presented the council with an overwhelming cry to leave it be, via online petition. Many of those who had signed the petition had since passed away. The demographic landscape of Far City had changed immensely in the last fifteen years. It was only a matter of time.

Daniel led Theresa past a bustling farmer's market and an array of local food stands that swiped customers from the restaurants, one of which was a small Chinese hole in the wall with a green awning and yellow letters reading "Wong's Garden." It stood out amidst the modern storefronts with its weathered sign and rain-stained windows. The two slinked discreetly into the frosted glass door.

The main dining room starkly contrasted the crowded farmer's market. Most tables were set, but a few still had the previous diners' dishes on top, flies bouncing from plate to plate. As for the diners themselves, they had left the place empty, save for the smell of cooking oil, fried fish and garlic that seeped into Theresa's nostrils. It made her hungry, and she realized that she hadn't eaten all day, even before Fern's call.

"Uncle!" Daniel called.

"Daniel! Thank God! Give me a minute!" returned a hoarse yell from the kitchen. "Just finishing up."

The boy sat at an empty table and motioned for Theresa to join him. She collapsed into a seat, famished, exhausted, speechless. They shared an extended silence, each collecting what coherence could be salvaged. Theresa called upon a prayer and repeated it in her head - the Holy Rosary. Her grandmother had taught it to her. She would pray it with her family, and often with Lania.

"When you don't know what to tell God, pray the rosary," her abuela would urge. It was more than just words to her. She repeated Hail Marys and Our Fathers and Glory Bes, hardly paying attention to the sounds emitting from her throat, though sporadically a word would dig itself into her mind like a tick, resting there and spawning a new idea that carried through her meditation. *Sinners. Hour of our death. Daily bread. Trespasses.* Now, the words *who art in Heaven* halted her prayer like a barricade.

Our Father, who art in Heaven... The prayer she and Lania had recited that night in the city sewers. The prayer her father had taught her as a young girl. Those words swung at her with a different might — the might of a question. *Our Father, who art in Heaven.*

Is he? Theresa thought. *Is he in Heaven? Is he on Earth? Is he anywhere? Is he?*

She didn't hear an answer to her question. She expected one. All her life, an answer had come to every question she had about her faith. Some voice would eventually go off in her head, granting her permission to keep believing. And if not a voice, some sign would manifest where God would show his face in an interaction with a neighbor or her missing a bus after getting off from work — some cause that produced an epiphany of an effect. This time, her question went unanswered, and she didn't bother looking for one.

She had watched people pass by on the sidewalk, watched the traffic creep along with absolute ordinariness on the bus ride. No sound, no sight, and now, no words. She tried again to start the Rosary.

I believe in —

She paused, then tried again. *I believe...* She could make it no further. The rosary was done, two words in. Following those first two words was a blank she could not fill. She knew the words, but would not give them life. She held her faith ransom for her son. *At least* her son. Yes, people faced tragedy all the time, but the price of her faith was Abraham. To have him back. In that moment, she decided. She decided that God could not have her soul if she could not have her child.

Her memory scratched all the way back to everyone she had ever loved — her mother, then her father, then Lania, then Abraham, and finally August. Even he, at one point, she loved. These were the people closest to her, and they all had one thing in common.

They were gone. Theresa felt like poison. A death sentence to anyone she grew to love. She had loved God. Perhaps that is why he too seemed missing.

She twitched as though she'd been shocked by a prod, but it was only Daniel's hand reaching across the glass table top to hold hers. The physical contact — she needed it. Every time he let go, her mind would fall off in a tailspin, and he'd bring her back to the present moment with a touch.

"I'm sorry, Theresa. I can't imagine how you're feeling right now."

His words now found the emotion that was lost in their urgency earlier. Theresa examined Daniel's face. The pools of sepia in his eyes, the newness of his skin, the thin tranquility of his lips — he appeared so calm as though nothing had happened, but then Theresa remembered what he said on the bus. *I don't want to go back.* His countenance was that way because everything had already happened to him.

"Where?" Theresa began.

Daniel raised his eyebrows.

"You said you didn't want to go back," Theresa expanded.

With a pained sigh, Daniel exhaled the words, "City Interrogation Center."

"And Lania," she said. "You saw her there?"

"I did," Daniel replied. "They put us in the same cell."

The simple way he spoke about Lania, spoke her back into existence from the moment he uttered her name back at Anna's, began the resurrection process. Theresa had assumed the IF agents had taken her life that night, but never with absolute certainty.

"I — I thought they killed her. The night of the baptism. I heard them. Beating her. I heard her crying out. Then nothing. That sound. The sound of her falling on the grate. The Elites. They said —"

"They said what they wanted you to hear." A man's voice from the kitchen revealed that he'd been attentive to their conversation. Daniel stood up and they hugged. The man, whose name was Marcel, buried his head in Daniel's shoulder and whispered something into the boy's ear. Then another long embrace — one that said *I've missed you* and *thank goodness you're safe*. Then he turned back to Theresa, abbreviating the moment with Daniel. Theresa wondered how they were related. "Thinking your friend is dead would make you less stable, more likely to make a mistake. You probably should have left town with your baby."

"Marcel!" Daniel scolded.

"No — he's right," Theresa admitted. "I'd been thinking about it. If we skipped town, we'd be fugitives, but at least we'd still be together. I underestimated the Intervention Force. Actually, I underestimated everything. We did it by the book, the baptism. No one ever saw me, and even if they did, I was in full disguise. How could they have known where I'd be? About August, about the Daycare?"

Daniel didn't respond, yet she looked to him for an answer.

"Lania?" she asked. "She wouldn't have said anything."

"She couldn't help it, Theresa," Daniel said. "Whatever she said, it wasn't because she wanted to say it."

"What do you mean? That she was tortured?"

Again, Daniel didn't say anything, but looked away. His arm twisted behind his back and he rested his fingers at the base of his spine.

"What did they do to her?" She paused, uncertain if she wanted to know, but the words escaped before she decided to speak. Then she realized. "They tortured *you*."

They had all been tortured in one way or another.

Before Daniel responded, the ancient man named Marcel broke the silence and emerged from the kitchen. He was an Asian man with cobweb hair bunched on top of his head and smeared around his chin and neck. His skinny body skipped and hopped around, nimble as a fortysomething. Theresa looked at him with the eyes of a mother who watched her toddler attempt to walk down the stairs. He was the fittest old man she'd encountered, but he appeared so fragile. When he spoke, his hoarse tone leapt out like a trumpet solo through crooked and stained teeth with intent and conviction.

"This is her, then — the Last Baptism?" he asked. Daniel delivered another chiding look.

"Yes. Theresa, this is Marcel. Maybe he'd like to introduce himself."

Marcel smiled and put his hand toward Theresa. "Pleased to meet you."

Theresa afforded a forced smile, the first one she managed all day. His quirkiness was intriguing as well as distracting.

"My godfather, I guess you could say," Daniel added. "We've been through a lot."

"And that's understating the matter," Marcel said. "So, you driving?" He looked straight into Theresa's eyes.

"Huh?" she replied. "Driving what? Driving where?"

"My car. We need to leave this restaurant. And Far City. Elites are only eight minutes away. Can you drive a classic auto transmission?"

"How do you —" Theresa started.

"A classic auto transmission," Marcel said with haste.

Theresa nodded, confused and disoriented. She had just started catching her breath from the afternoon. And she knew nothing about the teenager and the ancient Asian man prodding her out the door. But the circumstances emboldened her, and what more had she to lose?

"I didn't know you had a car," Daniel said as the three of them made for the back door.

"I don't," Marcel smirked. Daniel's face flashed disappointment but not surprise. "I didn't steal it. Not this time anyway. I'm borrowing it."

Daniel rolled his eyes, perplexity plastered itself on Theresa's face, and Marcel was already through the door.

JUSTICE

Central City, 2085

"Look at this" my dad says, handing me a copy of the Central City Trib-
*une. He has folded the paper so the article he calls to my attention is
framed evenly.*

*I stare at the headline: Ousted MAU professor a potential AFL risk. The
paper feels so thin in my grasp, as though I could rub my fingers together
and watch the words dissolve away. My head shakes from side to side in
apparent disapproval, but really, I'm disheartened. I always thought it
could happen to ProTruth, but never thought it would. He was too good at
his job. A warm body sat in every seat in his classroom. Hate to see a good
teacher fall from grace, especially a man whom I consider one of my best
mentors. And a friend.*

*I pick up the newspaper and peruse the text, sliding my finger across
the print and studying each of the words and their implications. It says
ProTruth is an underground faithie. That he orchestrates baptisms. That
he organizes prayer groups and has been quietly circulating religious
points of view to a hidden community of bapticks and Godseekers.*

"I said to drop his class," my dad's told-you-so tone pesters me. "I told

you not to associate with that — that fucking Godman. You did exactly the opposite. Now do you see? Makes me wonder how much garbage he's put in your head over the years. You know, I'm not stupid. I know you still visit him. If I ever catch you with him, I'll make sure to it myself that you never make it anywhere near Elite status. And you can kiss your job on the IF goodbye."

My father's words seem harsh and antagonistic. You wouldn't think he's my father — more like my boss. He's actually both. Were I still a college kid, I might have rebelled against his words. But I'm an adult now. I know what I want. I want to be Supreme Commanding Officer, and if I'm to attain that, I need to be hunting people like Truth, not meeting them for afternoon coffee.

As condescending as he is at the moment, my father is right. If I see Truth again, I have to bring him in. There's enough against him now. I gave him a free pass a year ago. But in the wake of this news story, I'm going to have to revoke that pass. If I see him again, I'll be an IF Elite in no time.

"Where are you taking us?" she asks as if she has a right, but I give her the answer.

"The City Interrogation Center," I reply.

I focus on the road in front of me. The stoplights and flashing pedestrian signals, the wayward cyclists swerving outside the bike lanes — I swear there's more space for bikes than cars on this street and about ten times as many vehicles. Many of the businesses look brand new and inviting. Bet I don't see them in a year or two, max. Such is the way of Far City. I play pinball with thoughts of the milieu, anything to get my mind off the creature in the backseat and his mother sitting next to him.

In all the Godseekers I've arrested, exactly zero have been babies. I expected to hear the child crying, and I planned to endure the wails with a stone heart. What I didn't anticipate was hearing him laugh and seeing his smile in my rearview mirror. The way he waved his arms in a rhythm as if he were dancing to some song I couldn't hear. He made noises, not words, but noises that communicated wonder and amusement. No, I didn't make arrangements for this sentimentality that subtly swept over my stone heart, melting it away into a puddle of, well, what is molten rock? Lava. Yeah. Melting my heart into lava.

Yet, I keep my course. I have no other destination in mind, not that I would veer from my objective if there were any other option. Also, what was I supposed to do? Turn them loose after my colleagues escorted them into my car?

Every time I check the rearview mirror, I can see the child looking at me and I know he can see my eyes. Even though I'm certain he has no idea what is about to happen to him and his mother, he projects a sense of shame onto me like burning sunlight searing my skin and setting my humanity ablaze.

Almost there. I just have to make it to the CIC and drop them off. The less I think about it the better, but the longer I'm in here, the more I ponder what will happen to this child. I have just met this baby and he is no one to me. No one except the most innocent person I've ever arrested. The *most* innocent person I've arrested. And that is how we are connected. He is as vulnerable as a victim of mine can get. What does that say about me? What I'm willing to do to get what I want? And that I'm questioning myself, what does that say about my commitment?

His eyes are brown like mine, deep and calm as soil. He will probably end up in Anti-Intervention Foster Care. A good home awaits. He'll grow up, just like I did, in a loving family, except with parents who will be meeting him a few months after his birth. And his mother. I can stand to see her punished. She broke the law. I'm just having trouble seeing the two of them separated. The way she's holding him in her arms. Even when she asked me where I was taking them, she never broke engagement with her baby, and he never takes his eyes off her, except to stare spears of contempt at me through my mirror.

Ten blocks left. I could turn my sirens on and bolt down the street to my destination, but I have a baby in the car and have been instructed to keep my speed and sirens down. There is no emergency, and these aren't violent criminals. If ever I could break protocol, now would be the time.

I believe I can make it. But then she starts talking.

"I know what will happen if you take us to the interrogation center," says the prisoner.

It's a statement. I don't need to respond. Who am I kidding? Even if it were a question I wouldn't need to say a thing. This woman hasn't got a right in the world and I'm letting her speak.

"I know you know exactly what will happen," she pauses to let the words frost over me. "They will take my baby from me. They will separate this child from his loving mother. Not a negligible mother. Not an abusive mother. I'm a mother who's committed to her child in every way. A mother who would die for her child at any moment."

She pauses and waits for my response, only, I say nothing. I figure that's the safest bet. If I say nothing, this discussion — or non-discussion — can go no further.

"I know you hear me," she proceeds. "I know you're *listening*. You wouldn't know what it's like, having to hide who you are to live in

161

society. You're a Freespeaker, yet you have no concept of others' freedom. I've never put my child in danger, and you want to deprive me of my freedom to raise him."

"Yes you have," I snap back. "You're here aren't you? You broke the Freedom Laws with your baby. I'd say that qualifies as putting him in danger."

"And who is responsible for that danger?"

"We've been doing it for decades—"

"That's exactly how backwards we are. You don't have children— you couldn't hope to understand."

"Don't assume that because I don't have kids that I don't understand," I realize I just gave away too much. And how does she know?

"Then you *do* understand." She pauses. A trap to get me to reveal some sense of vulnerability. Her tone changes from chastising me to something almost pleading. And I have no response. Because I do understand. Taking children, even baptized children, never felt right to me. But I've done it because it's regulated. I do it without a second thought. The State gives me the power to do my job, and I'm going to do my best at it. But deep down, I know. I know that separating this woman from her child is *wrong*.

"Then why?" she breaks the appropriate silence.

I just answered her question in my head, but I'm not willing to share. I just shake my head and ignore her, only she's gotten to me. I'm thinking now. Thinking about how this unknowing infant is going to scream for his mother. How this moment will be with him his entire life and he'll never know it, like a quiet cancer, embedding itself in his cells, waiting for the right moment to uproot his entire understanding of life. He'll be placed in a foster home with loving parents never knowing that he has a loving parent who, if she stays alive, is living in anguish everyday.

"I have dreams for him. Every parent dreams for their child. It is a right of a parent. I dream for him to be kind and loving to the people around him, and to work hard for the good of society. What dreams do you suppose are more worthy? Tell me? What do you suppose his new parents will teach him?"

"I —" It's all I can muster. "Just shut your mouth!"

All I can manage is a forceful command to quiet her. That and the deepest sigh I've ever let out in my life. And I feel stupid and defeated for making the command because deep down, I know she's absolutely right, and I'm absolutely wrong. My retort says it all. She wanted my vulnerability. She has it. I wish there was soundproofing in these cars. I need to get through this. I've done this hundreds of times before. But she's in my head. She has no idea, but her words strangle me with a co-incidental timeliness. That is because they remind me of all the lessons my old professor taught me about having an open mind, the importance of caring for my fellow human beings, being selfless over being selfish. Ideals that seem to contradict many of the values I was taught.

I notice my hand reach for my tranq gun, but then I realize that would leave me alone with the infant. Plus, it feels like cheating the situation. The easy way out. And I don't believe in shortcuts.

"What about my freedom, officer?" she continues. "What makes my freedom any less valid than anyone else's? Than yours? See, that's why you are what you are. A *freedom killer*."

"Where did you hear that?!" she shocks me with the insult and taunts me with a subtle, sly smile. I turn around and face her. We're not moving anyway. Haven't moved an inch in ten minutes. "I'm serious. You can work with me now, or in a few minutes, you'll never see your baby again, and that's just what's what. Tell me. Where did you hear that?"

"Why don't you answer at least one of my questions then? Why are you doing this? For you? For your country? Why are you *really* doing this?"

"It's my job, okay. I believe in it." I give her the scripted answer. I want to hear her say she knows Chameleon and Beamer. And then I want her to take me to them.

"Oh, you believe in something after all? Because it's your job? That makes it okay to —"

"You're getting off topic. I told why you're under arrest and why I'm taking you in. It's your turn. 'Freedom killer.' Where did you hear that term?"

"Just because you call me a baptick doesn't mean I am above calling you names as well."

Her answer is as scripted as mine. And she's lying. Godseekers like her *are* above making up slurs for people on the other side. "Don't bullshit me," I say.

"Well, isn't that what we're doing anyway? Bullshitting each other while we sit in traffic? I think I'm done talking to you. I don't want to spend my last few minutes with my baby talking to a freedom killer."

"You know Chameleon. You know Beamer. You know Truth too?" I'm past all these subtleties. My eyes are glued to my mirror to gauge her reaction to the litany of suspects, but she concentrates on her baby and ignores my questions. I resort to a threat. "We have plenty of time, you know." From my belt, I withdraw and hold up a vial of eternatae, again peeking at my mirror to see how the prospect of a little psychological torture makes her feel.

That sly smile still wears her motherly face.

"You see this?" She holds up her cuffed wrists, one of which is encircled by a jade bracelet. "This bracelet is laced with another drug which will make me forget just about every long term memory I have."

"The F drug? God's answer to eternatae? No way you're going to use that! You'll forget your own child."

"What difference will it make when you separate me from him? When you raise him in some backwards Freespeaker home where they teach him to hoard hatred and discrimination? And if I ever get to see him again, he won't resemble any vision I had for him as my son. He'll see the world through someone else's eyes. I almost think I'd rather forget."

Now that, lady, is some bullshit.

"You might as well go ahead and use it," I call her bluff. "I'm pretty sure I can track down Chameleon without your confession. Wouldn't be the first time I've had to find someone. I found you just fine."

"True. I've heard much about you, Agent Justice. You're the best there is, as I understand."

I flinch at her mention of my name. A card up her sleeve. But it's too late, for her anyway. Finally, we come to a lurching halt at a stoplight just half a block shy of the CIC. Finally, I can unload this baggage. I check back in the rearview, and the child's eyes are again fixed on my own. The light changes and I pull into the incarceration loading area. An escort approaches the car.

"You know, as soon as they open this door, I'm going to administer the F drug to myself."

"So?"

"So also in my vast collection of memories is the *current* location of your old partner and professor. And that tag-a-long Chameleon."

She holds up her wrist and places her finger on a small slit in the bracelet that could finely sever her skin and allow the drug to enter her bloodstream. It doesn't take much. I physically turn around and look into her eyes. What does she know? This has got to be some type of ruse. But the reality is, this is the only lead I've found in two weeks. It never takes me that long to track down a Godseeker.

The escort working at the Interrogation Center leaps back at the screeching of my tires as I peel out of the lot and make my way back into traffic. I slam on my sirens and lights and cut through the congested streets, thinking to myself how convenient that escort would have been a few weeks ago.

"How far?" I ask, as if I have a right.

"It's out there. Like you said, you're the best at tracking Godseekers. No one's gonna stay under your nose."

"Except you apparently," I quip, and she chuckles.

"Eight hours on the road."

"Now that is some bullshit. There's got to be a faster way."

"Please," she scoffs. "There's only one of us in the car who is full of it. Unless the Intervention Force has a private jet, let's get going. ProTruth is waiting. And don't cuss in front of my baby anymore."

This is complete madness. I have no basis on which to trust this woman. The last thirty minutes in the car have been grueling on my mind. To do that 16 times over again sounds awful.

"Royale? That's your name?"

"Absolutely not. My name is Maria."

"Of course it is."

Theresa

Traffic clogged the lanes of Interstate 5 during midday along the thirty-mile corridor between Far City and Newhill. Rush hour lasted from six in the morning until eight at night. For Theresa, Marcel and Daniel, they were used to the constant stand-still. Far City's population had skyrocketed over the last forty years to the point where it became known as the West's New York City. During the renaming procedure, a few variations of the east coast metropolis were on the voting ballot, but a far more generic name won out.

The air conditioner in Marcel's car — the loaner, so he said — was busted, so they cracked the windows just enough to keep a low profile while inviting air into the car. The air wasn't flowing because they weren't moving.

"We should take the next exit and go on side streets," Marcel recommended. "Just until traffic dies down. The further away we are from Far City, the better."

They had put about twenty minutes worth of distance between themselves and Wong's Garden, but in Far City Traffic, twenty minutes didn't garner much distance, and that's what they needed.

As Theresa drove, Daniel caught up with Marcel about the previous weeks — his lonely cell at the City Interrogation Center, meeting Lania, and figuring out how to cross paths with Theresa before the Intervention Force got to Abraham.

"Damn," Marcel said. "A day late."

"A couple hours, actually," Daniel lamented.

"How did you find Theresa?"

"The daycare. Lania mentioned it to me in the cell. I wasn't sure if Abraham or Theresa would be there, but I had to try. It was only a matter of time before the Intervention Force would show up."

"They knew?" Marcel asked.

"Lania had a replay. She was out for a few days. They must have drugged her pretty bad. She was talking in her sleep."

Marcel shook his head, gazing out the window. He had his own memories of eternatae and knew exactly what Daniel had gone through — every moment of it. He had been there himself. "I'm glad you're safe, Danny. I missed you."

"I missed you too, uncle."

Theresa scanned the road, weaving through traffic until the gaps between cars closed and they reached a dead halt, still half a mile from the nearest exit.

She caught an unsentimental glimpse of the Far City skyline in the rear view mirror. It was her home, the only one she'd ever known. She felt betrayed by it, a long, drawn out betrayal throughout the course of her life. *All these years*, she thought. She left bitterly.

When she was a child, she was in love with the city. The blue of the bay that shimmered magenta when the sun would set behind the Olympic Mountains, broken clouds in streaks and clumps blushing overhead.

The Governor's Mountain, so named by the Generic Name Act for the tallest mountain in every state, would tower over the entire landscape, above the trees, above the roofs of skyscrapers, above the clouds. Theresa still addressed the mountain by its former name, Rainier. Most pre-GNA locals did. At some point, when the name faded from common usage, Theresa's love for Seattle set with the sun over the Olympics. Lost in thought, her glance back at the city turned into more of a stare. A hateful one.

A horn blared and when she looked up, open road lay in front of her.

"Are you okay?" Daniel asked. "Want me to drive?"

She laughed anxiously.

"I'm fine. I just lost focus." Theresa was not in the best shape to drive, but between an emotional basket-case, a fourteen year old boy and an eighty-something, basket-case seemed to be the best option.

"What will we find in Portland anyway?" Theresa finally asked, just pleased to get away from Far City.

"Friends," Marcel replied. "Ones who might be able to help us find your son."

"How?" Theresa asked, immediately recognizing the skepticism in her tone. She cringed at first. Her voice lathered itself in hopelessness, and she became embarrassed. What kind of mother, they must be thinking. But could they blame her? Could any person of faith fault a little despair? In the last four hours, Theresa increasingly believed that hope came in waves and crested with poor decision making. Hope was fool's gold. Then at the most critical moment, the Intervention Force appeared, as if they knew all along, and a friend would disappear, not before a little blood and pain. In a moment, her feelings changed her initial question, and the skeptic had won.

"Why?" she asked plainly.

Marcel looked at Daniel, and Daniel looked at Marcel, both confused.

"*Why?*" Daniel repeated. "Don't you want your son back? Don't you want to rescue Lania? Aren't they —"

"I guess I should have been more specific. I meant what's the use? I mean, really. Why do we even try? It's over. The IF has Abraham. They have Lania. They took my father. Oh and they have my ex-husband, who I could give a damn about, only they took him from me too."

Her heart raced, she caught a breath, then continued. "What is the point? God? Is God the point? Don't you see? Without God, none of this would have happened. I'd still have a son, I'd still have a friend, and for Christ's sake, I'd probably still have a father. I don't even know if you've lost anyone — I'm sure you have in this shitshow. So why don't we just stop? Why don't we just give up? Why don't we just —"

Her voice rolled and thundered like a herd of prey. No response except her own heavy breathing. They reached the exit. Theresa turned off the ramp. The first lot she found, she pulled in and parked. Deep breaths, but no tears. She was mad at the world. Mad at life. She cursed it all. The skies, the afternoon sun, the concrete, the happy couple walking out of the mattress store, and most of all, the young mother she saw in the rear view mirror eating lunch outside of a taqueria. Theresa scowled. Why should this woman get to raise her child, while her son sat in some government facility waiting for his fate to be decided by someone in a government uniform. This woman became her latest tormentor, simply by holding her child, and when she brought the baby's laughing face to her crinkled nose, Theresa lost it. Lost it all. Her own son was contraband to them, but for her, her entire life. What type of room would he be in? Who was feeding him and changing him? Who would hold him

170

when he cried? Who would smile at him when he laughed? Theresa crumpled up on herself like an old piece of paper, sobs and shaking overwhelming her.

Daniel reached toward her, but Marcel shook his head and stopped him from touching her.

"Let her," he said in an aside. "She needs to be in this place right now."

Every part of Daniel wanted to reach out and give her comfort, but he remembered a simple lesson Genjin taught. Sometimes, laughter is the best medicine. But silence will let an open wound clot and heal itself.

They both sat patiently while Theresa felt the dark world crumble beneath her. In the parking spot next to them, a large black SUV pulled in. Marcel checked the license plate in the window reflection in front of them. A habit of paranoia that served him well.

IF93, it read.

They had been tracked.

JUSTICE

"Turn here," Maria says almost a moment too late. I swerve off the highway onto the perpendicular road, which resembles the same mundane stretch of asphalt we've been traversing for the last eight hours, going on nine, going on a lifetime.

The baby is asleep, thankfully, and Maria has been staring out the window in silence, also thankfully. Most of her words during the ride have been directions, though we remained on I-90 for a good long while, crossing a state border, not to mention acres of plains and trees and an occasional river.

She gives the most attention to her son, like a star in the sky she watches him, an eye forever, and when she looks away, she remains attached, always there, like someone told her to never let him go, and she took it at face value. Her arms have been statuesque, barely shifting or moving while the baby slept. On occasion, she would drift into a nap, but never for long, as her son would stretch and turn, and she'd respond by waking and smiling, silently communicating, *we were almost separated, but I bought us time. How much time, I don't know. Maybe a few hours, maybe their whole lives.* I realize that I hold the answer to that uncertainty, a power that I'm uncomfortably uncomfortable with.

"How much further?" I ask. She responds with a pause that lasts a little too long, and my patience swings into belligerence.

"How long!" I yell. Eight hours on the road will do that to a guy.

The baby stirs and cries. My rearview mirror captures a scornful look on Maria's face just before she attends to her child, and her cold eyes transfer from the glass, through my own pupils, and deposit themselves into my long-term memory. I don't know why the image stands out so vividly, out of all the moments I have had with Maria on this road trip, it's those eyes of bitter judgement grating on my guilt that make permanent residence in my conscience. I will never forget it. What can I do but feel like an asshole for forgetting not to use my scary voice in front of a child?

I back down and make no pursuit of my query, nor do I apologize; certainly Maria can see my ears glowing red with fury and embarrassment. The closest I get to *I'm sorry* is a conciliatory glance to the backseat, though she takes no notice of my unfolding face — her concentration rests fully on her child. She brings him close to her heart, presses his ear to her chest, and I see he attunes to the beat of the drum. She hushes him, sparing no lapse in attention, smiles at him, then sings to him. She hums a lovely line of melody, one bearing a melancholy so ornamented in her airy soprano timbre that I feel my skin collect and sprawl throughout my body like bubbles in a bottle of soda. Her baby responds by lowering his voice and relaxing his limbs. She has healed one wound, but is quick to return the daggers in my direction.

"You. Are. An. Asshole." I know. I said so to myself already. Her tone freezes the car cabin and I wonder if such contempt won't wake up the baby again. "My mama never raised her voice at me like that."

"My father did toward me." Her daggers dull a little at my openness, and once again, I'm shocked at my offer of vulnerability. She stares a little longer. I know she can read my eyes in the mirror, and she peruses them like a thief, usurping my most precious and guarded commodity. My humanity.

"About an hour more on the road." She rewards me. "Maybe more."

I shake my head. "You said eight hours in Far City. Another hour makes nine. What gives?"

"You drive like a cop." She reads my confusion. "Legally."

"I don't think you know many cops," I refute.

A snicker. "No. I don't."

The golden lines of the arterial whisk by a little faster after she critiques my driving habits. "There's a kid in the car," I explain. "I'm not going to top a hundred with a baby on board."

"His name is Isaac," she responds.

"Don't you two have approved names?"

"No. And you better get used to it."

"Why? You think we're gonna be friends or something?"

"Nope." But her reply comes after a noticeable hesitation — long enough to swallow some words before her definitive answer. I choose to ignore it.

"So. This place. Secret bunker? Godseeker central? ProTruth's secret hideout?"

"I didn't think Truth would tell you about the place." Another smile. A smirk, this one.

"All guesses, honey."

"Not anything less than what I promised you. And Jesus, don't call me honey."

Small droplets of water begin to dot my windshield. I hadn't noticed the change in sky, but above us hovers a mantle of grey, heavy and threatening. The green headlight indicator on my dashboard illuminates, and I fumble to set the wipers at the right speed, but can't get them just right. They end up moving too slowly for the water that begins to stream in tributaries atop the glass, or too fast so the rubber blades trip on the dry glass. I can't afford to get frustrated at such little things, and yet, I grow irritated at this struggle fest for such a simple action. I set it on auto mode, which I hate doing. Beamer once witnessed me undergo the same hostility toward my wipers. Later, he told me that was the moment he first realized how much of a control freak I am. He was always smarter than I give him credit for.

"Look at that," observes my company. "All you had to do was set it on auto, and voilà."

"Oh shut up already," I say. She giggles in condescension. Sometimes I forget how lucky I was to be an only child.

"You have some issues, you know," she says.

"Don't we all?" I counter.

"Don't we all."

"So what are your issues?" I invade. A stab in the dark. A conversation starter. Something. Anything. Like I said, we've been on the road for hours. But a deeper impulse than boredom inspires the question.

"You mean besides you and your Freedom Laws?"

"Sure. Seeing as how I'm giving you temporary immunity on the two."

She sighs deeply. "My father left my mother for another woman. My mother's first husband left her a widow. I inherited one of the two scenarios. I'll let you guess which."

I peel my eyes from the road and back to the mirror. Her gaze reaches out the window with nothing but longing and honesty. One heart broken by sadness, one by anger. She strikes me as angry and bitter, but not because her husband cheated on her.

"Widowed," I concede. Her hatred for me is a thin disguise for her own past. "A Freedom Law widow."

"And orphan. Half, anyway."

I'm silenced.

"That enough issues for you?"

I nod. She receives the acknowledgement via the mirror, then returns to the scenic road.

"What about you?" she asks.

"Nothing like that. Besides, I think you've got me pegged. If my biggest problem is keeping up with the tempo of the rain —"

"I don't think that's your biggest issue, Justice."

"How do you know so much about me? I know you know Truth and Beamer. But you seem to know a lot more than an acquaintance of theirs."

"What do you mean?"

"Like the wiper thing. Beamer tell you about that?"

That smile again in the mirror irks me. She has me dangling on a hook.

"The wiper thing. Yes, he told me about that. It's a great story. I had prayed for some rain on this drive. Just to see what you would do."

I shudder. "So you're all friends."

"Yes. The 'I hate Justice Club'." She laughs at the evident insideness of the joke.

I shake my head. "Whatever," I spit sourly.

"Lighten up. You're not as hate-able as you think."

If hate-ability were measurable, I'd say I have my fair share. And somehow, Maria knows this, and she's using it to break me, or at least bend me. It's already worked. Here we are, hours away from civilization. She practically has me trumping the law, only repairable by a shift in my motive. What could I tell my CO? That she is my prisoner who offered to lead me to high priority suspects in severe violation of the AFLs. I could be making the bust of a lifetime. The wolf in me still salivates at the thought. Only at this point, the wolf is no more than a figment of my imagination, because something much deeper has triggered my decision to drive so far from home. The search for answers, not suspects. The longing for friendship and counsel, not fugitives destined for the Truth Committee and a death sentence. Maria knows this. Knows there's an uncertainty inside of me that has grown into a self-loathing and now blossomed into full on desperation, a desperation to find something new about who I am. Something that challenges what I used to tell myself every morning with the utmost confidence — that I have it all figured out. Some people strive to have a firm understanding of their own lives. But lately, I've been waking up in the morning, staring at that corner of my room. Remember that spider's web? The one that has pressed on my self image like finger in a wound. I look for that web every morning, and a few days ago, I noticed that it had been abandoned. Left clinging to my walls and ceiling, sagging and forsaken, just as I knew it would. I suppose it had enough sense to find a better place to make its home. More sense than I have. Or perhaps it died before its survival instinct pulled it in some other direction.

"Hey —" Maria interrupts my spiraling introspection. "I mean that."

"Mean what?" I say, her last statement a distant memory by now.

"We don't hate you, Justice."

"Well that's reassuring." It is.

"It was ProTruth's idea to lead you out here. He's always thought very highly of you, even after you cut him off."

Really? Because I did cut him off. Everything he taught me, I pretty much rejected after making the decision never to speak to him again. From his point of view, I would think me a complete disappointment and failure. That doesn't add up to being thought of very highly — definitely not in my book.

"The place is sort of a refuge if you practice religion. Truth founded it with a few other religious leaders."

"That is incredibly outside the law," I say as old strings of mine are pulled by her remark.

"You do know that throughout history, laws have been found to be less than just, some much more than others. Some laws are universal, like don't kill people. Other laws reflect cultures and cultures can veer from what is right. Doesn't mean that laws should do the same."

"ProTruth turn you into a lawyer now? "

"He leaves a significant mark. I was in Beamer's class. He introduced me to my husband."

"Chameleon," I say, a wild stab in the dark.

"His name is Leonardo."

I smile, wondering if he's descended from the owner of the popular diner, then I remember that first names aren't passed on.

"You know that many students in Freethought 101 practice some type of religion or fragment of it or at least believe in God. It's a class that's geared for Godseekers, but he did a really good job of pushing the edges of what the law will allow without stepping outside those boundaries." She pauses and returns to the mirror. "Which begs the question — why did *you* choose to take his class?"

My regular excuse is that I just needed to fulfill an elective requirement and I heard the class was easy. I meet her at the mirror. Maria's eyes, still sharp and unwavering arrows, look into mine. Her question is sincere and genuine, and I listen to myself in awe as honesty escapes my lips again.

"I heard the class made students think differently. I had thought the same way throughout my entire life, being brought up in the Freespeak Education System. The way my parents brought me up was in line with my schooling, which was in line with how our society thought, behaved, and enacted laws. I never once considered that life could be different from how I viewed it. I wanted to see this different angle. I wanted to be challenged. That was my favorite part of college — why I chose an independent university instead of state run. The classes I took were mine to choose, and the selection of classes was much wider than at a state school."

"That's uncommon. People who are brought up in Freespeak Ed usually attend a like-minded school after secondary."

"Yes. My parents wanted me to start making major decisions for myself right out of high school, and the less risk, the less reward, they always taught. So in true rebellious fashion, I chose a college that would be my best bet at challenging everything they taught me. I took a risk in straying from a track that every other person in my graduating class followed. That's how I found myself at the university.

"To be honest, I knew I'd probably run into religious sympathizers there. I wanted to gain insight to their psychology and use that to my advantage when I became part of the Intervention Force. That way I could make my way to the top faster by capturing more Godseekers. And that's exactly what I've done."

She's leaning forward, engaged in my past, my psychology. But as I scrutinize her through my rear view, I find zero fear. I just told her how I planned to use Truth's class to manipulate and deceive Godseekers. Yet, there is no regret in her eyes. No reconsideration of her choice to lead me to this oasis of interventionists. She knows. Knows there is nothing to fear. She is *that* confident in what I will find out. It unnerves me just a bit, yet I proceed to unveil more of my own truth to this stranger.

"But Truth's class was the one that reached through my Freespeak way of thinking and filled it with the possibilities of something else. Something deeper than what I'd been fed my entire life. He struck down everything I learned. Destroyed it. But then built it back up. Or enabled me to. He wasn't feeding me information and dogma and rhetoric — he only set the stage for me to think for myself."

"And?"

"And, I guess, I've been thinking ever since. Until..."

"Until you took a chance on me. On me and Isaac."

The mirror conveys my affirmation.

A crest of silence peaks in the car as we proceed down the straight road. She continues her focus out the window, watching the trees, one after another crossing the glass that separated her from the fresh, free air. The sunlight strobes on her face and her eyes twinkle in the light. She looks satisfied for being "detained" in the backseat of an IF squad car.

"What happened then?" she asks. "What made you go back to your Freespeaker education?"

"I had the trajectory of my life planned out way before I took Truth's class. I had to honor that."

"Did you? People go through life changing experiences all the time. Why couldn't Truth's class do that for you?"

"I had a goal. I worked hard at it. I couldn't just stop."

"Fair enough. But then you had to forget everything he taught you."

"I did. But I didn't. That's why I'm here, with you. With Isaac."

I find myself pulling the car over into the dirt shoulder, and forgo the mirror. Incredulity has grounded the car. I can't believe how far we've come. How foolish I am. I turn around and physically face her. She looks right into my eyes, still fearless, but completely void of enmity. Instead, curiosity and compassion replace her earlier condemnation.

"What will I learn?" I ask. Silence. "What are you hiding?" Silence. "Why would Truth have me come all the way out here?" More silence. I don't get angry. "What are you planning to do to me?" All of a sudden, I feel victimized. At the first screech of my tires away from the interrogation center, I had it all planned out. My biggest bust ever. Supreme Commanding Officer in a week. Mission accomplished. But that was never my sole purpose. Now, the shells of my motivation for putting my future in Maria's hands have fallen to the ground. I'm here to find out what Truth had in store for me back at the Golden Garden. Perhaps back in Freethought 101.

The what-ifs and worst case scenarios would plague me right about now, only I have no idea what those may be. Just darkness. No better than where I've been.

"What do you know about Godseekers, Justice?" Maria finally breaks her silence.

"This a trick question?"

"You know a lot about us. You know ProTruth. You know Beamer."

"I *thought* I knew Beamer."

"True. I guess, then, there really isn't anything I can say to set you at ease. For all you know, you could be walking into a trap." She interrupts herself to scoff at what I'm assuming is the absurdity of the notion. "But, in all honesty, there's nothing I can say to make you continue on this road. Only that it's just about twenty minutes further. And..."

Another silence. I scrape my eyes from the distance and look back to her. "And what?"

"And try to have a little faith."

Theresa

"Is everything all right," the man said after stepping out of the passenger side of the Ford E-Force. The look on the officer's face, sincere and concerned, bounced from Marcel to Theresa and back again. He wore all black, and his pants were decorated with pockets, his belt with clips and slots. Most prominently was the holster for his firearm and just behind it, three black vials with thumb release injectors. Marcel saw them and knew immediately. One vial of eternatae for each passenger in the car. Better answer quickly.

"Theresa, a peacekeeper - he's checking on us," Marcel said. Peacekeeper was the favorable title for Intervention Force agents used among free speakers. Marcel used it as a warning to Theresa. She gathered a deep breath and rolled open her window.

"Thank you officer. I'm just having a — a rough day. My — my father's really sick and we could lose him at any time."

"Is he your father?" the officer asked. He stooped down and peeked into the car, catching Daniel's eye as well.

"No, he's my uncle," she replied with tears for Abraham rolling down her cheek. "We just came from the hospital. I — It's really hard to talk about, to be honest."

"I'm sorry ma'am, I just wanted to make sure you were okay. Is there anything we can do?"

Theresa lifted her shimmering eyes into those of the young IF officer, who wore an elite badge. His eyes were blue and steady. He reflected some of her sadness on his face. *There is one thing you could do. You give me back my son.*

"Thank you officer," Marcel said. "We'll be okay. We just need each other right now."

The young man reached into his pocket. From it, he pulled a small rectangular card with his name, phone number and media handle. He handed it to Theresa. "If I can ever help, you let me know."

He walked into the taqueria four doors down. Theresa and Marcel shared a look of disbelief. A close call for sure, but more shocking to both of them was how civil and kind the officer was to them. She looked down at the white letters written on the black business card:

Sandy Wichman
Intervention Force Elite Detective
@ifesandwich
(206)-555-1207

"Sandwich," she laughed. "Guy must have a sense of humor. Or his parents." She shook her head, breathed deeply, started the car, and drove out of the parking lot.

Theresa did not rejoin the interstate, but instead navigated arterials until she turned onto a southbound country road well away from the more heavily trafficked suburbs. She felt safer, but more frequently than usual, she scanned the road ahead and behind.

Daniel fell asleep in the back seat. Marcel struggled to keep his eyes open as well, but managed to stay awake to keep Theresa company. He worried about her, held her in his sights like a glass of water filled to the brim.

"Do you mind?" Marcel asked, reaching for the audio system power button. Theresa gave a nod. Marcel turned on the radio.

News. *Thorn Rivers is about to get a skin shine revitalization, a new treatment developed in Hollywood City to shave years off of older actors. We'll keep you updated on —*

Next station. News. *It is all part of the Great Plan. President Greatness' unprecedented fourth term in office has led to immense changes in our society. And this new candidate seeking to take his place will undo* all *of his work. That's basically terrorism. The end of Freespeak as we know it. Not only that, but...*

Next station... *the Far City Sonics lead the Central City Bulls, 83 to 53 at the half. More basketball in sixty seconds as we pause for station identification.*

Marcel smiled. He remembered the Seattle Supersonics well. The child in him still took pleasure in beating the Chicago Bulls. The one year in his lifetime that the Supersonics made it to the championship just happened to be during the reign of one of the greatest basketball players ever to set foot on the court. And he was on the other team. The Reboot Sonics, as many old Seattleites deemed this new team, had finally made it to the NBA championship again, fortuitously against the same team. Game four was on the radio. The Sonics were on the verge of sweeping Central City, and Marcel hadn't missed a game until Daniel came to his restaurant with the last baptism of Far City. Some things are more important. Good thing his team was up by thirty.

Next station. Marcel adored Jazz Hop, a blend of bass, percussion, and instrumentation looped on a regular beat. It resembled the hip hop music he'd listen to back in the 1990s and early 2000s. He'd make up lyrics in his head as he listened to the rhythmic cadence of Jazz Hop. He had a lot to say about the world.

"This okay?" he asked Theresa.

Another nod.

Theresa wasn't as much a fan of Jazz Hop, but the tune that played wedged itself in her growing despondence. Over the snare of a drum and long, warm stretches of bass, swelling horns and flutes carried the melody, sad, hopeful and angry all at the same time, expressing for her what words could not. It went major, and there her memories flourished. It went minor, and there her world collapsed. The piano, an ethereal jaunt, caught some, though not all the stray fragments of herself, and with its playful line attempted to stitch her back together. Not the same, but scarred and functional. Not powerful, but alive. It was as though the song knew her, and not just for her sorrow. It knew her past, as well as her present, and communicated it back to her. As the song came to an end, the beat broke down and the horns faded, and a simple harmony of guitar and piano intertwined to acknowledge the sad story that had been told, and ended on some happy chord rang out to silence.

"This afternoon," Theresa started, breaking the silence in the car. She didn't know how or why she felt ready to say anything. Marcel shut the radio off to listen. "I lost... I lost everything..." Between her words, pauses wedged as she figured what would be appropriate to say. "Everyone in the world who meant anything to me. I — I can't tell you how it feels... It's like silence... Anything I have to say... Gone... Any feeling I have. Meaningless. Any love I have in me. Powerless. Because they're all gone." And with that, she realized just how alone she was.

Her words drilled themselves into Marcel. He reached back, not too far, to a time when he felt how she described. Daniel thought of the night his parents were taken, and a stranger showed up at his door. A stranger who would never replace his mother or father, but a stranger who cared. And over time, Marcel became a friend, then like a father. The boy wanted to offer Theresa this hope — fast forward her vision to a time when perhaps he and Marcel might feel like family to her. The day would come, he believed.

"You are not alone," Marcel said. His words were less than extraordinary, but he was a master of tone and pacing. He knew just what words to emphasize and just how much. He could make a whisper seem like a roar. He could comfort a suffering woman, because he knew what she was thinking.

"You'll never be alone, I promise." Daniel spoke those words, and never in his life would he say something more definite, more sincere, more passionate. Marcel had grown on him, but so had his own experience. He too, could empathize.

But, Theresa could only gaze at the long arterial in front of her. She heard their affirmations. Only sounds. She nearly forgot to breathe, then drew in a hefty gust to her lungs. She shut her eyes for longer than a driver ought do such a thing, and in a moment opened them with a twisted look on her face. That skeptic's look that had chiseled away at her childlike faith. Ruined. That's how she felt. Like an old building, crumbling in the corrosive heat, each brick becoming more and more brittle. Like an apocalypse. Like the Church.

187

"Theresa?" Marcel decided he'd let her daze proceed long enough.

"I'm sorry — thank you both," she said.

"You sure as hell don't need to apologize," Marcel said.

At last, Theresa broke eye contact with the road and shifted her sight to look at Marcel sitting next to her. A short glance, she afforded. Two seconds to take in the old man's eyes. They were lodged in oversized pockets of skin, sagging downward, a result of time and tragedy.

"Me too," the old man nodded. "Not a child. Not like you. I never had kids. But people I loved. My nephew was the first, then shortly after my brother and sister-in-law. Dozens of friends. Christians, Buddhists, Muslims, Jews, — I knew many people of different creeds. My best friend was taken about five years ago when I met Daniel for the first time. He was Buddhist." Marcel's mind filled in a moment of silence with faces of the people he'd just mentioned. "Who else did they take from you?" he asked.

"My father. He was the first. He was killed by Freespeakers at a protest in Far City."

"I remember that," Marcel said. "That was almost ten years ago. It was all over the news. Abram Torres. That was his name."

"You knew my father?" Theresa again took her eyes off the long straightaway.

"I didn't know him, but the vigil outside Lourdes church — I was there. I was there with Daniel's parents. They were avid Catholics, just like your family."

"Were." The word was a statement. Theresa understood the past tense. "They were taken? Or killed?"

Marcel's lungs deflated as he screwed his head around to see if Daniel was listening. His eyes were closed and his mouth wide open.

"We don't know," Marcel answered. "Just that they were taken. They were going to take Daniel too, but I got to him first. His parents made sure he wouldn't be placed in Freespeaker Foster Care if they were taken."

"How long ago?" Theresa asked.

"Five years. I've been his guardian ever since. So long as he or I don't make any public religious displays, we're safe."

"But he said he'd just gotten out of the City Interrogation Center."

"Daniel doesn't really have much regard for the Freedom Laws. Do you, Daniel."

"Fuck the AFLs," Daniel's groggy voice muttered from the back. "I met Lania at the interrogation center." He yawned. "Turn the A/C up a bit?"

"That's mah boy," Marcel responded. He tapped his finger on the glass thermostat and made the air howl from the rear vents. The cold draft blasted Daniel in the face.

"I told Marcel we had to find you. Lania said you just baptized a baby and that you would probably be on the run."

"So Lania sent you?" Theresa asked.

"Oh, no," Daniel sounded adamant. "We were only swapping stories. She didn't send me, and the Truth Committee had gotten all that info from her already. I had to find you. It was only a matter of time before they got you and your baby." He realized how matter-of-factly he acknowledged Theresa's situation. "I'm sorry. It's just true. The IF — they don't miss."

Theresa hated that phrase. Not that Daniel said it, but the truth it carried. That she was a target, Abraham was a target, August was a target, and all the Intervention Force had to do was fire, and they nailed two, right in the bullseye. One more shot, and she'd be gone too.

"You're a boy," Theresa said. "You've been incarcerated. Why? Why would you come after a fugitive. Especially after you just got released?"

"Because, I hate the Intervention Force," Daniel started. "And since I'm a youth, they can't put me in a camp for violating the AFLs. Though, the CIC was a new experience. Usually I just spend a few nights in a de-tention center. But mostly, I went after you because I *hate* the Intervention Force."

He said so with unequivocal finality. He spoke as though no law, no bullet, no camp, no myth, and no truth could break his statement.

"Marcel," Theresa said, " if you knew about my father then you had to know Lania. Keep your circle pretty wide?"

Marcel kept his eyes on the road. "My job, like Lania's, is to keep Godseekers safe. I do it for Daniel, I'm doing it for you, and I've done it for dozens of others. I suppose you meet a lot of people that way. It's a good way to spend the twilight of one's lifetime."

"It's gonna be my job someday," Daniel said confidently.

"You've thought about it then," Marcel asked, and Theresa recog-nized that their conversation dipped into some previously arranged plan that she knew nothing about.

"I'm almost there," Daniel responded. "I don't know if I'm ready. If I can handle leaving you. Leaving the city. Leaving everything I know. Starting all over again."

"We'll have to talk about this when we get to Portland," Marcel said. Theresa chose not to let her curiosity get the best of her.

"I wish it didn't have to be anyone's job to keep Godseekers on the right side of safe," Theresa said. "But thank you. Thank you both for finding me."

Then Theresa felt at ease. Not completely, but in the moment, as she returned her full focus to the empty country road and the trees alternating with grassy embankments at either side of the car, she felt something filling the void within her. A drop in the bucket. But trust heals one cell at a time.

"So. How *do* we fight back?" Theresa asked the car.

"Portland," Marcel gave the answer. "Let's start there."

Theresa laid into the gas pedal a little more heavily.

The lights of Portland rose to the sky and fell on the river, a bath of color on a clear summer night, not a breeze to be found. In recent years, Portland's Sanctuary City status waned in much the same fashion as Far City. Refugees and immigrants found safety amidst strictly enforced government regulations and restrictions. Over time, it became necessary to open the municipality other outcasts of society confined by law, from religious followers to LGBTQAs to first generation naturalized citizens, to many elderly. The regulating of social status grew too powerful too quickly, and uncontested by a disinterested public's vote, many of whom were now imprisoned by laws set by leaders who walked into office. Now, only Portland and Music City, formerly Austin, TX, provided a safe haven for those whom common society rejected. An influx of Far City natives had migrated to Portland over the last few decades to escape the nationalism of their hometown, looking for a more peaceful habitat.

Portland kept its original name, and refused to identify itself by its relative distance from the nation's capital or geographic location. The City Council figured that "Portland" was not a traditional name, but a functional one, so why change it? Before gentrification transformed the city, citizens passed a number of preservation laws. Now that Far City's skylines were choked and its limits were populated only by those who could afford million-plus dollar homes, Portland clung to its quirky population. That meant longevity for restaurants and small businesses that had been in the neighborhoods for decades, some for generations. Many homes were retrofitted and renovated, but still maintained the same exterior charm as the year they were crafted. Microapartment towers housing over 200 residents were prohibited from being built in city limits to prevent high population density. Consequently, no big business found interest in developing offices on the Northwestern River; the residents of Portland had no problem with that.

Marcel directed Theresa to a longstanding Thai and Vietnamese provincial restaurant in the Division neighborhood. The River Market, it was called. A bamboo fence surrounded the outside seating, and string lights the colors of autumn warmed the space to the eye. Marcel had Theresa turn off the arterial and park in an alley behind the building.

"Another restaurant, huh?" Theresa asked. "Are you all part of the same franchise?"

"You might say that," Marcel said, smiling.

"Thank God we're here," Daniel sighed. "I'm hungry. Tyriq cooking? Chicken wings with that fish sauce glaze. You're going to love them," he said to Theresa, who just noticed that her stomach had been eating itself all afternoon and evening. Rather than going through the front door, Marcel led them up an old set of wooden stairs. Each plank creaked like a cackling old witch, and Theresa worried that at any moment, she would step right through a board and wind up with a broken leg. The door was the same as the stairs. Rotting wood, a brass knob that jiggled in its socket, and a bawling shriek as it slid open.

Inside was a dining room — not a restaurant dining room, but a residential one — and a kitchen where all sorts of spices and bottles and jars rested on the countertops.

A man who looked about a decade Theresa's senior stood at the stove, jerking a wok full of garlic, onions, carrots, cilantro, and other miscellany. His lanky limbs, shiny dark skin and bald head almost danced while he moved about the kitchen. In fact he hummed a popular tune that Theresa had heard before, but couldn't quite recall its name.

"Good timing! Dinner's almost ready," the man hollered out, as if he knew who had walked into the room.

"Good, we brought appetites," Marcel shot back.

"Marcel? The hell are you doing here!" he said before he even turned around to see with whom he was speaking. The man left his wok on the burner and peeked to verify. "It *is* you! Come here!"

"Ay, you're burning your stir fry," Marcel said.

"Man I don't burn nothin' unless it's supposed to be. But yeah, let me get this real quick."

He returned to his post and shook some of those small jars over the steaming pan. Coriander. Curry. Black lava salt. White pepper. Chilis. A spray of vinegar. A squirt of fish sauce. Chili oil.

"Just relax," Tyriq called over his shoulder. "Can't wait to hear your story this time," he added as he reached into the refrigerator to collect more vegetables, more prawns, more noodles. All of it was destined for the wok. Theresa grew up eating all kinds of foods from different parts of the world, but had no idea what this man was making.

"Tyriq is a freestyle chef, in his spare time, at least," Marcel explained, seeing Theresa's befuddled stare into the kitchen. "He loves fusing flavors and making new dishes out of them. Don't always work though, and the best ones, he never remembers how he made them."

"Ninety-five percent of the time, buddy!" Tyriq shot back.

They settled over dinner, which looked like a beautiful garden of greens and reds and oranges and yellows and meat and noodles all intertwined with each other. Shrimp, chicken, mushrooms, eggplant, young corn. It smelled spicy.

"Wow, what's not in this dish?" Daniel exclaimed.

"It's all inclusive," Tyriq grinned. "I call it the Garden of Eden." All the chef's dishes had names based on how the end product looked. Bird's nest for deep-fried noodles, turmeric typhoon curry, the Uluru steak — the chef was as much an artist as a painter.

"Ty, you remember Daniel," Marcel began formalities. "And this is Theresa, the last baptism in Far City as of about two weeks ago now."

"Wow - two weeks?" Tyriq looked at Theresa as if she were a relic. "You dodged IF for that long? Incredible."

"Not so incredible as you might think," Theresa said. She herself was not at all impressed. Had Abraham still been with her, then she'd allow for a feeling of accomplishment.

"I understand," Tyriq replied, not needing to hear her whole story. "My sister is like you. The IF stole her daughter a few years back. You'll meet her — my sister — she's on her way over for dinner."

His tone was so matter-of-fact. Jovial even. Theresa wondered how such subject matter could ever be that easy to recall. At first she felt offended, but upon further review, she was inspired by Tyriq's ability to find a shred of post-tragedy normalcy.

"She escaped the Intervention Force then?" Theresa inquired, her own future in her mind.

"Not really. They held her for a couple of years, but then the State released her in favor of using tax money for things other than locking up faith mothers. You'll find you're pretty safe in Portland. In fact —" he paused and thought about how ill-timed retroactive advice would be. "In fact, you might even like it here."

Marcel forked a prawn off the main sharing platter.

"I want to talk to your sister," Theresa said, eager to meet another mother who had gone through the loss of a child.

"I'm sure she'd want to meet you too," Tyriq said, catching a glimpse of an old stainless steel clock hanging on the dining room wall. The time triggered a sense of anxiety. "You two will have a lot to talk about. And that girl can talk. But she should have been here about a half an hour ago. She can be late sometimes. I wouldn't worry."

But he was worried. She may have been released by the Intervention Force, but that didn't erase the target off her back. And now he was harboring a fugitive. Playing chicken with the bull. He kept the conversation moving to curb his anxiety.

"Did Marcel tell you about our little group?"

"He's hinted at it," Theresa said.

Tyriq glanced at Marcel to make sure they were on the same page. The old man nodded.

"We all practice religion, underground as it's called," Tyriq explained. "I practice Islam, Marcel practices Tibetan Buddhism, and Daniel is a cradle Catholic."

Theresa marveled at Daniel. "You were baptized then?"

"I was."

She stared awkwardly long at the boy, wondering what Abraham would look like as a teenager. Surely the Intervention Force had legally changed his name already. That was always the first step. Soon after, they would find a family to raise him. A staunchly, unyieldingly free-speaking family that would ensure her name would never be mentioned to her boy. Abraham would never know he was the last baptism in Far City. In Seattle. The last baptism of Lania Langston. Lord knows if they've changed her name, but Theresa was still thankful that she was alive.

"Do you still believe?" Tyriq asked.

The direct question shocked Theresa.

"You know, we've all lost loved ones to the IF," Tyriq followed up. "I only ask because faith is often the first thing to go. And that's okay."

"I don't know," slowly escaped from her lips in a meek volume. Meek, but honest. "Part of me wants to say yes. But — I don't feel like I can say yes. Yes, I do. Like I can say that God is here. Because I —" She fumbled for the truth, and as a Catholic her entire life, her own words surprised her. Not their truth, but that she even uttered them aloud. "I don't know if God is here, and I can't get that thought out of my mind. And I wonder if God ever really *was* or if it was all just an illusion."

"Aaliyah said almost the same thing when they took Madiha," Tyriq stated. Theresa expected some perspective altering advice to follow. None did. "Sometimes God takes everything from us, and then we wonder, if he wasn't there to protect the ones we love, was he even there in the first place."

"And we're supposed to understand that it's all God's plan," Theresa added.

Tyriq chortled. "But who says you getting pissed at God isn't a part of God's plan as well?" Theresa felt reassured, pleased that if there was a God to be pissed at, at least there was still a God.

"It's easier when you don't have a god to blame," Marcel chimed.

"Yeah, just good ol' human beings." Daniel nestled himself comfortably in the banter.

"That's the truth though," Marcel agreed while Tyriq nodded his head.

They spent a few quiet moments just eating. Tyriq stood up from his chair and excused himself. His sister was nearly an hour late. Walking back into the kitchen, he pulled out his comm device and disappeared from sight.

Theresa's curiosity about the underground network of Godseekers was still not satisfied.

"So, Marcel, what did you know about Lania?" Theresa asked, picking up the conversation from the car, as well as the serving spoon to add another two scoops of mostly vegetables onto her plate.

"Lania Langston," Marcel observed. "She was a firecracker. *Is*, I should say. Baptizing kids in sewers was something new for her. But she said she always wanted to try one. The sacraments are very important to her."

"You're pretty connected. I still can't believe you know all these people."

"I'm old, and old people know everybody," Marcel laughed through an incomplete toothy grin. It brought a rare laugh out of Theresa, and the table relished it. Hopelessness needs a bit of humor to light the way back. Theresa took the moment's levity to ask what she'd been dreading to ask for the entire drive south.

"Do you think I'll ever see Abraham again?" The thought arose quickly, and she blurted it out before she could prevent the idea from taking physical form. She wished she had held her tongue, ill-prepared for whatever answer followed her question.

Marcel finished chewing his last bite of broccoli, and looked Theresa with softly creased eyes. She wanted Marcel to never mind, but still, she waited for his perspective. "I wouldn't lose faith," he handed her. "And if my knowing about your family and friends shows anything, it's that, like I said, you are not alone, and the world is smaller than it seems."

That was comfort for Theresa. Padding around the word that invited profound fear into her chest. Alone. Losing everyone in her life whom she loved, she felt her life's purpose had been robbed from her. She felt the deepest sense of *alone*. The type of *alone* where you have no one to love you, and no one to love. The words, the genuine words of this old man, a stranger this morning, alleviated that much of her pain. At least she would not face the rest of her life by herself.

"Thank you, Marcel," Theresa said through gathering tears. "I don't know how to move forward."

"One day," Daniel interjected, feeling his time for wisdom had come. "One day. Marcel would always say that to me after I lost my parents. One day of letting others love you. That will bring you back from the dead. Not all the way, but enough to stay alive. Alive with purpose. Enough to do something good."

Slow, deep breaths cushioned the conversation for the mother. "That's good. Thank you both. I —"

Tyriq interrupted the room as he lurched back toward the table. Their first challenge together wouldn't wait for Theresa's moment of clarity to sink in.

"They have her," he said. "Intervention Force from Far City. They've taken Aaliyah. Called me from her phone. We are no longer safe here."

"Were we ever?" Theresa muttered, but noticed Tyriq still frozen in place, fixing his ghostly eyes into hers. "What else?" she asked.

"They want to exchange her. For you."

Then Tyriq stretched out his hand toward Theresa, the cell phone in his palm illuminated with a call in progress.

Theresa

"They want you, Theresa."

August's voice sounded small and tinny through the receiver. It met Theresa's ear and stirred the volatile catharsis boiling inside her.

"You." Her voice was deep and frigid. "You idiot. You took my son. *Our* son! And handed him over to the goddamn IFs. Anna's? Que estupido eres? What were you thinking! We were on the run — you knew that!" A good portion, but not the rest of Theresa's tirade exited her system with a heaving sigh that quickly swelled into a shriek.

"You need to listen Theresa," August halted her, his voice unworthily firm. "They'll let you see Abraham again. They will. But you won't get to keep him—"

"Oh no shit, I won't get to keep him! I swear to God if you did this on purpose — if you're working with the IF —"

"Theresa!" this time August sounded offended. But before he went on the defensive, he empathized. "Look. I swear to you. I am just as much in custody as Abraham, and they are definitely using this other woman as a bargaining piece. I'm only relaying the message."

"What message," Theresa demanded, her face flushed.

"Turn yourself in. They don't need the others. They release this other woman who is here in custody. Once they have you, they will let you see Abraham one more time. Portland Intervention Force Headquarters, tomorrow morning at 8 a.m. You have all night to think about it."

Theresa started to speak, but she had nothing to say. Her mind raced like a shaken bee hive, and before she could conjure any question or statement, August took the last words.

"Theresa," her name stumbled off his lips, weighted with August's guilt. "I'm sorry! I'm sorry! I —"

The call ended.

"August! Wait!" No follow up, just the silence of an empty phone line, and Theresa realized anything she could say or had said made no difference. The only thing that mattered was the decision she would have to make.

Marcel, Tyriq and Daniel had witnessed the entire conversation, Theresa like an actress delivering a one-woman show. Their eyes gazed on her, part shock, part pity, part wonder. Theresa's grip on Tyriq's phone prompted her palm to develop slight film of sweat. She approached the dining table and set the device on the splintered wood. Three men's eyes, captivated, wondered what the star of the show would do next. Her eyes fixated on nothing, a brick perhaps on the wall in front of her.

Her eyes shut tightly and again, tears squeezed out. She was exhausted, trying to corral so many extreme emotions. She longed for a clear head, but all capacity to empty her mind had escaped. There was one truth, however, that remained constant. In the midst of her mind's chaos, it was the ground on which she stood. She had made the decision. Made it well before August conveyed the deal. That decision was clear from the moment she stood looking at the Intervention Force SUVs in the reflection of the tinted windows back in Far City. When she chose not to run, turned around and stepped toward the lion's mouth only to be near Abraham one last time.

"Tomorrow morning at 7:15," she said in a clear, steady voice, eyes now looking right at Marcel. "You have to bring me to the Intervention Force Headquarters."

"No, Theresa," Tyriq said. "This isn't the right choice. Ali's been on the inside for two years. She knows the system. She can handle her own."

"She's been a prisoner too long then," Theresa retorted. "Also, they will let me see Abraham if I turn myself in. I'm going. I want to go."

"You can't trust them," Daniel said. "You know you can't."

"I don't care. It's the only chance I have. And I'm tired. If they want me, they can have me. I don't know much about anything anyway. Take me there tomorrow. Get your sister back. Maybe I'll get released in a few years. Learn a few things too, like your sister. Maybe I'll find Lania. But I am done. I'm done running and hiding. And if I see August—"

She bit her lip, but the vitriol she thought she possessed had dissipated. Something to do with August's last words. And not just what he had to say. It was how he said it. Sincerely, with conviction. Her words on the phone, bitter and violent, were regrettable now and out of character for her, and she became aware of how much she was changing. It frightened her. The Freedom Laws had already taken so many whom she loved, but now, Theresa recognized, the Law was infiltrating the core of herself. Her faith. Her hope. Her compassion. Her gentleness.

She didn't wish ill towards August, but anger still moored within her heart, and it felt as real as a stone. Where love used to be, the law replaced it with something dark. So many words at the thought of August's name. Idiot. Asshole. Traitor. Incompetent. Irresponsible. She wrestled with the rage at the thought of his perfect, unbearable face. Then another face would slip into her mind and freeze like an image on the wheel of a slot machine. Abraham. And her mood would soften. Lania. Again. Her father. The mob. Sandy Wichman. Daniel. Marcel. Tyriq. The snorting IF officer above the grating on the night of Abraham's baptism. Then it all started over, right back to August.

It was people. People did this to her. She wondered if she might consider being a hermit. A monk. Trappist? Buddhist? Somewhere in a cave in a mountain or on an island in the middle of the ocean. She romanticized the possibility. But for now, all she considered was that the prospect of loneliness didn't sound as painful if it came from her own volition. Maybe she would find God again in silence and isolation. Maybe.

She shook her head at the future. Shook from side to side, then realized the action was involuntary. Her hands shook too. Her breath was jittery as she let out a choppy sigh.

Marcel took her hand, and brushed the errant strands of hair from her face.

"It's all natural," he said, slipping a small joint in her palm. "I don't know if you smoke, but just a little bit helps me calm down. Don't smoke the whole thing though. Too much weed is like too much booze. Could make the headache worse, you know."

Daniel looked at Tyriq, and they shared an unlikely chuckle for the moment. They both knew Marcel wanted to smoke the rest of it when

Theresa had enough to clear her mind. She did not smoke. But she looked down at slender twist of paper, twitching unsteadily in her hand. *What have I got to lose,* was the popular thought at the moment.

"Got a light?" she asked.

———————————

Sleep became her after a few long drags. If not for the weed, she'd have been a wreck in the morning, but between the tranquilizing effects of the drug and her already spent body, Theresa found nearly eight hours of sleep before the alarm woke her at six o'clock. The faint light of summer's dawn softly lit the room and she stretched and stirred, her head still fuzzy from the high, her limbs, light and slow to move. She slowly unwrapped herself from the soft covers of the bed in a room above The River Market, rolled over and grabbed her mobile media device. Her father's face smiled at her from the lock screen, then Abraham laughing on her home screen.

She had been silent on her social media since the baptism, except when she surveyed Fern's cryptic messages. Theresa wondered, what would she post now? That she had been a fugitive for the last two weeks? That her closest friend had been abducted? Or that she was about to turn herself in to the Intervention Force? She thought maybe she should have her neighbor pick up her mail. Or message Fern and update her. She desired to communicate. To tell her story to someone. To make her situation relevant to the world. It didn't matter much anymore, secrecy, because in less than two hours, her evasion from the law would be officially over.

She rotated onto her back and fixed her eyes on the ceiling above. But it wasn't the quiet yellow paint she saw, it was a blurry image of her son, the only remaining image from the previous night's carousel of faces. What would happen when it came into focus — when she would have her last look at the baby boy? How would he sound? Would he cry? Laugh? Or just sit there silently with that infinite gaze full of empty wonder? She wanted to answer all his questions about life. At first anyway. Then she wanted him to answer the questions himself. Wanted to teach him what was right and what was wrong and what was in between.

All of that was replaced with a single moment when she would look upon Abraham's face one more time. Would she still recognize him as a 10 year-old, or as an adult? Would some elevated power connecting mother and son allow her to just know that some stranger was no stranger at all, but her son? Perhaps in his eyes, or in his smile. Maybe in his touch. Or maybe he'd look at her, and he just would know. The thought, the speculation gave her hope, and she was caught off guard. It was the first sign of hope she had in weeks.

A knock on the door. A soft one. A whisper.

"Theresa?" She couldn't tell who it was.

"Yeah. Come in. It's okay."

It was Marcel. The ancient man moved at a groggy pace, wobbling as he stood by her bed, then took a seat in an easy chair.

"Did you sleep?" he asked.

"I did. Thank you for that, the smoke. It helped. And thank you for, I guess everything."

"So. Are you still going to turn yourself in?" He wasted no time with morning pleasantries.

"I want to," she replied and Marcel nodded. "It's odd. I don't want to be free. I want to give up. For all the animosity that I have for the IF and the AFLs and everything our society has become, I just want to surrender. All because I get one last look. That's all I want at this point. When

Daniel intercepted me yesterday, I knew Abe was gone, but I thought I could steal one last look at him. That's all I wanted. It's all I thought I had left. That's not giving up, is it?"

"No, Theresa. I would do the same thing. I'm sure Daniel would gladly turn himself in for one more moment with his parents. You are not giving up."

"I don't know why I thought giving him to August would be a good idea," she thought aloud. "I was so sure that Lania was dead. I didn't know they kept her alive. And that she would tell them who I was or where I'd be or give them any information."

"Don't be hard on yourself, Theresa," Marcel interrupted. "None of us are the criminal masterminds the IF seems to treat us like. And Lania — she had no choice. They probably drugged her with *eternatae*."

"With what? Is that Latin?"

"It's a truth serum. A mind altering drug. It's painful, and it works like hell. When the Truth Committee asks you a question, the answer falls from lips like ripe fruit from a tree."

"Truth Committee?" Theresa asked. "never mind. I don't really care. If I knew all this, I would have left Far City right after the baptism."

"Anti-intervention is getting tighter," Marcel explained. "The regulation has been there for a while, but with this new administration, the enforcement is getting more and more strict. Information is a commodity. They buy it, trade for it, or they take it."

The claims were lost on Theresa. She got up off the edge of her bed and went to the chair where Tyriq had left some of his sister's clothes.

"That drug — *eternatae* — did they ever use it on you?" Theresa asked as she fit on a pair of blue jeans in front of Marcel.

The old man stood up, turned around and revealed a scar just above the back of his neck. It was a horrid dark spot like a bruise that never healed.

"The CVI — craniovertebral injection — is a form of *eternatae*. The strongest form of the drug. People like myself and my friend Genjin, we have learned to meditate out of the gas form of *eternatae*. But not the CVI. It's too much. I bet your friend Lania has a similar scar now. Daniel does too."

Theresa could only shake her head.

"So. Still want to go?"

She studied the old man. He was still trying to convince her to stay. But practicality and self-preservation were no match for Theresa's longing for Abraham.

"I'm ready," she said, pulling a black sweatshirt over her head.

"Okay." Marcel lifted his skinny arm and rested his skeletal hand on Theresa's shoulder. He looked her square in the face. "But we're going to get you out."

Theresa smiled for the first time since she could remember. While every tragedy unraveled, it had been difficult to notice a small group of strangers showing her a great deal of love.

"Thank you." She spoke her words toward the sky.

———————

Tyriq drove. Marcel accompanied. Daniel hung back at The River Market. Stories of Portland's Intervention Force Headquarters circulated among Godseekers, particularly ones who had been incarcerated. The department was infamously corrupt, by anti-intervention standards. In the last year alone, the branch had undergone two changes at the Commanding Officer position, and a total of four doublers were found to have been previously employed, each now since disappeared, apparently from the face of the earth.

The deplorable track record drew the attention, then the ire of the Supreme Commanding Officer in Capital City. She had recently — not more than a month ago — taken a visit clear across the country to the Portland HQ to run an evaluation of the newest CO. A week she spent overseeing the new leadership, and after interviewing the rest of the staff, nearly 60 percent of the force had been relieved. But not replaced. Many openings for field agents and file clerks and even cafeteria workers still remained. The department was in disarray.

Tyriq relayed the latest information to Theresa and Marcel on the way to the facility. The information itself came from Aaliyah, his sister. Ever observant and resourceful, she learned much while imprisoned. She spent a good seven weeks in the Portland IF Detention Center, and once released, she had Tyriq make a few additions to their roster of friendlies within the prison walls. En route to trade Theresa for his sister, Tyriq was hopeful that the latter would have a plan.

"I know Ali," Tyriq said as they pulled away from the restaurant. "She won't be empty-handed. She'll know how to get you out."

He turned back to check his blind spot, but spared a moment for Theresa. She wore a look not of anxiety, but eagerness. Tyriq knew the face. After Aaliyah's daughter had been taken, her driving purpose in life became to tear down the system from the inside, even if she scraped at the flesh of anti-intervention like a slow illness. She would methodically undermine its authority until her last breath. Her hatred of the IF was calculated and patient. Now Theresa. *That same look*, thought Tyriq.

"You'll be fine," Tyriq said. Theresa nodded, and Marcel, who sat in the back with her, took her hand and squeezed it without looking in her direction. Seemed everyone had a surplus of confidence.

Theresa's mind was as blank as she could make it. As the car crept through traffic, she preoccupied herself with erasing each thought as it arose. The faces of everyone who had preoccupied her mind the night before — the wheel, that awful wheel of love and loss. She fought, fought hard to replace it with the same emptiness that formed a cavernous space in her chest. White. All white. When she closed her eyes, that was all she wanted to see. Auto-pilot. She had her directions. When the car came to a halt, when Tyriq activated the power brake and the engine hum faded to silence, she would release the door handle, step out of the vehicle, and walk toward the doors. She would meet whomever stood waiting for her — a man with a badge and belt, a woman with cuffs and a baton. They would don the same black suits as the elites who came for Abraham that day. That day at Anna's — no! Her mind drifted. Theresa erased the ladybug logo, erased the black suits, erased the memory of yesterday, the day before, and everyday before that. Until emptiness. Only emptiness, and once again, all white. In the cabin of the car, she breathed deeply and colored her mind with a new thought. She would approach whomever stood waiting for her and say the words, "I am Theresa Torres. The mother of the last baptism of Far City. You have my child. I've come for him. And you have a man's sister whom you promised to release." The exchange would be made. And from there, she had no inkling. But she didn't care. Because what would come next, what *should* come next, would be a moment with Abraham. At that, she smiled, and rehearsed the actions again in her head. Park. Exit. Approach. Say. Abraham.

The only nerve that caused her to twitch was the one that knew it couldn't possibly be that easy. *But*, she thought, *I have nothing to lose, and just a moment to gain.*

The doors were made of glass. Theresa opted for the revolving door between two hinged gates. At 7:50 in the morning, a trio of agents awaited her. She eyed them with enmity. Here was the enemy, right before her. How she wished she could attack them, bully them, take from them as they had taken from her. In that moment she began plotting her revenge. How would she make them pay?

She laughed. Vindication would be sweet, but vengeance would be sweeter. These thoughts were part of a new emerging Theresa, one she knew she would have to find a way to quell. They opposed everything her father taught her. Everything Lania stood for. The rule of nonviolence and forgiveness was the rule of Jesus and her Catholic faith. *Turn the other cheek*, is what she was taught.

Well, let someone else do that, Theresa's mind snapped back. She was done turning cheeks. She figured if she wasn't able to pass on the same values to her son, the values might as well end with her, and they would burden her no longer.

She thought of what people deserved, and judged them accordingly. The three Intervention Force Agents in front of her wore field gear with protective garb and utility belts. They noticed her, and one approached, his eyes locked magnetically to hers. She did not break the connection. She conveyed a frigid fearlessness and anything as far from the frail mess of a woman she had been.

"Theresa Torres," he said as though he knew her. He had an accent. Not from the northwest. Likely somewhere on the east coast. She nodded at him in reply. "Come with me," he said.

"Aaliyah. Where is she. She goes free before I take another step forward."

The man looked at her contemptuously. "You know, we could just take you in right here and now."

He was right. There was nothing stopping him. Her bolstered confidence had become reckless, and she realized she needed to play by their rules. Every indicator from her experience with the Intervention Force stabbed at her naivety. What was she thinking? Was she as gullible as August? All of a sudden, she felt a sliver of sympathy for him. Her nerves began to twitch once she realized she was defenseless in the lion's den. But an interior door opened and out walked a woman about her age. Long, curly black hair rested on her shoulder blades covering a bold insignia on her black leather coat. She nodded at Theresa, took her hand and thanked her. Then she walked out the door. Was that even her or a decoy, Theresa thought? She wouldn't know without Tyriq, and he and Marcel waited back at the car, parked three blocks away. They, along with Daniel, all seemed like distant memories anyway.

"I want to see him," Theresa said with a voice, cold as a corpse. "My son. That was the deal. Take me to him. *Now*."

The agent looked back at the other two who were already heading into the interior door from where Aaliyah emerged.

"This way," he said, leading her past the threshold, through the stale air of a brief hallway and into a holding room. "Sit here. I'll be right back. In the meantime —"

After a brief moment, August walked through the door and sat across the table from her. Theresa turned her head back toward the agent as if to say, *what in the hell do I do now?* He responded smirk and left the room. Theresa was all kinds of ready to see Abraham. Again, that was the deal. Quality time with her former husband was not expected.

Neither said a word, but she just examined him in astonishment.

"How did you get here so fast?" she asked.

"You'd be surprised how much they know and how fast they know it. Your car was tagged back in Federal Way. At the strip mall. An Officer Sandwich called you in." He chuckled. "Some details you can't forget."

The silence between them expanded like hot air, and neither one of them could breathe comfortably.

"Theresa, I'm —"

"Don't!" she cut him off. "Don't start. We don't need to have a moment right now, and I honestly don't know what I will say to you. I don't want to start screaming. Especially right before I'm going to see Abraham for the last time."

August shook his head.

"What?" she asked. "Why are you shaking your head? Stop shaking your head, you're making me —"

"You'll get to see Abraham, Theresa. But you won't get to hold him. He's not here."

Her heart sank. She knew there would be a catch. The deal would be good, but there would be a catch. This didn't feel fair. One last look should be in person. That would be worth it. With every ounce of faith, she tried to disbelieve August's words. But of course Abraham would not have accompanied August on his little road trip. She wanted to be angry at him. He lied to her, she thought. But no. He didn't lie. He said the IF wanted him to say, and it was true. She would get to see Abraham one last time. She should have known that it would not have been in the flesh. She gave the Intervention Force too much credit. Too much credit for being human.

Sure enough, the agent returned with a flat screen tablet, one that could project a three dimensional hologram of the image on the screen.

He laid it flat on the table, and there Abraham was, hovering in the air like an image pulled directly from Theresa's dream. Abraham. Their son. A live feed. The moment was delicate. Almost as delicate as the child himself. The agent was decent enough to leave the room and let Theresa and August share the last look together. Theresa fumbled for August's hand resting on the table, and clutched it tightly.

"Our son," she came undone. "It's our son... Our baby... Our son."

With her other hand she reached out to touch his cheek. The light bounced off her hand and reflected onto the wall behind her. She didn't blink. August remained silent as he tightened his grip on Theresa's hand. *I'm an idiot*, he told himself. *I have a son, but no idea what it means to be a father. To be a parent. But she knew. Theresa. She knew.*

She knew the painful collision of her parental dream and the rule of society, and now she was the wreck left behind.

She wore a yoke of wounded joy. Abraham's brown eyes looked as though they had been distressed, but somehow, he smiled. He was okay, for the moment. Maybe he could feel their presence. Theresa told herself that it was so, though she couldn't fathom how the tech could convey such a feeling to a baby so far away.

The image flickered. It had not been more than a minute. It flickered, then disappeared. Theresa collapsed on the table. August stood from his seat, walked around and knelt next to her. He put his arms around her, and she received him, his warmth and the love he offered in that moment. Then he leaned to whisper in her ear. She thought he might profess his lingering love for her.

"We won't be here for long," were his words, careful not to be too loud.

She smiled. *Yeah, gullible me,* she thought. She raised her eyes to him, red blood vessels spread like cracks in a shattered mirror. "You have a way out?" she whispered back.

"Who said anything about getting out?" he responded. Theresa was confused. He had a plan, but it was not what she expected. "The only way to trace your friend Lania is from the inside. And I know where she is. So does Aaliyah."

"That was really Tyriq's sister then?"

"I made sure of it. Unless meeting her was a big ruse itself."

A sigh of relief blew from Theresa's lungs. "How did you find Lania?"

"They're not very tight on security here." August pulled out a mobile media device.

"Your phone? How?"

"Not my phone, but *a* phone." He fiddled with the touch screen and pulled up a photo of a prisoner inventory report. "They don't seem to be heavily staffed here. Saw it just lying on a desk."

There it was in plain sight. Lania Langston. NI (New Inmate). A check in the box next to *Eternatae CVI*. Destination Location: Eastern State Interventionist Camp, WA.

"We're going to be transferred there. Then Aaliyah and the others will work on getting us out. She has some connections."

The prospect of seeing Lania again restored Theresa's spirits, but even that was a drop in the bucket to fill the void left by Abraham's absence.

"What about Abraham? What about our son, August?"

"You taught me this little prayer once: 'God, grant me the serenity to accept the things I cannot change; courage to change what I can, and wisdom to know the difference.' I guess — it's time to start accepting."

She looked directly into August's eyes. He was still kneeling beside her. This time, she embraced him, tightly.

"Thank you, August," she said. "I'm glad you remember something about the faith." She kissed his cheek, then returned to his eyes with a stern look. "But if God wants me to accept that I will never see Abraham again, then I don't see the point. I mean really — faith, hope and love? If love is the greatest, then I have to believe that I'll see him again. Hold him. If not, then God is dead. I'm dead. You're dead. And nothing else in the world matters. So to me, right now, that prayer means nothing. I'm gonna get our son back. I'm going to see him again in the flesh. I'm going to hold him and tell him my name, and your name, and his own name. If it's the last thing I do before I die, then I'll die a happy woman."

He smiled at her and that familiar fire, the determination he fell in love with when they first dated. It radiated.

He wanted to kiss her.

He didn't.

Theresa

The Eastern State Interventionist Center was Lania's new home, though everyone within its walls — prison guards included — called it the ESIC and knew the last letter should really stand for Camp. The dormitory where Lania and her cohorts took their nightly respite smelled of fresh linens and old onions left on a heat vent. Showers had been out of service for a few days, and the guards at the ESIC swore the plumbing was getting fixed.

The hygiene center was attached to the sleeping quarters, a mundanely long room where bunk beds lined the walls. After every third bedframe, a window offered a view to the outside world. Lania found herself in close proximity to the natural light, a blessing to her. Oftentimes, when all the ESIC lights would go out, she would stare out the single-paned window and partake in a staring competition with the stars. She would lose over and over again, especially on a new moon. Tranquility would visit Lania late in the evening. She knew the heavens had something to do with it.

One night early in her tenure, as she lay frozen on her thin mattress, the light of a full moon shone white through each of the four windows in the barracks. Just as Lania was about to say a prayer in her head, the dwelling came alive with whispering voices. At first, she was pulled back to the Truth Committee's interrogation room. Had the room been gassed with eternatae and the hallucinations followed her into the camp? Then she sat up and panned her surroundings. In moonlight now pouring through the intermittent glass, she observed her comrades, some with their eyes closed, all with their lips moving. The whispers engulfed Lania's hearing, and after a few minutes, died down like a slowing rain. From the bed above, a head leaned over the edge and grinned over her like the Cheshire Cat.

"We pray here," she said. "For me it is Isha. For you, the Our Father, I would guess."

Puzzlement contorted Lania's fresh face. The woman, Hadeeqah, introduced herself.

"I don't understand," the priest said. "Aren't we in here for praying and practicing?"

"Yes."

"What about the prison guards? Don't they monitor us? Aren't there cameras?"

Hadeeqah shook her head. "No cameras here. Just fences with barbed wire. Bars and locks. And some guards don't care, like the ones assigned to our dormitory."

Lania, still disoriented and confused, turned her head left and right, anticipating a cluster of IF officers to bust in at any moment, round up the prisoners, and send them off to a torture chamber. But torture chambers cost money, and funding for anti-intervention went almost entirely to the apprehension of Godseekers.

"Come on priest — I will pray with you." Hadeeqah stretched out her hand toward Lania, who lifted her arm.

217

"How do you know I'm a priest?" Lania wondered.

Hadeeqah only smiled. "I will start then, okay?" Hadeeqah began praying in the words Jesus had taught Lania, and the Catholic woman joined at the second line in a meek whisper. They recited the words without rush, without worry, and allotted room for breath and pauses. At the conclusion, Hadeeqah once again smiled down on her cohort.

"Next time, you pray with me, okay?" Lania smiled back and nodded. "Good night."

"Good night," Lania whispered back.

She awoke to the strength of the sunlight now beaming on the other side of the cabin. Lania had arrived in the late afternoon the previous day, and was told that her orientation would begin at eight o'clock sharp. *Orientation.* It sounded so ordinary. Several times in her life, she would call herself out for sugarcoating a situation. Others would make the same judgment. For her, it didn't matter. The optimism helped her keep a positive frame of mind when she faced adversity. Most of all, it was her choice to look at life in that way. But having someone else sugarcoat her situation — that infuriated her. An infringement upon her right to interpret injustice as injustice. Orientation. More like a condemnation.

The clock in the dormitory read 7:44 and all the prisoners stood next to their bunks, awaiting summons, which came promptly as the clock changed. Lania, along with two others, were held back by two sentinels. One was tall, a dark-skinned Asian, while the other man stood shorter with chalky white skin and searing red hair. *A Filipino and an Irishman*, thought Lania. One of them has to be Catholic. Gently, the pair marched the new inmates to the Camp Warden's Center, a small

218

complex with a failing roof, prominent in name alone. The warden was away at the moment, which was a common circumstance. So, the second in command emerged from his office to meet the trio of new inmates. She uttered an under-the-breath exchange that lasted a mere moment, then ordered each to their assignment. Orientation over. Lania wondered if it was even necessary. The two guards both tried to cover their looks of bemusement as they ushered the three out of the Warden's Center.

The tall one brought the other two inmates toward the field, while the short man led Lania to the mess hall, which wasn't too far off. In fact it was only one of four complexes in the hub of the camp, but it was the largest. There wasn't much of a need for construction. Most of the ESIC was farmland, and with the exception of the harvests used to feed the residents, the grain, fruit and northern cotton — a modified plant — were stored in the fourth complex, and shipped out on a weekly basis. The mess hall was quite possibly the cleanest, most comfortable building in the camp as well, and within its doors, past the wide open cafeteria floor and into the confines of the kitchen danced a happy man. He was old. Older than Lania, for sure. At least she thought so. His black hair was matted on his scalp, haywire and greasy. The man's eyes peered out from wrinkled, sagging sockets, no doubt aged from years of being too elated for his circumstance.

"Sup G," the guard called out casually, as if they were teenagers from Lania's childhood.

"Red, you brought me some company?" replied the happy man. "Hope she can cook. Don't want another prison riot."

"Yeah me too. I'm off. Warden's out again. They want me to step in."

"Mmm, right. You gonna let me outta here then?"

"Maybe — only if she cooks as good as you."

The guard turned to Lania. "You —"

"Young man, please," Lania decided to join the raillery, walking into the kitchen. "Where's the meat?" The fridge was full of vegetables and starches.

"Guess the jokes on her," happy man said as the man named Red floated out of the space. "Sorry honey, we're all vegetarians around here. Didja see any livestock outside?"

"Oh Lord," was all Lania could muster.

"Name?"

"Lania."

"Ah, no GNA?"

"Nope."

"They didn't give you one at orientation?"

"You mean the 60-second encounter I just had at that building over there? They barely told me what to do."

"Well, guess that's what I'm here for."

"And you are?"

"G. They let me pick a name. But if we're going by originals, you can call me Genjin."

A pause and a look of shock paralyzed Lania's face. "You don't say."

In the coming days, Lania would find out that life in the ESIC wasn't always so bad. Only when the warden was around did the staff perk up and pay attention. Nightly prayers turned to silence. Playful banter died down. Formalities, generic names, and posturing all of a sudden became the norm. But during those frequent stints when the warden was traveling to anti-intervention regional meetings in Far City or Capital City, the atmosphere at the ESIC relaxed.

That sun pressed its heat, a molten footprint on the campgrounds, draining and drying out the inmates who labored in the fields. The two kitchen staff were not spared either. Radiating heat from the stoves and ovens compounded the heatwave. Lania asked Genjin to write up a service order for the air-conditioning. He held up a handful of tickets.

"Been submitting one every week this summer," he said. "Don't know what's taking them so long. One time Red came in and said they installed a new one. Just had one small manual element."

From beneath the counter, he lifted a piece of paper folded like an accordion, and began fanning himself. "Ahhh, air conditioning," he said with exaggerated relief.

She took a moment to look for any sign of distress or bitter sarcasm on her companion, but there was none. Only the genuine joy of entertaining another human being. His face withered and creased as he fanned in graceful delight. Hair spotted his cheeks and chin, long strands that twitched stiffly in the wind, much like the elusive hair on top of his head that curled and looped like cursive letters, spelling his age.

Meeting Genjin was no coincidence, Lania believed. Their crossing filled her with hope that God was still paying attention to her, and if God's eye was still on her, it must be on the world and on all those who lived under more dire conditions than she. Yes, God was real. How else, out of all the possibilities, would she have met a boy in the City Interrogation Center, speak with him briefly, then end up working alongside his teacher in a prison camp? The providence astounded her, and she believed even more that people are all connected.

Ten days into their friendship and spending large volumes of time with each other on kitchen duty, they each learned some personal details about the other's life.

Lania explained why she chose to become a priest, one of the first women ordained by the Catholic Church. She craved a life, not of solitude, but one of community. In all her romantic relationships before entering the priesthood, she felt a deep solitude, one she could only escape by separating and being alone. A great paradox, she said.

Genjin, a Buddhist, talked to her about his divorce.

"Well, everybody's doing it, these days," he told her.

"But you got divorced thirty years ago," she said.

"I tried. To love. But I guess I'm like you. I love to be in relationships, but with lots of people at the same time."

"Wow, *lots* of people huh?" Lania said, arcing a single eyebrow.

"Oh, no, I don't mean, wait—"

Lania burst out laughing. "I like to make people feel uncomfortable by making them question their moral fiber. Annoying priest habit, I guess."

He smiled back at her like an innocent creature.

Genjin had been in this particular camp for over a year and knew most of the guards by name, and certain ones by badge number. He knew which faces to avoid, which ones to entertain, and which ones practiced religion themselves. It seemed that some of the staff found the ESIC a stepping stone to the Peace Force, with the ultimate goal of becoming an Intervention Force Elite. Then some people just needed work, and they took on lower level security jobs. Others worked at the ESIC in order to be around like-minded folks, and to be decent toward them.

Lania wondered about their futures, if the ESIC was the last stop for her, for him, and for anyone else who was confined in the prison walls.

"Why are you thinking about 'last stops' already?" Genjin

questioned. "You're still young. Well, I'm still young anyway."

"You're older than me," Lania shot back.

"I'm 67. You?"

"Ha! 63."

"Well you act like you're 78, so I think I have you beat."

"What does that even mean, acting like I'm 78? What does a 78 year-old act like? Tell me — I want to know."

"For starters they complain a lot. Think they're younger than they actually are."

"You're kind of an asshole aren't you."

"Them's tough words for a priest."

"Too harsh for your soft ears?"

The banter kept them going. Back and forth they went, and they cooked mac and cheese with steamed broccoli. Again, back and forth while they were plopping scoops on trays and while they washed and put away dishes. Like childhood friends, they went at it. Any outsider wouldn't have guessed that they had just met. Once a guard asked if they were married.

"Friendships form fast when you're old," Genjin responded.

"It's not like you have a lot of time to figure out if you actually like someone," Lania advised. "Gotta just go for it."

"So, the priest likes me, eh?" Genjin smiled and winked. The guard slunk back into his post, blushing.

Lania rolled her eyes. "Wouldn't the monk like to know."

"I'm a Buddhist. Not a monk."

"Too bad," Lania said. "Monks are my type."

They went on and on.

Theresa woke up in her third bed in as many days. Still, the previous night, she managed to sleep well. She woke up pleased, finding peace knowing that August had something to do with her mood. She still harbored resentment for him, but wanted to find a reason to love him again. He wasn't the same idiot she thought he was. Something had changed in him — or her. It began once they looked upon Abraham.

In August's mind, he sought to preserve himself and Theresa. Gaining freedom and potentially locating Abraham. Someday. He lost the boy, and he was determined to be the one who got him back. At least he and Theresa were on the same page.

With minimal effort, August was able to learn that the two of them would be transferred to the ESIC that morning. Three hours north back to Far City to pick up more inmates, then a five hour train ride to the ESIC across the state.

"How did you manage to find out?" Theresa asked him through the bars in her cell.

"It's Portland," he said. "Aaliyah befriended the watch guard last night. He told me. He's like us, or like you. A Godseeker."

"That makes none of us," she reacted. The statement was large and cumbersome for Theresa. She had difficulty wielding the words. August flashed a look of surprise.

"What do you mean, *none* of us? Aren't you the one who risked everything to baptize Abraham?"

She glared at him with hurt and anger.

"I don't mean that in an accusatory way," he softened his previous statement. "I guess I'm just confused. I thought your faith meant everything to you. Now it sounds like you're renouncing it. I mean, are you sure, or are you just mad?"

"Well, I know I'm definitely mad," Theresa whipped. "I also know I'm not ready to talk about it yet. At least not with you."

August nodded and looked away. At one point he was her husband, but that was a different time He didn't explore the possibility of reuniting. It would never work out, he figured, after they got divorced. Her faith and his lack of it doomed their marriage. Even now, as Theresa questioned her own beliefs, August numbed himself to any feelings he may have for her. Friends. That's all they could be now. At least, that's what he told himself.

"Fair enough," he replied. "I guess, if anything, I want you to know that I still care about you. And that's all."

Instantaneously, he changed his mind. He knew — didn't even have to venture to the depths of his heart to know that in saying he cared about her, what he really meant to say was that he loved her and would always love her.

Before the silence hung too long, two IF elites entered the cell block corridor and ushered Theresa and August onto a transport van, along with three other prisoners.

"It's a silent ride, or you get gagged," warned the agent in the passenger seat. "It's that simple."

"Asshole," one said under his breath, but a little too loudly. Theresa was taken aback. She didn't expect a Godseeker to be so bold. The IF agent scoffed as he exited from the passenger seat. The back door of the van abruptly opened, and he pulled the prisoner by the collar and threw him to the ground. Three kicks to the gut, then he opened a storage unit beneath the bench, pulled out a roll of duct tape, and wrapped it around the prisoner's head. One kick to the face. The man was out cold. The agent tossed the unconscious body onto the floor of the van.

"When he wakes up, make sure he's seated just like the rest of you." He inspected the prisoners with his own pools of blue, hovering above a condescending snicker. "Anyone else got something to say?"

Silence. Except August's face. It made no noise, but still spoke volumes. His eyes bulged and he wore an exaggerated frown.

"You? You got something?"

August shook his head frantically like a child who did not want to get in trouble. The agent peered at August for all of ten seconds, but August tilted his head down and fixed his eyes on the floor. He wasn't afraid, but acted as such. He knew the type. The agent wanted to feel powerful, so he let him feel powerful. Pride's not worth an unnecessary beating. Plus that duct tape would hurt coming off.

He was always a man of practicality.

The sun set behind a flat horizon. Trees and water. Somewhere they grew, somewhere the scent of salt and the white noise of waves rolling on the shore filled the air. Lania loved those features of Seattle. Everywhere she looked, there was green, and she couldn't drive for five minutes without a glimpse of a body of water. Here at the ESIC, fields lay dry in the distance and the scorching sun baked the earth beneath her feet. The barracks were hot at dusk, but the cool night air would begin circulating, and it would be cool enough by the time she went to bed.

In the mess hall, she and Genjin prepared two large cauldrons of pasta to feed nearly 300 prisoners and staff housed at the camp. Everyday, they cooked, and they were the last to eat. Then they did the dishes. Most of the time, other inmates would volunteer to help serve the meal, but on particularly long and hot days, the overworked and tired laborers would enter the mess hall and not think twice about solidifying their spot in line. Any food sufficed, as long as it filled the void in their bellies.

No extra hands volunteered to help this evening; the day was extraordinarily hot, and a new order for recycled cardboard had come in from an online retailer.

"Hope you're ready for a busy night," Lania shouted at Genjin. "No one's signed up to help out."

"New faces today," Genjin hollered. "If they arrive in time, Hillman said he'd send them our way."

"New faces? You mean we'll have to train them? We might as well just do this meal ourselves and train them tomorrow when it's supposed to cool down a bit."

"Just have them help serve food. That won't be too complicated, as long as they get the portions right."

"Gotcha," Lania was more opposed to the idea of help than she was to tackling the monumental task alone with her new friend. A sense of self-competition pushed her will to getting it done on their own, but not as much as her growing affection for Genjin. Help would be welcome, but if none came, she wouldn't be upset.

The industrial-sized pots boiled with hot water and salt. Lania and Genjin filled makeshift colanders made of chicken wire — they looked like large crab traps — with penne, hurled it into the pot for about eight minutes, then pulled them out and emptied the contents into serving vats. While the next batch cooked, they poured tomato sauce from a pitcher over the noodles. The vegetables, frozen peas and carrots, had sat at room temperature for an hour. And dessert, well, there was no dessert in the camp, except on rare occasion, Genjin said, when a kind guard would come off a stint of off time and bring in some warehouse-bought cookies.

"Got some help for you!" yelled Hillman, a friendly guard. "Just arrived and we're putting them to work!"

Genjin laughed. "Good, they'll find out real quick we don't waste any time at the ESIC!"

Lania was filling the next colander with bags of pasta when Genjin spun her around to meet the company. She had grown not to expect much from God's plan, especially those obvious blessings when what you want most is delivered right to you. But lately, with the meeting of Daniel and Genjin, she felt as though God was giving her more and more reasons to keep her faith strong.

He had just delivered another.

Looking exhausted from the journey, Theresa's tired eyes found their way into Lania's.

"Let's get to work," Genjin said with unknowing enthusiasm.

Theresa

The farm extended to the west until the leaning stems of corn and wheat blurred into the horizon. To the east, tangled bushes of berries, blue and black, formed orderly lines, the kind that resemble pages laying on top of one another if you drive by fast enough. The north housed the camp, and to the south stood the gate, but the biggest problem of the day came from above. It was fire and weight and air that laid its heavy body on top of all the farm workers and their taskmasters. The tang of salty sweat breached the corners of August's mouth as he pulled and plucked, bending and stretching his muscles as he would when working on a wall canvas. His soft skin snagged, but held remarkably well against the scratch of thorn and jagged leaf. He wasn't used to manual labor, but made no complaint.

Blueberries were the order of the day. Summer stretched on and the green bushes soon colored themselves with bunches of indigo. A bucket full and back was his pattern for the early morning. His command was every ripe berry for five rows of crops and more if he didn't fill twenty buckets that rose just above his knee. The rows extended to an unseen end, and August had to temper efficiency with thorough attention to the bushes he left behind. Should his surveyor find a single ripe blueberry left on the stem, August was told avoiding the consequence was worth meticulous effort.

Demand was great — blueberries were in food fashion, and now that their season had come about, people frenzied at local markets and pastry shops. Neighborhood bars featured blueberry mojitos and other such mixtures to cool the tired tongue after a long day at work.

August remembered going out to happy hour after a long day of painting and wandering about his estate. He'd go with Theresa and a few other friends of hers or his. His favorite drink was a blue mule, stingingly cold in a copper cup with crushed blueberries, vodka, ginger beer, and absinthe. He recalled its flavor, or rather the feeling of the soothing drink and the satisfying smile it produced on his face. That carefree smile.

The memory didn't make him long for freedom. As he rolled his thumb over a cluster of blueberries, an unlikely wonder came about: he wondered whose hand had harvested the fruit in all those blue mules he had enjoyed. The lack of thought about where his food came from was a luxury of freedom and wealth. So many illusions, he realized, because now at the end of his day, only simplicity waited. No alcohol. Not even a single naked blueberry. ESIC protocol deemed them reserved, as in reserved for the paying customer. When the harvest was through, the thousands of pounds of blueberries and apples and grain and barley and cotton would leave the ESIC grounds for those paying customers. A slim portion would remain to feed the prisoners and staff. Nearly all the fruits of his labor would go to another person, somewhere out there in the free metropolis. A person like he used to be, one who would have no idea that the blueberries in his drink of choice came from a prison camp in Eastern State 42.

Tomorrow's calendar called him to pull weeds. He felt more at ease with that task.

———————

At the end of the day, August processed to the mess hall in one of two lines bearing scraped faces and arms, burnt and dusted skin, and weary eyes. But there she was, standing clean and somehow full of radiant beauty with serving tongs in her hands and a net cupping a ball of frenzied black hair behind her head. He smiled at her as she filled his tray with fresh vegetables from the fields, and she would look back at him with a quick and hesitant grin, sparing any eye contact.

He thought about Theresa and his son. Not of the past, but of the future. The past was a forgettable whirlwind of error. He married Theresa too hastily, he understood. Had a child without a plan. But he had always imagined a life with a family. Someday. Someday crept up and sat under his nose for a good long while, too long for him to realize that Theresa and Abraham were all he ever dreamed of. That his art must become secondary, and so must his independence, because now he was depended upon.

Such were his musings under the body of the sun throughout the day, and he dragged them into the mess hall behind him, hoping Theresa wouldn't notice. Being around his former wife, he remembered her drive and her selflessness — her voice, that lovely voice he fell for at the youth shelter in Far City. Theresa cared for others, not just herself, not just him, not just for her child, but for everyone. This was why he fell in love with her. *A wealth of love*, he thought. *Richer than I'll ever be.*

Even though God wasn't a part of his life, God was the root of everything he loved about her. That day in the Portland Intervention Force Headquarters, what she said about her faith worried August. A fundamental pillar of Theresa's life had crumbled in tragedy, and for her, his heart broke. At the same time, guilt amassed and sat in his stomach like a bucket. A bucket of useless fruit he would never have the joy of tasting. He wouldn't have survived unless his purpose stood right in front of him at the end of each day, putting steamed vegetables on his lunch tray. Now, her purpose was in doubt, and he worried.

No. It was definitely not the past that occupied his mind. Not now that she was in front of him. That past would reflect only shame. *Why did I take my son to that daycare,* he asked himself. How he wished he could uproot and dispose of that shame. It planted itself deeper than any weed. He bowed his head as he passed Theresa and found a seat with his farming cohort.

Night's curtain pulled back and dawn greeted the ESIC. Theresa had volunteered with Lania and Genjin almost everyday until she convinced the ESIC Assignment Coordinator that a third hand in the kitchen was necessary. It was the only time and place she could catch up with Lania since they resided in separate barracks. They had spent the last week exchanging stories, with Genjin being a fly on the wall for most of their discussion. He listened to their conversation, piecing together as much of the story as he could. Lania took note of his interest and made sure to color in some context.

"Oh no. He *didn't.*" Lania needed a moment to believe that August would actually take Abraham to Anna's Ladybug Daycare, knowing full well that the child and Theresa were fugitives. Theresa shook her head and sprayed another tray clean, then continued her story. Lania's feelings of providence swelled when Theresa got to the part about Daniel.

"He found you," Lania said with a fleeting feeling of relief. "Well, I guess you ended up here anyway. He was adamant about finding you. We only spoke a few times in the City Interrogation Center before they released him. I bet they released him to —"

Theresa knew immediately where Lania had stopped speaking, and where she was going. Intervention Force followed Daniel. Probably knew about Marcel, probably about Tyriq. Probably knew about every detail about their lives.

"It's not his fault Theresa — I should have been more careful. I should have told him —"

"It's no one's fault, Lania," Theresa said. "At least none of ours. Not yours, not Daniel's. Not even August's. They've taken one thing after another from me. From you — from all of us."

"And what about God, Theresa? Did *they* take God from you as well?"

Theresa shut down. Leave it to her friend to go straight for the jugular. She took the scrappiest tray in the stack and began spraying and scrubbing vigorously, pretending that Lania hadn't asked the question. Dried rice had caked on and stuck to the tray. Theresa dug in with her nails. It wouldn't budge. Harder she scratched, her muscles tensing until finally the residue gave way, jutting under her fingernail and causing blood to trickle from behind her fingertip. Another distraction. Finally she turned to Lania who was still engaged with the question, but hadn't said a word. She was good at that.

"It's okay, honey," Lania said.

"I know I just need a bandaid and —"

"Oh, I know your finger will be fine. I'm talking about how you feel. About God. We all have reason to be upset. I am too."

Lania's advice strayed from the path Theresa expected it would take. Theresa expected a pep talk. A 'don't give up the faith' monologue.

Not approval of her damaged faith. But like Tyriq, Lania expressed only openness to her struggle.

"I thought out of everyone, you'd be the most disappointed that I'm mad at God."

"You know how close I am to your father, Theresa."

Her dad and Lania were childhood friends whose relationship transcended transition, distance, disagreement and heartbreak. It's why they would spend so much time together, why Lania wasn't just a priest, but a family friend.

"I remember when your mother died. He lost his faith in God, for a good long time. And I was right there with him. Your mother was a beautiful woman, not just in appearances, but in the way she treated others. She had a way of making you feel like every word you said mattered. Had a way of making you feel loved, even if she had just met you. You're more like her than you could imagine, Theresa. Not everyone has that gift. In fact more people are better at making you feel inferior when you first meet them. Feels like that anyway, these days."

Theresa's memory of her mother was spotty. She was barely in kindergarten when she died. The moments were far removed, and so few, but they were vivid. She knew exactly what Lania was talking about. Her mother, Daisy, was aptly named. A name that would have survived the Generic Name Act all on its own. A name consistent with the flower, flourishing and bright.

"She was good for your father, and she accepted and trusted me to be a part of your lives."

"Trusted?" Theresa asked.

"He never mentioned to you, and I suppose for good reason. Your father and I were high school sweethearts. We loved each other very much. But I — I couldn't — I couldn't commit to him — I had other ideas." Lania looked wistfully at the floor and took a shaky breath. "When he was murdered, I felt much like you probably feel now. I was angry. Angry with society, angry with government, but also angry with God. I wondered why, just like everyone else when we are unexpectedly separated from something we love. But I kept on going through the motions of being a priest. Some of the worst preaching of my life."

"Well, you hid it pretty well," Theresa said.

"I guess. I kept up a front for my community. They needed me, and they didn't abandon me like I thought God did when Abram was killed. But then I began to see it again."

"Dad?"

"*God.* I started to remember why my community came together. We all shared the same faith. Had the same acceptance of one another. The same values. Love one another. Serve those less fortunate. We all centered our lives around God. That's why we were together, and why I was so close to your father, and why I am so close to you."

Lania's story made Theresa dwell on her own struggle. Yes, Lania found God again, but she herself had not reached that point. Not yet. Too many people, too much love shattered. Couldn't God have spared her one family member?

"You'll find what you need, Theresa," Lania reassured her friend. "You're a strong woman. A loving woman. You've lost so many, but you haven't lost everyone."

She hugged Theresa tightly as August entered the kitchen.

Theresa

No one had shown up to volunteer in the kitchen over the past few days. The perpetual heatwave cranked itself up to 110 degrees, and the kitchen sizzled. The staff served only cold foods; Lania made the stoves and ovens off limits. But a new face greeted Genjin in the early afternoon, about an hour before volunteers usually showed up.

"Can I help you?" Genjin asked. It was August's inaugural visit to the kitchen.

"I'm here to help out before dinner," August said. "Finished my harvest quota a bit early today."

"An hour early? Either you're a superhuman or maybe fifteen minutes away from getting caught." Genjin surveyed August's arms, scraped and still perspiring.

"I just got it done," August shrugged.

"And you want to volunteer in the kitchen instead of taking an hour off at the camp spa?"

It took August a moment to process Genjin's sarcasm, a moment long enough for Genjin to pour and hand him a glass of water.

"Gonna need a few of these," the old man suggested. "If the warden doesn't murder you, the heat will."

The cold water shocked the back of August's throat, and he drank the frigid liquid so fast his head stung. Adrenaline carried him through the day. He needed to talk to Theresa. Volunteering to help in the kitchen may have been suspicious — Genjin was right that no field worker with a clear head would give a second to an extra task. But Theresa was worth it, and even more so, he had some important news for her.

She stood on the opposite end near the dishwasher where her frazzled hair and clothes mimicked the anxiety running around her insides. Since the Portland EFHQ, he had not once seen her smile or even portray a semblance of normal. Melancholy sculpted itself in her eyes, mouth, cheeks.

He stepped cautiously in her direction. Lania recognized him first and stepped aside, indicating that Genjin had needed her help with... something.

August didn't get too close, afraid that Theresa may still harbor negative feelings toward him. He would never forgive himself for signing in Abraham at Anna's Ladybug Daycare, but that night in the Portland EFHQ had given him enough confidence to start rebuilding his relationship with Theresa. He had seen her just about everyday at mealtime, but had no opportunity to converse with her. All he knew was that she was far from happiness, and he was part of the reason why.

"Wanna get out of here?" he started with an awkward smile.

Theresa rolled her eyes then shot him a cold look.

"That's not what I mean —" August backtracked, giggling and reaching for Theresa as she spun away. "Look, I'm here for two reasons. You want out of here? Out of the ESIC? That's what I meant to say."

"To wind up back here or run around out there as a kill-on-sight?"

237

Theresa snapped before taking a breath and recomposing herself. "I'm tired, August, and being back here with Lania has been good for me."

"Has it? I know you've found Lania, but I also know a part of you is out there in the world, and that's all you've been thinking about for the last month."

He was right. Abraham could be anywhere in the country by now, but one place he made permanent residence was in the forefront of Theresa's mind. The boy accompanied her with every rising sun, every action and interaction, every breath — there was the face of her baby.

Weariness consumed her, and to a degree, she was established. Worn by time and trampled by a force she could not overcome, Theresa leaned on the kitchen counter, deflated. She felt like she had given up. It had only been six weeks. Even if an escape was possible, she would have no idea where to start if she got out. Every aspect of her life had disintegrated in the last month. She wouldn't dare contact her friends or even distant family — that would only put them in danger. No. Her only hope was to dream of slow-cooked progress, think about her son everyday, and serve food in the ESIC mess hall. Perhaps the pain and longing will go away someday, she thought, and the thought made her tear up at its own absurdity. She faced a poverty of possibility. The only moments she could afford were spent in the kitchen with Lania and Genjin. Comfortable moments. Easy ones. But without Abraham, they were empty ones.

August was right. Abraham had never left her mind or her heart.

"You've given up?" August said, unaware of Theresa's internal monologue. "You'll never find Abraham from behind the gates of a concentration camp."

His challenge shook her. Jolted her back to reality, to the Portland

EFHQ where she said she would do anything to see her son again. She loved the work of the kitchen because it was constant and had nothing to do with a plan. A plan that appeared less and less favorable to the lure of menial routine. August had a point, however. If there was a chance, even a small one, to reunite with Abraham, she would risk her life — spend its entirety — pouring all her blood, sweat and tears to make it happen. Only, she wondered if she had any left to spend.

"What then?" she blurted.

"Some of the guards in the field are just like you — Godseekers. Did you know that? Some of these guards don't even care if you pray. Guess you just gotta know which ones are friendly and which ones will whack you with a baton."

"I noticed, and Genjin pointed it out to me. There are friendly guards. So what? They gonna bust us out of here? Set us up with a getaway car? Give us a ride to freedom?"

"Well, partly. They'll get *you* out. The ride is already coming. It's Aaliyah and your new friends. They'll be in this area within the next few days. The plan is for you to get out of here tonight. That's why I'm here. Well, one reason anyway. Oh, and Aaliyah and Tyriq, they have traced Abraham's location. He's still in Far City."

"They found him," she said in disbelief. "How do you know all this?"

"Like I said. The guards are friendly. No time for hows. You need to —"

Theresa caught her friend in the corner of her eye. "Wait — what about Lania?"

"I'm sorry Theresa, but the plan only works for one of us. It has to be you, and you have to get Abraham back. I know you will."

She rested on an uncertain pause. What about Lania? What about

239

August? What about Genjin, for whom she developed an affinity and recognized Lania's affection for him extending beyond a simple friendship. What about everyone else in the camp?

"I know what you're thinking, Theresa. You always think of others. I love that about you," August said, stepping closer to Theresa. "Why are we in here? Why is Lania in here? It's for Abraham, and now he's in their custody. If any of our sacrifices meant anything, we have to get him back. Think of our son, Theresa."

Theresa stared into that long thought. That dubious decision. She'd made many in the last several weeks. None of them to her gain. All of them to her loss, she believed. She felt a closeness to the most hopeless characters in the Bible. Often, she thought of Job, the man who lost everyone and everything, yet somehow retained his faith. A better person than she, Theresa conceded. She barely had the chance to get her footing on life at the camp, let alone consider her faith beyond her evening prayers with Hadeeqah and Lania. Now an escape plan? Maybe God was reaching out again, giving her a means. Maybe she could believe one more time. If anything, there was absolutely nothing left for her to lose.

"Okay," she said. "What do I have to do?"

"A new crop of inmates arrives tonight from Portland. One of the field guards has been coordinating with Aaliyah and the two doublers who will be transporting them. When the new inmates arrive, you'll be leaving with them under pretensive recall to the Far City Interrogation Center," August explained. "They have official orders to extract a prisoner, but the name on the orders has been changed to yours. After they take you out of here, you'll rendezvous at Mountain Town 32 with your friends. That part, the transporters do not know, and you have to relay that to them. Just in case they get found out, they won't be able to divulge the meeting point via eternatae. Three days, though. Mountain Town 32 — about 100 miles away. After that, your search for Abraham begins."

It all sounded so easy. An escape where she wouldn't have to sneak around, but doubling transporters would simply pluck her from captivity and bring her to freedom. The doorway to the kitchen burst open. A guard. Not a friendly one. Genjin and Lania tried to signal August and Theresa to no avail. The man rumbled across the kitchen like an agitated animal, rattling the kitchen counters as he stomped by. A bull, he had his eyes set on August, who upon noticing the beast closing in, widened his own eyes and wore his panic on the hairs of his flesh.

"Oh shit," he whispered in an exhale.

"Oh shit is right," the man's voice hammered. He grabbed August by the collar. "Putting rocks in your harvest containers? You're going to the yard. Then it's the shed for you."

The yard and the shed made Theresa think of an old horror film. Tearing through the yard only to find a shed where the victim would be slaughtered. The guard yanked August away and barked at the three others to get back to work. He gave the back of August's knees a swift kick, causing him to collapse to the floor, then he bound his wrists and ankles before pulling him up and gusting out the door. Theresa couldn't handle it. She ran to him and shouted.

"August!" she cried. The guard unexpectedly offered a moment for a final interaction. "Is there another reason?" she whispered in his ear.

He only looked at her with a broken longing, one past due. The guard jerked him out of the kitchen.

"You," he exhaled to himself as the forceful hand shoved him back out into the heat of the sun. "The other reason was you."

Theresa took a stack of clean trays to the front of the food line where Genjin and Lania stood.

"What's going to happen to August?"

Genjin let out a heaving sigh as he lifted a serving bin of rice and placed it on the distribution counter.

"You'll find out any moment now," he said. And right on cue, an all call over the public address system blared in the kitchen.

All prisoners, report to the yard immediately.

Theresa and Lania shared confused looks. Genjin shook his head, covered the rice, still steaming hot from the pot, and headed for the exit.

"C'mon," he said. "It's best not to dilly dally when they call us to attendance."

In a haste, Theresa put down another stack of trays and Lania put the evening's dinner on hold. They scurried after Genjin who was already out the kitchen door, but waiting for them in the main hall. He wouldn't make eye contact. His sloped forehead tilted downward and before Theresa could ask again, Genjin turned and started walking briskly toward the yard.

Outside, the prisoners were already accumulating. The yard was a large open space, scattered with sun-crisped grass and bent over dandelions. The dirt was a fine powder clouding the scene in the middle of the docile crowd who formed a semi-circle and appeared as though they were preparing to watch a night of theatre in the park. After the dust had cleared, Theresa saw him. August already bound to a post with three guards attending to him, each holding a club of a different nature. One was a heavy steel, another had a sharp grater-like texture, and the last glowed with the white light of an electric charge.

"They're going to beat him publicly?" Theresa whispered in Genjin's ear.

"Shhh!" he snapped back.

She wanted to leave. *I don't want to watch this*, she thought. But that was the point. To remind prisoners every so often that even in the comfort of the ESIC where some guards might be lenient, there were those who were barbarous, and no time was a good time to cheat on your work, or break any other rule. August gave them an opportunity. His ruse cost him dearly, and now the whole camp had to watch.

The last trickle of inmates made their way into the semi-circle, and the guard with the electric baton stepped toward the front center. He wore a full uniform, long pants and long sleeves, and not a drop of sweat accumulated on his forehead.

"In case you forgot," he began without amplification. He didn't need it; his bellowing voice was a booming scream at the ESIC body, and he glared from left to right like a jaguar. He towered monstrously above the other guards. "You don't *fucking* cheat your quotas! You do as you're told. Or this."

At once the guards with the steel and the serrated club began striking August who yawped and writhed and winced and wailed. The sounds he made extended his pain to the gut of every prisoner in attendance. Theresa couldn't watch. She closed her eyes and turned away, but then herself was struck by one of several guards in the audience. It was a soft blow, and she looked up and saw that it was Hillman, a decent man, the one who directed her to the kitchen on her first day at the camp. She looked into his eyes — his face was stern and cold, all except for his eyes. His eyes were forlorn. August's pain reached him as well.

"Look," he said, firmly with a vulnerable reverb. It was his job. Just like it was the job of every other guard cycling through the crowd, en-suring that the terror of the yard was absorbed in its entirety.

Just beyond the scene was a line of small boxes made of dark metal. Small slits at the roof allowed air to flow inside. Each box was too small to be an outhouse, but large enough to fit — to fit what, Theresa won-dered. Storage from the field's harvest? Tools? At the long stretch of the afternoon it had to be 200 degrees in there. And why would they put it —

Theresa nearly threw up when she realized what she was describing in her head. Each one was a tiny metal shed.

Theresa

A kind of mud formed around August's body — pools of his blood and sweat meshed with the ground, and the residues that streaked along his limbs and torso made his skin resemble granite. He was unconscious and his eyes swelled shut. Two guards, formal and stone-faced, marched on either side of him, dragging the living corpse to the nearest of the five sheds. They stuffed August's body in the capsule, and he contorted, groaned and then breathed. Now flanking the shed, the guards surveyed the crowd still gathered in the yard, the metal door wide open so all could see the living thing curled up in the shed. The man with the full uniform approached the scene, satisfied at the terror and unblinking awe of the inmates at attention.

"This is the shed," he spoke in a collected voice. Every prisoner strained their ears. Many of them had never seen the shed used, or the yard posts, during their tenure at camp. Genjin and a few other longtime inmates had witnessed an identical scene only once. "You cheat. You disobey. You step out of line —" The last word hung on his theatrics as he turned his back and slammed the door shut, punctuating his warning. A heavy double latch lock clanged into position, reverberating on the skin of the audience. No one turned an eye from his. Then he and the two guards at the front filed away, leaving the crowd to survey the five sheds. They stood there in the late afternoon sun, still burning high enough in the horizon to draw sweat and consciousness. And there, they felt a heavy thirst stacked on top of their weariness from the day. Hunger, shortness of breath, and the utter terror of the last thirty minutes captivated them. But not a single complaint.

The one occupied shed made certain of that.

Another thirty minutes transpired when the tower of a man returned to the front of the field, this time appearing more relaxed. A proud close-lipped smile stretched into his folded cheek.

"Enjoy the show?" he asked. "Back to work. An extra hour. Go."

The prisoners sauntered back to their stations while some of the guards commanded a faster pace. One had a whip in his hand and lashed into the crowd, and the people scattered like a startled school of fish.

Except Theresa. Her attention froze on the small enclosure that surrounded August. The configuration perplexed her. How will he move, once he awakens? He couldn't spread out his arms and legs — there was not enough room in either direction. Leaning against a wall would be horrid, as it would burn his skin. Sitting straight up, standing, or lying down curled in the fetal position would be his options. Maybe he'd sleep through it all, she hoped. The night may be tolerable, but the next day's wave of heat put her stomach in a blender.

He was in there for one reason. To make sure she knew she was getting out that night and where to direct the transport. He was in that shed, making good on his promise — to do anything he could, not just for Theresa, but to get Abraham back. Just like he said in Portland.

She finally looked away and went back toward the mess hall, where Genjin and Lania were already entering the complex. She swiftly made her way back inside and found Lania profusely weeping on Genjin's shoulder.

Theresa floated in their direction like a ghost.

"I am getting him out," she said with calculation and surety.

Lania looked through her tears and Genjin shook his head.

"How Theresa?" he wondered as he stirred the rice and added water to the dried grains. "Since I've been here, that was the most gruesome thing I've ever seen. They're not taking these things lightly. Not any-more."

"I don't care!" Theresa nearly shrieked, but caught herself and re-peated the statement immediately in a whisper. "He's in there because of me. *For* me. I'm going to get him out of there."

Genjin sighed.

"What do you mean he's in there because of you?" Lania asked. "What did he tell you when he visited?"

Theresa spied around, saw no one, but was still paranoid. "He came to tell me something I need to know."

She was getting used to the secrecy game. Don't tell even her friends the plan, only that there was one, lest the guards use the truth serum to pull the information from them. In her case, she was prepared to take the rendezvous location to the grave if she had to, only to protect her friends.

Then she took inventory. The only other person who knew the ren-dezvous point was August. They could use eternatae on him and he'd —

Slowly, in front of Lania and Genjin, it all made sense to her. They would not have the opportunity to use eternatae on August. She had been thinking about this since staring at the shed in puzzlement. He won't make it. He won't last the day tomorrow. In the heat. They would give him water. Would he refuse it? Did he mean to kill himself before then? She didn't know how he would do it, or even if he meant to do it. The only conclusion she could draw was that she needed to get August out of that God forsaken shed, and out of the ESIC.

Genjin and Lania didn't ask anymore questions. They both knew that with less information circulating, everyone would be safer. Instead they continued preparing dinner for their neighbors who would be starving for the late meal, especially after a punitive hour of work. Lania snuck in extra portions.

Theresa did her best to help, but her mind was pulled in all directions, anticipating a guard or two to show up at any minute to take her away. Her feelings for August engulfed her mind, even more than her hunger, which pained her stomach. She couldn't let him die, and didn't intend to let that happen. But how? How could she get that door of the shed to open? How could she pull him from those walls, the walls of the ESIC, the walls of Freespeak, to freedom? Getting him out the shed was the first step. At any cost.

"Genjin," she said, as an idea struck her. "What will they do to you if you're caught praying in here? I mean, by a guard who actually cares."

"They'll kill you," he responded. "Probably on sight. What they did to August — that had nothing to do with AFLs."

Theresa nodded, and Lania caught the gesture.

"No way," the priest sailed in. "No Theresa, whatever it is. You can't

248

get yourself killed. Abraham. *Abraham.* Honey, he's still out there. And you — don't — just — I need you. I need you to *live.*"

"I know. Don't think on it any more. Please. You've got to trust me."

In the kitchen utility drawer, Theresa found a pad of paper and a pen and began writing intensely.

Masses of exhausted workers filed into the cafeteria. Genjin and Theresa served while Lania thoughtfully prepared additional rations. By the end of dinner, all the food was gone despite Lania's extra helpings and the kitchen staff was turning away hungry bellies.

Theresa didn't eat. Every so often, her hand would slide into her pocket to confirm that the piece of notepaper with her writing hadn't fallen to the ground. She pulled her hand out, careful to push the paper deep in her pocket as she did. August engulfed her thoughts and she wondered if she could sneak him some food, just wedge it through one of the slits in the wall of the shed. Then again, she wondered if he would even be conscious to receive it. Her concern for him was overshadowed only by the fact that the transport to take her from the ESIC had not yet arrived. She grew anxious, and every time someone passed the window of the kitchen, she looked up expecting to see a uniformed Intervention Force guard moving in her direction.

But no one showed up. The three cleaned the kitchen and prepped it for the next morning. Still no sign. Theresa went back to her barracks, showered and readied herself for bed. She sat up on her mattress, eyes shifting to the window every minute. No one.

Hadeeqah leaned over her bedside, and Theresa's anxiety softened. The smile was absent from the Muslimina's face, replaced with solemn grimness. But not despair. Despair had never sewn itself into

Hadeeqah's countenance or the tone of her voice when she prayed. She was living hope, Theresa decided. If she was to miss anything about her experience at the ESIC, it was her shared moments with Hadeeqah at the end of each day. She pondered what would become of her friend, of Lania and Genjin too. In spite of their situation, none of them adopted despair.

"I will pray for you tonight," Hadeeqah said, then the smile returned before she rolled back on her bed.

The full moon cast a white light on Theresa's bed with a sharp brightness that singed her eyes as she stared at it. She reached in her pocket and held in her hand the folded up piece of paper she had prepared before dinner. She needed her own escape plan to initiate. The transporters would be part of the plan as well.

The day's exhaustion lay heavy on Theresa's consciousness, and she slid onto her back, her eyelids no longer willing to keep watch. Even the thought of August couldn't prevent her from slipping into slumber and into a dream. He was there, though, in her imagination. It was a good dream. The two of them were in a cabin, warm in front of a fire beneath a winter's snowfall. The flurries spun and whisked downwards and upwards, the wind howled, but inside the cabin the joyful mood of Christmas music and dinner filled the air. They sat, separated on the couch, and there with them was Abraham.

The two of them talked about leaving Far City and moving somewhere in the middle of the country. It would have to be near a river though. No lakes, she said. She had had enough of lakes. She wanted a river. Or the ocean, August suggested. The Islands of Hawai'i were still an American territory, but they did not observe the American Freedom Laws. Their connection to the gods and goddesses of the earth was too powerful to be overturned by legislation.

He leaned into her arms and she held him. He spoke of the heat and how relaxing it was, and the rhythm of the ocean's waves. They mused about their future as if the past had never happened. And that was all. The extent of her dream was just the two of them talking in comfort with their infant child in the living room, and all was as it should be. And she drifted off, releasing the folded piece of paper from her grasp.

A squeeze on Theresa's shoulder woke her. Abruptly, she quaked into consciousness, immediately snatching the small piece of paper she had released as she fell asleep. She stirred with relief to see that a guard had finally come to pull her for extraction. At least that was the hope. Over every encounter with a Freespeak official hung a stench of paranoia. She had to appear clueless as to what was going on, and in fact, she had no idea of what was about to happen. For all she knew, the plan could be thwarted, and this guard could be taking her to be neighbors with August.

"Let's go," the guard said, urging her off the mattress.

An interlude of groggy sounds escaped Theresa's mouth, and she rose with her wrists together, waiting to be cuffed.

"No cuffs," she was told. "Just come with me."

The guard's voice was light and airy and her hair hung like a black mirror, straight, silky and shiny. Her brown skin in the moonlight was the color of raw sugar crystals, spotted with moles among her smiling eyes. She smiled with her lips as well, and Theresa felt at ease.

"Rivera," the guard said. "That's my name. But I assume you know not to call me that around here."

Theresa nodded. Knowing her name also calmed Theresa.

251

"You're going to be extracted for further interrogation in Far City."

Theresa nodded again, still half asleep.

Rivera pulled her close. "Hey, you gotta wake up. You can't let on that you know what's happening to you. Come on."

Adrenaline zapped Theresa into awareness. She nodded once more. "Okay. Got it."

Rivera led the way and Theresa stumbled to keep up. They were headed toward the ESIC's administrative office. The camp appeared remarkably peaceful in the light of the full moon.

The two of them walked. Past the other barracks. Past the mess hall. Past the field. Then past the sheds. One, two, three, four, and one left. Rivera was a good five paces ahead, and even though she seemed friendly, Theresa didn't want to get her in trouble. This was her chance. With a clear shot at the air hole in the roof of the last shed, she removed the paper from her pocket and crumpled it into a ball. A simple five foot jumpshot. Just like throwing away a scrap in middle school. Just like tossing a coffee cup in the recycling repository. All those years practicing with the Heathland Seagulls basketball team were finally going to mean something.

She approached.

The shot was up.

She said a prayer.

The paper wad hung in the air, then bounced off the roof of the shed, rolling forward on the ground. Theresa panicked, but fortunately, the ball landed in front of her so her progress was not impeded. One more shot. She past the shed and put up the shot as she faded away toward the ESIC office. Another prayer. She knew immediately that the shot was skewed. It landed on the roof of the shed, just short of the air slit.

Theresa bent her head up to the sky. Frustrated with herself, she could only hope that the note would not be found. But of course it would be found. There were no other scraps of paper anywhere around the field. It would stand out, at least in the morning, like a lily in a field of dirt.

It's not like she signed the paper. And with any luck they wouldn't find it until morning when she would be halfway to Far City. Or Mountain Town 32.

She turned and gave one last look at the shed. The ball of paper was still on the roof, and the moonlight bounced off its white fibers, causing it to glow. An asterisk, calling to attention a scheme.

Rivera was now a good ten paces ahead of Theresa, but did not look back. Negligence was more favorable than collusion. Theresa stretched her stride and quickened her pace. It wouldn't look good for Rivera to be so far from her prisoner, and by the time they reached the ESIC office, she was right behind.

As they ascended the steps to the main door, a brisk breeze whipped the pair in the face. Rivera's glimmering black hair waved in the wind and the moonlight shimmered off the strands like a reflection in the water. Theresa's knotted locks twitched and hopped.

"Brr!" Rivera said. "Better enjoy the cold now. It's gonna be a hot one tomorrow."

Theresa administered a fake giggle and felt all the more sympathy for August. Meanwhile, August himself awoke from the gentle wind and the tap of a small crumpled up piece of paper on his forehead. A curiosity, he thought as he unfolded the wad. The moon shone through the opening of the shed, just enough for him to read Theresa's handwriting.

Theresa

A harsh fluorescent light drilled through Theresa's head and its beams were amplified by the bright white laminate walls in the windowless room where she was contained. Claustrophobia made her queasy, but she kept imagining the shed immuring August, and thusly her holding tank became a suite by way of perspective.

Rivera dropped her off not fifteen minutes before the door opened, and Theresa was escorted out by a familiar guard, whose name she didn't know. She recognized him as the one who held the serrated club in the yard. As he grasped her arm, her bicep fibrillated, causing him to grip her tightly and yank her arm behind her back so he could bind her wrists.

At the door stood Rivera and a third officer, an older man with a black and white goatee. Theresa wondered if he was with Rivera or the ESIC. She had never seen him before, but it wasn't as if she had inventory on the prison staff.

All four of them exited the building. Theresa inhaled the outside air, cool in the settling of the night, and it refreshed her. Some kind of hope filled her as she inhaled, one that she trusted, and she hadn't trusted a hope in a good long while. She carefully hid the hope from her face. In fact, she looked at the ground, tilting her head so low that her hair covered the sides of her face, though she peeked at the roof of the shed, then the ground surrounding it. No sign of the wad of paper.

The group approached August's shed. If by some miracle the wad of paper made its way into his hands, the time was now. Like a needle stitching her plan together, the wind picked up again, feeding an allergen into the nostril of the ESIC guard who cuffed her, and he let out a strident sneeze.

Inside the shed, August read that as his cue. He waited a prolonged moment, then began.

"Hail Mary!" he shouted.

"The fuck?" the ESIC guard said.

"Full of grace!" August continued. "The Loooooord is with thee!"

The ESIC guard broke from the troop and marched toward the shed. From his utility belt, he removed a baton — unserrated — and struck the steel of the shed, clanging painfully loud. The noise shocked August into momentary silence, but he persevered.

"*Blessed* art thou among women, and *blessed* is the fruit of thy womb, *JESUUUUS!*"

He knew just which words to emphasize. The ESIC guard became enraged. Completely ignoring the convoy, he sprung to the door of the shed, swung it open, and dragged August out under the moonlight.

"Holy Mary, *Mother of God*," he said those last three words directly into the guard's eyes with a pointed disregard and disgust.

"You're going to die for this," the guard said. "No harm in starting a little early." And with that, a blow to August's face. And another. Again and again.

Weary on the ground August muttered between kicks to his

stomach. "Pray for us – sinners — now — and at the hour — of our — death."

Then the officer with the black and white beard aggressively pulled the ESIC guard away from August.

"What the —" the guard said.

"Don't speak to me without respect," the man said. "I'll have you released. Without severance." Then he turned his attention toward August, squatting next to his broken body. He turned August over, revealing a grinning blob of dirt and spit.

"He's right, you know," the man said to August. "You are going to die."

Theresa kept her head down.

"But he's not your toy," he looked at the ESIC guard. "He's coming with us."

"What for?" the guard asked, confused.

"He'll be publicly executed in Far City. The SCO will carry it out on live stream. He'll be an example to all the bapticks who are still out there.

"Pick him up," he ordered the ESIC guard. "Shouldn't be too much trouble from the looks of him."

Back in the ESIC office, Theresa and August were placed in holding cells while the latter's transfer got processed. The moonlight had shifted its angle, but still managed to illuminate the room, enough for Theresa's eyes to adjust.

The cells were adjacent, but she withheld any look in August's direction. August was incapable of exerting such effort. His eyes were shut, his body a pile of bones on the floor, his skin a punctured sack. He

256

knew about Theresa's exit. He knew who was picking her up. And he knew he had just joined the party. Somehow, Theresa had orchestrated his extraction. It was her scratched and fluid writing on that sheet of paper on which was the prayer to the Mother of God. With all his knowledge and the luxury of a more spacious cell, he stretched his limbs, then curled back up into a ball, falling asleep before he could think another thought.

Theresa, on the other hand, was wide awake, enthralled that August had received her message and hopeful that he had ripped it into a hundred pieces and buried it in the dirt. He must have memorized the prayer, she thought, and her mind again filled with all sorts of mysteries. Why did August risk everything to tell her of the escape? Could no one else relay the message? Was there no contact between Aaliyah and the transport? Why did *she* herself have to be the only one who knew about Mountain Town 32?

Trying to figure out the plan kept her preoccupied as she tried not to pay attention to August, but she couldn't not look at him. First her eyes, then her head turned to the man she once loved. She saw him sound asleep and she was pleased. If anyone deserved to be sleeping deeply and peacefully at this moment, it was him. His sacrifice gifted her with an opportunity for freedom, and yes, made her love him again. He was not fighting so much for his rights, or even to reclaim Abraham. He fought for her. Fought for her love. He was doing everything he could to get her to love him again. At least that was how she saw it. Because as she looked upon him, satisfied at his state of comfort, pleased at how her own plan was panning out, she realized that he was winning the fight. That she was falling in love with him once again. His was a love that she needed more than anything right now. It was immediate, proximate, and genuine. And she wasn't about to let the Freespeakers take that away from her. Not again.

The lights came on, and this time, only the bearded man and Rivera entered the room. Both Theresa and August's cells were opened.

"Follow us," Rivera said to Theresa, as she and the officer stooped to inspect August. "Blue, we're going to need to lay out some covers in the van. He's pretty messed up. Blood all over the place."

"Let's see if we can't clean him first," replied Blue, scratching his goatee. "You're right. Can't have all this blood."

The guard who beat August had been replaced. It was Hillman. Theresa breathed yet another soft sigh of relief. Blue and Rivera both seemed decent. They were doublers. They had to be. A sense of security eased her mind, but she wouldn't allow herself to enjoy it fully. There was still no room for trust without ample time.

"Here, why don't you just wait a little longer while we try to get this guy cleaned up," Rivera told Theresa, who backtracked into the cell.

Half an hour later, Rivera picked up Theresa and escorted her to the van where Hillman and Blue were helping August into the prisoner's cabin. He was seated, chained, and then Theresa followed suit. The transport was similar to the one that had taken her to the ESIC weeks ago. Eight seats total, all with appropriate restraints and a supplies kit. Theresa imagined this ride would start off much more pleasantly than her first voyage across the state. No batons and no duct tape.

Rivera and Blue entered the front of the van. Their seatbelts clicked. The engine started. They were off. Just like that. Theresa could hardly believe it. It all seemed so easy. But after the yard and the shed, even if Rivera and Blue were taking them to a new circle of hell, she figured it couldn't be much worse. Famous last thoughts.

A slit in the front wall slid open about thirty minutes after the van started moving.

"Are you familiar with this part of the state?" Blue asked. Theresa assumed he was addressing her since August had drifted back out of consciousness.

"No actually, I've never been out here," Theresa said.

"That so? Well, I guess we'll just have to keep moving toward Far City then."

Then Theresa picked up on the hint.

"Well, I had an aunt," she fabricated. "Estranged from our family. My dad said she moved to Mountain Town 32, but that was years ago. 'S around here, I think."

"As a matter of fact, it is," Blue said, shutting the sliding panel.

Theresa

The term 'Martyr' had gained traction in certain circles of Godseekers. Daniel would throw the title around whenever he had the chance, which happened rarely. Marcel rebuked him.

"Don't call us that," he would say to the boy. "The movement should simply *be*. It doesn't need a name. Just like religion."

Daniel sat at the edge of his bed, leg bouncing like a piston. He, Marcel, Tyriq and Aaliyah would soon crowd into a small shuttle van and head for the rural town where they would rendezvous with Theresa and August. Two people to rescue, one for the second time. The teenager felt a sense of accomplishment and pride.

His role exhilarated him. Over the last year, he had worked with Marcel to support doublers who wedged their way into anti-interventionist enforcement. *Handlers*, they were called, unofficially, and Daniel looked to the title as a badge of honor.

Heavy on Daniel's conscience lay his failure to save Abraham before the Intervention Force abducted the baby. He also felt the sting of Theresa choosing to hand herself over to the authorities. She had no choice, and that was a problem. Now, Daniel would begin collecting the scattered pieces of each failed mission, and put them back together.

Marcel tried his best to instill a sense of realism. "We are not trained agents," he said. "Just everyday people tired of turning the other cheek." Even though Marcel had been handling Godseekers for years, he was no pro at working the system, which constantly changed. New rules, heavier sentences, and extended branches of enforcement made it hard to keep up. He and Daniel used what information they found to help Godseekers under duress.

Today was a big day to that end. Extracting a person from a Freedom Law camp presented an unprecedented challenge for everyone in the group — an act with real martyr potential if anything went wrong. Daniel continued bouncing on the springs of his mattress, then up to his feet, then back down.

This would be practice, he thought. Practice for a greater purpose, something he and Marcel had discussed in the last year. Getting caught by the Intervention Force for a minor offense was part of the plan. Possession of a religious icon brought him into the City Interrogation Center with Lania, but would most likely not lead to any further detention. It was a risk he took in order to understand the greater risk of doubling. What was it like to be in the custody of the enemy? Not only did his mission bring an answer to that question, but it brought him to Lania, to Theresa, and to Abraham. Most of all, it taught him that there would always be someone in need of help — in need of a martyr. For that, he loved the title.

The discussion about Daniel's future ended the night he returned home from the interrogation center. Daniel would become a doubler, working his way as far up the Intervention Force chain of command as he could. Marcel had instigated the plan, but underneath his enthusiasm for Daniel's acceptance lingered hesitation. Five years, he had spent caring for Daniel, and he had grown attached to the boy, even depended on him for certain daily tasks. Most of all, Marcel loved having a protege. Perhaps, he thought, a little too much ambition made its way into Daniel's mind. Too late now.

"If you're going to be a doubler," Marcel would say, "the most important thing is to hold on to your own truth, because you'll be constantly surrounded by people trying to take it away from you."

Marcel's words, at times, frightened Daniel away from exploring a life as a doubler, but the boy was now adamant about going through with the process. A safe family would adopt him and place him in Freespeak education. He would learn how to hate people like himself, his goal to become a very high ranking doubler. The hate must be believable. More than believable. It had to be real. Only not as real as his true purpose. And that is what Marcel's words of caution meant. If Daniel succeeded, no one would question his allegiance. He'd be the doubler no one saw coming. One that no one would question. One who could protect people from the inside. One who could manage networks of Godseekers within the confines of Freespeaker prisons and camps. And no one would die. Not for their beliefs. Not under his watch.

He would often get ahead of himself, but for now, one thing held Daniel in place like an anchor. Marcel. He was now Daniel's family, his only family. There was a reason for that, and Daniel sought to find out. As a doubler, Daniel planned to search for his parents. Whether they had been killed, camped, brainwashed, or anything — as long as they weren't forgotten. As long as he could reclaim their story.

Daniel prayed every night. He thanked God for Marcel, who didn't just keep him alive, but kept him going with a purpose. Marcel had been like a father, grandfather, uncle, friend, co-conspirator. Just like he would never forget his parents, he would never forget his guardian.

The weathercast called for another eighty plus degrees. Mid-socks and running shoes were always on his feet these days. He was used to running. Even made it a part of his daily routine. He'd wake up before everyone and go for a jog. Marcel commented that in his eighty-seven years of life, he'd never encountered a teenager willing to wake up with the sun, and not only that, go for a run. How odd, Marcel would say. Daniel would just shrug.

Daniel was not preparing for his morning exercise this time. Just a long road trip. In a small backpack, he had a couple changes of clothes, a spare battery for his comm device, and some car snacks. He threw some water on his face before emerging from his room at Tyriq's restaurant apartment, and found him, Aaliyah and Marcel already sitting around the dining table eating breakfast.

"Ready to go?" Daniel greeted the group. He typically didn't eat breakfast.

"You should probably sit down and eat with us first," Marcel suggested. He cleared his throat and stumbled through his invitation. "I cooked this time."

"Really?" Daniel said. "Ty let you work in his kitchen?"

No one said anything, and this time the silence was more awkward than reverent. Marcel stood up and walked Daniel to a seat at the table. They both sat down, and Marcel looked at Daniel, his eyes painted with bad news.

"Tyriq and I are going to Mountain Town 32 to get Theresa and August."

"You and Tyriq?" Daniel responded. It was all he heard. "I thought all of us were going."

"After you told me you were ready — ready to become a doubler — I put out a request. That request got answered much faster than I had expected. A safe family in Central City. They've been fostering doublers for about seven years now. A few of their kids are grown up and already doubling on the Intervention Force. There's a narrow window for them to accept another child. This is your opportunity. Do you still want to go through with it?"

Daniel had no appetite to begin with, but he picked up the serving spoon and dished himself some fried rice and a couple links of Portuguese sausage. He started eating. The rice flourished with the flavors of garlic and smoked paprika, yet he ate with a crooked face, the instantaneous realization that this could be his last meal with Marcel. Ever. The man was 87. All that determination he flashed for the past few months, and even more so in the previous week, seemed to deflate as the reality of his decision settled in.

Marcel cautioned Daniel that if he ever said yes to a life of doubling, that the transition could come as fast as when he lost his parents.

Daniel chewed both food and thought. The table was eating patiently. Even carried on other conversations while leaving him to his doubts. Then Aaliyah spoke to him.

"Daniel, you don't have to. Not if you aren't ready. This is the rest of your life we are talking about. You still have a choice."

Her consolation had a reverse effect on Daniel. He knew if he wanted to impact the world of Godseekers as a doubler, the time was now. Fourteen years old was the legal maximum to be adopted before being put in state custody, and if he missed this window with the family in Central City, there was no telling if he'd have another chance. So it was now or never.

"Marcel." The man didn't want to look in the boy's direction, but he did, eyes incapable of holding back emotion. "Thank you —"

It was all he knew to say. All he could say. All he had to say.

The last five years came rushing with the saltwater that streamed from Daniel's eyes. Everything happened fast in his world. Everything, temporary. He supposed he had better learn not to grow too attached to anything. OR anyone. Something the old man had taught him. Marcel, the Buddhist. Letting go of attachment presented a sincere struggle to Daniel, a Catholic. He'd always seen Jesus' message as one of attachment — a message saying, build a relationship with others, and love them. Love them forever. It was an ideal not meant for mortals.

Marcel stood, his knees abnormally wobbly as he hobbled over to Daniel. He draped his arms around the boy, which felt warm and smelled of fried things and ginger.

"I'm gonna be great," Daniel proclaimed. "I'm gonna do what you did for me. Protect people."

Marcel didn't speak, but his spirit was attached to his young friend like a father's to his son.

Theresa

Theresa studied August, his body jumping and sliding along with the vehicle, despite the straps of the restraints keeping him in his seat. She felt relieved to see the smeared dirt and blood washed away, revealing his clear, brilliant skin, though torn and scratched. His dark brown hair splattered over his forehead like a muddy waterfall. Theresa reached and combed the loose strands over to the right with her warm fingers. Just the way he liked it.

She had always loved August for his creativity, passion for justice, and the way he treated others with respect and dignity, no matter who they were.

They didn't know each other long before getting married — only ten months. After a long stint of singlehood, her extended family, friends, and co-workers all buzzed about her boyfriend, and quickly, questions about her marital status arose from the captivated audience. Someday, she figured, she would wed, though she was in no rush. It would happen in God's time. Losing her father steered her heart toward a companion. Before he died, she would have been content living alone and devoting her life to her social work. But a void widened in her heart, and when she met August, he filled the empty space.

Sometimes she wondered if she had waited to baptize Abraham, maybe August would not have been scared away. Or maybe she would have just determined he was not the one for her. But *the one* was never just one to Theresa. She didn't believe in a soulmate — didn't want one. Just a person who respected her and didn't drive her crazy.

Breaking the law didn't fit into August's plans. She understood his choice to leave, though it didn't stop her heart from breaking and being disappointed in herself for putting too much faith in him. Turns out her faith wasn't misplaced.

This morning, as she pulled the strands of August's hair from left to right, as she witnessed his broken physique losing the battle against even the bumpiness of the country road, she felt drawn to him in yet another way, because he had just shown a new level of love to her back in the ESIC. That ultimate, self-sacrificing love. That type of love that few have the opportunity to share, but many say they possess. To die for another. For her. For Abraham. August may not have believed in Jesus, but he sure as hell understood him.

This morning, she still loved August for his creativity, for his passion for justice, and for the way he treated others with respect and dignity. Now, she loved him for the sake of loving him, and no other reason, she found. Maybe, she thought, that counts as a soulmate.

The van came to a halt. Two doors opened and shut. The back doors came apart, and Theresa leaned out to get her bearings. It was still dark, but she could see the sky lightening, the moon nearing the horizon ready to set, and the last few stars that hadn't faded away in the sun's approach. Rivera sprung in the back and relieved Theresa of her binds, then August, who stirred at the handling.

Blue climbed in as well and helped August out of the van. Theresa exited and found that they were parked in a sprawling gravel driveway. An old farmhouse stood in the middle of acres of fields and a few nearby apple trees giving the landscape some texture. In the growing dawn, Theresa could make out tints of brick red paint on the siding of the structure. It reminded her of how a farmhouse would appear in a children's book. A row of rectangular windows extended from the front door, while a massive semi-circular glass panel crowned the home on the second floor.

Outside on the porch sat a woman in an adirondack as if she'd been stuck there, frozen in time. She wore a coat, zipped up all the way to her neck. A blanket fell over her legs and she sat silently beneath the simmering yellow glow of the porchlight. Her hair, swift and short, dark brown and magenta in the light, huddled on her scalp like cotton candy, thin and airy. Theresa could read the woman's age from afar. A hunched back, boney fingers, and movements, unhurried and dainty as the snow, revealed the woman's age. She paused from her apparent prayer and greeted the company with a crooked wave. Rivera acknowledged the pleasantry, but halted Theresa while the woman finished her morning prayer.

"There are safe houses all around this part of the state," Rivera leaned in and explained to Theresa. "I have a feeling you're going to have to get used to places like these. At least in the foreseeable future. They're off the grid — no electricity. Usually, they're self-sustaining. As out of sight as they can be."

Theresa looked around. She saw no neighbors. Only the trees and tall fields of wheat and corn. The driveway they had pulled into was part of a dirt access road. They were exactly in the middle of nowhere. In one way, it made Theresa feel safe. In another, the seclusion felt eerie and lonely, like how it would feel to be forgotten.

Blue remained at the van, still assisting August from the holding cell, while Rivera walked Theresa toward the house and the woman who sat in the adirondack. Nearing her, Theresa could see she was wearing a royal blue hijab, but the head covering was pulled back. Her eyes were shut.

"Fajr?" Theresa asked Rivera, who nodded, and they stood patiently at a distance while the woman finished her prayer at dawn. Her reverence was not lost in the fact that she remained seated. Her face conveyed concentration, the wrinkles around her eyes hung loosely like clumps of dough, and her hands, still and soft, rested on the wooden arms of the seat. At the close of her prayer, she stood up and scanned Theresa from top to bottom, then managed a smile behind her wrinkles.

"She has a bit of a glow for a woman who has lost her baby, and I'm sure much more," the woman said to Rivera. "That's reassuring."

"She managed to get her husband out of the ESIC," Rivera explained. "I think I'd be pretty happy about that too."

"Ex-husband," Theresa clarified out of habit, though the woman's observation was right on target. "I'm Theresa," she grinned.

"Diyaa," replied the woman. "Salaam. My friend Aaliyah told me your story, though I think you're quite famous enough in the circles of Martyrs now."

The word 'martyrs' made Theresa recoil for a moment. Death was an inherent part of the word, and dying for her faith was not something Theresa was prepared to do. For Abraham, yes. For August? Yes. If he could do it for her, she would do it for him. But for God? Theresa was still undecided. She nodded in spite of her reservations, but no more than a simple acknowledgement for the story Aaliyah must have relayed to Diyaa. It was a story of acclaim, yet one in which she took no pride.

Even though finagling August's release from the ESIC was a small victory, she would have been happier curled on her sofa with her husband and son. And God would be there too. In the walls of the house where she grew up, in her heart. Only, God would not dwell in the silence. God would fade away eventually, had she followed the law. From her own heart, she would lose God. But as it was, the Intervention Force, the AFLs — they had taken God from her. So she spared herself some of the blame. God was given to her by her father, by Lania — that God had shattered and fallen. Now she would have to find God again, all by herself. The last several weeks, she had felt abandoned by God. But then, remembering the note she had written, hanging on the edge of the shed, Theresa caught the inkling that God may yet have a plan in the works. The thought didn't comfort her, however. Quite contrarily, a profound fear infected her. The trajectory of her life was not that of kings and queens, or followers of the faith leading wholesome and happy lives. No. Her life took the direction of the prophets. Of those who spoke against the overwhelming majority. Of Job. Of saints and martyrs. And yes, they lived lives worthy of remembrance. But Theresa didn't want to be remembered. She just wanted her son back.

The green front door had a circular stained-glass panel eye-level with a visitor. In the center of the abstract design was a small brown cross, a blue moon, a star of David, a yin and yang, and a deity with four arms standing on one leg — Shiva. Most of the icons were familiar to Theresa. In the middle of them all was a fully bloomed red rose, its stem ornamented with leaves and thorns.

Blue and August finally made it onto the porch, and Diyaa took them all into the living room. On top of the coffee table sat a large stainless steel flask filled with black tea. Diyaa made a quick trip to the kitchen to grab an extra mug for August, whom she was not expecting.

Theresa took in the moment, which felt awkward. It seemed a pleasant simplicity, drinking tea with strangers and her ex-husband. August was a lovely distraction on the ride to the house, but now her focus went right back to Abraham.

"So you know my story?" Theresa asked Diyaa, who nodded. "Then are you going to help me find my son?" Theresa asked with all the courteousness of an improper house guest.

"I'm sorry, my dear. You won't be seeing me for long. I'm only here to get you settled. Then I've got to disappear myself."

"You're all leaving us here?" Theresa wondered.

"That's the idea," Rivera explained. "Blue and I, we're doublers. Transporters. Diyaa is a Ghost. Marcel, I believe, is your Handler, and that's pretty much it in the game of extraction."

"This house is completely off the grid," Diyaa said. "I procured it and swept it for bugs and cams. I've also stocked the refrigerator and pantry with four days worth of food."

"Four? I thought —" The hospitality made sense in Theresa's mind. "Thank you. You're very considerate."

"Of course," Diyaa said. "Food is very important, you know. But I'm afraid I was only aware of one guest in the house, so I hope you and your former husband are on good terms."

August had been quiet. Still exhausted, he was less interested in questions and more fixated on the cushioned rocker in which he sat, but he did keep an attentive ear to the conversation, which went on for about an hour. Diyaa explained a few details. Marcel — and likely someone to drive him — would arrive in three days to take Theresa and now August to the Tri-Cities, which sprawled along a river in the middle of the state. There, they would begin the search for Abraham. In the meantime, she and August needed only wait in the house and keep a low profile until the handler showed up.

Theresa's paranoia commanded her first question.

"If Marcel doesn't show up, then what?" Theresa asked.

"Then I wouldn't hang around here," Diyaa instructed. "Extraction protocol is to be strictly followed. If something goes wrong, you must assume the worst. We can't rely on comm devices, unfortunately. It's too easily monitored by the Intervention Force, and we can't afford good enough technology to have private lines of communication. You should know that all of this is quite new to us as well."

"First time for me," Rivera added.

"I've been a transporter on a couple other occasions," Blue said. "But yes, extracting people from the ESIC or places like it? It takes some high tech hacking. Definitely above my paygrade."

"Well, we're on the other side of the wall, so you all must be doing a good job," August chimed in. "Are we just having tea for breakfast?"

Theresa took the initiative and walked to the refrigerator and pantry. There were two dozen eggs, some bread, bacon, an array of vegetables, and other non-breakfast foods.

"We've got plenty here. Are you all staying much longer? I'll cook."

"We can't," Diyaa replied. "In fact, we've overstayed. It's already light outside."

The sun had been shining over the horizon, and Rivera and Blue got up to go, Diyaa with them. August lay asleep already in the rocking chair, but Theresa resolved that he'd wake up to the sound and smell of crackling bacon. She met the three Martyrs at the door.

"You all do a lot of work for someone like me," Theresa said. "Thank you."

"It's work we believe in," Rivera said.

"Yeah, me too," Theresa said, noticing the sincerity supporting her words. Dying didn't sound appealing to her, but fighting back did, and that's what martyrs do, especially when it came to Abraham's justice, her own, and everyone in the ESIC. "Sounds like a pretty complex network of spies and doublers. I feel like my life is in front of a camera right now."

"It's not often that we can orchestrate this," Rivera said. "Marcel has been working the extraction syndicate for years now, ever since the Intervention Force began taking AFL violators. But even he hasn't run extraction that often. He's getting old. His words, not mine. But he said you were special. 'That last baptism in Far City,' he said, 'We need to make sure she makes it. If we don't even try to reunite a mother and her child, then we have no business doing what we're doing.' He's right. I believe it."

The conviction in Rivera's voice reassured Theresa, and a trust, a faith, one she felt absent for quite some time, made itself known to her.

"I'd like to do the same thing, someday," Theresa said. "Thank you. So much. For everything. From the ESIC to here. In the last few days, I've felt that friendships are forming much faster than normal, and it's all because people are willing to sacrifice so much to keep me safe. I want to do the same thing for others."

"Spoken like a true Catholic," Rivera said.

The words didn't quite find a landing pad in Theresa's heart. Instead, they hovered over her, in a purgatory of self evaluation that would have to be determined once this was all sorted out. Or at least once she had a chance to think.

"Goodbye, Theresa," Diyaa said. "And remember, stay in the house."

Theresa

Theresa took in her latest surroundings, adding it to the album of containment she had experienced since she left her childhood home. There was Marcel's restaurant, Tyriq's restaurant — thank God her company was comprised of foodies — the Portland Intervention Force HQ, and the ESIC. She counted the car rides too, for they were filled with just as much mundane adventure and time as the notion of staying in a penitentiary or safehouse.

Theresa wondered if Diyaa found this latest accommodation on a vacation app. The countertops sparkled, the showerheads burst with full and direct streams, the toilets were warmed electronically and came with built in bidets, and the corners of every room were clean without a hint of dust. Most striking was the morning sun pouring in through the half-circle windows above the family room. The lights were off inside, and the great room colored itself with the warm filtered yellow of the morning. Theresa meandered to the couch and took a seat in the sun-light. It felt embracing. Her body was cold from the night, and instantly the light, the intense first light of dawn flooded over her skin — through her skin — and proceeded to heat her insides. She shut her eyes and crafted a smile of relief, the kind that flirts with sadness only because of how deep the longing for comfort was, and how far the real comfort desired still seemed.

Solar power converters provided the small amount of electricity needed to light the home and power necessities, as well as a few luxuries. A small library invited Theresa to pass the time away, and August came upon a collection of blank canvases, oil paint and brushes. Board games, journals, athletic equipment, knitting needles, and a tool shed with lumber — all options for keeping themselves busy while waiting for their handlers to arrive.

The first evening, Theresa sat outside on the porch just after sunset. The empty landscape called to her, and she toyed with Diyaa's warning to stay inside. *Did she mean stay in the house, or on the property?* The cornfield stretched as far as her eye could see, and it tempted her. The utter freedom tempted her. A simple walk outdoors tempted her. A narrow trailhead into the field opened as she scanned the edge where the cornstalks ended and the front lawn began. Her eye stuck to it — couldn't break loose. Then it reeled her in. A small voice in her head whispered caution while the rest of her being glided forward in an eager, ignorant waltz. To stroll freely and take in the fresh air — what risk? What caution? The moment was here. The moment was now.

She entered the field on a flattened path, and sure enough, it was a trail of sorts. A corn maze, she thought. Best not to get lost, but already she found herself under layers of thought. Not the distressing variety that had been plaguing her, but thoughts of the moment. Observations. The direct rays from the sun, the song of sparrows, the hum of the wind, and the shuffling of the stalks of corn culminated in an opus. An opus of the moment. A frozen moment that belonged to her. It felt special to Theresa. All other moments in time before this one seemed to belong to someone else. Someone she loved. Someone she hated. A stranger. A friend. A God. But now, it was only her and the earth, and as she did so many times before, Theresa wandered among the living song of nature, now questioning if God had composed this very moment, or if it just happened to come about — found its own way into existence without the hand of a creator.

After about an hour of meandering, she emerged at the exit about sixty meters from the entrance, but still within the massive yard of the farmhouse. She peeked to the left and to the right. All was as she'd left it except the sun and the clouds.

When she returned to the house, August was frantic.

"Where were you?" he asked. "I thought you were taken. I was ready to go looking, but I remember what Diyaa said."

Theresa understood his panic and apologized. "I just got caught up in a walk. I'm sorry, I didn't think it would take that long. It was lovely, actually, and it still counts as not leaving the house. Well, the property anyway. You want to go tomorrow?"

August shook his head, still nervous about their circumstance, and incredulous as to why Theresa didn't share the heightened alert. He didn't want her to go either, but he kept his tongue. He felt no claim to Theresa. Not enough to tell her what to do. Not again.

On the morning of the third day, Theresa awoke just before dawn. She hated sleeping through the morning, but made an exception for herself and rolled over, intent on falling back asleep. She had grown amiable to a single bed in the last few months, stretching out her limbs and curling in on herself under the covers. The rest was glorious, and she had enjoyed three days of it.

August took the room across the hall, but spent most of his time lying awake pondering the plausibility of his living. How a few days prior, he was prepared to exhaust himself to the heat inside a small metal container, and how now, he lay in a bed with fresh, clean linens. Free. About as free as he would ever be. Death had found him, yet because of Theresa, he slid through Death's fingertips like scurrying fish in the water. *Not today*, he thought. But upon further review, "Maybe today," he whispered to himself.

Still groggy, Theresa hatched from the covers and found the ensuite bathroom she had enjoyed the previous two mornings. She let the faucet run for a few moments, then cupped her hands under the stream and splashed warm water on her face, rubbing the dryness from her eyes. She dabbed the beads of liquid, then drew from the bottle of lotion on the counter and began massaging it into her cheeks, her forehead, then around her eyes until it had all dissolved. She inspected the skin around her eyes to see what wrinkles had formed in the past month, and slid her hand on her cheek to see if it was still soft. Her body could no longer sustain its youth, and the recent events assaulted her longevity. The more life she lived, the more time she'd spend in front of the mirror, not admiring herself, but feeling concerned. She felt the anxiety in her heart and mind, but her body wore it — wore it all — like new scars.

Satisfied that she had done all she could to preserve the youth of her face, she left the room to find August. His door was closed. She stood outside and stared at it. The last time they were a couple, this was exactly how she felt. Standing behind a closed door with him on the other side. She wanted to open it without reservation. Affection had sprouted in her like a new sprig growing from the soil in a houseplant, and she nurtured it as it grew. *Too fast*, she would tell herself. *Just like we started out.*

She didn't want this segment of their relationship to be like the first. Exciting, but rushed. Genuine, but unfamiliar. Loving, but foolish.

The door in front of her looked brand new. Freshly varnished wood with a nickel knob that she wouldn't touch. She felt the awkward minute pass and stepped away.

"Not gonna knock?" August hollered from inside. "I knew you'd come around sooner or later."

Theresa rolled her eyes, then barged in as if the last sixty seconds never happened.

"Come on," August continued. "There's room." Then he shimmied over, tapped on the bed and tried making his eyebrows hop.

"You're stupid," Theresa laughed. "The eyebrow thing? Really? You know it works a lot better when you're not healing from a prison beating."

August frowned like hurt puppy, a clear over-reaction. Theresa modestly sat in the easy chair next to his bed. She took his hand and examined his arm and all the wrappings she had applied and reapplied.

"You look like a —"

"Mummy?" August tried.

"Like roll of toilet paper about to run out. You see, you can't finish my sentences anymore."

"I guess not."

Then, just silence. For a good long while. One that they used to share. At their wedding, Lania said during her sermon that you should be able to be silent with the one you love, and that shouldn't be a problem.

279

That's when you know that even when there's nothing to say, you don't need to say anything.

Theresa again lifted August's hand and read his wounds. This time, she didn't let it go. She held him, and it felt good.

"I regretted leaving you, you know," he said as she listened with a gulp of air. "The moment I left the house, I knew I shouldn't have. I just wouldn't let myself go back."

"Why not? We needed you."

"You know why, Theresa. I don't mind that you're a Catholic. I love you for that. But what you did, what you were planning to do at the time, was dangerous. And look at us now."

Theresa shook her head, overwhelmed with guilt, and August took notice of his inability to have grace in conversation.

"It's not your fault though," he said, just before realizing again how poor his choice of words were. But he couldn't stop. "It's the world we live in that has the problem. It's the AFLs and the freespeakers. It's intolerance and hate. I'm not fooled into blaming the woman I love for being courageous."

The word fell out of his mouth inadvertently.

"You still love me?" Theresa's voice solid.

"Yes." The word didn't travel or hang in the air. It was as though August merely opened himself for Theresa to witness his own conviction, immovable as a mountain.

"Then why did you —"

"Because I was afraid. And looking back on it, I was selfish."

"You're not selfish, August. Look at what you did to get me out of this mess. To help us get Abraham back. You were about to die." A gap of silence. Then she asked with curiosity, "What did that feel like?"

"What, the beating?" he giggled with an obvious answer at the ready.

"No — being ready to die for someone else. For something else."

"Exactly how it sounds, I guess" August replied. "Scary as hell, noble, painful, full of purpose. Mostly foolish. But who says you don't do foolish things for the people you love."

Love. He used the word again. Theresa let go of his hand and the window became her distraction. She could look directly at the sun, which was now muted by an influx of haze from surrounding wildfires over the last few days. It was a soft orange disk, like a blister in the sky.

"I love you too, August." Her words were like the two of them — fugitives freed from the captivity of her lips. And they kissed as the morning sun broke through the haze.

Theresa

Theresa spent the afternoon preparing a just-in-case meal, just in case they had time to sit and eat. But she knew that was about as likely as the AFLs being overturned tomorrow, and the food she cooked — a mix of sautéed vegetables, hand made tortillas and queso fresco — would sooner spoil on the counter as they tore to their next destination. Despite the warmth and grandeur of the farmhouse, no place felt like home. Only checkpoints. The next location to avoid bindings and fences.

Theresa longed for a home — a place where memories could be absorbed by the walls, capturing spirits in engravings and wall paint. Mostly, a place of stability and safety. Maybe someday. Someday far off in time, when Abraham would be a man, and she would be granted obsolescence by the Intervention Force.

There was no ETA for Marcel and his accompanying party, but Theresa wanted to be ready. She had no personal effects in the house, but part of the safehouse package was a convenience backpack with essentials for the fugitive lifestyle. She stumbled upon it earlier in their stay, and rummaged through curiously. A smoke bomb. Useful. A taser.

Perhaps best to keep that in its case. A thin black bodysuit. That would benefit one of them, at least. Some food, some water, a compass, a two-person tent, and a fresh change of clothes. Women's. Lucky for her. Fortunately, the house was stocked with clothes for both men and women, and they packed a few extras for August.

The backpacks rested next to the front door, ready to scoop up upon their extraction.

This is my life now, Theresa thought. Life in a backpack. Moving from place to place, evading anti-interventionist law enforcement, and calling nowhere home for long. Theresa picked up the realization as though it were a wounded wolf. She felt drawn to it in living her life as she desired, but fearful that it could terminate her existence at any moment.

She sat alone in the living room while August napped upstairs. His condition had improved, but still, he needed to regain strength. She understood her ex-husband was probably realizing much of the same things himself. She wanted to talk about it with at that moment, while he was there and she was there, and quiet and time made themselves accessible. Instead, she put her faith in the future, and decided the only one available to hear her thoughts was her own mind. Still, she craved for someone to listen. And again, that absence, that new void left by an evicted faith, came knocking at her heart's door.

Outside, the sun had nearly fallen from the sky. A familiar unnamed urge pulled Theresa from the couch, out the side door and toward the cornfield where the path extended out. She wouldn't have time for a full walk. Marcel could arrive, the Intervention Force close behind, and either the window would be missed, or she would lead to the death of all of them by making them wait. Still, she wandered into the stalks of corn, promising to stay within earshot of the driveway so she could run out if her handler showed up.

The smoke from the wildfires had gotten substantially worse from the morning. She could stare at the sun, just over the horizon. It was still an orange disc, smearing the immediate sky around it shades of yellow and tan. *Rain*, Theresa thought. We could all use a good rain right now. On second thought, the last time she heard rainfall, she was in a sewer with Abraham and Lania, doing the unthinkable. The ruination of three lives in one night, under one storm.

Keep your rain, God. Theresa thought, cursing the Heavens. She resolved to brood in the dirty air. That's how her own soul felt. Ashen, unclean, unclean. It longed for a breath of fresh air, for the expanse of a clear blue sky and a sun, like God once was to her — bright, obvious, warm, reassuring.

If her own faith wasn't enough, August consumed her thoughts, and of course, Abraham and Lania, then society, then Rivera and Blue, Diyaa and Aaliyah, then the Martyrs, then anyone who felt faith in their own hearts. Too much. Too many people all caught in the web of Freespeak, which lurked like a venomous spider — at least that was her perspective. That hate. She perceived it as clear as the ears of corn in front of her. But anger? Anger, her previous anger, had abandoned her as well. Now she stood alone in the midst of her thoughts, no God to pray to, no August to lean on, and no anger to fan the flames of her own sickness. Only herself. And what was that worth? She hoped to live long enough to find out.

Then, she took her eyes of the sky and off the ground and looked behind. She had strayed too far, walking for at least twenty minutes, and twenty minutes in an undetermined schedule could mean life or death.

She hurtled steps toward the house. She could see the roof outline the sky. Cornstalks brushed against her side, and at one point, she twisted her ankle on uneven ground. An expletive squeezed out of her mouth, for she had grown accustomed to not making loud noises. Forward and forward she went, the rhythm of her pace slowing down as she grew tired. Her body favored adrenaline over the pain from her fall, and she pressed on. *God I hate running*, she thought.

About 20 yards from the entrance to the corn trail, a force from the side launched itself into Theresa's ribs, throwing its arms around her, but keeping her upright. She felt as though she had run into a tree, but it was Rivera, whose eyes were wide open. Then slowly, the transporter's face revealed itself to Theresa — scrapes, a bruise, a laceration under her ear, and fragments of earth from wading through the cornfield.

"Back." she whispered.

The word broke every hope that Theresa spent the last three days building. Rivera said it again.

"Back!" she spoke hastily through her teeth, and this time, she dragged Theresa the reverse, returning to the center of the cornfields, then diving among the stalks when the trail turned toward the farmhouse. At first she guided Theresa methodically off the trail and through the tall stems, enough to preserve the shape of the plants as they appeared from the path. About fifteen feet in, she plowed through the corn with recklessness, trying only to get further and further away from the house with Theresa dragging her feet behind.

Then she stopped. Theresa was dazed and baffled, but pretty sure of what Rivera was going to say. And then she said it.

"We've been made. I'm sorry Theresa. I'm sorry. Marcel, Tyriq, August — they're all at the house. And the Intervention Force. About a dozen of them. We have to get further away. This field goes on for about a mile. They're going to look for us. We may have to hide and wait for them to give up the search in this area, or trek through the wilderness for a while. I don't know."

"What about —"

Before she could ask her question, a gunshot pierced the muddled atmosphere and roiled the blood in her veins. She felt it, like an earthquake sending a wave from her heart to the tips of her fingers and toes. At first she lay as still as a cob, fallen to the ground and undisturbed by the wind. Then she found herself running. Running faster. Running back to the red farmhouse. Back to the kitchen where her sautéed veggies and tortillas and queso were kept warm in the heat of the summer evening. Back to the living room couch where she should have been the whole time. Back to the porch, where Diyaa sat three days ago, frozen in her prayer at dawn. Back to Anna's Ladybug Daycare. Back to her childhood room where she and her father painted lilies and butterflies on the wall.

Fear and a hope crescendoed. The fear projected the inevitable before her eyes. Someone was dead, and with utter certainty, it was a person she loved, a person who loved her. Hope scraped and clawed for life inside Theresa. It cried like a dying animal, hoping desperately that the shot was merely a warning, merely a threat. That hope told her she could save a life, emerging from the corn field, extending her hands, and welcoming the chains and the labor camp. Life wasn't so bad there. If she and August and Marcel and Tyriq could live, she would take a week in the shed.

Her step proceeded unwaveringly. *How much further*, she thought? She wouldn't turn her head back, but no sound of Rivera from behind.

An image of the doubler didn't even occur to Theresa. Her mind ran on a single track. Almost there. The house was bigger. A few more turns. Then another diving body hit her. Not Rivera. It was Daniel.

"With me. They're all gone. Marcel... With me, now, Theresa!" A face, white as cotton with eyes like nectarine pits begged her to turn back. In his face, she saw that hope never had a chance. She swallowed hard then jogged behind Daniel. Rivera wasn't much further ahead. She slowed her pace and joined the two in their dash away from death.

"You — Daniel," Rivera said, her voice shocked and disturbed. "Why are you here? What are you doing?"

"Come on!" he urged. "The farm access road, about a mile and a half outside this corn field. Aaliyah — she's got a —"

"Attention!" a screechy male voice called out from an amplifier. "This cornfield is surrounded. Return to the farmhouse, and no one else will die. Do it quickly. You have two minutes before we kill another one."

Theresa stopped, and to her disbelief, so did Daniel. Perhaps he laid claim to the same hope she had.

"No —" Rivera cajoled. "Keep going. They are lying. It's a kill mission. I heard it myself. I wouldn't have come all this way if they were only going to take you back in. You go back that house, and you're all dead."

Theresa could only think of the seconds drifting away like seeds from a dandelion. She looked to Daniel. He seemed to know better in these situations.

"No way they have this field surrounded," Rivera rationalized. "It's far too massive. That much is a bluff. But killing all of you, that is a promise. They've already lost you twice. They're not interested in taking you as a prisoner anymore."

Daniel shook his head. "Come on Theresa," he said. "I saw them shoot Tyriq. I saw them do it. Right in the head. No questions." Daniel was sobbing already. Then shaking. "Come on. Rivera is right. You can't save August... I can't save —"

Then that very voice took command of the megaphone and rooted Theresa's feet in the ground.

"Theresa." August's voice was even and low, calm and almost sedated. She took a step forward, but not toward August. It wouldn't have mattered anyway. Two minutes had passed.

"*Run* Theres —" August yelled.

Her incomplete name echoed in the air and hovered over her. The sound of August's last word was a memory she would carry for the rest of her life. She memorized it, its timbre and pitch; like a song that would play over and over in her head, she heard it and replayed it. Punctuating her name was the sharp crack of a gunshot. Like a leech, it sucked the last syllable — the life — from her name, it ruined the song, the sound of August's voice, and the memory. It was the only track she would hear, day after day, until her last day. It was a song of sacrifice. Regrettable sacrifice. A song she swore she would never hear again because now, they had everyone. Everyone she loved.

———————————

She stood in place as she imagined a spirit might stand the moment it wakes up in purgatory, not knowing where she was or which way to go. Then Daniel again captained her ship. He pulled her, not urgently this time, but gently, with empathy and humanity through his own weeping eyes. It was all Theresa could respond to at that moment. And then, a third shot rang out, and Daniel's grasp went limp as he fell to the earth. In a flash, Theresa retrieved the boy's energy, and picked him up.

The three Martyrs carried each other like crosses toward the horizon where the sun had lain its head not an hour ago. Darkness had won over the day, the cloud of smoke ensuring not a single star could be seen.

Theresa

Hours, they drove, all of it in shocked silence. Aaliyah stayed on a web of unmapped farm roads until the tires of the pickup truck met a paved arterial. A few turn offs, and they were on the highway. The passengers stayed below window level to avoid suspicion.

The truck in which they rode belonged to a man. A Martyr himself. He was a wealthy man who had heard stories like Theresa's, and upon hearing about the network of Godseekers, he asked how he could help. Aaliyah, who met him at an interfaith service, said she needed a transport that could take them off the beaten path if necessary. The truck had lived in the man's yard for nearly seven years, waiting for a purpose. It was one of several vehicles he owned, and not the least travelled either.

In luxury lost on all of the passengers, they traversed east toward the state border, spent a night in an old motel under Aaliyah's pseudonym, then carried on the next day, passing through more plains before meeting the towering Rocky Mountains. No pursuit attached itself, but a few nervous moments left the cabin a bit shaken when law enforcement followed the truck. Time, they needed.

Aaliyah turned off the interstate, then off the paved street and onto an ill-managed path that ascended a mountain. About eight miles into the ascent, she found a landing tucked around a switchback that was decorated with overgrowth. Trees shrouded the site. If they weren't safe in such seclusion, they never would be.

In the truck bed was found a generous supply of food and camping supplies. Martyrs were always prepared.

Theresa found Daniel sitting on a rock next to the pallid glimmer of a camping lantern. He gnawed on a patch of jerky with a can of soda next to his sneakers, looking dazed, focused or perhaps just staring listlessly at the tree trunk in front of him. Adjacent to the rock was a stump of a tree, smoothed from cycles of seasons. Theresa sat and tried to stare at the same target on which his eyes rested.

"You found me again," she said. "I owe you twice now."

Daniel shook his head. "No. Maybe if I wasn't late all the time, then you could buy me a pizza or something. Just a few minutes behind Abraham, now a few behind Marcel, Tyriq, August." He sighed mightily and the breath shivered out of his lungs, echoing in the valley below. Grief strangled him. "I—"

Then he realized he had nothing to say. Theresa didn't pry. Whatever was said would be honored, and nothing more.

"Martyrs, huh?" Theresa said. "Couldn't we just be heroes? They get to live in the end."

"Yeah," Daniel broke. The sadness contained inside him found its way out, and Theresa held the bawling teenager in her arms. Marcel wasn't such a distant memory, and though Daniel had lived a life amidst the Martyrs for five years, no experience could callous his feelings toward the man who rescued him from orphanhood and a state governed life. He always came back to that fact, but facts don't always matter, especially when it comes to people you love. Feelings do, however, and they are more oft brought about by the little things, like the fact that Marcel never greeted Daniel without a smile, or the fact that Marcel would cook him chicken with ginger and glass noodles whenever he got sick, or the fact that Marcel was his shoulder for the last five years, and whenever Daniel missed his parents, Marcel's shoulders would lift him up, his ears would listen and turn pain into peace, and his wisdom would make hope out of despair.

Now, Theresa rocked him. Rocked him as though he were the son she lost. She took the opportunity to be a mother — she didn't know when it would present itself again. For now, at least, August wasn't her mind's occupation. Not even her own son, Abraham, engulfed the thicket of her mind. Only the immediate, present need of Daniel, the boy who rescued her twice and was now scratching at the walls of his world, trying to dig himself out.

"Today is the worst day," Theresa acknowledged. They weren't even her words. She spoke like a prophet, as though the spirit of God moved the air through her vocal chords, making the sounds that Daniel and she needed to hear. "They've taken the last from us. They may take more, but not before we take back."

He heard her words. He believed them. Still, he cried on.

"You and I, Aaliyah, Rivera — we're not going to be martyrs. We're not going to die for what we believe in. We're going to live for it. And only God will take us away from this life. I promise you, Daniel. We have each other. And we always will. I promise."

"Don't make promises you don't have the power to keep," Daniel uttered through his sobs.

"I have the power to keep this promise, and the Intervention Force or the president himself couldn't stop me."

Her determination was stout, and her will as solid as steel. Her embrace, however, embodied the warmth and comfort Daniel sought.

Aaliyah meandered near, her eyes streaked red from an episode of her own. Her brother, Tyriq, had joined the ranks of martyrs as well. She sat next to Theresa on the stump, and without hesitation, Theresa latched onto this woman to whom she hadn't spoken even a hundred words in the time they'd shared each other's company. Yet, actions and experience made them family. Some families share words and they mean nothing — ornaments strewn along false branches of a family tree. But their silence was sincere, and they knew their friendship had an unshakable foundation.

Rivera was, at the moment, the only one with dry eyes.

She had never stood at the edge of a cliff, watching from a distance while, fragment by fragment, her soul broke apart, each piece shriveling as it detached itself from the whole. It was evening, and the luminescent full moon clawed through the cloud of ash and smoke until a deep red orb revealed itself like a mystery whose last question was finally answered. It produced no light, just color, subdued behind a frosted case of atmosphere.

There she stood on a mountain forest road, too old for maintenance to be a memory. Too old for memory. The elements had erased any tire track or footprint made from a wilderness enthusiast. It *was* the perfect place to camp for the night, she observed.

Her black hair had grown long, and over the last year, it was the only vanity of hers that she appreciated. Her mother had always admonished her whenever she didn't take care of her hair, but would do so by yanking a handful and pulling Rivera close to scold her negligence. She hated the irony of her mother's discipline, but in her better moods, which were more often than not, her mother's soft fingers would run over her scalp and trace down her long hair. *Only because it's beautiful*, her mother would say. In the still summer air, she could feel her mother's soft fingertips, the warmth of her hand, and the perpetual pout upon her face. It wasn't a look of disappointment, just merely her natural face, and Rivera always thought her mother the loveliest picture of a person she had ever seen.

Rivera freed her hair to the wind. It whipped and flapped and tangled. It embraced her cheek, covered her eyes, even constricted itself around her throat, but soon, the wind had collected its prize all in one heap, and in unison, Rivera's locks merged upon themselves, and stretched outward to the west as if chasing the sun. Then, like her mother scolding her, she clutched the full body of her hair as close to her head as she could. From her jacket pocket, she pulled a pair of long office scissors.

When she finished, she had surrendered all of it to the earth, the wind carrying it as if the hand of God were reclaiming each strand of her beauty.

"My hair is not me," she whispered to herself.

Some strands disappeared instantly, while others lingered in the moonglow, like spun silk from newborn spiders. It mingled with nature, as though it were meeting an old friend, once again familiarizing itself with its origin, returning to the earth amidst the rest of the ashes floating through the air.

The crunch of dirt and rocks neared, and Theresa stood just behind her. Theresa's eyes were now dry too, and she felt they would never be flooded again. At least not for the same reasons as in the last month of her life. She had no more tears for blood, though she anticipated much more blood to be spilled. *Let the callus form, the numbness take me*, she thought.

Neither she nor Rivera spoke, though Rivera lifted her hand and passed the scissors to Theresa, and in the same swift motion with a buzz and a snap, Theresa's hair joined Rivera's in the wind, intertwining themselves with the fragments of their souls in the old Cascade Valley.

Then Theresa found words worth saying. "Our revolution starts tonight."

Together, they stood before the moon, the only other ears to hear Theresa's words.

"Daniel told me his plan," Theresa said.

"Central City," Rivera acknowledged. "Aaliyah will take him, but not us."

"What will we do?"

"Stay hidden. Hidden for a good long while. It'll give us time to figure out what this revolution looks like, and who can help us."

"I just want to help people. People like us. People who believe. People who don't believe. People who are innocent, but broken."

In that moment, Theresa realized she had invited God back into her life. She had grouped herself among people who believed. Because they needed her, she needed them, and they all needed God. What better ally for deliverance? What better friend when all friends had been taken? Though, one person was left. Theresa's desire was simple and modeled off Daniel's actions toward her.

Theresa concluded her thought. "And," she spoke with a thoughtful breath, "I want to find the one person alive whom I love more than anything."

Rivera nodded. "He's out there Theresa, and the world is much smaller than it seems. You'll see him again."

"I know. I know I will."

Someday soon, she hoped.

JUSTICE

"Slow down," she says more readily than I expect, and I tap the break, allowing my speed to decrease well below the speed limit. We haven't seen a car in at least an hour.

I glance at my rearview, and Maria is scanning the edge of the highway. Her finger is raised and she counts, silently moving her lips. *One. Two. Three. Four. Five...* Outside my windshield, I survey the forest bordering the edge of the road. She must be counting ghosts because all I see are facsimiles of trees. Right as she whispers the number twelve, she gives the command.

"*Stop!*" she says firmly, careful not to yell in front of her child who has fallen asleep. My screeching brakes fail to stir little what's-his-name. "Forward, real slow." A few moments, then she orders me to turn left. I bring the vehicle to a halt and look at her directly.

"Into the dirt? There isn't even a road."

"There will be," she assures. Curiosity moves me forward. Paranoia keeps my acceleration gradual as I split two unassuming evergreens cloaked in moss. The soft earth beneath my tires coaxes my Ford into automatic off-road mode, and we proceed over roots and rocks, pushing on a good five minutes before the ground beneath evolves into an access road with fresh tire marks visible between potholes and large stones.

We ascend, climbing to a clearing where a massif of stony peaks casts a long afternoon shadow into the valley before us. Here, Maria has me park the car.

"We walk from here."

I shake my head skeptically. At the same time, my mind absorbs all the natural landscape surrounding me. Part of me can't help staring dumbfoundedly into the horizon, wondering what lies at the end of this road.

"You think Truth and a bunch of Godseekers would set up shop in a flashy pavilion off the freeway exit? It's a safehouse, Justice, not a casino. We're supposed to be hiding from people like you, remember? Don't worry, I've hiked this path dozens of times. It's only hidden from the highway. The rest of the way is maintained. Now where are your flashlights?"

I wade around to the trunk of my car and pull out a pair of lumens, along with a pack and some waters. I'm starving though. Haven't had a bite since lunch, and all that driving drummed up a serious appetite. And stiff legs.

"They have any food at this place?" I ask, half joking.

"You kidding? Truth wouldn't set up a place like this without a full kitchen." I can't tell if that's sarcasm or not, but I seem to remember Truth mentioning he was a foodie back in college. I'm already putting one foot in front of the other, negotiating a switchback up the steep side of a slope of boulders and scree. Maria leads the way, going no slower than I would if I were alone, and I'm impressed, shocked even that she's moving so swiftly with Isaac in her arms. That's his name.

Darkness erased the day and became full blown night in the time it took us to hike up the mountainside and arrive at a meadow. The lupine and bear grass glow in the moonlight, their scent teasing the air around my nostrils.

Maria extends her hand and asks for a bottle of water. Together, we pull up to a rock and sit in silence, nothing but the heave of our breaths and a slight breeze providing the score for the moment. I want to ask her a question, but the words don't reveal themselves to me.

I want to ask her if it's okay. If it's okay that I'm here. But I have no idea what that means. I only know that it's a question I've been asking myself with each step I have taken into the realm of the American Freedom Laws. Every cautious step. And I've verified with so many people. My parents. My family. My friends. My co-workers. Everyone around me says, "Yes, yes Justice. The Intervention Force is where you belong. You were made for it." If that's true, then I have no idea why I keep asking myself that question. Is it okay? And now I look to this woman. My adversary. I want to offer her the question of my life. Like telling a foe my weakness. Am I trying to sabotage myself? Here in the night, in this moment of silence, I'm ready to offer the question.

But instead, she hops up from her seat and practically bounds into the center of the meadow. At first I think she's running away, but she squats and begins stretching her hand over the grass and earth as though it were a wounded creature. As though it were her own. Then her hand finds traction — a latch — and she pulls. A steel hatch. An underground bunker. She waves me over.

"The hell is this," I say below my breath but above her ear. I don't expect her to answer, and she offers no reply. Long story, I'm sure. I walk toward her, and stand over the hole in the ground. A stairway. Only this one is going down. Down toward that other place. Not heaven. I know that much. It is the place where the question eating away at me will get answered by my own demise. A strange panic strikes me, while my body descends the steps, following my prisoner. My prisoner. Right. Joke's on me.

At the bottom of the stairs, a long corridor extends forward, endless like the straightaway that led us here. Warm yellow lights ensconced in glass protruding from the walls grant our path a soft effulgence. It feels almost cozy.

Isaac is still sleeping in Maria's arms. I envy his peace. I would have had it if I had just done my job. Dropped these two off at The Box. My day would be over. Probably would have taken the rest of it off. Probably could have had a good lunch and been at home watching the Thursday night game.

But no. I got tempted by big fish. ProTruth. Beamer. Chameleon. Too good to be true. Or judging by how out of the way this place is, too true to be good. Who knows what secrets are buried under this mountain, and I am only one man. One confused man. The question I am wrestling with had me in a choke hold back above ground. Now that I'm in this underground whatever, I can't help but lick my chops at how easily I could turn this trip into the catalyst I need to become Supreme Commanding Officer. All I know is that it will end with a decision. One that will determine the trajectory of the rest of my life. I don't know if I'm ready for that.

Maria interrupts my midlife crisis as we turn a corner into some type of waiting room.

"Welcome to ETHOS," she says.

"Ethos?"

"Ecumenical Truth Hall Of Seekers."

"What a name," I gasp, almost rolling my eyes.

The space is commodious, dimly lit and populated with an assortment of antique furniture — plush rockers, fabric couches, and some armchairs with ornate embroidery and shriveled upholstery. A handful of people congregate in a small seating area eating pastries and drinking tea. I scan the room for a barista. Two of them wear yamakas on their heads, another a cross around his neck, and two women in hijabs. Reminds me of that mural back in the Hills District. I wonder if they staged the scene, just to tempt me. Or mock me.

That voice in my head grows larger by the minute, screaming that I've hit the jackpot. I could raise my stats well above 400 if I just camp out here and let the faithies come to me — a predator in the hive.

One member of the group makes eye contact with me, and his face is stricken with dread. He recognizes me and alerts the others. They stare at me, and I remain composed, glaring right back at them. I sustain my attention long enough to let them know I'm aware of their presence, but then return to Maria and Isaac.

They're gone.

"You have a reputation around here," says a familiar voice, its owner standing next to a bulletin board. It's Beamer. His eyes, for a moment, fixate on a particular graphic posted at eye level, and instantly I recognize a face in a photograph. An all too familiar one — one I see in the mirror on a daily basis.

Instinctually, my hand launches toward his neck, but he grabs my wrist and brings it down slowly.

"None of that now," he says with a smile I want to punch off his face. "We don't condone violence at ETHOS."

"You. Backstabber." My voice is almost tranquil as I speak through my teeth.

"Quit bitching and follow me. You look like you need a drink."

I relax my arm and he releases my wrist. He walks in front of me and seems strangely confident. A half thought surfaces in my mind telling me to pull out my gun and fulfill the promise I made after he drugged me. But he's not looking back. That would be too easy, and no matter how much of a doubler Beamer is, I won't kill him with his back to me.

We enter some type of social hall. There's a pool table and ping pong. Also a few old arcade games - the giant ones that are the size of a telephone booth, one of which happens to be in here too, along with two vending machines. It feels like a rec room in a century-old college dorm.

If Beamer was right about one thing, it's that I needed a drink. After the nine-hour detour with Maria and Isaac, I could use a couple shots.

"Whiskey?" I say as he whips out a bottle of Jameson.

"Good Catholics carry wine. Great ones have Irish whiskey."

"Is that in the Bible?"

"I wouldn't know. I'm not Catholic. I know this is whiskey though."

He pours me a glass and sets it in front of me. I snatch it off the counter and down it as if I'm trying to put out a fire in my throat. Of course, it's whiskey. Wouldn't help much.

"So what are you then?" I ask as he refills my glass, this one I sip slowly.

"What am I?"

"Cut the bullshit, you know what I mean. What religion or cult do you belong to?"

"Justice, I don't believe in God."

A moment of silence develops. He's not making sense, to me at least. I take another swig and my glass is empty again. He pours me one more shot.

"Didn't see that coming, did you?" he says.

"You don't believe in God? Then what are you doing here? Isn't this place pretty much a church?"

I'm a bit confused. Is he a doubler on my side? Did he bring me here so I could round up all these faithies? I'd still be pretty pissed at him for not keeping me in the loop, but that would make his jabbing me with a needle twice in a day forgivable.

"Did you fall asleep during our last conversation? I was a student of Truth's years back. Just like you were."

I admit, I wasn't exactly paying attention to what he was saying back at that Chinese restaurant.

"Only you and I took extremely different paths," he says.

"Not so different. I thought we were partners. I thought we were friends."

"I'm not an idiot, Justice. You never thought we were friends and we were only partners because our CO assigned us that way. We worked together for a couple of years, and all I ever heard you talk about was becoming Supreme Commanding Officer. If I were any better at my job, I know you'd just use me to get what you want in the end. But I'm not here because of hurt feelings."

"Then for what?" I challenge. "To make sure I don't bring in Truth? You his bodyguard now?"

He pauses and downs the rest of his drink. I look at my glass and wonder if he's laced it with a drug.

303

"No Justice. I'm here because of you. Because this was my only option. Because I'm a nonbeliever who supports a believer's right to believe."

"So, you've been a doubler all this time?"

He nods. I shake my head. He gave signs, but never any red flags. I question myself, wondering if my ambition blinded me to my own partner's secret life. I make up my mind that no matter what happens with Truth, I'm going to take Beamer in. The liar. He deserves to be locked up.

"I honored the system," I tell him. "You cheated it."

To my disgust, he scoffs and starts to laugh. "Screw the system, Justice. It's a bad system."

I get up from my seat at his words and lean in, wearing a scowl on my face. "You can't speak like that —"

"You 'Freespeakers' are some of the most hypocritical people around," he interrupts. "I hope you're smart enough to at least realize that."

I open my mouth to retort, but again, nothing comes out. All of a sudden, the defense of the law seems powerless. Maria's voice breaks the silence before it gets too awkward. Isaac is still peaceful in her arms.

"Look who found each other," she says. "Good thing you took him out of the hall, Beamer."

"You don't have a pre-GNA name?" I ask, hoping to put distance from our last interaction.

"Are you kidding me?" he replies. "Beamer is a badass name."

"You're like the grim reaper," Maria says to me. "You freaked out everyone in the lobby. We Godseekers think you're out to kill us. Inviting you here is like inviting the devil himself over for dinner."

That's a little harsh. The devil himself? I'm not religious, but everyone knows who the devil is, and I'm definitely not him. Not evil. How is that even a perception of a representative of the law?

She leads me out of the rec room, but before we make it into a hallway, Beamer calls at me one last time.

"Justice —"

I look back at him and the enmity and smugness on his face thaws into something much more human. It almost looks like a face of concern. For me? For Truth?

"You're still armed," he says. "We're putting a great deal of trust in you. We know that Truth means something to you. Please. Don't screw him over."

I peer into him, wanting to crush his request like an insect beneath my shoe. But I can't. He's sincere about it, and no matter what I have against Beamer, I have nothing against my old professor. Only everything I stand for opposes Truth.

What a name.

Back in the hallway, Maria ushers me past door after door, every 20 feet, one on the right, one on the left.

"What's in these rooms?" I ask Maria.

"Mostly dorms, but some are private prayer rooms furnished with symbols and artifacts from different religions," she offers honestly. "There are also a few adaptable rooms where patrons can bring in their own icons or symbols of their faith."

"And which of these doors will we be walking through?"

"Anxious?"

"To get out of this sewer pipe you call a hallway? Yes, very much."

We halt at a distinct door.

"Red, huh?"

"This room is special," Maria explains. "Truth comes in here a lot. It has many relics he and some of his old friends have collected over the years. In this room are artifacts from just about every religion you can imagine. We call it the catholic Room — with a little c."

"Catholic? Interesting name. I don't see why a room housing items from so many traditions would be named for one religion. Is that a Catholic's doing?"

"You know what the word, 'catholic,' means don't you?"

"It's a branch of Christianity."

"It is. But it also has its own meaning. It means 'all-embracing,' which really was what Jesus was about, if you think about it. Not always reflective of the church carried on in his name. But for the most part, we Catholics do our best to welcome all people. Even you."

I let her words sink in for a moment, then iterate my eagerness.

"So Truth is behind these doors?"

"You know, there have been so many times when I've appreciated the appropriateness of his name."

I shake my head. Again.

"Ready?" she grins eagerly.

I take a deep breath and nod.

The door opened, and there sits my old professor on the floor, eyes closed and meditating. Or sleeping. I turn to Maria.

"Now what? Do we wake him?"

"I'm not asleep," says the figure on the floor in front of me, and I almost jump. "I've been waiting for you."

He opens his eyes to me, looking up at my face. He's all sorts of vulnerable and I have every ability to apprehend the man, just like I was about to do back in Far City over a week ago. But of course, I don't. I didn't make this trip with only one objective in mind. I have questions, my own questions that need answering. And the only man who can answer them, I believe, is sitting on the floor at my feet. I join him.

"Thank you, Maria. And you too, Isaac," he gushes with all the human emotion effused in the presence of a giggling infant. "You two have been instrumental in making this happen."

"Making what happen?" All of a sudden, I feel like I'm caught up in something much more intentional. Something intended specifically for me. The photograph of me on the bulletin board. I scarcely paid attention to the description that accompanied it, but remember the word "priority" residing somewhere above my hairline. The faces I saw in the lobby — maybe their looks of panic and dread also contained something else. Something more of an awe. Making *this* happen? That's an answer that intrigues me as much as it terrifies me. Truth proceeds anyway, and I'm sure he knows exactly the dialogue rattling off in my head.

"'This is a very long story," Truth says as Maria and Isaac depart. "You're going to need a more comfortable seat."

JUSTICE

I saw a meme once that said the more wrinkles around your eyes, the more you must have smiled throughout your life. I sincerely hope that's true for my old professor, who surveys his cup of tea through weathered eyes, carefully adding pebbles of sugar to the brew. He stirs slowly as if it were the most important task of his life, and he had all the time in the world to accomplish it.

What a maelstrom he must have lived. My imagination pieces it together — this place, his association with doublers, his class. At first, I'm certain that in the scheme of his life, my contributions make a mere scratch, but then I realize the extent to which he is reaching out to me. I must know more about him. He clearly knows more about me, and any moment now, whenever he decides the rocks of sugar have sufficiently dissolved, he will color my own canvas with who knows what. I can't tell if I'm anxious, frightened, excited or indifferent. Only one of those sound like the choice of the future SCO, a position that is growing more distant.

Truth reaches for a small white pitcher and pours some cream into his tea, a thin white line dips in slowly, and not once does he lift his eyes or say a word. Is he stalling? Is he making me wait? He stirs his cup once again, distributing the milk evenly.

All the while, I scan the blank room. A green glass cross hangs from the wall opposite me, a singing bowl next to the sitting pillow supporting Truth, the rug beneath us, and the tea set are the only items inside the room, except for the two breathing bodies coping with silence. Maria led me to believe there would be more artifacts in here. I admit, I'm a little disappointed.

At last, he sets the spoon down on a plate and picks up his mug to taste his tea. I swear, if he starts adding more sugar or milk I'm going to lose it. Right as a coaxing word is about to dive off my lips he inhales deeply and looks me right in the eye.

"I was just about your age when I had you in my class for the first time," he finally begins. "I didn't always want to be a teacher, you know. In fact, my aspiration resembled yours when I was a youth. I wanted a career in civil service, and from there, I thought I'd make it to the top."

"You? SCO? I don't believe it. You're a faithie. Wait — aren't you?" I pause thinking of Beamer who just outed himself as a sympathetic who doesn't even believe in God. Could Truth be the same? "You seemed so adamantly opposed to my ambition. That's why I left you. That's why I never looked back, because I knew that if I did, my life would be ruined. Why didn't you ever tell me you thought the same way I did? If I knew at least that, I might not have, you know, disappeared."

Who am I kidding? I needed to disappear in order to get to where I am today, but I can't help wondering what my life would have been like had Truth convinced me to follow him.

"You went your own way," Truth states in a voice stripped of judgement. "I understand, and I respect that choice. In fact, I wouldn't have encouraged you differently. Justice, my goal was always, is always to teach people how to think more so than what to think. Meddling with others' beliefs never served me well. Only shedding light on truth." He rolls his eyes. "I never really liked this name. It puns way too often."

"Heh," I chuckle. "Your name suits you, but I never really liked my name either."

"I thought you would have it tattooed on your arm by now. You seem to embody at least an idea of Justice."

"An idea. Yes. I suppose that's what's wrong with my name. I don't want to be attached to an idea."

"You know, when I was growing up, traditional names hadn't been entirely phased out. They were still more popular than generic ones."

"Did you have one?"

"I did."

"What was it?" He pauses while scrutinizing my face. He's looking for the inevitable betrayal, just like the last time we had a conversation like this, back at Wong's Garden. I don't blame him. I'm not ruling it out. But I'm not taking any prisoners at the moment.

"Daniel," he says, as though he just uttered some kind of incantation, waking the dead. Air evacuates his lungs in a shaky gust. "I haven't told anyone that name in — how old are you?"

"Thirty-six."

"Yes. About thirty-six years now."

"Well, at least you didn't break the GNA. That's one thing you have going for you."

He chuckles. "Well, some things die with a name," he says with a wistful sigh. "And some names die with the ones we love."

"What are you talking about Truth?" He shakes his head and sniffs.

"You can't deny that the AFLs have wrought more pain than peace, Justice."

"Well, actually —"

"You don't need to respond to that. I'm not here to debate our views on the American Freedom Laws."

"Then what, Truth? Why am I sitting here? Why am I sitting here, listening to you instead of taking you in. You and everyone in this building should be delivered to the ESIC."

He shakes his head again. It bothers me.

"Okay, this is mounting up to one colossal waste of my time —" I say, irritation mounting.

"He is not ready," he speaks into the collar of his sweater.

"Ready for what? For *what?!*" I reach over to grab him, but my hand goes right through him. A projection. Shit.

"Truth!"

I'm on my feet now.

"Open this door!"

It's locked, by the way.

"What are you hiding from me?!"

I let out a frustrated scream. I should have dumped Maria and Isaac at the damn Box. The early evening I could have had sounds so much more preferable to this moment I'm currently enduring, but I realize the pain isn't coming from being contained in this room, it's from being so close to the truth. The one he is hiding from me.

"Come back!"

Desperation in my voice. I'm not even hiding it any more.

"I know you know me. Come back, Daniel!"

His name escapes like a jailbird. I collapse to the ground, blindsided by my own manifestation of an illegal name. Am I on his side now? Then the door unlatches, and the knob turns. Truth enters. The real him. I know it's really him because he touches me. He puts his hand on me and turns my curled body around to face the lights on the ceiling.

"You called me by my name," he says.

"I know you have more to tell me than your real name, so what? What is it? Why did I drive all the way out here? Why didn't I lock up Maria and Isaac?" I'm using everyone's illegal name now. Sure, he's got an old name. What fifty-something didn't have a traditional name back in the 50s?

He lifts a large envelope that I didn't notice in his grasp when he walked in the room. "I'm not the only one with a traditional name."

"What is this? Is this about Maria? Isaac? Beamer? Chameleon —."

"It's you, Justice. You, too, were named like me. It was given to you by your mother — a friend of mine."

Disbelief colors my face red. Red with embarrassment. No way would *I* have a pre-GNA name. I'm not old enough, and my parents would never even consider it. Unless there's something I don't know about them.

"Here. Scan this." Daniel, or Truth, hands me the envelope. I pull out a plastic sleeve containing a parchment with a silver emblem in the middle beneath the seal of the president. I recognize the emblem. It's a code pattern for Anti-Intervention Foster Care.

"What is this? How did you get access to this? *I* don't even get access to foster system files. This is more than just practicing religion out here in the wilderness. This is theft of confidential government property."

But my XT-reader is already out. No way I'm ignoring this file. Consequences don't quell my curiosity, because I should not be looking at this file. It's one of the top rules of Freespeaker Foster Care. All files are to be handled by approved staff. I'm approved for a lot of things, but not even SCO gets access to foster files. How Truth managed to get his hands on this, I have no clue. But in handing me this file right after claiming I once owned a non-GNA name makes me anxious. Not anxious enough to avoid the writing that appears on my screen.

In plain, encrypted text in front of me lies a story I had never heard before. A story in which I am the main character. My eyes run about the file like a child on a playground, bouncing from end to end, taking an interest in one section, then taking notice of another and moving on. Pieces of the official record begin to brand themselves in my mind, and I feel my heart start to pound more and more rapidly with each new hoax of a history that reveals a truth that I never would have known.

Name: Abraham Torres...

Date of Birth: October 29, 2059

GNA/Permanent Name: Justice Flint...

Origin City: Far City, Hills District...

BioParent Name: Theresa Torres

BioParental Custody Violation: Freedom Law Violation (initiation) ...

Date of initiation: May 28, 2060

Date of Collection: June 5, 2060

FosParent Father: Sycamore Flint

FosParent Mother: Dream Lewis

FosParent Address: 3978 Westcrest Hill Road, Central City, State 21, 60611

Brick Jones, Peace Force Detective

On 5/28/2060, a squadron of 43 Peace Force Officers... dispatched to the East Hill of the Hills district... located the suspects beneath a storm drain on the south sidewalk along E. 48th Street between Hemlock and James Avenues... suspects included two women, one a clergy member, the other matched the description of our target, Theresa Torres... she held a baby... suspects were clearly in the middle of a religious prayer of some sort, reciting words simultaneously... entered the sewer system... pursued the suspects... priest emerged at Garden Avenue ... woman and child escaped... apprehended the priest, dressed in a priest uniform... priest identified as Elania Langston...

Song Witherspoon, Intervention Force Squad Leader

The date is 6/5/2060... arrived at Anna's Ladybug Daycare... suspect Abraham Torres was marked present for the first time in seven days... three Intervention Force Elites remained in the lobby, two outside the nursery door... I entered the nursery and apprehended the child... returned to City Hall... Child Relocation Department... expedition label... the extent of my involvement...

The narratives go on, but these two capture my attention. They seem to play almost the exact same role in my most recent case. Immediately, I think of Isaac. He is me. I am him. My eyes keep going to the names, both familiar and unfamiliar. There are my parents, Sycamore and Dream, and my name, Justice Flint, along with the address of the house where I grew up. Adjoining my past as I know it are three strangers — Theresa, Elania and Abraham. Then the narratives that tell a story like something from an alternate universe.

The word, "initiation," drones in my head — what I just worked so hard to prevent, I was a product. What does this mean, that I myself was a failure of the Freespeaker Law Enforcement. A success of the Anti-Intervention Foster Care Program. I can't help but think I would have, if I could have prevented my own initiation, taken my own mother into custody, and put myself into foster care.

It's preposterous. There's no way this could be a legit file. There has to be some type of new tech, the way Truth was able to forge such a document.

"How did you get this?" I ask. "How did you get this?! There is no way you could access this."

"When I was in law school, I took an internship with the Freespeaker Department of Foster Care. I did that for one reason. To locate this file. It had been moved to the archives 10 years after it was made, and no one ever bothers to look through archives that old unless there is a criminal record attached or you are a suspect of violating the Freedom Laws. I doubt anyone at the Central City foster care office even knows or cares that it's missing."

"You stole my file? Mine specifically? Why? Why was I a target?"

Daniel looks me straight in the eye and says, "Like I said, I knew your mother. After you were abducted, I helped her escape the Intervention Force and brought her to safety. Your mother was a remarkable woman, Abraham."

"Don't call me that! That's not my name!" I shut off my XT reader and throw it at the wall. It's sturdy. Doesn't break at all. But the green glass cross? Pieces on the ground. Truth looks at it, horrified, then again, a deep sigh and his head shakes once more.

"Justice," he says my name, and I hate the sound of my name in his voice. I hear it, and it sounds like a lie. Because I know now that every time he has spoken to me, he's never seen me as Justice, only this Abraham.

"Don't speak to me. This is a ruse. Another test or one of your mind games."

Without giving Truth a chance to explain, I kick open the door and burst from the room. At my top speed, I run from him and the fable he exposed. Retracing my steps I make my way from ETHOS, up the staircase and out of the buried hatch, across the open grass field, bathed in moonlight. I sit on wide tree stump and start breathing heavily, hyperventilating. Activating my sat-comm, I'm ready to call in an order to wipe out the coordinates of the facility. But before it boots up, I see Maria jogging toward me, holding Isaac in her arms.

"Go back!" I command, but she keeps her approach.

"I said go back!" And this time I see my fully loaded pistol lock on to her. She slows, but does not stop. She saunters grimly, moonlight shimmering in her wide eyes aiming right back at me. I hold my gun less than steady, but she holds Isaac like a statue. We possess two different weapons — one with the potential of life and the other with the power to take it away. The few moments I spend thinking about the situation are enough to help me see the absurdity of what I'm doing. Immediately, I holster my weapon. I fall onto the earth and duck my head in my arms. Maria finishes her advance and sits on her knees next to me.

I'm crying now, riddled with guilt from aiming a firearm at a baby and plagued by the uncertainty of who I am and where I come from. I know that my character comes from the people who raised me, but what could I have been had I the opportunity to... to... well, to grow up like Isaac can. In the arms of his mother who loves him. Did my mother — this Theresa — love me? For some reason, the answer is obvious to me. She did love me. No question. And she would have spent the rest of her life looking for me. Maybe she still is. I know this because I believe that Maria would do the same thing for Isaac. And even more so is an odd feeling in my gut. And my gut is never wrong. It tells me that she loves me. Somewhere, after thirty-six years, she still loves me, more fiercely everyday.

Maria sits next to me. Isaac too. She waits several moments before saying a word, just letting me sit and let the new truths of my life sink into my skull.

"You don't have to return if you don't want to," Maria consoles. "But there's one thing I want you to know."

"I don't know if there's much more I can stand to learn about myself today."

Respecting my distress, she says nothing.

"But, like I said, I guess I didn't come this far to leave important truths unclaimed." I hate that word so much right now. *Truth*. It unravels me, spins me around into nothingness, and takes all I once knew as my truth and disintegrates it. Truth destroys truth. Only one truth was a lie. All this time, it was a lie, and all my life, an urge to find my real self has led me to this moment. I am not sure if I'm happy with the outcome.

Maria rests her arm around me, and lays her head on my shoulder. A little too comfortable, but I need the physical contact right now. I feel an odd sense of comfort.

"Will you hold him?" she asks, eyes still twinkling in the moonlight.

I've never actually held a baby.

"Sure," I concede.

She hands him to me. He's incredibly warm and fixes his tiny face on mine. Full of sadness, joy. I stare at his mystifying features and he coos and ahhs, extending a hand with crooked fingers toward my face. His eyelashes curl, just like mine, and he has a birthmark just below his right ear. I do too. I look up at Maria, who's been watching our silent exchange so gracefully.

"He's your nephew."

Theresa

Daniel had never lived outside of Far City, never even traveled beyond the northwestern United States. So, the concrete beneath his shoes felt foreign as he stood in front of Lakeridge Elementary School in a suburb of Central City. The air smelled cooked and overripe, like the ground, the cars, the bricks, the bodies, and everything around him had been baked by the sun, left to settle, then reheated the following day. The resultant aroma stung bitterly in his nostrils, but he wouldn't long for the crisp air of Far City. Even amongst the dense population of his hometown, the marine breeze often cleared out the stagnant particles mingling about, and a deep summer breath could be refreshing. Daniel put it out of his mind. This was his home now — sour oxygen.

He took his first step forward, away from Aaliyah and the truck. His leg trembled as though he were shaking off his past. The engine revved, and in a moment, the only connection to Daniel's history was gone. Ahead, the stainless steel sign of Lakeridge Elementary glimmered a greeting. Daniel didn't flinch. Forward. The stucco siding of the building and beige paint was ordinary, but he was struck by the pronounced windows stretching from the ceilings of the classrooms all the way down to the floor. He could look through the reflection of the glass, empty desks stacked one on top of another and towers of chairs leaning precariously near the glass. *School. That's for normal kids.* Such were Daniel's thoughts plus one more as he approached the double metal doors.

I'll never be a normal kid.

Not with helplessness or self-pity did he wear this thought, but with pride. Fourteen years old, and already he had found his purpose in life. He pressed the green intercom button.

"Can I help you?" a convivial voice greeted almost instantly amongst audible laughter in the background.

"Hi there, umm…" Daniel wasn't sure how to introduce himself. He only knew what Marcel relayed to him, and that was the school address where his new adopted family would meet him at this time on this day. Maybe "Hi there, umm" would be enough.

The door buzzed. He pulled it open, the handle warm and the door heavy. As he looked up, he noticed an older woman already rounding a corner at the end of the hallway, her white curls springing from her head and bouncing with her step. She smiled.

"Hi dear, can I help you with something or are you looking for someone?"

"Yeah — er yes. I think. I'm looking for the Singer family." It sounded more like a question, but he was quite certain of his purpose. No other reason he'd be so far from home.

Her greeting smile had transformed into one of acknowledgement. Less happy, like a last look you give to someone about to do something courageous. Someone you know you'll never see again.

"Come on," she said. "We have breakfast."

If there's one thing Daniel loved about his people, it was that they were always feeding each other, but the more times he ate with his co-conspirators, he came to the understanding that it wasn't the food he loved, so much as the company. Of course, the food was good too, but if he had to choose between one or the other.

"I'm Claire, by the way," the woman said.

"Daniel," said the boy, still transfixed by the unravelling newness of his life. "My name is Daniel."

"We'll have to change *that* first," she frowned. "A shame, I know."

"But isn't Claire a traditional name?"

"It's a short. Clairvoyant is the long form. But you know, too many syllables." She winked.

Through a hallway, through an office and into a break room with a kitchenette, a few sofas and a stunning view of Great Lake 2 behind a massive panoramic window, Daniel gawked at the luxury afforded to school staff from the Future in Education Act. On the long table, he found nothing modest about the aforementioned breakfast. Hash browns, eggs, sausage, and pancakes. A stunned look scribbled over his face.

"Marcel had a few things to say about you, including your breakfast favorites," Claire said.

A woman sitting at the table scrutinized a tablet and typed on the interactive tabletop surface.

"Just a second!" she yelled, playfully exaggerating. A few taps and one final swipe on the table and Daniel found an image of him right between the pancakes and eggs. The woman who made it happen rose from her seat, tall as a post and walked with purpose toward Daniel. She peered at him over her glasses, squinting a little bit to examine the boy.

"I'm Windy Dixon. I'm the principal here at the school. And you are Daniel Cipher." He nodded, his eyes occasionally bouncing toward the feast. "I think he's ready to eat," Windy said to Claire.

"That makes two of us," Claire replied.

"Three of us," the principal said.

Claire pulled out a chair for Daniel, who knew the drill. *Everyone seated, everyone eated* — an old mantra Marcel used to say, and one that was common among friendly company. Between bites and pleasantries, Daniel read snippets of the profile beneath the glass on the table. A biography, biological statistics and a photograph. Daniel was astonished to see such a collection of information about himself. Paranoia entered his mind, but then he noticed that much of the profile was written in Marcel's handwriting.

"Did you know him?" Daniel asked, still following the rules of meeting new people. No information shared until it was given first.

"Marcel Wong came to visit us about two years ago now," Windy said. "We've worked with him to coordinate a network of doublers from Far City to Central City. He also sent this to us. It just arrived yesterday. It's for you."

An old fashioned letter. Stamp and all. Daniel held it like a relic. An antique from the past. But he wasn't sure he wanted to open it. He spent the majority of the car ride committing himself to the future and detaching himself from the past.

"The Singers are a great family," the principal continued. "They have two other children, a bit younger than you actually. They're on their way right now. Should be here any—"

The intercom buzzed. A few moments after Claire long-pressed a green button to unlock the door, a couple walked into the office and found the break room. Daniel folded the letter and tucked it in his pocket. The first man appeared to be in his late 40s, bulky and swift in movement, followed by a woman with jet black hair down to her waist-line. She grinned, eyes full of love at the sight of young Daniel. The way a mother would look at a son. How could she manufacture such a look, he wondered.

The thought entered his mind, but never really took root: *these strangers are now my parents*. It felt odd to him, especially since his life had never really known much structure. But structure was all he would know from this moment forward.

"Daniel, it's good to meet you," the man said. "My name is —"

"Dad. And you're Mom."

He hadn't said the words "mom" or "dad" in the five years since his own parents vanished. Though Marcel was a father figure, he could never bring himself to call Marcel *dad*, not that Marcel ever desired it. Daniel was, if possible, more surprised than the Singers and Windy. No one in the room expected him to dive into the plan so readily.

The four moved to Windy's office, and the Singers unveiled the larger scope of Marcel's and their plan — an intricate plan for Daniel to go through the Freespeaker education program on track to become anything from an Intervention Force Elite Commander, or even the Supreme Commanding Officer someday. Figuring out how to use that position to change people's hearts and minds — that was Daniel's job.

Sitting in front of him now was his new team. A group committed to broadening the perspective of freedom, something society needs a reminder of each generation.

"I guess Marcel knew what he was talking about," Mrs. Singer said. "You seem quite ready."

"I am."

"Well, I suppose you know what the first step is," she followed.

"I've thought about it. An old teacher of mine told me his name always meant a lot to him, especially as a teacher."

"What was his name?" Mrs. Singer asked.

"Genjin. He was a friend of Marcel's too. His name meant something along the lines of revealing our true humanity."

"I don't think you can use his name, unfortunately — it sounds foreign, and for your role, you're going to need something a little more standard."

Daniel nodded. He closed his eyes, and strangely, he went to a memory that evoked a long-steeped pain, but now seemed more than appropriate for his life-long undertaking. Taking a deep breath, he exhaled, "How about Truth?"

JUSTICE

Theresa Torres

August Bolden

I hand wrote my birth parents' names on a sheet of cardstock paper, framed it, and propped it up on my nightstand. I'm a side-sleeper, so, when I open my eyes and wake up each morning, it's the first thing I see, the first thought I think. I'm hoping that if I practice enough, I won't need to look at the words to remind me. One day, I'll wake up and just know that this woman was my mother, and this man was my father. I don't even know what they look like, and the closest I'll get is what I see in the mirror each morning. They're my only authentic connection to what I feel is right.

I've never met my birth mother. To me, she is just an idea. But how can you be so attached to an idea — love it even, without knowing what she sounds like, her embrace, or how she would love me?

But I look at Maria and how she holds Isaac, how she speaks about him, how she would die for him, and I have my answer. She must have gotten that from somewhere. She must have gotten it from her. From my would-be mother. That's been the latest thought to haunt me. I had two foster parents who were compensated to take me in through the Freespeak Foster Care System. They did their best to love me and raised me with good intentions, from their perspective. But somewhere in the world, I had two parents who would have given anything, everything, just to raise me as their own.

I don't know if my mother is still alive. Even though I've kept in touch with Maria every few months or so, I never talk about it. I haven't been ready.

I did learn from Maria that my birth father had died. Was killed, rather. Executed by the Intervention Force. My own people. To think, had I nothing to do with the man, I would have done the same thing, not caring whose father or husband or son he was. I have made a lot of arrests, but I have never killed. It was not in my blood. But I could tell I was getting there. Angrier and angrier, I grew. I realize now that it was because I had strayed further and further off track, pursuing a goal I never really wanted. Only one other person understood the truth about my ambition, and he did everything in his power to help me see through it as he did. It took him over a decade, but finally, he has succeeded. It only took the biggest revelation of my life to knock me off my high horse down to reality.

I always believed that we are products of our environment, and that the only things we are "born with" are simply hereditary. My foster mom was Filipina, and seeming that my birth mom was Latina, I held some of the physical characteristics one might expect in a child with foster parents like mine. But maybe there are less tangible traits that could be born into a child. Ones that keep us rooted in our familial legacy. No matter how sure I was about being the Supreme Commanding Officer, a dreadful uncertainty brewed in my imagination. The kind of uncertainty that makes something impossible, unless you're willing to tear your own fabric of integrity. I wonder what that would feel like.

Part of me always rebelled against the values I was taught. The American Freedom Laws were bars and fences, not foundations, and so was every way they made me think about people around me. Not just Godseekers, but everyone. That some people are better than others. Some deserve to live freely, while others should live in a quiet corner of the world in darkness, perhaps underground, beneath the surface, the only place where God could be found by anyone — even a headhunter like I used to be.

No, I don't follow God. I don't seek "God." I'm saying that if I'm honest with myself, I don't mind one way or the other if people do or don't. In fact, I think it's better to believe in something rather than nothing, even if it's just in yourself.

That agreement marked the end of Justice, and the beginning of Abraham, though, I don't like that name either. I still introduce myself as Justice Flint, but I *have* thought about adding the Torres surname to my identity.

My acceptance of Godseekers didn't happen overnight, especially the night at ETHOS that seemed to stretch on for days. I'd never been more contradictory toward Godseekers than I was right after Truth showed me the foster care file. Only the prospect of my true identity kept my rage at bay, like a lid over a pan of splattering oil. I had nowhere to direct all that anger, because I was angry at the truth. Not my old professor, but the truth itself. I was angry at something real, for being real. Even I could see the absurdity in that. So I had to direct that energy toward another end. Toward figuring out what to do with this new story, and that required space.

It took a year to get to where I'm at today. Off the Intervention Force. Can you believe it? Beamer used to think I'd try to take over the world as Supreme Commanding Officer. But once my world changed, so did my dream. A dream can't stand without a foundation, and like the American Border Wall, those foundations crumbled mightily.

I left Far City too. Left America. I got a work visa and have been living in Northland, or Canada, for the last nine months. Crazy, right? A year ago, I would have slapped someone suggesting to me to move up north. And here I am. I needed to get out of there. That place where I felt the plasticity of my existence, but covered it up with the law. Rules are not meant to be scapegoats, and the only ones used as such are probably frivolous or unjust.

God, I sound like Truth. Only this time, I'm not struggling with words like this. I'm finding myself in them.

"Come back when you're ready," Maria said before I stormed away from ETHOS. At the time, I would just as soon have called in an air raid to the facility.

Ready?

For what, I wondered. But that is exactly what I spent the last 12 months deciding — that I'm ready to go back.

Why? To fill in the holes of my story. To find out more about that intangible part of my mother passed on to me. Mostly, however, I want to see Truth again. The last time I saw him, I could have torn his face off — at least that's what the look in my eyes conveyed. I can't leave a man hanging on that image of me, especially one who could return such a look with disarming love. My old professor. A great man.

Only the monotony of the road is familiar; no tree stands above another, except when I make the count after the 312-mile marker. One... two... three... all the way to twelve. A hard left a few moments later. A short wander through the woods and I reach the old forest road, which looks more travelled than the last time I made this trip.

The hatch makes no effort to hide itself from me. I half expected to wander around like an idiot, looking for the opening. But there it is, the front door, as if I had come here every week for the last year.

As if I belonged.

Down the stairs. Through the corridor. My arms rest on the front desk and a young man is on the phone refraining from eye contact, but obviously talking about me.

"Yes, I'm sure it's him," he says. That makes one of us.

He hangs up and greets me like a long lost relative. Who knows?

"You must be Justice, or Abraham," he says, a bit hesitant.

"Justice is fine," I clarify.

"Well, Justice, Maria is on her way over. It will just be a minute."

Talib is his name. He motions for me to sit down in an adjacent waiting area. It reminds me of visiting the doctor, some earth-shaking news waiting for me on the other side of the door, and now I start wishing for the day to be over. The same butterflies that disturbed my stomach a year ago have resurrected, and my palms begin to sweat.

I try to distract myself by zeroing in on the bulletin board, the same one I glimpsed a year ago. The one with my photo pinned at all four corners to the cork. The same picture remains. This time I read it completely.

Justice Flint. ETHOS top priority. Volunteers needed to assist in setting up an initiation in Far City. Please contact Daniel directly.

Daniel. Weird. You may ask what's in a name. Well, more than you might think.

"You don't look much like that picture anymore," Maria says from behind me. Her voice is unmistakable.

"The hair, I know."

"I was actually thinking about your eyes. The anxiety and anger — it's gone. And it appears you've been smiling a lot more." She touches my cheek, which makes me uncomfortable at first. I'm not much for physical contact. She stretches the skin around my eyes, then releases it and gives a nod.

She moves close into me, and it takes a moment for me to realize what she's doing. I open my arms, and in she walks. She hugs me tight, and again, I feel strange. It's like coming home to a house you were born in, but no memories surface. You have no association with the place, but it has laid claim to you. It's your point A. Your alpha. No matter how unfamiliar you are with your beginning, it's still your beginning, and that matters. It is part of your story, and what good is a story without a beginning?

"It's good to see you, Maria." Finally, I offer her words.

"I've thought about you, brother. Prayed for you everyday since you left." I smile with sentiment at her familial acknowledgement. I have a sister. A sister who prayed for me everyday for the last year. Her prayers feel comforting, if not foreign. What would a man like me do with a prayer?

"How is Isaac?"

"He's taking a nap, so this is a perfect time to talk."

"And Truth — or Daniel?" She turns away and continues down the corridor, the same one she led me through one year ago.

"Come on. This way."

Finally. Getting somewhere. This whole year, I've been wondering what this moment would be like, sitting with Truth and ironing out the details of my life. Not that I expect him to figure it out for me, but just to hear his wisdom. I have so many questions for him, I know I do, just no idea what they are. More than anything, I want to tell him my story. The story of the last twelve months of my life. Most importantly, how I've changed. I want to tell him he was right about me. That the person he saw in me was always there, and how I fiercely tried to hide it behind my ambition. He deserves to know. After all the times he stuck his neck out there just to help me find the truth about myself, I owe it to him. I owe him my truth. It's the least I can do.

Maria reaches the catholic room and its unmistakable red door, but she passes it, only gracefully gliding her fingertips over the bright lacquer finish, then withdrawing her hand and placing it over her chest.

"Not in the catholic room today?" I ask, a bit bemused.

Maria stops, pauses a moment and then turns around. A trail of reflected light crookedly cascades down her cheek.

"Three months ago." Her voice trembled, then she collected all the words and poured them out at once, barely breathing as she spoke. "Three months ago, Daniel was found by the IF. He was running an operation with Beamer, trying to facilitate another baptism. God, those two." She pauses and looks upwards. An aside to God. "After you left the IF, you know how I told you about rumors spreading that you were a doubler? They figured Beamer was a doubler too. I'm pretty sure they knew once he left the Force. They took them both."

"Have you traced them yet? Maybe I can help."

Her tears flourish, and I know. In fact I knew as soon as she passed the red door, I just wouldn't let the thought rise above the surface. I spent enough years on the Intervention Force to know that two fugitives like Beamer and Truth would be KOS. Kill on sight. No ceremonious execution. No Truth Committee. No life sentence to the ESIC.

The realization cripples me. My legs lose their strength, and I topple over. Maria catches me and holds me, and for a moment, I feel comforted, warm and cold, lost and loved at the same time. I begin to eulogize him in my head with flashbacks, the stories as fresh as his ghost is for me, even though it's been three months since he... it's even weird to say it. Died. Or was killed. Truth. Was killed. What a name. *What a name.* I find myself envious of it, but no way could I ever live up to it.

I still remember the first day I walked into his class. I knew I was playing with fire, registering for Freethought in a Freespeak Society, but I had no idea what I was getting myself into. I had heard the rumors about how liberally he peppered his ideologies into the course and how counter-cultural they were. I thought I'd learn about Godseekers so I could lock them up. He disarmed the practice of religion for me. Made it seem harmless. It took me a career to believe him.

Images of his younger self and I discussing my future — I let them flood into my head, pouring over, burying less favorable recollections like that day at the Golden Garden. I wonder what he remembered most. And I know it's selfish, but I wonder what he remembered most about me. That matters. In this moment, in Maria's arms, that matters to me more than anything.

How many times had I given up on him? Decided that I would arrest him. Lock him up. See him to a prison labor camp. It rips me apart to know he died at the hands of the IF, and there I was, that same badge of the law that would have ushered him to the exact same fate.

What a hypocrite I am.

"He loved you, Justice."

I hear Maria's words. They fall on me like wet cement, heavy and immobilizing, and like a madman, I start to cackle and cry, wail and shrivel into myself in pure disgust at what I've done with my life. Maybe he'd roll his eyes at this self-loathing, but I'd tell him I need it. It's something that's been festering inside of me that I need to expel.

Because I can't move forward until I acknowledge this. That he was right about me. I've done it logically. I've done it emotionally. For all practical purposes, for all human purposes, I've recognized that, yes, Professor, you were right. You knew me, better than I knew myself. But now, on the warm floor in a hallway of ETHOS, I'm weeping for the man who gave every ounce of his energy to help Godseekers, and saved enough for a defiant, freespeaking pupil. I didn't deserve any of his effort. But with that thought, I realize why. Why he'd give so much of himself to help an enemy find himself. It was always his greatest lesson, and I understand it now. Maria, Beamer, Chameleon — they were all extensions of this lesson. To sacrifice who you are, even for someone who doesn't deserve it.

In my sister's arms, I'm the beneficiary of that lesson. I feel it surrounding me. It pulls me further and further from grief and isolation.

My head is no longer bowed in shame. Instead, I look upward. That's where people like him believe you go after you die, right? I think maybe I believe he's up there too.

———————————

"If Truth is gone," I start once my fit of tears begins to fade, "then where were you taking me?"

Maria smiles. It must be good. A grin like that after my outburst?

333

She helps me to my feet, and we continue down the hallway, just a few doors further.

"Isaac," she hushes me, clutching a door knob and pushing it open.

A soft blue light gently illuminates the room, and Isaac is asleep in the arms of another woman. I recognize Isaac instantly, and fixate upon him while keeping my distance. His head lies on her chest, his small arm stretched across her stomach. His entire body inflates and deflates in a steady rhythm. In contrast, the woman appears frozen in place, still alive, but her breathing is much less labored as if the oxygen swirls around her cavernous lungs and is expelled by its own devices.

Maria doesn't enter the room, rather, she urges me forward to my nephew. As I approach, something distracts me from Isaac, who is sound asleep in the woman's arms. It is she who catches my eye. Slowly, I un-wrap each wrinkle from the woman's face. Behind them, I find intense and deep brown eyes. Her skin is brown too, like Maria's. On the left side of her nose, a birthmark. The more I stare, the more I realize she's doing the same to me, peeling back the years that have masked my counte-nance, that have weathered down my innocence and curiosity that one day in the past swaddled my appearance. I feel her burning layer after layer of Justice, until at last she finds what she's looking for. She found me in my own eyes, not staring, but entering.

Maria takes Isaac from her arms, which stretch toward me.

"Abraham." She says my name and it's like a song — one she's been singing to herself her whole life. She speaks my name slowly, carefully, with the same broad skepticism that I harbored my entire life, the kind that belongs only to those who have suffered an immense fracturing of trust. She calls me by this word, this word to which I have never felt a connection, until this moment.

When we long for the dead, when we speak their name, nothing, no despair nor ignorance, no distance of time or space can muddle the appearance of true love. I may not believe that there is a God out there, but I sure as fire believe that this woman is my mother. From the composition of her face to the voice she uses to utter my true name. I would never ask this woman to call me Justice. She is Abraham's mother. She's my mom.

I walk to her bedside and kneel to be at eye level with her. I want to cry, but I can't. This moment belongs to her, not to me. Her tears are profuse and unyielding, tempered only by her victorious laughter. I hold her and she holds me. Clutches me like she'll never let go, and I would never ask her to. Then, I call her by name.

"Mom."

Acknowledgements

My family always push me to do great things with my life – to be adventurous, unorthodox, and most of all, they dare me to be happy. They are the greatest source of love in my life.

Anyone who read my book and gave me feedback – there are several of you – helped me discover myself as a writer. You gave me ideas, some I accepted, some I questioned, and some I rejected. That entire process may not have made me the most skilled writer, but now I know better how to critically think about my work (and my students' work as well). My mom also read my book three times before I published. Love you momba!

Lastly, my church and faith. I grew up Catholic, a title I wear more as a culture than a religion. I don't think everyone should be Catholic. I don't think everyone needs to believe in God, especially in the same way I do. I only believe that people need to be good, imperfect, and grateful. The concept of God is what you make of it, as is the way you live your life. I just like Jesus because he teaches us to love each other, *no matter who you are*, and I can roll with that.

And speaking of which, love and gratitude to all of you for reading.

THANK YOU, PROFESSOR

A Memoir

There is a story behind this story.

Kellen, the young man to whom I dedicated this book, was my 8th grade student when I unshelved the first chapter of this story and began to shape it into a novel. With my horrid sense of self-discipline and spotty attention span, I handed the reigns to my student, who gave me writing and revising assignments over the course of four years. From the first chapter to the last typesetting action, he pushed me to work hard for this accomplishment. With his dedication to me, I published my first novel and attained a dream I've had since middle school.

Together, we are writing our own story of how anyone can change anyone's life, regardless of age or role. You simply need to care about a person and have a certain willingness to work hard. Perhaps all the stars aligned to make good chemistry between myself and Kellen. *Thank You, Professor* is a shout out to teachers of all ages.

Made in the USA
Coppell, TX
06 February 2020